ROSALIND JENKINS

Smell of]
by K. R. S. Foster

C000115809

Drawings by Maddison Jane

Smell Of Lavender
Copyright @ (Kirk Foster, 2020)

ISBN: 978-178456-753-8

Paperback

First published 2020 by UPFRONT PUBLISHING
Peterborough, England.

An environmentally friendly book printed and bound in England by www.printondemand-worldwide.com

Dedication

This book could not have been written or even have seen the light of day without the help, guidance, encouragement and assistance of my beautiful and clever wife, Jo.

For
Cassie & Nathan

My sincere thanks to…
Glyn Doggett, Maddison Jane, Carolyn Marsh, Peter Webber, Gill Dawson, Reginald Hine, David & Bridget Howlett, Pauline Humphries, Gerry Tidy and all the members of the Hitchin Historical Society for their advice, help and inspiration, through the wonderful work they continue to do in bringing the history of Hitchin to the wider public.

Smell of Lavender

By K. R. S. Foster
Time: The summer of 1851

Preface

This book is not unique, but it is unusual. Rather than a play written from a book, Smell of Lavender is the book behind the play.

Kirk Foster is founder and Artistic Director of the Market Theatre, Hitchin and he has written over two hundred plays for this venue. The theatre has a strong and varied programme of plays produced for Hitchin audiences and the company tours nationally to over thirty theatres. The genres include scary, thrillers, whodunits, comedies, farces, musicals, children's plays, pantos, adult pantos and historical plays, both national and local in subject matter.

July each year sees the vibrant Hitchin Festival take place and the Market Theatre produces a local historic story in conjunction. The play Smell of Lavender was performed in July 2017 and featured Claire Bowman, Bethany Filler and Lizzie Buckingham.

It was because of the impact of the Covid-19 pandemic and the uncertainties surrounding the re-opening of theatres around the country, that this book was written. (You don't need a theatre to produce a book.) Only time will tell if this book is successful or not, but if it should be well received, there are another couple of hundred books that could follow this one!

9 Cock Street, home to Perks Pharmacy & Distillery

Chapter One

It was the breeze that finally awoke Sarah and gently led her back to the present. That sensual breeze we have all felt at times, that sings of August and flows at the most perfect of temperatures. A balmy breeze that heralds a sought-after Summer's day, enabling joy and bestowing bliss. She lay still, as still as she could, listening to her own breath, faint but unencumbered by cough or stress. Determined not to rush the moment she had awakened to, she refused to move and simply basked.

Now confident that she was no longer dreaming, she tried to recapture the moments just before the breeze had entered her life. In her dreaming she had been up at the field off Gaping Lane, breathing in the night air and savouring the crop's aroma. The lavender lay cut upon the ground, drying and awaiting collection. Then her thoughts meandered to more morbid territory and she pondered whether this was what the last moments of life felt like. Aware, conscious, but unable and unwilling to move or interact.

Ridding her mind of these darker thoughts, she remained torn between residing in that semi-conscious state where lucid thoughts whispered 'stay a while longer', and the knowing that there were things to be done and another day to be conquered... finally, the 'knowing' triumphed over the temptation to remain...and she opened her eyes.

The window was latched wide open, immediately in front of her and thankfully the breeze did not fade but continued to blow gently upon her face. It was early, maybe four thirty, maybe five o'clock, but the sun was already doing its work.

She turned her head towards the far side of the room, expectantly. Hopefully. But to no avail. There was a slight pause, as she let her mind drift to another day and then...she rose from the bed, with an urgency that proclaimed she would ensure that the day would go well despite all doubts. She washed and dressed, pinning her long auburn hair up as was the fashion, then - only momentarily - took note of herself in the long looking glass. One inch over five feet, slim waist, well defined bosom, and freckles that had haunted her since a child. She was attractive, she knew that, but to avoid feeding her vanity, she brought her brief examination to an end.

She went to Edward's room. He slept still. Though she stood beside him, he did not become aware and neither did the four-year old stir as Sarah crept silently from his nursery. In another room, she found Eliza, her housekeeper-cum-nanny-cum-everything, slumped in her chair, hand still resting upon the side of John's cot. Perhaps, in her dreams she still rocked him. Peering past Eliza, her eyes alighted upon her youngest child, who slept unashamedly, as only an infant can. He too was being cooled by the same breeze that had awakened her. Yet, despite his comfortable repose, he was not well. She knew this to be true because the stocky Doctor Hawkins had told her so and he was a knowledgeable

Doctor, whose words could not be ignored.

"He is not well, Sarah, not well at all. I tell you this for, if I do not, I fear you will cling to false hope,"

It broke her heart to think the child would never reflect on the simple joy of a breeze that wakes one from slumber. As she dealt with that possibility and vowed not to grieve before the event, an inquisitive fly flew in to investigate the sleeping cherub nestled in the cot. She watched it flying closer to his delicate nose and, fearing it would settle, she waved her hand swiftly across its flight path and the annoying insect obediently left the room via the open window.

It may be that Doctor Frederick Hawkins, the town's most esteemed surgeon, was wrong. On subsequent visits he had been much less gloomy in diagnosis, more encouraging in tone.

"It may be that my original summary was incorrect." he confessed. "As my colleagues will readily tell you, Sarah, there have been the odd occasions where it has proved the case."

"Rest assured," he offered after another visit "that nothing is impossible on God's earth, and your son may yet survive." These words had been well received and most welcome. There had been enough doubts of late, and she had been trying hard to move on. She knew she must face another day and all the pretence that went with it. She would remain steadfast and then none would become the wiser.

Sarah washed, breakfasted, and gave instructions to her yard keeper, James, to wake Eliza by six-thirty. Also, that Eliza should send for her immediately should John worsen. Satisfied that all was in order, she left the sleepy household at number 62b, Bancroft, and stepping out through the side gateway on to the street, she was engulfed by the true power of the day's heat. There had been a mighty downpour of sunlight, which now lit up the sleepy town with the cheery promise of more to come. She turned her face to the sky, eyes closed and soaked for a second in the warmth. It was six o'clock and the intensity of the sun's rays could already be felt. 'The tribulations of life never seem so fraught when cloaked in sunshine', she thought to herself.

"Good morning, Sarah." Sarah turned to see Samuel, her brother in law; twenty-seven years of age, thin, tall, gangly with tousled hair and brown eyes and just two years younger than herself. She had not seen much of him over the past months as he had been completing his chemistry training in London. Due entirely to her efforts, he had not been required to cut short his apprenticeship because of the circumstances. For this, Samuel was extremely grateful.

"Today, I think it will exceed yesterday's heat, if that were at all possible."

"It most certainly feels that way. How is Catherine?"

"Well, thank you."

"And what of Samuel junior? He develops massive lungs, I hope, and keeps you both awake throughout the night?' Samuel laughed nervously. He liked Sarah very much, always had, but found himself becoming very much tongue-tied in her presence.

"He does indeed, yes, very much so. Yes, indeed, throughout the night." Sarah's inclination to playfulness took hold and she stood silent, forcing the nervous Samuel to speak again.

"Um … I understand that he is teething."

"Teething?"

"Yes. So, I am told, hence he cries continually ... but I understand your little John improves. I spoke with Doctor Hawkins yesterday. He seems much encouraged by John's progress and wages that he may well pull through. And that is good to hear." beamed Samuel, now running out of things to say.

"And what of Catherine…?"

"Catherine?"

"Your wife, Samuel… Catherine? Has she settled?'

"Oh, Catherine, yes, she is well…."

"I know she is well, Samuel, you have told me that she is well, but has she settled into the house?"

"Most certainly, she has settled, we both have…almost…"

"Then you are ready to take over the business?"

"Yes, most definitely... I mean, no, good heavens, no."

"I jest, Samuel, I merely jest…"

"Of course, you do, yes. But I will be ready, Sarah, within a few days. In all truth, I just need to get my head around a few issues, that is all, and I have great plans, Sarah, great plans. I have learnt much in London and with our new lines of communication there are great opportunities ahead."

Sarah started to move away from him.

"By that, am I to understand that you have been in discussion with Mr Ransom?"

"We are of a like mind, Sarah, yes, I think we are."

"And that is good." she said as a parting comment.

"You think so? Honestly?"

"Honestly!"

But Samuel wasn't finished. He was passionate about the plans he had for expansion, the acquisition of more fields, the increase of produce and he wanted to know that she was fully on his side. "Oh, well, I won't hold you up anymore then. But you are happy with the plan to use William's offer to distil?"

"Yes."

"That is good then, that is very, good, yes… We'll see you

later this afternoon!" But Sarah was away and the distance between them was growing as he called out… "Will you be walking alone later, or do you wish to accompany myself and Catherine?"

Sarah did hear him but decided not to respond as she had not the faintest idea what he was talking about. She continued south along Bancroft, smiling still at Samuel's charming awkwardness, that made him so endearing to all that knew him. But feeling somewhat guilty, she chided herself and reasoned that she would not tease him so wickedly in the future.

Glancing across the street at Hermitage House, grand in its appearance and a shining example of Hitchin's growing wealth, she slowed her pace. The street was beginning to bustle and rouse itself, ready for the day's work. Scruffy boys with barrows carted, sluggish horses pulling waggons clattered, master-less dogs barked and friendly folk called out the virtues of the day. Amidst the activity, door fronts were being swept, cleaned and, in some cases, scrubbed. Due to the weeks of dry weather and ripe sunshine, dust now caused havoc whenever the wind increased intensity from gentle to gust.

Several 'good morning's' greeted her as she passed the Waters' House and on into the centre of the town. She replied to all with courtesy, but a courtesy that made it plain she had neither time nor inclination to stop and chatter. "Good morning, Mrs Perks. A wonderful day, a majestic day and a great day for Hitchin!", bellowed the portly Charles Grey, a local farmer, as he trotted past on Waterloo, his ageless shire horse. Charles possessed a booming voice that could quite happily deputise for the town crier's, and on occasion had. "Don't you think, madam?" he said, tipping his hat and turning his attention to another unsuspecting pedestrian.

"Indeed," she had said in response, not fully understanding the meaning of his comment. A great day for the town, because the sun shone? The sun had shone on Hitchin before, and it would no doubt continue to do so in the future.

She cast the oddity of his words to one side and crossed the bottom of Brand Street. Rumours were circulating that this steep street was the proposed site for the new Town Hall. There were many new building projects in discussion and only time would tell if such grandiose ideas ever materialised. She continued towards number 9, Cock Street, home to Perks Pharmacy and Distillery. On the opposite side of the street, the shutters were being opened at the Three Horseshoes and huge barrels, almost too big to pass through the frame of the front door, were being wheeled in. Finally, Sarah arrived at the gate entrance to Perks yard and saw the girls already at work, topping bundles of lavender. Normally during the season, the workforce would have already been up for two hours or more, as cropping was always done before the sun got to work. This early start ensured the natural oils in the lavender heads were retained and not dried out by the day's heat. But now all work in the fields had been completed and the work in the yard always started a little later in the day. The men were gathered around the stills which were already ablaze, and the ancient process of turning the wonderful crop into oils, incense and perfume was in full motion.

"Good day, Mrs Perks." cried Davey Chatman, foreman of the yard. "We are much blessed with a fine crop this year, ma'am, and no mistaking." The other men respectfully took off their caps and stood as Davey continued. "Giles and some others have taken the main cart up to Mount Pleasant to load the last crop, should be back by noon at the latest."

"That's good, Mister Davey, excellent."

"Yes, ma'am, so all should be done in time, ma'am." He replaced his cap back on to his balding head, where tufts of grey hair surrounded his ears and refused to go.

Sarah looked for Lottie, her head girl, and found her talking to the Canning sisters, as they were busy stacking bundles taken from the cart.

"Lottie? One moment if you please?"

Lottie had worked in the Perks yard since she was eight and was Sarah's most trusted and conscientious employee. She was friendly, reliable, obedient, tall for her sex, with red farmers' cheeks and dark brown hair. However, she was never sluggish in expressing an opinion when she was invited to. She was also an outrageous gossip, which made for good sport on more tedious days of the year.

"Good morning, Miss Sarah. What a wonderful day it promises to be."

"Good morning, Lottie. Yes, a glorious day,"

"To my mind, miss, I couldn't think of how it could possibly be a better day for it!'

"Indeed, Lottie. Now, is all well and are we coping?"

"As well as can be expected, I suppose, miss. Though, we're still awaiting on those Royce sisters". Lottie's smile faded and her previous glee for the joys of the day subsided, as it always did when this troublesome pair were spoken of.

"I'm sure they'll be here soon."

"Yes, miss, but late as always, methinks, and with some lame excuse to top it all."

"I'm going next door Lottie, to check on Anne. I'll return in a moment and then we can go through today's schedules."

"Yes miss"

As Lottie returned to her conversation with the girls, Sarah headed next door to number 8, Cock Street, the home of her mother in law, Sarah Perks senior.

Sarah's daughter Anne, now six, sat in the corner with her slate, practicing her spelling. Sarah sat with her mother in law at the side table, sipping on morning tea. They both watched Anne for a while before Sarah senior decided to speak.

"Anne, dear, would you like to show your mother your work?" Anne brought over her slate, displaying a list of chalk-smudged words.

"I think they are spelt correctly, mother."

Sarah dutifully glanced at the list.

"They are all correctly spelt. Good girl, Anne, you have done well,"

"She has been working hard, haven't you, Anne? She's been a good girl for her grandmother."

Anne dutifully returned to her seat in the corner of the room to continue her work, leaving the two women to talk about things that adults talk about and little girls of six do not find at all interesting.

After a slight pause and additional sips of tea, Sarah spoke first of her daughter's well-being.

"How is she?"

Sarah senior lowered her cup to its saucer and turned away from watching Anne to answer.

"Well, very well, she is a blessing and no trouble at all."

"I am most grateful… you are most kind"

"Nonsense, it is my pleasure, in every way. It is not every day that I am so blessed with such intelligent company."

There was a slight pause and Sarah looked back at her daughter.

"What of the night? Does she sleep at night?" The fact that

her mother in law did not respond immediately, brought Sarah's eyes to gaze upon Sarah senior's wizened face. She was now sixty-five years of age, thick set and still a proud and formidable woman. Sarah felt her daughter in law's gaze but continued to keep a steadfast eye upon her grandchild, as she replied.

"Most nights she rests as soon as her head touches her pillow… but sometimes, on occasion, she still cries herself to sleep. But she never cries out for me, nor anyone else." Young Anne was now quite content with her spellings, and after glancing satisfactorily up at her mother and grandmother, wiped her slate clean and commenced with a new list of exciting words. "Those occasions grow fewer every day, Sarah, so you have no cause for concern. Time is a great healer."

Sarah senior knew of the workload that her daughter in law had taken upon herself. It was not easy for any woman to run a business and a family in tandem. She was well aware of the pressures that came with such a burden and would do everything within her power to lessen the weight. Having her beautiful and well-behaved granddaughter to stay was the least she could do.

Once the compulsory cuddles and kisses had been energetically exchanged between child and mother, Sarah headed back to the yard. At the front door, she stopped and turned to her mother in law.

"I know that you don't require gratitude, but I would like you to know…"

But the elderly Sarah stopped her before she could say more. "I know… and once Samuel has started work and all is well with the little man, your Anne will return to you. I am more than happy to have her here and will be struck extremely sad when she has to leave." Sarah smiled back and then turned to go.

As she heard the door close behind her, she was reminded of something her brother in law Watson Perks had once said of Sarah senior…. 'Make no mistake, my dear, and do not judge my mother wrongly. She may have a face of granite, but she also possesses a heart of gold. A heart of gold that is not immediately apparent because she keeps it hidden behind an iron corset'. In earlier days, this was no doubt true, but it was becoming apparent to Sarah that with age, the iron corset was showing signs of rust and the once hidden heart of gold was now shining through and revealing its concealed glory.

As Sarah returned to the coach drive that led to the Perks yard, she became aware of a woman moving towards her from the direction of the ancient Shambles. The frame of a large woman was waddling towards her, with her side to side stride reminiscent of a great galleon tossed at sea. "Mrs Perks?!" came the unmistakeable cry of Mrs Parker, landlady of the Beehive in Bucklersbury. Sarah stood and waited for the hefty woman to come alongside, breathless, cheeks puffed as if constantly blowing. Mrs Parker leaned against a gate post to give herself time to regain her composure; a composure that, to all respectable persons, would have been considered to have been in tatters. Sarah, whilst waiting for her to speak, threw a cautionary glance at the gate post, to ensure that it was still upright and wasn't beginning to bend in the middle. Intermittently, Mrs Parker, breathlessly repeated…

'There you are…there you are…' and sucked in great volumes of oxygen between each utterance. Sarah knew that she would eventually recover, for she had seen Mrs Parker in this lung-challenging condition before. There had been times, in the past, when she had seriously considered summoning Doctor Hawkins to administer help and the Vicar, in case they were witnessing Mrs Parker's final rush to stop someone in the street before they managed to escape. Eventually, she calmed.

"I hope you don't think this presumptuous of me, Mrs Perks?"

"Not at all." Sarah replied foolishly, knowing such a comment would be leapt upon as permission to continue…

'But I was talking to Mr Gatward, yesterday, and he was a-telling me, in passing like, that you bought the most beautiful necklace from him the other day." It had been a long sentence to render in one go and she was forced to breathe in heavily before saying more…

"'Mrs Parker', he says to me, 'It is the most beautiful necklace and you really, really must see it, you really must.'"

There was a pause. Her immense bosom lifted and fell with the recovery rate of a breaching whale. Her face beamed with smiling anticipation, desperate that Sarah would say...

'Of course, Mrs Parker, I'd be only too happy to show it to you.' But Sarah hesitated. Why should she show her the necklace? A necklace that Mr Gatward would most certainly not have told her about. A necklace that was in fact, a brooch. Unbeknown to Sarah, the nosey Mrs Parker had been across the road from Gatwards, at a window on the upper floor of George Spurr's department store and had observed Sarah exiting the shop.

Mrs Parker was obsessed with knowing everything that occurred in the town. Most nights she lay awake, thinking of all the things that she did know about and fretting unhealthily about the things that she had yet to learn. The fact that some folk in the town knew things that she did not, drove her into an uncontrollable frenzy of concern. This 'frenzy' was not good for her sanity and Mrs Parker knew it. But she found herself helpless to resist and, like most people suffering from an addiction, it was so much easier to just roll over and just accept it. Not literally of course, Mrs Parker would find 'rolling over' a near impossible feat to accomplish. She had to know quickly what it was Sarah Perks had purchased from Gatwards or suffer the mortal humiliation of hearing of it from someone else.

"Necklace…?" Sarah queried…

"Or perhaps it was a ring and not a necklace, possibly?" 'Ring…?' Sarah continued, demonstrating the most impressive signs of trying hard to recall. As Sarah continued to act the part, Mrs Parker's busy-body picture of optimism began to fall from her face. All the I-want-to-know-all-that-is-going-on-in-the-the-town-before-anyone-else-does obsession, began to eat at her conscience. The longer Sarah seemed to think, the more guilt began to rear its ugly head and sap Mrs Parker's appetite for 'being in the know'.

Mrs Parker had few friends, if any, and was, consequently, very lonely. Sarah knew this and understood loneliness. Especially the oppressive loneliness that torments even when one is surrounded by well-meaning people. Mrs Parker was a snoop, a snob and a tittle tattle of the highest order, but she had offered Sarah companionship and kindness in hard times. She had been happy to talk long into the night about herself and not try to dig deep into Sarah's soul, or to offer subtle therapy. Well-meaning people are not always the first to realise that to come out of the other side, you must first wallow in that which hurts. It is a simple fact that a broken heart is, by definition, broken and cannot be fully mended. Mrs Parker was of course, oblivious to any of these truths, and hence had proved the ideal companion during difficult times.

"Oh!" Sarah suddenly exclaimed, with the skill of a London actress, just as Mrs Parker was giving up on ever achieving her aim… "You mean, the brooch!"
"That's it!" screamed Mrs Parker, with a shriek that surprised even herself… "The brooch! That's it! The brooch!" In unison, a false sense of laughing-relief spilled from both ladies...
"Of course, Mrs Parker, it will be my pleasure. Please come with me and all will be revealed..."
So, saying, Sarah led the victorious Mrs Parker through the yard, into the shop and finally into the little office where the brooch had been kept safely since purchase.

Sarah took her apron from its hook as Mrs Parker poured compliment after compliment over the tiny brooch. Sarah hoped that her act of dressing for work in mid conversation might prompt Mrs Parker, who had now achieved her goal, to eventually leave. But life is never quite as simple as that. Evicting her from the shop would not be easy. Sarah eyed the office clock on the wall, as Mrs Parker continued to exclaim how beautiful the brooch was and how she was going to buy something similar but possibly not quite as expensive. Time was moving rapidly forward. Sarah had yet to start a single moment of work and Mrs Parker was going nowhere. The day seemed lost before it was begun when the ever-clever Lottie Greenacre entered the shop with a pitchfork in hand.
"Miss! Miss! Did it come in here, miss!?"
Sarah and Mrs Parker left the office and came into the shop where Lottie was crouching as if to lunge, weapon in hand, against some vicious assailant.
"Did what come in here, Lottie?"
"The rat!" answered Lottie, still looking at the floor.

"Rat?!" cried out Mrs Parker, now also scouring the floor...
"I didn't see a rat, Lottie, but it's hardly unusual..."
"You don't understand, miss, this was no ordinary sized rat!
It wasn't one of our ordinary ones that skip about the barns,
or the ones Mister Davey catches in his traps. Oh no, miss.
This rat what I saw was the size of a small dog!" Lottie
never took her eyes off the floor for one second, and for the
first time Sarah noticed that Mrs Parker's eyes did likewise.
"I must confess, I am no fan of rats, whatever their size..."
Mrs Parker backed slowly towards the shop door as she
glanced up to speak to Sarah, "I think, I should be going,
there is much for me to do at the Beehive..."
"There he is!" screamed Lottie, but not nearly as loudly as
Mrs Parker, who also screamed then turned and ran out of
the shop, almost forgetting to open the door before exiting,
and wedging herself momentarily between the door frame as
she did.
"I'm so sorry about this, Mrs Parker..." But Sarah's words
were pointless, for Mrs Parker was nowhere to be seen.
Sarah turned to Lottie who was leaning on the pitchfork with
an unmistakeable air of triumph. "And where is this rat the
size of a small dog, Lottie Greenacre?"
"Sorry miss, must have been mistaken."
"It's too bad, Lottie, it really is, you could have given the
poor woman a heart attack." chided Sarah, even though she
was, in truth, most thankful for Lottie's interjection.
"Better her have a heart attack than you have earache, miss.
Everyone knows she's averse to rats and I was aware that
you were struggling to be rid of her." Lottie placed the
pitchfork to one side. "Sorry if I done wrong, Miss"
"It's not so much that you done… did wrong, Lottie, so
much as you…. oh, never mind, it is done now, I suppose,
and no real harm has been caused."

"She'll survive, miss, but I'm not so sure you would have done. When she gets talking there's no stopping her, and that's the truth."

Sarah pulled a chair out at the central table to sit and encouraged Lottie to do likewise.

"Now Lottie, tell me where we are all at and the state of affairs."

"Well, miss..." Lottie seated herself at the table and continued to retell the opening-up of the yard that morning; what work had been completed and what was still to be done. She reminded her that Giles and some others had gone to the fields at Mount Pleasant to bring in the last crop that had been cut and left drying, and that they hoped to be back by noon. Finally, she broached her favourite subject, the Royce Girls. Not only had they not arrived when they should have, when the yard had opened, but they were still missing and in Lottie's opinion, were unlikely to be seen anytime soon.

"And why do you think that, Lottie?"

"Well, because of today, Miss... as sure as fire they won't be here this morning, but I wager you they'll both be at the railway station at three o'clock in their Sunday best."

"Railway station, Lottie, what on earth are you talking about?" Sarah stopped suddenly, as the importance of the day dawned upon her. "Lottie! I had forgotten what today was!"

"Forgotten, miss, how could you forget? It will be marked down in the history books as Hitchin's greatest day."

"How could I? I don't know how I could, but I had!"

"Oh, Miss Sarah..." offered Lottie, in the most understanding way she could think of.

Sarah stood and paced the shop floor. "What a foolish, foolish... forgetful woman I am. It completely went out of my mind."

"Not to worry, Miss Sarah, you've had a lot on your plate recently, what with everything. The business, and such… and little John, being not so well. It's no surprise, I think." Lottie continued to offer solace and a series of excuses that might make her beloved mistress not feel so foolish. But Sarah was lost in her own thoughts as other occurrences that had puzzled at the time, now all made sense.

Samuel's offer for her to accompany him and Catherine, Mr Grey's exclamation that it was a great day for Hitchin… 'It wasn't because the sun was shining' she chastised herself, 'It was because the Queen was coming!' Mister Davey promising all would be done by noon, it wasn't a promise that needed to be made on a normal day. But today was no normal day in the hearts of Hitchin folk, because today was the day that the whole town would drop tools, close shop doors, and congregate at Hitchin railway station to witness the Queen's visit to Hitchin!

"Don't let it plague you, miss, no real harm is done."

"I'm sorry, Lottie, I really am. You're right, I have had so much on my mind of late… but it matters not, for I am now back with the living."

"That's good, miss… and do you recall promising the staff a half day, miss?"

"I do Lottie, I do. And fear not, for it is merely a slip of the mind that has brought this about, rather than an irretrievable fall into senility. They shall have their half day, as promised. You are right as always Lottie."

"I am, miss?" exclaimed Lottie, pleased that she was right, but not sure why.

"Because as you say, no harm has been done. Nothing is changed, nothing is lost, I just need to get my head around it all and organise accordingly" She again paced the shop floor as if to cajole the brain into thinking faster. "And the brooch! The brooch I have just shown Mrs Parker, I bought that to wear today and... sprigs!

"Miss?"

"Sprigs. I had promised to make sprigs of lavender! You will help me, Lottie. Bring in an un-topped bushel and we will cut and bind the sprigs here at this table." Sarah began to clear the table of oddments and clutter, but quickly became conscious of Lottie still standing.

"Well, Lottie, did you hear me?"

"Yes, miss, but with those Royce girls not here and with Hilda away visiting her Aunt, would it not be best for me to help the girls do the topping in the yard, or they won't be finished in time?"

Sarah stopped her clearing away and vowed that neither Lottie, the girls, nor any of the Perks workforce would miss seeing the Queen at the station. With that assurance, the excited Lottie gave a curtsy bob, which Sarah had forbidden her from doing and exited quickly into the yard to fetch a bushel of lavender to make the required sprigs.

After the initial shock caused by her memory acting so inexcusably, Sarah's earlier positivity returned and enabled her to celebrate that it was indeed, a great day! The day, to be exact, was Wednesday 27th August 1851 and the Queen, yes, the Queen of Great Britain and the Empire, was to visit Hitchin! Actually, she was only to stop for several minutes at Hitchin Railway Station and there be presented with several gifts and to numerous dignitaries. To Sarah's knowledge there was no plan for her Majesty to stroll blindly through the dusty streets, breathe in the sewage of the River Hiz and be entertained by the unbathed and foul-smelling gypsy Draper on his violin.

Mr Draper was a gypsy of some notoriety who lived with his family in the woods around Hitchin. He was the scourge of the town's people, especially the Quakers; the strict Quaker, John Whiting, in particular. Gypsy Draper, being aware of John Whiting's feelings, would stand at the front door of John's house of an evening and play loud and lively jigs. This act of defiance would infuriate Friend Whiting, who would gather family and servants, retreat to the back garden and not return to the house until Draper had tired of his mischief and left. Not all townspeople, however, considered gypsies so lowly. Sarah herself for one did not.

For many years, an old gypsy woman would regularly visit the house in Bancroft to sell her wares, and this was much encouraged by the Perks family. Once a month she would arrive, whatever the weather. She would be invited into the yard and offered a drink. There she would sit and chat with the servants, telling yarns and using her dry humour to cause great hilarity. She was a popular character who had visited for more years than any could remember and had seldom missed a month. Sarah senior had said that the woman had been a feature of the Perks lives long before she had married her husband Edward. Why, when and how this tradition had begun was now lost in the mists of time. Regrettably, the old lady had not been seen for some time and it was presumed old age had finally caught up with her.

Nor did the town's artist and brewer, Samuel Lucas, think badly of them. He had told Sarah that he had spent many a happy hour chatting to the Drapers at their woodland encampments. Samuel had a sense of mischief to match Sarah's. In his wonderful oil painting of Hitchin Market, besides filling the square with figures of Hitchin's finest, he also featured, dead centre of the canvas, gypsy Draper and family! Sarah was sure Draper would have willingly played for the Queen, if asked, but because he had not been asked, the town's uncharitable dignity would remain unblemished. Sarah walked to the open door and shouted through the blinding sunshine to the far corner of the yard, "Lottie? Better that you bring two bushels and of the ripest stalks. I feel one will not suffice and beware that some of the older bushels have dried too much to be used for sprigs."

"Very well, miss!"

"And look lively, Lottie, there isn't time to waste!"

"Yes, miss!"

"However, Lottie, neither rush your choosing, for only the best will do, understand?"

Sarah thought to speak again but realised any more commands would only slow Lottie's mission and prove contrary to what was required, which was haste. So, with renewed confidence, Sarah entered the shop's office, returning quickly with several empty wooden trays, which she placed on a chair at one end of the table. Just this small effort had caused her brow to sweat and she took from her apron pocket a cloth, which she waved vigorously in front of her face to replace the almost non-existent breeze.

As she continued to cool herself with the improvised fan, her thoughts returned to the royal event and she reflected on the afternoon timetable. The Queen's impending stop would be made during her journey to Balmoral, her summer retreat in Scotland. With the opening of the railway line the year before, almost to the day, Hitchin's importance had grown rapidly. And now with the branch line to Shepreth open, a large corn exchange planned for the town centre and a new town hall being agreed, Hitchin was preparing to exploit its true trading potential.

"Here's one, miss, I'll just need to choose one more," gasped Lottie, dumping the bushel upon the floor.

"Well done, Lottie, excellent choice!"

"It's hot work mind, Miss Sarah, searching through those bushels."

"Well, you have made a good start, Lottie."

"Just as well we'll only be working the half day, miss, this weather will fry anyone foolish enough to graft a full one." Lottie wiped her brow with the back of her hand and once more ventured out into the burning sun.

Sarah continued to inspect the chosen bushel. "Good Hitchin lavender, if I do say so myself."

Hitchin had initially grown prosperous through the wool trade, but in recent years the excellent lavender produced in the town was placing Hitchin firmly upon the national map. Old Mr Harry Perks had started it all, back in 1790, by taking over 9, Cock Street and opening his pharmacy. Sarah had been told by a reliable source, as in Watson Perks, that the house and yard had at one time been in the possession of the Middleton family. At a gathering of the Perks Family not so long after she had married into the family, Watson had given one of his lectures on the history of Hitchin.

"John Middleton died in 1509…" began Watson Perks, standing in front of the winter fire that burned and lit the old drawing room in his Tilehouse Street home…but before he could continue further, he had been forced to pause as his nephew, Samuel, entered the room late. "John Middleton died in 1509…" repeated Watson, lifting his sagging frame, pulling in his well-fed stomach and altering his stance to replicate the headmaster of the British School, "…and left his substantial estate including 9, Cock Street to his wife, Alice. The same Alice that two years later in 1511 would marry Thomas More."

There was a slight pause before he continued with the

confidence of someone who is about to reveal a 'thing' of great importance. The pause had intended to be dramatic. But it was somewhat spoilt by the timid, mouse-like voice of his wife, Mary.

"Samuel, dear?" squeaked the timid Mary, "would you like tea and a scone?" All eyes turned from Watson to Mary and Samuel. Most of the eyes showed signs of holding back laughter but one pair glared disapprovingly. Mary and Samuel quickly became aware of this, so Samuel politely declined, Mary retreated to her chair and Watson continued with added emphasis.

"To answer the question undoubtedly on the tip of your tongues, yes, that was the same Thomas More who became Henry VIII's Chancellor, was knighted, tried for treason and beheaded in 1535."

The next best thing to an amateur scholar discovering interesting information, is being able to impart this knowledge to others. It would be fair to say that Watson Perks suffered from a more sophisticated version of Mrs Parker's disease. For it cannot be denied that the two of them shared the same thirst for knowledge, however, there the similarity ended. Watson would continue to be content working his way through rolls of ancient paper, even if he were never able to pass on what he had discovered. If Mrs Parker should find that no audience was forthcoming, she would shrivel inwardly, show severe signs of insanity and find herself admitted to the local asylum.

As Sarah smiled to herself at the absurd assertion that there were similarities, she dragged the bushel over to the table, ready to be cut. Leaning against the edge of the table, she once more fanned herself and continued to reminisce.

It was at this same evening talk, that she had found herself raising her hand in the air, just as an obedient child would. Watson had turned to her and, still enjoying the role of school Headmaster, had asked, "Sarah?"

"You said 'substantial estate', sir. Did the Middletons own other buildings and property in Hitchin?"

Watson smiled gratefully, for this new member of the Perks family had suddenly brought a new dimension to his winter talks; questions.

"Yes," smiled Watson, deciding that Sarah would now be his favourite relation of all time. "Indeed, Sarah, they owned several along Cock Street and Bancroft, as well as numerous fields on the outskirts of the town."

This stimulated others to also enquire for more information and the delighted Watson dutifully furnished everyone with more facts than he had intended. At the end of the evening, and when no one else but she would hear, he had whispered, "Thank you, Sarah, for your interest this evening. But remember, you are now a member of the Perks family and to ask a question, there really is no need to raise your hand."

Sarah had not asked the question out of politeness or to impress, that was not her way. She had asked because she was genuinely interested. Local history had always been of interest to her, and this coming together of minds with Watson forged a partnership of common interest. He was never a boring man and enlightened every gathering he attended.

'It is too easy,' thought Sarah, 'to say he is sorely missed; to say, he is greatly missed would be more befitting.' Hours of research and exchange of information had taken place over four years until his death in April 1849. In honour of his memory, when time would allow, she continued digging into any cellar or attic that may reveal more of the past.

Lottie returned with the second bushel, just as Sarah had finished clearing the table. "By the table, if you will, Lottie." Lottie did as Sarah requested and dumped the bushel down where Sarah had dragged the first one.

"Still no sign." stated Lottie.

"Still no sign of what, Lottie?"

"Of those Royce girls and I don't expect we'll see them today, neither."

"Over there in the bottom drawer, Lottie, you'll find scissors and binding…" Lottie collected these and returned to the table.

"I told the girls what you said about today, miss, and Mister Davey's going to pass it on to the men."

"History is being made today, Lottie, and we all should be a part of it."

"They're all extremely grateful, miss, and what with not being docked any money and all…"

"I suggest you top the lavender and I'll bind the sprigs, Lottie. We will do several trays. One I shall give to my lady friends, as I promised. The rest can be taken up by any of the girls that wish to sell them at the entrance to the station. Any monies taken the girls may keep."

"Thank you, miss. I know Lucy will be particularly liking of that, as her mother Dolly has been a-suffering with her teeth and there's a bill to be paid."

"Then see to it that she is given a tray."

Sarah did not look up from her chosen task as she spoke as she was determining the order of her work. She would cut the correct lengths of bind before she started bunching and binding, this would give Lottie more time to get ahead with the topping.

There was still plenty of time, but not plenty of time to waste.

"...not just lavender oils and scents, Sarah, but toilet soaps and even shaving soaps!"

Chapter Two

A few moments of silence passed as they both laboured in the heat. The door to the yard was open wide to allow any of the breeze still willing to enter to do so. The sun poured through the doorway and splashed across the stone floor as if a bucket of sunlight had been thrown upon it. The heat was intensifying and it was still early morning. 'It is going to be unbearable standing in all our finery up at the station' thought Sarah and made a mental note not to forget to take her favourite parasol. She would take her special white one decorated with tassels. Having thought that extremely sensible thought, she then realised that she could not recall what she had done with it. She had an ordinary everyday parasol, but it would be nice to carry her favourite one with her when seeing the Queen. Had she taken it next door yesterday when she went to see Anne? She was not convinced that she had and before she could dig deeper into the vaults of her memory, Lottie broke the silence…

"I know it's not my place to say these things, miss, but I'm thinking you are sometimes too kind of nature."

"You are, are you Lottie, and why is that?" replied Sarah still trying to remember the whereabouts of her parasol.

"I am, miss, because I think it true, and I'm not alone in those thoughts." This time Sarah did not reply. The whereabouts of the parasol had now grown in importance. Sarah was considering the possibility that she may have left it at Catherine's when she went round to check that all was well, and to update Samuel on the state of the business. "They says they have the fever." continued Lottie, bringing Sarah's attention back to what she was saying. Lottie became most annoyed when people took advantage of charitable persons such as Miss Sarah. Although she realised that the Royce family's lot was not an easy one, they were no worse off than many in Hitchin. In her view, Miss Sarah was being taken advantage of and the leniency shown to that idle pair was unfair on the rest of the girls.

"Perhaps they do have a fever, Lottie?"

According to Lottie all they had was an aversion to work. "They are wretchedly poor and according to Doctor Hawkins, the wretchedly poor are prone to fever."

"Yes, miss." Lottie, at the same time as topping the lavender and lying them in front of Sarah to bunch and bind, was deciding whether it was prudent to continue the conversation. But once Lottie Greenacre saw what she thought to be nothing more than blatant unfairness, she found it impossible not to speak out. "But begging your pardon, miss, and at the risk of sounding uncharitable, they wouldn't be so wretchedly poor if they turned up for work on a more regular occasion. That's my thinking, anyhow."

"Possibly… I'm going to put these first three sprigs to one side for Mrs Dalton." So, saying, Sarah walked into the office with the said sprigs. Lottie continued her work, still not satisfied that Sarah was taking the situation seriously enough. She had known the Royce family all her life, and she knew the whole family to be cunning and expert in deceit. It wounded her to see the kindly Sarah having the wool pulled over her eyes by the indolent pair. The infamous family were also known for being lazy, untrustworthy and light fingered. The town constables had paid more visits to their dwelling in Chapman's Yard than any other and it was not to congratulate them on their admirable work ethic. In her anger, Lottie accidentally decapitated a bunch of lavender so short that they now did not have stalks long enough to stand in a thimble of water. She quickly brushed the torso lacking lavender heads on to the floor to conceal her folly.

Sarah re-entered the room aware that Lottie's silence was deceptive. Lottie's 'silences' were intended to convey that she had accepted what had been said and that she had dropped the subject. But Sarah knew that this was not the case and to save Lottie from giving herself heart burn, she re opened the conversation.

"Besides, Lottie, you know that Mr Royce has constant gout and Mrs Royce is almost an invalid, being severely incapacitated by ill health. Both are virtually bed ridden...."

"That may be, Miss Sarah, but those ailments haven't prevented them from producing fourteen children." There was a slight pause, as Sarah was not sure how to counter this. "Of course, on the other hand," continued Lottie quickly, "that may be why they're so bed ridden."

"Lottie!"

"Sorry miss."

After a few seconds of quiet, Lottie changed tact.

"That younger one, Thomas, is always around where he shouldn't be. A sly eye and a slick hand has he. Do you know what they calls him, Miss Sarah? They calls him the 'Trouser Locksmith', on account of the number of pockets he picks. He were round here earlier, up to no good. I asked him, just before I chases him off, I says to him, 'Where are your sisters, you little rascal?' 'Fever' says he, 'They has the fever and won't be in today'. Fever, my foot, which is exactly what he got from me. My foot planted firmly up his…"

Sarah threw Lottie her 'That's enough, thank you' stare to save her stepping over the threshold of no return. Lottie took note and stopped before it was too late. They both continued to work the next five minutes in what can only be described as a subdued calm.

Eventually, Lottie decided that now was the time to change the subject completely. "Was Mrs Parker here to order some products, miss?"

"No, Lottie, she wasn't. She was here to view my brooch." Sarah continued to tell Lottie the story, assuring her that the brooch had not been purchased through a moment of vanity. But if the Queen was willing to take time to visit then the townspeople should endeavour to look their most splendid. As Sarah spoke of the Queen's visit, Lottie suddenly remembered something else that she had deemed as being most unfair. And before she could stop herself, her mouth had opened, and her voice had spoken.

"It shouldn't be young Mr Ransom presenting the bottle of lavender, miss, it should be you."

Sarah stopped what she was doing and looked at Lottie. "Mr Ransom distils just as good lavender, Lottie, and does it really matter who represents our town?"

"Yes miss, it does; to me it does and to many others I can name. Old Mr Harry Perks was set up here with his lavender long before the Ransoms got in on the act."

What Lottie said was undoubtedly true but Sarah always tried to be philosophical about it for it was not a fair world. In the wealthiest nation on earth, leaders of the largest

Empire ever seen and still expanding, despite George III giving great chunks of it away, yes, even despite that folly, there were still people in the town starving. The workhouses were no better than prisons, a working man's wage was pitiful, education for women was almost non-existent and health care for the poor just meant a half-decent burial. But for the generosity of the town's wealthy, especially the Quaker community, even more would suffer and die each year. It was also unfair upon the Quakers, for in Sarah's opinion their good works were not fully appreciated. Despite their willingness to put their hands deep into their pockets for charitable causes, they were still regarded by the rest of society as oddities. Religious fanatics.

"I'm afraid, Lottie, it isn't a fair world."

"Is it because he's richer, miss, or because he's a man?"

For a moment, which felt like an age to Lottie, Sarah stood silent. Lottie wondered if she hadn't heard, but Sarah had heard. Sometimes the simplest question has one searching for some reason and logic in the answer, that one knows one is going to give. All truthful answers are not given because they are necessarily right, but because that is the way things are. Consequently, a sad reflection on life.

"Both." answered Sarah continuing with her bunching and binding. As Lottie realised that Sarah wasn't going to add more to her brief and crushing answer, she followed suit and started once again to top the lavender.

'Yes' thought Sarah, 'The world isn't fair.' But she knew also that William Ransom was bright, clever and extraordinarily well educated. According to her brother in law, Samuel, who thought William could do no wrong, he was also an extremely clever chemist. Samuel and William had spent many hours discussing collaborations; areas where they could work together and not always be in a state of rivalry. Samuel and Sarah both knew that the Ransoms' farmlands were extensive, and that they had the type of financial backing that the Perks could never think to raise or attract. It made sense to cultivate good relationships with these Quaker farmers. Samuel may well be tongue-tied around Sarah and his punctuality suspect, but he was no-one's fool. He had his own plans for Perks pharmacy and lavender products, and…

"…not just lavender oils and scents, Sarah" he had enthused at a recent supper "but toilet soaps and even shaving soaps!"

Sarah was appreciative of Samuel's attempt to involve her in his decision making. In truth he did not have to. Besides, Sarah was no-one's fool either, she knew the Perks processes were archaic. The stills in the backyard of 9, High Street were still flame driven, whereas the future lay in processing with steam. Or so she was told, by Samuel.

"They'll have to go, Sarah, they'll just have to go. Or better still, we save money and time by not distilling our own lavender but sending it to William and pay him to do it."

"Is that what you intend to do?' Sarah had asked, repaying his determination to involve her.

"I think it is for the best, Sarah, I really do."

"Then if that is the way forward, Samuel, so be it."

"I'm so glad you agree, Sarah. I only wish I could explain the benefits to you better, but explanations are not really my forte,"

"Not to worry." breathed Sarah with a sigh of relief.

"I know!" beamed an unbelievably excited Samuel.

"It really doesn't matter, Samuel," she added quickly, hoping to douse his flame of enthusiasm, but it was far too late.

"I'll send William round to you! He is so much better at explaining industrial theories, mechanical systems and

manufacturing practices than I am. That's it! I'll send
William round!"
And he did.

It was a few days later, recalled Sarah, when the yard had
been closed and all had gone home. It was close to nine
o'clock in the evening and still full light. As she reached for
her summer shawl, there came a tap on the windowpane of
the shop door. The windowpane was frosted and although
she could make out a figure, it was impossible to tell who it
might be. Sarah unlocked the door.

"I am so sorry to disturb you so late of an evening, Sarah." It
was young William Ransom.

"William?"

"I know you are keen to end your day of business, but would
a brief word be possible?"

William Ransom was the eldest son of John Ransom, a
wealthy Quaker whose farm buildings stood towards the
north end of Bancroft, virtually opposite Samuel and
Catherine. William was twenty-five years of age but
possessed a maturity that belied his years. He had returned
home five years previously, after qualifying as a
manufacturing chemist in Birmingham. Since his return, he
had taken unused outbuildings and barns on the farm,
converting them into venues for expanding their farming and
lavender business. They were now packed full of expensive
and ground-breaking machinery. Amongst these he had
installed, at great cost, large modern stills in two of the
refurbished barns. Improving the state of the world was a
personal mission and a faith driven desire on the part of
William. As with all Quakers, he was determined to improve
the lot of his family and society by embracing modernisation
and new ideas.

A good-looking man in Sarah's eyes, he impressed her privately with his vigour, intelligence and love of archaeology. He was confident, charming and good-looking… Sarah paused, for had she not already listed that he was 'good-looking'…? It mattered not. He was not married because, as he had professed to Samuel, he was far too busy at present to contemplate such domestic luxuries.

"Of course, please come in." She stepped back to allow him to enter the shop, and as his medium height, slim frame passed her, she closed the door behind him.

"I will not keep you long, Sarah, as I'm sure I have stopped you on your way to see your daughter."

"Not at all. I see Anne morning, lunchtime and evening each day. She is a-bed now. I saw her earlier before her dinner."

"And she is well, I trust?"

"Quite well, thank you and quite content living with her grandmother,"

"And with Samuel now returned to Hitchin, it will not be long, I assume, before your burden is lifted and Anne can return home to you?"

"Indeed, not so long to wait now."

"And little John? How fares little John?"

Sarah knew his questioning was prompted by genuine concern and not conversational politeness. It was not the Quaker way to speak for the sake of it. Sarah had heard that their religious meetings were peppered with long bouts of silence. Opportunities to self-reflect as well as to engage with God.

'It might be an idea to send Lottie along one day.' thought Sarah 'Better not, for the experience would undoubtedly kill her.'

"In truth, John's health varies from day to day. We are never sure what each morning may bring. This morning, however, he was well. In fact, seemingly quite at ease."

"Then let us hope it is an upward slope to recovery."

"Yes, with God's blessing, it is. Will you sit?"

William accepted her offer, removed his tall stovepipe hat, placed it on the table, pulled out a chair and, having respectfully waited for Sarah to sit first, sat down. With William sitting close she observed truly for the first time his grey blue eyes, set beneath wavy black hair and eyebrows that matched. His face, she noted, wore an expression of humility and a desire to please in equal measure.

"Samuel has asked me to explain briefly how I, and he, very much see the sense in working together wherever possible." He spoke in a manner that Sarah perceived as being slightly patronising.

"You mistake me, William, I am not blind to the advantages." Sarah's intervention surprised William and he was taken aback.

"Please forgive me, Sarah, it was not my intention to suggest that you were. Please let me start again?"

"Samuel tells me that our stills in particular are old fashioned." stated Sarah before William could resume. "He is of a mind to send our lavender to you in the future. He tells me you have installed more modern stills than our archaic beasts, stills that work on the principle of steam rather than the naked flame. Is this true?"

"It is, Sarah, yes. Samuel and I have discussed this and many other things as well. In truth, I am looking to improve the process and in doing so continue to build Hitchin's reputation in the country. We are surrounded by fields that produce some of the finest wheat and barley in the land."

"And lavender."

"Indeed, and lavender, in particular."

"Tell me, William, why is it your steam method proves

superior to the open fire method?"

"The advantages are straight forward enough. Heating the stills by steam instead of naked fire avoids the lavender from being burnt or the oil gaining an empyreumatic odour through the application of too much heat." Sarah had received a basic education but at the arrival of the word 'empyreumatic' she suddenly wished that she had not shown such interest. An interest which had now been misinterpreted as a desire to be informed. On William's part, he had no plans to embarrass Sarah with convoluted words from the world of science. Partly because he felt she was not as interested as her question had implied, and partly because he had used Samuel's request to explain as an excuse to speak on a completely different matter.

"William, I will be honest with you. May I be honest with you?"

"Of course." answered William, thinking of how he might turn things round to what he had really come to speak to her about.

"It was very considerate of Samuel to ask you to see me, but I am really not as interested in the science of what we do as he would think. I love the lavender fields and what they represent for their own sake. It is history that moves me, William, not science. I understand why things must move on, for I am aware that there can be danger and folly in standing still. But for me it will be a sad day when a machine reaps the harvest and not men armed with sickle, scythe and pitchfork."

"That is good, Sarah, because..." Sarah, raised her hand slightly to stop him from speaking further.

"Please William, let me finish for I am almost done."

"Of course."

"Neither do I look forward to the day when, because of the

invention of the mechanical, steam-propelled 'topping'
machines, the girls in the yard are rendered redundant and
surplus to requirement. I do not want to be there when
Samuel is forced, through the advantages of modernisation,
to tell them that they are no longer needed in the Perks Yard.
That for me would be a sad day. I am a granddaughter and a
daughter of farmers, married into a farming family. A
farming family that now sell their many products through
this rickety, old fashioned store. I want to stand by a field,
William, and hear the swish of the sickle, the chatter of the
girls as they pick and see the contentment of dripping sweat
from every brow, when all know a good day's work has been
done."

William sat admiringly, waiting to see if Sarah was planning
to say more. But she was not going to say more, in fact, she
thought she had said quite enough and had opened large
areas of her heart to a young man she hardly knew.

"There… I have finished."

"Then I take it, that without being rudely intrusive, you are
not disappointed or regret your decision to step away
completely."

"I am far from disappointed and I can assure you, William, I
have no regrets whatsoever." She lied.

"I'm not sure Samuel is fully aware of this. I think he holds
hopes that you will stay on longer than you have agreed."
Sarah did not answer. "I only tell you this as a friend, Sarah,
to forewarn you." Sarah still did not answer. "Is it
presumptuous of me to regard you as a friend, Sarah?"
Sarah's silence continued, until she felt compelled to offer an
answer for fear of appearing rude and ungrateful if she did
not.

"William, I am quite happy for you to think of me as a
friend." Again, there was a slight pause and she did not look

at him directly as she spoke again. "And I hope I can think of you in the same way."

"I would be honoured if you would."

There was a silence that lasted no more than a few seconds, but to Sarah and William it seemed to last an age. Finally, the intense moment created was extinguished by William standing and taking his hat from the table.

"This is very wrong of me. I keep you from your family." Even as he spoke, he was walking towards the shop door. Sarah stood and quickly followed him, her two steps to his one. Outside on the doorstep, William replaced his hat and spoke. "I understand that you have a keen interest in local history, Sarah?" he asked, bringing lightness to a conversation that, inside the shop, had created an atmosphere of inexplicable emotion.

"I have William, very much so."

"Then you really must accompany me to Wilbury Hills quarry. The Great Northern Railway Company are digging there for ballast and many ancient bones and artefacts are being recovered. I have discovered a small iron age spear point and many coins." He turned for the first time to look at her since stepping outside. "Would such a trip be of interest, Sarah?"

"Well..." answered Sarah, confused, hesitant, but before she could stop herself… "That would be most agreeable, William. Thank you."

"Then we shall arrange it, as soon as is convenient to you. Goodnight, Sarah."

"Good night, William."

William tipped his hat graciously and walked away. Sarah went back into the shop and closed the door behind her. Instead of reaching for her shawl, she sat again at the table. She needed a few moments to collect her thoughts.

Outside, William had planned to return to the farmhouse, but seeing his friend, Samuel Lucas, opposite at the Three Horseshoes, he went and joined him. They spoke enthusiastically of their separate trips to the Great Exhibition. William purposely stood with his back to the public house, facing Samuel, who had his back to the street. He gave Samuel no clue that his mind was elsewhere. William, assured and confident in all situations, had been thrown by his conversation with Sarah. He had intended his visit to be an opportunity to explain to Sarah what was to happen on the day of the Queen's visit. Not only had he singularly failed to do that, but he had ended the conversation, by inviting her on an archaeology excursion to Wilbury Hills! The whole episode, to William's mind, had been quite odd. 'All very strange,' thought William, not being able explain his own actions.

Samuel Lucas, unaware of all that troubled his friend, related his glee regarding some Pacific Islands artwork he had viewed in London. William managed to make all the right noises, in affirmation and negativity, to convince Samuel that he was suitably impressed. Even when William mistakenly said 'No,' when he quite obviously should have said 'Yes,' he quickly managed to correct himself. Out of the corner of his eye, William caught sight of the Perks shop door begin to open. He watched Sarah appear in the shop doorway, now wrapped in her light summer shawl. She turned and locked the door, completely unaware that William watched her from across the road, and headed home.

William, still out of the corner of his eye, watched Sarah walk towards the Brand Street junction and on into Bancroft. He thought of walking after her to impart the information he had really come to offer but thought better of it. Yet, he reasoned, his farmhouse stood virtually opposite where Sarah resided, he would only be heading homeward himself. As he considered whether to go or not, Samuel Lucas bid him goodnight. 'Perhaps,' thought William… 'with Samuel's departure, I could walk briskly now and find myself catching her up without intending'. At that moment, a business acquaintance came out of the pub and, on seeing William, offered to buy him an ale. William, to convince himself that catching up with Sarah Perks was unimportant, said 'Yes' to the offer and followed him into the Three Horseshoes bar. Only for a second mind, for no sooner had he entered the building than he returned to the street, having remembered that he was a follower of an abstinent faith. Sometimes, when your mind is elsewhere and deep in thought, the most important of things can so easily be forgotten. With Sarah now out of sight, the decision whether to catch up to her or not had been taken away from him. Not certain how he felt about this fact and still somewhat confused, he began his walk home at a leisurely stroll.

"There will be some other opportunity to explain myself." he spoke aloud, knowing there was no one in earshot 'Besides,' he thought, 'it would be quite unseemly to be spied chasing down the street after any lady, particularly a lady so recently widowed.'

"Lottie?" asked Sarah, remembering something that Lottie had said earlier.

"Miss Sarah?"

"You said that Hilda was not present at work today? I know she asked to visit some relation who was ill, but that was a few days ago. I take it then that she hasn't returned?"

"No, Miss Sarah, not yet,"

"Do we know how her relation is doing? Is she likely to

recover?"

"Don't think she's expecting her aunt to recover, no, miss."

"That's a shame…" Sarah picked up the first tray, now overflowing with sprigs of lavender. "I think we'll lay the trays out over here by the wall, Lottie."

Lottie looked up from her topping. "Phew! The heat, miss," she moaned for the umpteenth time, and pulled the back of her forearm across her brow to wipe away the droplets of sweat. "I feel as if I've just stepped out of hot bath, look at me, miss? I look as if I'm on fire." Lottie was indeed reddening from the intense heat which seemed to be warming the skin from the inside out. "Even the bees are having a sleep today, miss. Mister Davey says some of them are doing their work, but they are moving much slower than usual because of the heat. Instead of flitting from one lavender head to another, they're settling on just one that they takes a fancy to and then refusing to move on to any others."

"Has anyone been stung?"

"Not as I know, miss. The girls and the men are all too clever as to get in the way. Didn't even have any bee injuries up at the fields when we were collecting the sheaves."

"That is good news, Lottie. I know a sting doesn't stop anyone working, but they can be nasty and uncomfortable to say the least."

"No, no-one stung, miss, although Daisy was taken ill for a while."

"She was? In what way, taken ill?"

"Almost fainted, Miss."

"She did?"

"And she was sick."

"Sick?"

"On more than one occasion, miss."

"That's not like Daisy, it was probably brought about by the sweltering heat."

"Possibly miss, possibly," murmured Lottie, not looking up from her work. Sarah became suspicious of Lottie's attitude and manner.

"Lottie? I take it you wish to tell me something about Daisy."

Lottie looked up, put her work to one side and excitedly moved closer to Sarah.

"Well, miss, it's like this. I thought to myself, that's strange, being as Daisy always seems such a hardy soul. Anyhow, I told her to rest awhile, but she insisted on keep picking up the sheaves with the rest of the girls."

"Well, Lottie, you told me the Royce girls said they were suffering from a fever. Perhaps they do, and if they do, that may be what Daisy also suffers from."

"Possibly miss, but I don't think so. Daisy's suffering ain't from no fever, miss, not the sort those lazy Royce girls say they have, anyhow."

"What do you mean, Lottie?"

Lottie looked over her shoulder, somewhat dramatically, before leaning back to Sarah to continue.

"I tell you what I means, Miss Sarah. I think Daisy and her Richard will be announcing some good news in the next few days, or my name's not Lottie Greenacre."

"You think so?" asked Sarah, finally realising what Lottie was referring to. "That would be good news, indeed. It must be over a year since they were married, and they are such Godly folk. Yes, indeed, that would be most wonderful news if they were so blessed.

"It's not only Godly folk that is blessed with children, miss. Them Royce's breed like rabbits, miss."

"Lottie! You really must stop this… uncharitable talk about

fellow townsfolk. And see that Daisy and Richard's good news comes through their choice and timing, Lottie, and not forced out because of some rumour spread through town gossip, however well intentioned."

"My lips are sealed, miss."

Sarah was dubious, convinced that the sealing of the lips, was something far beyond the physical power of Lottie Greenacre, even if she had made the statement in good faith. "I haven't mentioned or suggested it to anyone saving yourself…"

"That's good, Lottie, let us keep it that way." Sarah well understood the destructive power of the 'loose tongue' in a small and close-knit community. "Except, of course, my Robert. I had to tell him. And my father. And old Mrs Thomas next door."

Sarah paused her work and breathed an exaggerated sigh of disbelief. But Lottie wasn't finished. "Oh, and I did mention it in passing to Annie and my friend Lilly at the stores in Sun Street, but none of them won't say nothing." Lottie seemed to have finally finished her short list of recipients. But worryingly, Sarah could hear the cogs that powered Lottie's brain still working flat-out and was not at all surprised when Lottie added "Oh, and of course, Hilda. I had to tell her, just before she went away to look after her aunt." Realising from Sarah's deadly silence that this might be one person too many, she tried to reduce the size of her moral crime with a perfectly good excuse for having done so. "But I only told Hilda because she's unlikely to be back in time for when Daisy does choose to announce it. And you know how Hilda hates to miss out on any happy announcements. She's already miffed that she's not here to see the Queen."

"Lottie Greenacre, you're incorrigible."

"Thank you, miss. Although I'm not sure what that word means, miss, but seeing as you've never said a bad word to me in my whole life, I don't expect it means anything that I can't live with." Sarah decided it was no longer a case worth pursuing and instead decided to change the subject by asking Lottie to enlighten her on Hilda's poor Aunt. Lottie, never shy or reluctant in delivering gossip, duly obliged.

Lottie explained that the whole thing, in her opinion was a rum case from top to toe and to explain it fully, she would need to start from the very beginning. This, thought Sarah, was probably a good idea. And with the two of them never stinting from their appointed tasks of topping, bunching and binding, Lottie, ever good to her word, started from the very beginning.

Until a few weeks ago, Hilda had never mentioned this aunt to anyone. Then suddenly, out of the blue, she had taken Lottie to one side to confide in her. Hilda needed to tell her story to someone, and for some reason, she chose Lottie. 'Not the wisest choice, if she wished to keep it private.' thought Sarah…

Many years ago, Hilda had thought this aunt of hers had done something despicably wrong and quite upsetting. When Hilda's grandmother died, she had left a pretty little piece of china to Hilda's mother. Only small, it seemed; a shepherd holding a crook in one hand and a lamb in the other. Apparently, it wasn't worth a great deal of money, but it did hold sentimental value for Hilda's mother. But when it came time for Hilda's mother to receive her inheritance… the piece of china was nowhere to be seen. Hilda was convinced that this aunt had taken it for herself. Hilda's mother was devastated by her sister's action and seeing her mother so

distraught in turn upset Hilda. She was so annoyed that
Hilda told her mother not to have anything to do with her
sister and convinced the rest of the family to do likewise.
Which they did. For the next twenty years.

"Twenty years? Oh, that's very sad."

"I know, miss, but it gets even sadder."

Lottie continued with her story. Over the years and even
after her mother had passed on, Hilda had continued to make
the woman's life a misery. Then, a few months back, a clerk
at the solicitors' office that had dealt with the will was
arrested for fraud and theft. It materialised that the accused
man had been stealing clients' belongings for years and that
one of the pieces he had stolen, was the piece of china.

"So, it wasn't the aunt after all?"

"No miss, it wasn't. And that is why Hilda, now
overwhelmed with guilt and remorse, is doing everything
she can to help this old lady in her last days. Her aunt has no
one else, you see, and Hilda sees this as her opportunity to…
well, say sorry, I suppose."

"Poor Hilda."

"So, miss, none of the girls had a problem with Hilda
missing the work, even though it leaves us shorthanded."

"That's very kind of them."

"Yes, miss, but those Royce girls are another matter
altogether." said Lottie throwing her favourite subject into
the mix…

"Lottie, for heaven's sake, will you stop…" But Sarah's
admonishment of Lottie's crusade against the Royce sisters
was brought to an abrupt halt by the shop door opening.

"Why, William?" Sarah unconsciously changed her
disapproving glare to a warm smile.

"What brings you in today?" William respectfully took his

hat from his head. "I hope you, nor your family, are suffering on this day of all days?" continued Sarah, gently dabbing her brow with the dripping wet cloth taken from her apron pocket, seeming to only make matters worse.
"We are all quite well, thank you and in good spirits."

A 'moment' descended upon proceedings, with William thinking Sarah as radiant as when he last saw her and Sarah thinking thoughts along similar lines. The moment would have lasted longer had it not been for Lottie's artificial cough. And, as her artificial cough was far from subtle, the eyes of Sarah and William immediately alighted upon her. This glance in turn energised Lottie who diplomatically sprang into action.

"Another bushel of our finest lavender you say, Miss Sarah?" invented Lottie with a brilliance of mind that surprised even herself. "Of course, miss, I'll get it straight away," and with that Lottie exited out of the open door and into the yard. Having watched Lottie exit, their eyes once again turned back to each other. "We make sprigs." volunteered Sarah, explaining Lottie's departure.

"Sprigs?"

"Yes, we make sprigs of lavender. Some for my lady friends to hold later at the station and some that the girls may sell at the station entrance."

"Ah yes, sprigs. Which brings me neatly to the point of my visit."

"You wish to have a sprig?"

"Not exactly, no. The other evening, I meant to speak to you about today and then, not finding the opportunity, I thought it no matter, for another opportunity would surely arise."

"And did it?" asked Sarah trying to keep up.

"No, I'm afraid it didn't, which is why I am here now. Before it is too late."

There ensued an unhelpful silence.

"William? I must tell you that I really haven't the faintest idea what you are talking about."

"Of course, you haven't," answered William, slowly regaining his natural confidence. Then, feeling that he was now back in control of his instincts, he added, "Let me explain."

"Several weeks past, it came to my notice that information was circulating the town that was false. I understood why this information had come about as it has roots in some truth. I refer to the presentations later today being made to her Majesty and Prince Albert."

"Are you saying there will be no presentations made?"

"On the contrary, there will be presentations, most certainly. There will be some fine grapes from Joseph Sharples' hot-house, a plateau of flowers cut from Exton's flower beds and a bottle of lavender perfume that I've personally made for the Prince Consort." Having said this, William paused.

"That all sounds most fine," said Sarah, feeling she was expected to say something.

"Yes, a fine presentation from the town to the Queen."

"You must understand, William, I do not have any issue over whose lavender perfume is presented. It could just as easily have been Mr Bartlett in Sun Street who was chosen."

"That is unlikely, Sarah. Bartlett's lavender output bears no comparison to the amount of lavender produced by our two businesses."

"Are you then saying...?" Sarah had hardly commenced her question, when William politely raised his hand in the air to signal her to hold, as she had done to him the previous evening.

"Please Sarah, I have almost finished, but have yet to come

to the point. I want you to know that the board chose Ransom perfume over Perks perfume, not because of any difference in quality…"

"For there is none," interrupted Sarah, despite her earlier acceptance that he should be allowed to finish.

"True, none whatsoever. As I say, not because of any difference in quality, but for the simple fact that I am now producing eight times as many lavender products as the Perks yard. The board wish to show off the quantity of the town's lavender products not, I repeat, the quality."

"I see. Thank you for this information, William, but it really wasn't necessary."

"But it was necessary. I had strongly suggested that you were informed officially and though I was under the impression that would happen, I now know that it did not. For that I am extremely sorry." He paused for a second and Sarah mistakenly went to speak, but William's hand once again shot into the air, this time with even more speed, so that Sarah would not even start her sentence.

"I still… I still haven't quite reached the point I am here to make."

Sarah respectfully said nothing.

"Despite rumours in the town to the opposite, it will not be myself presenting these tributes, but the young Mary Exton."

"Mary?"

"Yes Sarah, Mary. This is not just a day to pay homage to the Queen, it is much more political than that. Today is an opportunity to lift the profile of the town locally, in London, nationally, internationally. As you know, Mary's father is the banker William Exton, her Uncle Joseph Sharples is also involved in the Hitchin Bank. This is the bank that holds the Great Northern Railway's local accounts. It is business that steers this venture today, Sarah, business and nothing else."

"I see." William looked as if he were hoping for more assurance, so Sarah added. "I really do."

"I'm glad. I wish it were otherwise. In my opinion, it would be more befitting if it were you doing the presenting, or even Samuel. After all, Harry Perks was the one to put the wheels in motion, so to speak." The silence that followed was profound but pleasant and for that William inwardly breathed a sigh of relief.

"Thank you for telling me this. I really am most grateful, William,"

"Thank you, Sarah. I did not want you to think me vain, Sarah."

It was an open question, one that Sarah could respond to if she so wished. But she never got a chance.

"Here we are, a bushel of the finest, the most-finest, nationally acclaimed Perks lavender!" cried Lottie as she entered through the doorway, struggling with the weight of the said bushel. But even as she entered, even as she spoke, she realised instantly that she would still be regarded as an intruder. So, with the most brilliant change of direction, she spun on the spot and returned out through the doorway, saying as she went … "Yet, I think I could find even better than this, if I really put my mind to it." And she was gone. But it was too late.

"Well," said William, replacing his hat on his head, "I must leave you to your sprigs."

"Sprigs. Yes, indeed, we have many sprigs to create and time is running fast."

"I take it you will be present this afternoon?"

"Most certainly, nothing in this world will stop me from witnessing this glorious day." She followed William to the door, which was fortuitous, because the low door frame caused William's tall and fashionable hat to be knocked from his head, which Sarah expertly caught. There followed a few moments of forced laughter until neither could consider extending it any further and it eventually subsided.

"I have my ticket, which enables me a place opposite where their majesties' carriage will stop. And… I have a new brooch."

"A new brooch? That is good. And I have my hat," quipped William, venturing to joke. The forced laughter this time was much shorter and borne of politeness rather than embarrassment. "I will look out for you at the station, Sarah. Good morning." He tipped his now firmly placed hat and walked away.

"Yes, good morning to you, William and thank you. Thank you very much." said Sarah, speaking to the closed door's frosted panel.

With his left ear un-mistakenly larger than his right

Chapter Three

"Miss Sarah?" Lottie's voice went unheard. Sarah stood still, deep in thought and still looking at the closed door in front of her. "Is there anything wrong, Miss Sarah?" This time Sarah was aware of the voice behind her but she was in that twilight zone, where one is meandering from the world where one's thoughts are one's own, to the world where one's thoughts are concerned with the moment. The sound of Lottie's voice was dragging Sarah back from the former to the latter. In this case however, Sarah's transition was proving slower than would be considered normal. "Miss Sarah?" repeated Lottie for a third time. Sarah turned to face Lottie and smiled.

"Lottie, you were saying?"

"Will we be needing this, miss?"

Sarah, with body and mind now firmly back in the Perks shop at 9, Cock Street, looked at the bushel Lottie referred to.

"Good heavens, Lottie," reproved Sarah, walking briskly back to the table. "We hardly have time to finish the two we already have, let alone start a third. No, you can take that back to the yard. I really can't think why you fetched it here in the first place." Sarah resumed her work at the table and Lottie, feeling slightly peeved at having disappeared with such ingenuity and not have her performance appreciated, picked up the bushel.

"Right, miss, I'll take it back then." With that, Lottie exited back into the sun, a sun that was now burning those working in the open yard and slow cooking those lucky enough to be sitting in the shade.

Sarah concentrated again on her work, grouping the fine stems of lavender and binding them with the pretty yellow bind. As she finished one, she held the complete sprig in the air, and bringing it to her nose, breathed in deeply. It must have been a magical sprig, thought Sarah, for with one intake of breath, the familiar odour transported her up to the fields. The fields where, not so many days ago, the ripening crops had swayed in the summer winds and added a splash of imperial purple to the lush green landscape. She found herself standing on the edge of the field at the top of Gaping Hills. Without knowing it she had closed her eyes, to enrichen her transportation. The gold finches and blue tits were applauding the day with their non-stop chatter and the lavender stalks danced excitedly in the gentle gusts of wind, as if to say; 'We are ready for you, we are ready!"

It was only the sound of Beggar, the yard dog, barking outside that brought Sarah suddenly back to earth. She realised that was the second time in but a few minutes she had allowed herself to be led elsewhere. She chastised herself for her idleness, affirming that there was far too much work for such idle folly. Though she determined not to forget the power of closing one's eyes and breathing in the lavender odour to transport one to enchanting places. Who needs a magic lamp or a flying carpet to reach one's favourite locations when one possesses the gift of seductive lavender?

"Beggar!" shouted Lottie outside in the yard "Stop your barking, dog!" From the sound of Beggar's continued growling, Lottie's command was falling on deaf-dog ears. Sarah was suddenly struck by stark realisation and knew that this incessant snarling could only mean one thing. Beggar rarely barked, in fact he only barked at one person to Sarah's knowledge.

But a word about Beggar. He was a mongrel who belonged to no-one. One of those numerous master-less hounds which for no explicable reason, choose to attach themselves to a place, person or people. Beggar was one of that mysterious blending. He had wandered in one rainy day, this time last year to be more precise and had lain down obediently in front of the girls as they were busy topping. He was of medium size, with his left ear un-mistakenly larger than his right; an errant ear that flopped over forwards as if it were exhausted or dozing. The right ear was of more normal proportions and stood upright for the most part, as if listening out for any danger whilst the left ear slept. Awake or asleep, he would stretch out on the cool cobbled stones in front of wherever the girls worked. Lottie tried to work out if he was offering his loyalty to any of them particularly. But it soon became apparent that the dog was assigning his loyalty to the herd and not to any one person.

Now, to Sarah's knowledge, there were only two things that would bring Beggar to life. The first, and this in spectacular fashion, was food. Whenever the girls stopped for a break and unwrapped their bread cloths, the seemingly docile dog would suddenly leap into the air, performing what one could only describe as a backward somersault. He would complete this feat of dexterity by landing upright on his hind legs and then would totter around in anticipation of reward. The whole astounding display was a show designed to encourage the payment of food, like a beggar performing for alms. Hence, he was named Beggar. In his upright position and with the use of his short front paw, he would flick the floppy ear backwards as if to put it back in its place, like one of the girls might if a stray curl of hair should escape their head caps. If Beggar did favour an audience to perform to, it would be little Lucy Hutchins. This was ironic, as Lucy's background was most unenviable. She would come supplied each day with quite meagre rations from her over-crowded home in Thorpe's Yard. If anyone would not have food to spare for a performing dog, it was Lucy.

It was obvious that he had been taught these tricks and all surmised that he had been lost by some travelling side show, a circus possibly, or even the companion of some organ grinder who had retired from the roads and set the dog free. Whatever his background, Beggar was now very much part of the Perks yard. He slept there, ate there, and refused most enticements to leave. Occasionally, he would be put on a rope lead that Lucy had fashioned for him, and then he would begrudgingly submit to accompanying the girls up to the fields of an evening. For the best part, Beggar was at his happiest performing, dozing and living in the yard.

The only other event that would bring Beggar to life, was one that did not involve any party pieces whatsoever, but just aggressive barking and growling. It was a sight not pleasant to watch, for his constant snarling would show a side of Beggar's character that was rarely seen. The cause of this frenzy was Lazzy Smith, the gypsy.

Sarah was convinced that Beggar had taken a dislike to this odious character, because he was just that; odious. Lottie, the girls and many of the men thought it was because

Lazzy Smith was a gypsy. Although Sarah did not agree with this assumption, she could understand their prejudice. The constables would point to an increase in crime whenever these nomads were camped close by. They had, as Lottie pointed out, a reputation for cruelty towards animals and that may explain Beggar's behaviour.

In defence, Sarah had pointed out that there were plenty of respectable residents of Hitchin whose reputation for animal welfare was suspect, to say the least. As for the regular charges of poaching lain against them, there would be little game left to poach by the time the Stevenage twins Albert and Ebenezer Fox had finished their moonlit work. 'No,' thought Sarah, 'not all crime could be placed at the foot of the travelling community.'

Sarah prided herself on trying to see things from both sides of the argument. "It is too easy" she had once told Lottie and her friend Annie, "to jump to false conclusions; conclusions invariably arrived at simply through prejudice and gossip."

Lazzy Smith had been shown in through the back door by a reluctant Lottie. She had Beggar by the scruff of the neck and was allowing him just enough freedom to scowl at Lazzy.

"Thank you, Lottie, please take Beggar outside and see if you can't get him to quieten."

"Yes, miss… come on Beggar!" shouted Lottie, as she pulled the indignant dog away. "Quiet now, he'll do you no harm…"

Sarah could hear Lottie calling for Lucy, who might prove more persuasive with Beggar. She looked at Lazzy with her stern face, a face that few ever saw.

"Could you not enter the shop through the shop door, rather than coming through the yard and causing our dog to bark?"

"I'm sorry, Mrs Perks, I'm sure. It was in order not to cause any offence that I came that ways." Smith leered sanctimoniously. "Being a Romany, I thought it best for your reputation if I enter your premises unseen, like."

"What can I do for you?"

"I comes from the Reverend Alington, as you knows, Mrs Perks and on an errand." Lazzy Smith finished every sentence with a look that combined the adverbs 'leer' and 'sneer', so possibly forming… 'Sleer'. No such word existed, as Sarah rightly knew, but it was a word she thought adequately described what would otherwise be indescribable.

"Very well, and is this errand in regard of purchasing some product?"

"Indeed it is, Mrs Perks…" sleered Lazzy Smith…But before he could continue, Lottie poked her head round the open door.

"Sorry to disturb miss, but Mister Davey says to tell you that they've finished what they was a-doing and he'll wait here just outside the door, with Silas and Bartholomew, for you to instruct them on what's to be done next, miss." informed Lottie with the subtlety of an innocent remark that was intended to convey a message of reassurance.

"Thank you, Lottie. Please inform Mister Davey that I don't intend to be detained for long." answered Sarah and Lottie's concerned face disappeared from the open door.

"Mister Smith, I am most pressed for time today, so please be brief if you will."

"Lavender, Mrs Perks."

It always annoyed Sarah that he should address her as 'Mrs' Perks, not because she was not 'Mrs' Perks, for indeed she was. But because everyone else referred to her as 'Miss' rather than 'Mrs'. To her, this sounded much less formal and right, somehow. But this man always managed to say 'Mrs' in such a disturbing way that he made it sound not only incorrect but grotesquely vile. "In what way, lavender, Mr Smith? Does the Reverend Alington require flower heads, tincture, oils, perfume?"

"Yes. He requires all of thems that what you just mentioned."

Sarah was astounded.

"Do you jest with me?"

"No, Mrs Perks," he reached for something in his waistcoat pocket. "Unfortunately, I cannot read, not through the lack of trying, you understand, missus, but more through having had poor education, or in truth, none." He handed Sarah the crumpled note and she took it to the open door to see it better in the sunlight. As Sarah lifted the note to read, she observed Lottie, Beggar, Davey, Silas and Bartholomew all standing by the doorway. Silas lifted a homemade cudgel and nodded supportively. They resembled a bunch of notorious villains about to ambush some unsuspecting persons on the highway. Suppressing an instinct to laugh, she bit her tongue and began to read.

'Dear Mrs Perks,
Please be kind enough to supply Mr Lazzy Smith with the following: Seven Bottles of oil, seven bottles of perfume and seven bushels of your finest lavender. I have a desire to bathe, then dry and scent myself before lounging upon a bed of recently cut lavender. This is to test a therapeutic notion of mine, let us say, an experiment. Mr Smith is in possession of the small pony and cart, with which he will transport the said goods back to Letchworth Hall. The monies due, he holds in the opposite waistcoat pocket to the one from whence he withdrew this crumpled note.
Sincerely yours,

Reverend John Alington JP'

Sarah looked up from the note, scarcely believing what she had read and to be certain of its contents, she read it once again. If it had been from anyone else, she would have discarded the request as some practical joke. But this was from the Reverend John Alington, the wealthy eccentric who held residence in Letchworth Hall, and it was said that nothing lay beyond that unpredictable man's cravings or wit.

The wealthy Reverend Alington's short spell as vicar of Letchworth church was brought to a sudden halt by several complaints about the content of his sermons. These consisted mostly of rantings, ravings and the constantly endorsing the virtues of free love. When finally stripped of his parish, he had set up his own pulpit outside the church yard. There he preached in competition with the newly appointed rector, Samuel Knapp, who valiantly tried to make himself heard inside the church above the rival sermons outside. Most of the congregation deserted the church and joined Alington, not out of any preference for his views on what the Bible required from good Christians, but through being Alington's tenants. They owed their living to this wild and capricious man and could ill afford to upset him.

He revelled in shocking and upsetting any he took a dislike to. He was scurrilous and provocative, caring not what people thought or said. He would often invite gypsies, villains and the ungodly to his home. There, he would provide sumptuous dinners which would be followed by bacchanalian debauchery. It was said of a night, one would find the hall and its bedchambers to be filled with all the whores of Hertfordshire.

Amongst the other offices he held as a member of the

landed gentry, was a position upon the bench as a Justice of the Peace. He professed that if anyone would see fit to press charges against him, he would see to it that he himself was sitting the day the case was heard. Considering himself to be a man of impeccable and sound character, he would then see no sane reason not to acquit himself. To avoid this occurring, he was seldom, if ever, asked by the bench to sit on any cases, in fear that he would make a mockery of its jurisdiction.

On another occasion, he thought to send his workforce to London to attend the Great Exhibition. They informed him that most of them had never been to the great city and were afeard they may get lost. To make sure that did not happen, he had laid out in his grounds, with lengths of timber, the complete street map of London from Kings Cross to Hyde Park. For over a week, he had taught them and drilled them into knowing the right roads to take, with those going to the Exhibition having hay tied to their right knees, and those heading home having hay tied to their left knees. This was to ensure that they would not become confused to which way they were going. At the end of the week, after what one can only assume was utter chaos and muddle, he concluded that they were all stupid and decided not to send them after all.

He delighted in causing outrage within respectable circles and had a distaste for the residents of Hitchin. It was not unusual to see him march along Bancroft, in a giant leopard skin, accompanied by gypsy fiddlers who could out-fiddle the best in the land and gypsy girls dancing to their heathen tunes, swirling their dresses provocatively. They would cry out profanities and sing songs so offensive that even the wickedest publican would turn red and blush with embarrassment.

According to Sarah, this man's antics were but another

reflection on the unfairness of the world. The wealthy that
are mad are designated 'eccentric' and very much left to
their own devices. Yet, the poor who are deemed mad are
taken from the streets to languish in some dreadful asylum.
'However,' thought Sarah, 'The sooner Lazzy Smith was
gone with Alington's required purchases, the better for
everyone.' Sarah moved back to the open door and called out
into the yard over the massed heads of her hidden
bodyguard.

"Mister Davey!" she shouted, pretending that they were not
close by, "Here if you will?" Davey quickly moved away
from the doorway, so that his reply did not sound too close.
"Coming, Ma'am!" shouted Davey, cupping his hand to his
mouth to sound some distance off. He had decided that this
might dispel any notion the gypsy might have had that he
was by the door, waiting to pounce if he were so required.

Lazzy Smith was rugged, of medium height, thin,
unshaven with dark, curly wild hair. He was a man renowned
for fisticuffs and general brawling. Rumour acclaimed him
as a decent prize fighter in his younger days. Apparently, in
some brutal bout, he had killed a man whose body was
rushed away and never found. He was overly polite for the
most part but could become argumentative and quite violent.
Sarah's gentle gender would not prevent Lazzy Smith from
lashing out if he were so minded, of this she was certain.
There had been a moment in her life, quite recently, when
this man had caused her to fear for her safety. Yet, following
the incident, she had decided not to make issue of it, as - to
her just and fair mind - it was more driven by alcohol than
genuine intent. That was what she had told herself, anyhow.

Sarah had moved away from the doorway in pretence of
still reading the note, as Davey entered the shop. "You
called, ma'am?" asked Davey, as if he had rushed from the

other end of the yard.

"Yes, Davey. Please be kind enough to see that these products are taken from the stores and are loaded on to Mr Smith's cart." instructed Sarah, handing Davey the crumpled note, forgetting that he could not read.

"Certainly, Miss Sarah" answered Davey, glancing at the note as if he could read. "If it's fine with you, Miss Sarah, I'll ask Miss Lottie to lend a hand?"

"Lottie?"

"Yes miss, seeing as she is more likely to know the location of these here products than me, miss."

He held out the note towards the end of his sentence hoping that she would realise. After a couple of seconds, Sarah did realise and agreed to his request.

"If you'd like to follow Mister Davey," said Sarah, not looking back at Lazzy Smith.

He had stood throughout, patiently looking around the shop when her eyes were upon him, but when her back was to him, she felt his eyes boring into her, mentally undressing her. Lazzy Smith was quite aware of the effect he had on her and gloated in the knowledge. He fabricated a slight attention-seeking cough to make her turn to face him.

"Begging your pardon, Mrs Perks," he sleered. She reluctantly turned to face him but avoided his eyes. He was holding out a pound note heavily disguised as another crumpled piece of paper.

"The Reverend says to keep the change if you will, Mrs Perks."

Sarah had already costed the goods in her mind and although she would not usually accept charity, especially from such undesirables as these men, she decided not to give him an excuse to remain any longer than was necessary. Besides, it was far too hot to search her money box for a mere farthing.

"This way, if you will!" almost bellowed Davey, to give time for the remainder of the protection gang outside to disperse. If Lazzy walked out into the yard to find them gathered and Silas with cudgel in hand, it might have led to an altercation of some kind.

"Thank you kindly, Mrs Perks." said Lazzy Smith, respectfully touching his cap, although lingering on the word 'Mrs'.

However hard Sarah tried to remain fair and polite, this one man challenged those instincts to their limits and she would feel much happier when he was gone. She was convinced Alington always sent Smith on these errands, in the knowledge that she did feel so uneasy in his company. Or perhaps, Lazzy Smith requested of Alington that he should be sent. Sarah would not put that past him, especially of late. He followed Davey out into the yard and Sarah took the dishevelled looking pound note into the office to store in the cashbox. As she did so, still with her spirit disturbed and uncomfortable, she sat down and reluctantly recalled her last meeting with Lazzy Smith.

It was late July when she was returning one early evening from the fields at the far end of Lucas Lane. The crops had been identified as being of an excellent quality and ready to be harvested. The small Perks work force had ridden back to the yard in the large cart. Sarah had elected to walk back. She was lowish in spirits, as she had been for several months and consequently was much happier in her own company. Visiting the fields during the day brought her mixed emotions. On the one hand, joy in seeing the beauty of the lavender and the ripeness of the crop and on the other hand, loneliness, as she sank deeper in the knowledge that during the day she walked alone.

She had stood staring out into the hills beyond, for what she believed to be minutes. Yet, an hour had come and passed before she finally shook herself from her daze and made for home. Turning a corner in the lane, where the hedges either side made little room for more than one person to pass at a time, a figure suddenly appeared from a gap in the hedge. A scream of terror escaped from her lungs and snapped the air.

"Did I frit you somewhat, Mrs Perks?" sleered Lazzy Smith. For it was he that stood before her. Hot and bothered, he undid his neckerchief and dabbed at his sweating brow, the evening sun causing the beads and droplets to glitter on his skin.

"Yes! You most certainly did!" replied Sarah angrily, holding her hand to her chest. There was a slight pause as she recovered her composure and assessed her situation. Lazzy Smith neither apologised nor mocked her for screaming out loud. He just stood and… sleered. She had her hat on, as she always did when out, firmly connected to her head with a long hat pin. But she did not carry anything larger that might substitute for a defensive weapon. He had never threatened her physically before, quite the opposite, he had always spoken to her with politeness and courtesy, however insincere. Yet, she had always felt threatened and unsafe in his presence. And she did so then.

"You'll be on your way home, I'm guessing, Mrs Perks?"

"Yes. Aren't you a long way from your master at Letchworth Hall?"

She was determined to keep some conversation going until she could find a way of moving on. He did not block her way as such, but his stout frame made it most difficult to pass, without her brushing against him or he having to move to one side. He did not move.

"You mistake things, Mrs Perks. Lazzy Smith has no master, save his instinct to do good. The Reverend treats us folk well and running a few errands for him is no skin off my nose and I sees it as a way of showing my gratitude."

Sarah felt herself growing uncomfortably hot, and she knew this was not just a consequence of the warm evening.

"As to being round here, ma'am, I have kin camped close by and I have just paid them a visit. A surprise visit if you may. We sat some hours and sang and reminisced of the olden days."

Sarah said nothing.

"Much fun was had, which is only right, I think, when the world be so ablaze with the sun." This time, at the end of his sentence, he did not sleer, as was his want, but visibly grinned.

"And swimming, Mrs Perks, we did some swimming in the river, as the Lord made us, so as a way of cooling down. Not as if I'm cooled down now, you understands? What with the undressing and the redressing and everything and the walk to here from the campsite, I coulds just as well go back and takes another swim."

Sarah still said nothing.

"Nothing so enticing as a swim on a day like this one, don't you think, Mrs Perks?"

"I really must be on my way…" began Sarah, looking to move past him. "Mister Davey and the others will be concerned as to my whereabouts."

"Then it would be only right that I should escorts you home, Mrs Perks. These is dangerous times and the lanes is full of villains, so I hears tell."

"Thank you, Mr Smith, but I have no need of an escort, thank you, I am quite capable…." As she spoke, she made ready to pass by him, but he swiftly and purposely shifted his weight to make her exit more difficult. Now he was close to her. She found herself wedged between him and the hedge. He was close, she could smell his clothes, she could smell his breath. Garments that carried the stench of the unwashed, breath that oozed, dripping with alcohol. Clothes that had obviously sat unwanted on the bankside, if he had indeed recently swum, which she sincerely doubted. She knew the gypsies swam the river naked but if he had swum, surely some of his foulness, that suffocated her now, would have washed away.

He had moved closer still, holding out his crooked arm for her to take. "If you should do me the courtesies of taking my arm, Mrs Perks," he sleered, "I will promise only to walks you back to the top of Bedford Street. I would not seek to embarrass you none, a-front of your friends now. It would not do for you to be seen out walking in the company of a… gypsy, I thinks." He was drunk, Sarah knew him to be drunk. He had the unmistakable sway of one trying to prove otherwise. She had vowed not to look him in the eye, but now she found herself doing so. But he was looking elsewhere. All through his speech, his eyes were no longer on hers but staring unrestrained at her neck, eyes that were being pressured to focus on the top button of her dress… as he stared, he moved into her and she was forced back, almost to be buried in the hedge.

"Mr Smith, I must be gone… please let me pass…" Her words faded on her lips, she could feel him against her, he had now dropped the courteous arm and she felt… she felt… she could not comprehend what it was she felt. She felt vulnerable, helpless. Her conscious screamed to be saved but her sub conscious said nothing. It remained silent, unmoved. She sensed her whirling and confused mind transporting her to that hideous, pleasure seeking world that inhabited his master's hall. She saw herself semi naked, her clothes being softly pulled from her as if she were wrapped in tissue. The hands that took her clothes from her belonged to faces; wicked faces, but wicked faces that did not frighten her. Faces, contorted and ecstatic, promising and possessed, pressing into her face and neck. Helpless and losing all strength, she abandoned herself, now guiltless, to whatever may ensue. Her eyes shut tight, dreading, yet yearning, desperate, yet wanting. She saw herself falling gently, in slow motion, from the gallery in the great hall, as if lowered by a thousand searching hands, on to a bed of shining purple… And at the very moment that Sarah's energy was being irretrievably sapped, her brain turning fit to swoon, she heard the familiar sound of barking. Then the just as familiar voice of Lottie Greenacre calling out in the short distance. "Beggar! Now what's started you a-barking? You caught the scent of something, have yer?!"

Lazzy Smith, jolted by the sounds, looked back down the path, his face changing, his mind sobering. Stepping away, he looked back fleetingly at Sarah, his passion chilled but his sleer intact.

"Ah," he said, stepping further away from her and touching his forelock… "I think's you're now in safer hands, Mrs Perks, so is best I bids ye a good evening." Another stint of loud and ferocious barking in the air accompanied the arrival of Beggar.

On seeing Lazzy Smith, the faithful hound stopped momentarily, growling determinedly, as hunter and hunted eyed each other. Then Beggar darted once again up the dusty lane with Lazzy his intended victim. The speed of Beggar running up the lane towards them, was only matched by the speed of Lazzy Smith disappearing back through the gap in the hedge. As Lottie also came into sight, she saw Sarah for the first time who, feeling foolish, had taken herself out of the hedge to greet Lottie with as much dignified pleasure as she could muster. Meanwhile, the fully focused Beggar had disappeared through the gap in the hedge and after Lazzy Smith.

"There you are miss," called out Lottie as she came closer, "We was a-wondering where you had got to, so I decided to come and meet you and at the same time walk Beggar, who grows fatter and porkier every day."

"That was very kind of you, Lottie, but there really was no need." Sarah had answered, straightening her lopsided hat, "I had just tarried a while longer at the fields than I had intended."

"No trouble, miss, it will be good for the dog, although he came with reluctance. All the way up here he did nothing but dawdle. But just a back a bit round the corner, he suddenly acts like a beast possessed. I thinks he must have caught scent of a rabbit, or the likes."

"Yes," answered Sarah, deciding not to relay what had taken place, as her soul was seared with guilt and she did not want to upset Lottie. Besides, the fair-minded Sarah told herself falsely, he had not actually attacked her and he was no doubt driven by drunkenness. Such an incident, raised in the right circles, would no doubt see him imprisoned. Transported even. Her conscience, ashamed of her own indecency, questioned whether he was totally at fault. She could have passed by him, threatened him with arrest. No, she had good reason to cast the whole unsavoury episode from her mind. But she knew, that even if unspoken, the memory would return to haunt her. And it did, often.

"You alright, miss?" queried Lottie, looking at her mistress more intently and seeing Sarah's mind not completely present. "You seems to have more hedge on you than the hedge has, miss."

"Yes, I'm fine," over enthused Sarah who, in trying to conceal the event, only managed to make Lottie more suspicious. "I foolishly stumbled, but I'm alright now. No injuries, save to my pride."

"Right you are, miss." Lottie, unconvinced, turned to the gap in the hedge, shouting out for her four-legged companion. "Beggar! Here boy! Beggar!" There was a slight pause whilst they listened, but no bark was forthcoming.

"Not like him…. Oh well, not to worry, he knows well enough where he lives. He'll catch up, no doubt." With that, Sarah and Lottie began their walk home in the faint illumination of the dying light.

Beggar did not catch them up on their walk home. He was already inside the yard by the time they arrived back, eagerly awaiting their arrival.

When he enthusiastically welcomed them home, Lottie noticed blood on his nose. But it wasn't Beggar's blood. "I think this hound has had himself a rabbit!" concluded Lottie, ruffling his neck "Is that right, Beggar, you four-legged poacher, you! Has Beggar had himself a rabbit!?"

It was a memory that Sarah had fought hard to supress. It tended to raise its ugly head whenever Lazzy Smith appeared, or she, in moments of sinful weakness, allowed it to surface of its own accord.

Her thoughts were disturbed by the sound of the pony and cart leaving the yard via the cobblestoned coach drive. The welcome departure of her unwanted customer was accompanied by the reassuring sound of Beggar's farewell barking.

"No Beggar! Come back here you… Beggar!" Sarah heard Lottie shouting.

"Beggar! You villain! You comes back here, now, do you hears me!" It was Lucy's little voice, trying to add weight to Lottie's command.

"It ain't worth you chasing him, Lucy!"

After a slight pause, Lottie re-entered the shop to explain what had happened.

"Begging your pardon, miss, but that hound of ours has gone a chasing after that gypsy and Lucy's gone a chasing after the hound, but I doubts as if she'll catch him up."

"No, nor do I. But we can't be concerned with his antics today. No doubt he'll be back when he's ready, he usually is." Lottie had wandered over to the shop window, looking down Cock Street. After a moment, Lucy came into sight.

"Well, Lucy's back miss, but no sign of Beggar,"

Lottie came away from the window and absent-mindedly watched her mistress at the table.

Sarah had picked up a small bunch of the delicate stems, spilt the bunch in two and placed one half on the table close by. With the other half in her hand, she took up a piece of the yellow binding already cut to length and continued binding as before. It was something that Sarah had done many times over the years and now the operation had become second nature.

"Come on, Lottie" commanded Sarah, looking up and seeing Lottie lost in thought. "We have much to do, I think."

Lottie returned obediently to the table and resumed her work. The topping of lavender was something she had practiced since a small child and there was no one more competent or expert. Although, in this case, they were 'heads' with 'stems' being topped to enable the sprigs to be formed.

For several moments they worked in silence. Although the

front door was unlocked, the shop was closed for the day. Sarah had not anticipated much trade, on a day when all would be readying themselves for the royal visit and she had seen no point in opening. It was now nine-thirty and the heat was becoming unbearable. The sprigs would be ready in plenty of time, but as for the topping in the yard…

"How are the girls faring, Lottie?"

"As good as can be expected, miss. Hopefully, they'll be done in time." answered Lottie, but then added, because she could never resist the temptation, "But what with Hilda away and them…"

"I know, Lottie. I know and you know I would hire extra hands if I could."

"I know, miss."

"But who is looking to be hired on the day the Queen comes to town? Any other time the loss of three workhands would not create such an issue. As I said earlier, if the girls are not finished by…let us say one o'clock? Yes, one o'clock should give time enough for everyone to return to their homes and put on their Sunday best… if they are not done by then, they may all down tools on the clock's striking and leave what they do as it is. What is more, tomorrow's work will start at noon and not a minute before."

"Yes, miss. Thank you, miss."

"Good. Now, no more… 'Thank you, miss', Lottie, for I have made it plain enough and so it is done. For I swear, if I am obliged to say it once more, I shall surely faint under the weight of my own repetition." Sarah and Lottie laughed, both now content.

"I do not like that man." said Lottie after a several minutes of quiet. Sarah knew of whom she spoke but chose not to answer. A few more moments passed but, like a dog with a stick, Lottie would not let it go. "I like not that he comes here and worries you, miss." Sarah opened her mouth to reply but Lottie gave her no chance. "It's true, miss, I sees you whenever he is here, he unsettles you somewhat and quite understandable too."

"He is a customer, Lottie…" began Sarah, but once again Lottie cut her off.

"…He's a gypsy, miss!" snapped Lottie with a venom that surprised Sarah.

"Lottie!"

"I'm sorry miss, but they are not to be trusted. And it does not hold well that anyone should see him in this shop. It's an embarrassment miss, and not one that you are deserving of."

"That is very prejudiced, Lottie."

"I'm sure it is, miss, whatever the word means, but I knows I'm speaking the truth and if that's what the word means, then that is what I am."

There was a slight pause.

"Prejudiced."

"Sorry, miss?"

"The word was 'prejudiced', Lottie and it means having a preconceived idea about someone or something without any reason or personal experience."

"Does it, miss? Then that isn't me. It isn't me because I have good reason and experience to make me think the way I do. In fact, the whole town has cause. I'm not alone in this thinking. So, you'll have to agree, miss, that I'm not that word you just said."

"Prejudiced."

"Exactly." Lottie was content and felt justified "That is definitely not what I am."

Sarah decided to rationalise the subject. Lottie was always of a strong mind and Sarah liked that. She also encouraged debate amongst the girls, as she saw it as a form of added education. To be able to hold an opinion and have the words to justify it in conversation was good, instead of just making wild and unsupported statements.

"On a personal basis, Lottie, I try hard not to be…that word. It is too easy to hate and dislike, thinking you have good cause, when in truth you have not. I find if I slip into the mind set of disliking people for no obvious reason, I then find myself inventing evidence to justify those feelings."
Silence.

"Like Lazzy Smith? For it is quite obvious you can't stand the man…and don't deny it, miss, there are others think as I do. We see it in you and you don't even try to mask it."

"What on earth are you talking about, Lottie?"

"I know he's not here very often, but when he is, you have on your 'stern' face. I never sees your 'stern' face unless he is here or his name be mentioned."

"It is true, that I do not like the man…"

"And is that because you have good reason and personal experience, in order that you are not… that word?"

There was a slight pause as Sarah struggled to choose the appropriate words, but failed.

"Lottie, I really do not want to pursue this conversation."

"There it is."

"What do you mean, 'there it is'?" queried Sarah.

"Your 'stern' face." Having spoken and before Sarah could comment or defend herself, Lottie had branched off down yet another route.

"Besides…" said Lottie beginning the case for her defence against all things 'prejudiced'. "…they are ungodly folk, all of them, behaving as they do. None of them are in church of a Sunday, none of them. That's maybe why you loathe the man so, miss, what with you being a good Christian woman and what have you, you finds he turns your stomach whenever he's close..."

"Can we drop the case of Mr Smith, please Lottie?"

"You see, miss, it may not be anything to do with you having any of that word about you, it's just something you can't help when you're near him. Something that's just natural in you and that something you can't help."

"Lottie?" Sarah had stopped work and looked worryingly at Lottie "What do you mean?"

"What I say, miss, the way you feel about him, you know, that man that you don't want me to mention anymore, you just naturally feel the way you do about him, and you can't help it."

Sarah stared at Lottie.

For one horrifying second Sarah seriously considered that Lottie had access to her mind, her thoughts, her sins, her shame. But Sarah need not have worried... because as Lottie continued her evidence, Sarah realised her sins and shame were quite safe.

"Because you being so good, miss, and standing so close to something evil."

"Evil?"

"Alright miss, something bad," corrected Lottie, "a coming together of two things that are... opposites... that's it! You are naturally stern with that man because you know you are opposites. That's what disgusts you."

Before Sarah could consider this further, Lottie was off again on the subject that Sarah would much rather drop. But she could not even chastise Lottie for talking instead of working, because Lottie was working faster than her tongue. She must search for another reason to quell Lottie's enthusiasm.

"You take Daisy and her Richard, miss. Now, they're Godly

people in anyone's eyes and they done what Godly people should do. They got themselves married and here we are just over a year later, and they are having their first little 'un."
"Remember Lottie, we don't know that yet,"
"Not entirely true miss, because I do, you do and they do. It's just the rest of the world that is still ignorant of the fact. Oh, and saving for those good trustworthy friends and relatives of mine that I also told. But my point is, miss, them gypsies don't behave that way."
"You don't know that, Lottie…"
"Like them that are forever camping down at Oughton Head. Them gypsy girls find themselves expectant and then thinks about binding themselves together in the eyes of God, just as an after-thought like…"
"I hope you realise that God is listening to your gossip this very moment, he doesn't sleep Lottie." warned Sarah, but Lottie was undaunted.
"I know that, miss, and I don't think those gypsies get much sleep neither… besides, miss, it ain't no gossip, it ain't just me saying it, everyone knows it."
"They worked hard in the fields, Lottie."
"They did and credit where it's due, miss, but they're a strange folk. Living on the edge, having no permanent abode and making up their own rules and morals as they go along."
"They do us no real harm."
"Not in the fields, they don't, no, but if they come into town of a night-time, you'd best lock the doors and board up the shop. It's known, miss. A few weeks ago, they stole two dogs from West Mill Farm. But bless me if the villains didn't come back the following night and steals their empty kennels as well. The Constable investigated and even visited their encampment at the Little Spinney." Lottie paused for added thought before continuing. "I suppose the gypsies'

logic was as the farmer had lost both his dogs, he wouldn't be having any use for their kennels, so they may as well have them as well!"

"Lottie!" exclaimed Sarah. Lottie was slightly taken aback by the ferocity in Sarah's voice.

"Miss?"

Sarah took a little time to compose herself and then looked to how she would reason with the passionate but, in her view, misguided Lottie, "They have a reputation, I know Lottie, but it's probably much exaggerated by certain people who have no cause or right to speak badly of them."

"Yes miss."

"Have they ever stolen anything from you?"

"No miss." admitted Lottie.

"Broken into your home in Park Road?"

"Can't say they have, miss."

"And what about your back yard, have any of them trespassed and stolen belongings of yours?"

"Not of mine, miss…"

"… Or anything belonging to your father, mother, or any other member of your illustrious family, however distant?"

"No miss." confessed the crushed Lottie. But Sarah was not finished.

"Or from any of your friends?"

"No miss."

"Well then." concluded Sarah, triumphantly. There was a very slight pause before Lottie mumbled.

"Well, nothing that I could prove, anyhows…"

Sarah, now having achieved what she perceived to be a complete victory, summarised civilly, not wanting to rub Lottie's nose in it, but looking to conclude with reasoning. "Thinking how you think, Lottie, is exactly… what that word is."

"You mean, prejudiced?"

"Yes," answered Sarah, slightly taken aback that Lottie had finally grasped the word, "but I do not condemn you for it, Lottie. I have no right to. I am nowhere as saintly as you would like to paint me. I know that and God knows...God knows that." Sarah hesitated for a few seconds and Lottie was not sure whether she had lost her line of thought or not.

"Miss?" prompted Lottie.

"I just look to point out that so much friction, anger and unfairness in the world has roots in, well, prejudice. We feel threatened by people who have not necessarily shown any signs of threatening us. It is perceived that engaging with these people, whoever they are, will harm us in some way; spoil us, ruin us, destroy everything we treasure... Do you understand, Lottie?"

But Lottie did not understand. And although they had been Sarah's own thoughts and words, she did not fully understand either.

Arthur had a falling out one night at the Three Horseshoes

Chapter Four

The door to the shop opened and the friendly face of Samuel Perks peered in. "Do we disturb?"

"Of course not." beamed Sarah, pleased to feel the atmosphere change from heated debate to friendly conversation. Samuel was followed through the door by Catherine. Two inches taller than Sarah's five foot one, she was slim, elegant and regal with hazel hair and warm, soft brown eyes that captivated all that had the good fortune to meet her. If told that she was descended from Russian royalty, you would believe it.

"Catherine."

"Sarah, good morning to you… Oh, no, I can see now that you are indeed busy and we disturb you."

"You do not disturb" replied Sarah looking back at Lottie, who did not relent from her labour. "You see that Lottie is busy and it is impossible to put Lottie off her stride. Isn't that true, Lottie?"

"Yes, miss. Good morning Mr Samuel, Miss Catherine."

"And good day to you, Lottie." Catherine lowered her white tasselled parasol and, releasing the catch, closed it down. Sarah thought it bore a remarkable resemblance to hers and wondered if it indeed was.

"We have just purchased this parasol for Catherine."

'Ah…" thought Sarah, 'apparently not'.

"It's a fine parasol, Miss Catherine," commented Lottie, regarding the parasol but never ceasing the topping of lavender, as if she had eyes under her chin.

"My old one is so tattered and grubby, that I could not even consider using it today. But likewise, neither could I contemplate standing out in this sweltering heat without protection."

"Indeed." agreed Sarah, moving closer to Catherine, still eyeing the parasol.

"Whatever you do, Sarah, ensure you have yours with you later or you will most certainly regret it."

Catherine was sincerely concerned about everything and in every way; whether regarding the well-being of her family or the welfare of complete strangers who may have fallen upon hard times. On several occasions, she had taken baskets of apples and pears picked from her orchard and distributed them amongst the poorest souls in Dead Street. The street had earned its ghoulish name after becoming a burial overspill for plague victims. Those families living in the notorious 'yards,' especially Chapman's, Barnard's and Thorpe's dwelt in the worst poverty to be found within the town's precincts. The town's picturesque facade hid the disgraceful fact that far too many families were living in total squalor.

Two years earlier, William Ranger had published a report so damning, that it prompted the Hitchin local Board of Health to be formed. 'The area poses such a health hazard,' Ranger had written 'that with inadequate facilities, over-flowing privies, open dung pits and defective drains, sadly it aptly deserves the name of Dead Street.'

In Davies' Alley there are seven houses, one occupied by seven people, all sleeping in a tiny room with no window, back entrance or means of ventilation. In Hewitts' Yard off Back Street, there are twenty-six houses, inhabited by one hundred & twenty-nine persons sharing three privies! These three privies were built over the river Hiz into which they directly discharged. In most places the town continually smelt of undisposed excrement. This human waste was stored in cellars, backyards and - if lacking the possession of these two structural luxuries - a dung heap was simply created outside the front door. These are cleared at irregular intervals by the night cart and deposited in pits at the Dirt House along the Bedford Road. For the socially conscious it was an abomination that could not go unchallenged and plans were already being made for its eradication. For the poor, this squalor and spreading of constant epidemics were the companions that they lived with. It had always been that way. They were born into it and had grown up with it. Sadly, yet, inevitably, these deprivations that dogged their every waking day, would invariably be the cause of their death.

It was into these areas, which were also home to the town's worse criminal elements, that the charitable Catherine would enter unafraid. She was like some angel of Nightingale stature, with scant consideration for her own health or the dangers her visits might pose.

Her husband Samuel was as angry as Samuel could be,

which was not very angry at all. On one occasion, during a fit of being the nominal 'head of the household', he forbade Catherine from visiting the areas ever again. Not because of her charitable nature, far from it, that was something Samuel was proud of and fully shared, but because of her insistence on going unaccompanied. It was eventually agreed that she would continue to visit, but in future, she would take a female servant with her. She was convinced that any man servant accompanying her, would antagonise the male occupants and hurt their pride.

Privately, Samuel doubted that any of the male occupants had any pride to hurt, but he kept this thought to himself and acquiesced to Catherine's compromise. Consequently, order and tranquillity were quickly restored to No 27, Bancroft. Sarah glimpsed them smile at each other, like only newly-weds do and felt pleased yet envious.

"May I speak with Lucy? I have some good news regarding her mother's dentist bill." asked Catherine with a smile so warm and persuasive that Sarah could understand why Samuel had agreed to the continuation of her charitable work.

"Lottie, would you be kind enough to take Miss Catherine through to the yard?"

"This way, Miss Catherine, we'll find her in the shade of the top barn, I'll shows you the way." The two of them exited, with Catherine raising her parasol as she went back out into the sun.

"Sarah...?"

"Samuel...? answered Sarah with the exact same emphasis to tease. Samuel, of course, was completely unaware of this and continued unaffected.

"I understand William has been to see you?"

"Indeed, earlier this morning."

"And he managed to make sense of what I could not?"

"Yes, and now I am the richer for it, Samuel."

"That is good, excellent..." Samuel hesitated "... Do you mock me, Sarah?"

"Not at all," answered Sarah, deciding that it was far too hot to mock, even though teasing Samuel was one of her pleasures in life. "William was very informative and yes, it makes sense to me, but in truth it did when you explained."

"But how could it have? I failed miserably to explain..."

"Nonsense, you do yourself ill justice, Samuel Perks. Your explanation, however brief, made me quite conscious of the common sense in what you have planned."

"It did?" Samuel was not completely sure whether Sarah was once again gaining humour from his benefit. "In truth Sarah, the problem is, I have everything in my head, but whenever I try to impart this knowledge, to you in particular, it becomes a jumble." Sarah did not reply but smiled sympathetically, "Catherine says it is because you look to tease me."

"Does she?"

"Yes, is she correct in that assumption?"

"Yes, Samuel, she is."

"Oh." exclaimed Samuel, a little in the dark as to why she would admit such a thing. But before he could ask for more information, Sarah continued.

"And it is something I am not proud of.... but you must know, Samuel, that I do it because I am fond of you, not because I look to ridicule you." She could see from his blank and innocent face that she needed to expand her reasoning. "You have always been so kind to me Samuel and I am extremely grateful for that kindness. I think of you as a younger brother, which of course you are through marriage. Yet, I mean as if you were my real younger brother, you understand?"

"Yes." said Samuel, because he thought he ought to and, "of course," he added, to give his answer substance.

"Know that I tease you for honest reasons but, from now on, I will make it quite obvious to you when I do, so that we can both share in the humour."

"That would be most helpful, yes, as I am not always as sharp as I might be with reading people's intent."

"You're doing it again, Samuel. You have the sharpest of minds. I know of no one who possesses one sharper and I will not stand by and see you put yourself down."

"Perhaps I just need to be more confident. I know my mind can appear hesitant, but Catherine tells me that is because it is so crammed full of ideas."

"And she is right."

"But my brain is not always at its best transferring the information to my mouth. There the transmission of my thoughts seems to collide chaotically with my tongue."

Sarah was forced to break into laughter at this. "Oh Samuel, you are so adorable!"

"I am?" and he laughed with her even though, as usual, he was not sure why. They were still laughing as Catherine returned.

"And what is so funny, pray?"

"Catherine, I have just told Samuel that he is adorable."

"And he is, I most heartily agree."

Catherine knew what Sarah alluded to; character virtues that had helped her to fall in love with him. Virtues that incited feelings of fondness and endearment and turned most hours of the day into joyful ones. Catherine was an intelligent woman, astute and quick of mind, and she knew from their very first meeting that she loved him. She also knew that Sarah was very fond of him because he reminded her so much of her late husband. 'That constant reminder,' thought Catherine, 'must bring Sarah mixed blessings. The similarities between the two brothers bringing both happiness and pain.' Catherine looked kindly at Sarah and wondered if she realised why she was so fond of Samuel.

"Husband, we must be away and disturb Sarah no longer."

"Yes, Catherine, you are right, we have dallied long enough."

"And you will travel to the station with us later, Sarah?"

"If I may, Catherine, thank you."

"Will you come round to us, or shall we collect you?" Catherine asked, once more propelling her new parasol to open.

"I will come to you."

"Then it is agreed. We shall see you later and together we will enjoy this auspicious day… and for heaven's sake, Sarah, see that you come armed with a parasol."

"I will, Catherine, I most certainly will, and thank you." Sarah followed them to the shop door. As Samuel was about to step outside, he suddenly turned back to speak.

"Sarah, my mind! What am I like? I have not mentioned what I was asked to convey to you!"

"And what was that?"

"William tells me that he asked you whether you would enjoy a trip to the Wilbury Pits, in order to observe some of the excavations." he stated quickly, knowing that Catherine was waiting for him, frying beneath her new parasol.

"He did."

"But he inadvertently failed to nominate a day for the excursion."

"Samuel?" called Catherine from the street.

"He asked me to say, would this Sunday suit?"

Sarah hesitated. She wanted to say 'Yes', but for a moment her mouth would not open. The decision area of her

brain froze and she stood silent, with Samuel waiting for an answer. She contemplated all the alternatives to the affirmative, saying she would have to think about it, or consult her diary or anything that would delay her final answer. But a combination of Samuel's expectant face and Catherine's impatience in the heat, prompted her to give voice to the words... "Yes, Sunday would suit very well."
"Good, that is good. Oh, and he has asked us to accompany you both. He also suggests, weather permitting, that maybe a picnic would be agreeable?"
"A picnic?" exclaimed Sarah, continuing to mask her reservations, "An excellent idea. Yes, a picnic would be most agreeable, I will see you all later!" she shouted to the waving Samuel, who was now quickly trying to catch up with the disappearing Catherine. Sarah closed the door and returned to the relative coolness of the shop. There, at the table, beavering away in deep thought stood Lottie, once again at her work.

'A picnic' thought Sarah, contemplating the proposed outing. She was not entirely sure if she was more pleased about the excavations and picnic, or about seeing William. If she admitted to herself it was the latter, then guilt would inevitably raise its torturous head. She immediately admonished herself, as if she had been consumed with some inappropriate resolution. It was a nice friendship they enjoyed and that was all, she assured herself. It need not be more. In truth, she did not want it to be more. In her confused mind, she could not detect truthful thought from wishful thinking. However, she decided that nearer the time she could always feign illness and avoid placing herself in a position she would later regret.

The darkness of self-questioning was returning to cloud her mind. Energy sapping guilt that laid her upon the rack of repentance and stretched her mental sinews. It had not surfaced to taunt her for two days now and, consequently, she had fooled herself that she had regained control of her troublesome mind. Yet, whenever she looked to joy, she saw John's face. Loving. Loyal. She saw it now but did not see him reproaching her nor did he look at her hurt or disapproving.

Sarah looked to Lottie to see if she had heard her inner screams, but Lottie had not looked up. Sarah suppressed her raging guilt and returned to the table. She thought now of things that owed no allegiance to either side. The more mundane things in life. What would Eliza prepare for dinner that night? Would the Queen trip whilst stepping from the railway carriage? Where had she left her favourite parasol… a parasol that looked amazingly like Catherine's?

At that moment, God decided that it was the right time for Lottie to start yet another conversation, one that would engage Sarah's mind elsewhere.

"Miss?" started Lottie, as she often did, "I has a question for you."

"Go on... what question would that be, Lottie?"

"What we were saying about Mr Ransom doing the presentation and not yourself…"

"Ah… I understand from a reliable source that he may not be..." Sarah began to explain, but Lottie was on a roll and was not going to be put off by a simple incorrect fact.

"Well, say he was miss, for argument's sake, and you weren't chosen because you're a woman and that's not fair. But as you said earlier it's not a fair world…" continued Lottie. Sarah knew this was leading somewhere but at present she was not sure where.

"Yes?"

"Well, to my mind, that doesn't make sense, because the top job in the country is being the Queen, right? Well, the Queen's a woman, isn't she?"

"Yes, Lottie," conceded Sarah, "at least she is to the best of my knowledge."

"And being a woman didn't stop her becoming Queen, did it?"

"Of course not."

"Well there you are then, miss."

"But it did stop her becoming King." joked Sarah. But it was obvious from Lottie's blank face that she did not realise this was an attempt at humour. On another day, Sarah might have found time to explain, but it was hot. Baking hot, far too hot for a lesson in irony. "It doesn't matter Lottie, I jest, that is all."

"Oh, I see… very good, miss" Lottie made an admirable attempt to show that the penny had dropped, but Sarah was not fooled.

"No, you don't see Lottie, so that is why it is best forgot. It was a poor attempt, on my part, at humour and it deserved to fall upon stony ground." Sarah held up a final bouquet and placed it on top of the second tray. "There! Another finished tray. We are making good progress, Lottie, you and I."

Lottie paused in her work, picked up the sprig that Sarah had just placed on top, holding it to her nose and breathing in deeply.

"What a smell, miss, it right takes you straight up to the fields, stone me if it doesn't!"

"My thoughts exactly, Lottie." Lottie replaced the sprig and Sarah took the tray to join the earlier completed one.

"Fit for a Queen," enthused Lottie. "I can't believe it, miss. Her Majesty Queen Victoria of all England and most of the world coming to visit sleepy old Hitchin!"

"On her way to Balmoral after several weeks of hard work supporting her husband at the Great Exhibition. To my mind they richly deserve their rest." observed Sarah, with an air of patriotism. Lottie had picked up more lavender, but with less energy than previously, as if she were carefully considering another question. Unknown to Lottie, Sarah was watching her, waiting for the inevitable query that always followed such pensive actions. Lottie continued to struggle and the intuitive Sarah came to her rescue. "What is it, Lottie?"

"Prince Albert is married to the Queen, yes miss?"

"That's correct, Lottie."

"And they're married, proper and all, just like anyone else civilised would be, yes?"

"Of course." answered Sarah, curious to know where Lottie was heading.

"Well, if that's true miss, and he's married to the Queen, then why isn't he the King?" exclaimed Lottie, pleased that she had finally managed to vocalise her thoughts. Sarah breathed in deeply, knowing that explaining this peculiarity to Lottie was not going to be straight forward.

"Well…"

"He's married to the Queen but he's not a king?"

"Correct, Lottie…" There was not time for a long, detailed answer and so Sarah was hesitating. She would need to keep the explanation brief. That way, Lottie would have time to grasp it fully before the Queen had come and gone!

"But he is German?" queried Lottie adding more difficulty to Sarah's mission.

"Yes, he is German and before you ask Lottie, it isn't because he's German that he is not called 'King'."

A similar line of conversation had taken place before. Where Lottie had informed Sarah about her father's attitude to the royal marriage.

Arthur, for that was Lottie's father's name, was a well set, burly man in his late fifties. He was one of those many individuals in the world that have a view on most things and not afraid to let everyone know. Many would readily listen to Arthur Greenacre, not because he was always right, far from it. In Sarah's humble opinion, he was invariably wrong, but people listened because he was basically a nice man. That is not to undervalue him, for there is a lot to be said for such a compliment.

On occasion, Arthur's forthright opinions had been known to change rapidly. This would often cause a great deal of confusion to even his most steadfast supporters. It was not unusual for him to promote a theory at the beginning of an evening and be championing the completely opposite view by the end. Lottie had told Sarah that Mister Davey and Arthur had a falling out one night at the Three Horseshoes. There had been far too much drinking, of course, which is often the cause of most 'falling outs.'

Arthur had just finished a lecture on the virtues and vices of breeding prize cattle. At the end of his unofficial speech, there had been a pause which Arthur had mistakenly interpreted as being the silence of an impressed audience. 'Arthur Greenacre?' Mister Davey had said, standing up from his chair, 'I take the liberty of speaking on behalf of many gathered here this evening when I say that you talk more hogwash than can be gathered from a fat pig's bath. But on the other hand, you're a nice man.' Lottie had explained that it had taken her father's sozzled brain some time to decide whether he had been complimented or insulted. Yet, after consideration, all ended well, as fisticuffs did not ensue. Instead they had laughed, shaken hands and after several more drinks, had walked home together singing 'Rule Britannia'!

"That's what my father calls him miss, you know, Prince Albert 'that German' that's what he calls him." continued Lottie. "My father loves the Queen dearly miss, as of course we all do, but I think he's not too keen on her husband because he's a German."

"Does it really matter which country he heralds from as long as he cherishes the Queen as we do?" suggested Sarah, as she felt the sign of prejudice once more resurfacing.

"Suppose not, miss, but my father says that he speaks with such a strong accent that the court can barely understand him, is that true, miss?" asked Lottie, looking to find another way of justifying her beloved father's dislike of the Germanic race.

"Having never met the Prince Consort, I cannot confirm one way or the other, Lottie."

But Lottie was not keen to let the subject drop. "Do you think it might be true though, miss?"

"As I say, Lottie, having not met him, I really have no opinion on it."

"My father hasn't met him either, miss, but that doesn't stop him having an opinion on him." said Lottie, confirming the world's unanimous view of Arthur Greenacre.

'Obviously not.' thought Sarah to herself as she did not wish to upset the loyal Lottie by voicing it.

"My father says, 'If he can't be understood and no one knows what he's talking about,'" continued Lottie, misinterpreting Sarah's silence as encouragement. 'Victoria may just as well have married a Prince from Timbuctoo and have done with it.'"

   Sarah stopped what she was doing and found herself coming to the Prince's defence, as she did for all those maligned for no good reason. "I think the Prince is much misunderstood Lottie, by your father as well as others. I hear he is a man of great intellect and innovation. A modern man whose clever brain envisaged and encouraged the Great Exhibition and the building of the Glass Palace."

"He did?"

"He did. We should congratulate any person that can envisage and bring such marvels of engineering to fruition. It is an image of beauty that contains most of the great innovations from across the world and Empire. It is not just an Exhibition, Lottie, it is also a thought-provoking experience. By far the most amazing sight on God's earth, I think. An awe-inspiring example of British ingenuity and British craftsmanship. Truly the eighth wonder of the world. It is an event that every Briton can feel immensely proud of."

There was a slight pause.

"And have you seen it, miss?"

"No," admitted Sarah. "but I intend to do so in the very near future."

Sarah expected the sharp Lottie to politely counter with something along the lines of 'But how can you have that view, miss, if you've never seen it? Is that not a sort of prejudice…' although Lottie would no doubt have struggled with the word 'prejudice' once again. Or she may have said something on the lines of 'If it's wrong to say gypsies are villains without evidence, isn't it just as wrong to say something is great, when not having seen it?' Thankfully, Lottie's mind was not travelling that path, so Sarah was spared.

"So, it was all thought up by a German, miss, this Great British Exhibition in its glass house?"

"Yes Lottie, or at least conceived by a German. Yet, only this country could have made an innovative conception become a reality." There was a slight pause before Sarah pre-empted

Lottie by adding, "Of course, at present this is just hearsay, opinions of friends whose views I respect and trust. I will, of course, reserve my final judgement until I have seen it for myself." Feeling content that her final statement had covered most corners, Sarah resumed her work.

"I'll tell that to my father, miss, what you have just said." commented the impressed Lottie, who believed Miss Sarah the only person in the world wiser than her father. "It might make his mind rest easier, with his disappointment that Prince Albert is a German rather than a more acceptable British Prince. I don't think he's so keen on the mixing of blood in marriage, you see."

"Although you say that Lottie, the Royal line is already…." Sarah stopped herself, deciding that this was not the ideal time to lecture on the bloodline of the British monarchy. It would cause poor Lottie's brain severe angst to learn that lingering in Queen Victoria's blood stream were bits of France, Holland, Spain, Austria, Germany and most other European countries - and beyond into the deepest Mediterranean.

"Is already what, miss?"

"It matters not, Lottie… see?" exclaimed Sarah lifting a finished sprig to put Lottie off course. "…Another is done. We are making excellent progress, Lottie!"

"Yes miss, unlike the girls in the yard. They will struggle to finish. Although, as I knows, you said it won't matter and it can all be finished tomorrow."

   Lottie knew that the girls were keen to finish as a sign of their gratitude for having been given the half day. Mister Davey was also keen to finish before the designated hour otherwise he would have to relight the still again the following day. As he had pointed out to Lottie, the flame lit stills took so much time to achieve the right temperature.

Besides not being nearly as efficient as, in his words, 'Them new-fangled steam heated stills, that they has at Ransom's Yard.' He had recently suggested to Sarah that she consider investing in one, being unaware of Samuel's plans. Sarah had answered Davey politely that she would 'look into it' but would make no promises.

"My father also agrees with me that it is you that should be making the presentation, rather than 'shaking' William. That's what he calls Mr Ransom on account of him being a Quaker."

Sarah did not answer. Consequently, Lottie continued, "Because that's what they do, miss, at their meetings. They all stand in silence shaking away as if there's no tomorrow. Rum lot, miss."

Sarah again chose not to answer. Explaining to Lottie that there were different sects within the Society of Friends, as in all religious fraternities, would be pointless. Lottie was confusing 'Quakers' with 'Shakers'; a minority sect whose demise would eventually be brought about by their strict code of celibacy. Refraining from having children had always seemed to Sarah a misguided policy for a sect that looked to grow in numbers.

There ensued a short silence, where Lottie's thoughts returned to the magnitude of what was going to happen later that day. "It's a bit like I'm dreaming, Miss Sarah. I mean, I know it's true like, but... the Queen of England... comin' to little old Hitchin!"

"Indeed, Lottie, it will be something for you to tell your grandchildren in years to come."

"Fat chance of that. The speed my Robert moves. I'll be my great grandmother's age before I've had children of my own."

"He will get round to proposing before long, I'm sure. He's

probably just waiting for the right moment."

"That's exactly what he says, miss, 'I'm just waiting for the right moment, Lottie' he says. I told him, I says 'if that right moment you're waiting for doesn't turn up very soon, Robert Kitchener, you might finds that when it does, I says 'no' to you."

"I don't believe you, Lottie."

"And neither does he, miss, and that's the problem. He doesn't need the right moment, miss, he needs one of them Chinese fire-crackers up his rear end..."

"Lottie Greenacre!"

"It's the truth, miss. I also hears there's an invention of this cable that gets connected to something or other and if you touches the end, you gets the most almighty shock. I'm thinking of buying one of them cables, miss, as a present for Robert. That's assuming the fire-cracker doesn't have the desired effect first."

"Lottie... you are outrageous!

"Thank you, miss." replied Lottie, with her usual statement to Sarah when a word was used that Lottie didn't understand. "Perhaps today might be the 'right moment', Lottie? Had you thought of that? Robert might see the Queen's visit as the ideal moment to propose."

Lottie dwelled on the idea for a few moments. "Do you think so, miss?" asked Lottie, becoming quite keen on the idea.

"Why not? A few subtle hints might help of course. What with 'men being men' and not always in touch with a woman's romantic ideals. But I have always thought of your Robert as a sensible and sensitive boy, and it would not surprise me to hear that he is contemplating such thoughts."

"I suppose it's possible, miss. Quite possible. Although, I think I might still take a fire-cracker with me just in case it hasn't entered his head."

The two looked at each other as they laughed and continued their labour. Sarah, now twenty-nine and Lottie approaching eighteen, had grown close over the years. Even though their positions were worlds apart, their relationship had become a fusion of fondness, loyalty, respect and trust. This strong bonding had been able to manifest, due to Sarah's liberalism and Lottie's confidence.

"In truth though, miss, I can't see it happening."

"No, I suppose proposing on a railway platform engulfed in a fog of steam and choking smoke does have its drawbacks."

"And I still haven't got my head round this 'railway' thing neither. All noisy, smelly and dirty. My father says it will all end in disaster. When they opened it last summer, miss, he said he wouldn't be seen dead near it. 'Their screeching is the heralding of the end of the world', he said."

"It's the future, Lottie."

"Not as far as my father's concerned it ain't, miss. All that grim smoke and thundering noise. He reckons it's enough to turn a cow's milk sour in her belly. He says, 'Why would he want a train when he has a perfectly good horse and cart?'"

There was another short silence as they both reflected, from their own perspectives, on the 'wisdoms of Arthur Greenacre'.

"Will he be at the station today?" asked Sarah innocently.

"Oh yes, miss, wouldn't miss it for the world. But because of the Queen, miss, only because of his love for her Majesty. Nothing else would see him dragged up there. I think, that although some might say that my father is quite convinced in his ways, he is also a man that will look at both sides of an argument."

"He is?"

"Well, he says he is and I have no reason to doubt him, miss."

"That is good, it is good that a person is willing to see both sides of an argument."

"And although he has been quite harsh about them railways and the evil they brings, there is the argument, I suppose, that it will be good for the town, what with them links to London and Cambridge."

"And is that what helped him to change his mind?"

"Not exactly, miss, no. It was as soon as he discovered that the Queen herself had her own engine and carriage."

"I see."

"As far as my father is concerned, if it's good enough for the Queen then it's good enough for him. In his eyes, miss, Her Majesty can do no wrong."

"That's very patriotic of him, Lottie"

"Despite the fact that she is a woman and married to a complete foreigner who can't be understood by no one." added Lottie. "I mean, according to other people, it's a fact, miss. I, of course, have no personal knowledge of these things, so I will reserve opinion until I might meet him. You know, so that I won't fall foul of that word you said … that word that I've now forgot again."

"Prejudice?"

"That's the one, miss"

Feeling that her line of thought was starting to make her sound foolish, Lottie thought it might be best if she fell silent. Which she did.

After a few seconds, they both became aware of someone's presence and looked towards the open door to the yard. There, dripping with sweat and surrounded by a slight haze of heat, stood the petite form of little Lucy Hutchins.

"Begging your pardon, Miss Sarah, but Annie told me to tell you Beggar is back"

"Thank you, Lucy."

"Not that there was any doubting it." added Lottie.

"He looks a mite exhausted, miss, but Annie's giving him some water and he's lying down in the shade." said Lucy, turning to go and then stopping to add, "I don't know much about nothing, miss, but what I do know is that Beggar ain't at all keen on that Lazzy Smith, miss."

"No," replied Sarah.

"There ain't many that is, Lucy, ain't that right, miss?"

"Yes," answered Sarah and quickly changed the subject. "How's your mother, Lucy?"

"She's fine, miss, thank you." replied the little waif, stepping back into the coolness of the shop, "She's had all her remaining teeth taken out and Miss Catherine kindly collected some monies from the generous folks to pay the extraction fee. She's hoping to get hold of some Waterloo teeth soon. But failing that, father says he'll carve a new set out of some wood he'll be buying from Mister Newton's wood yard."

"That is good news, Lucy. I trust she's not in too much pain?"

"Not too much, miss, and she says the gin 'elps a lot." With that age-old explanation, Lucy returned to her work in the furnace of the yard.

"She'll be lucky to get hold of any Waterloo teeth nowadays, miss, unless someone's died and the family is looking to hand some down."

"Lucy's family have much to deal with, I think."

Sarah had heard much about the hardships suffered by the Hutchins family from Catherine. They were a family of thirteen, with parents and eleven children sleeping and living in two rooms. Sisters and brothers, some in their early teens, slept in the same bed. Sarah felt uneasy as she remembered Catherine telling her of this and shuddered at the horrors this undoubtedly brought about. Lucy's mother, Dolly Hutchins, was a legend in her own lifetime, renowned for many other things beside the ability to continually produce children. She was as hard as cobbler's nails, selectively deaf and able to drink any woman or man under the table. She could also bend brilliantly with the breeze.

When constables called looking to caution her unruly sons, she would produce a homemade hearing aid and holler to the officers to speak up. This she continued to do until they were forced to shout so loud, that those standing at the top of Windmill Hill could hear their every word. On the other hand, when charity was offered, she was attuned to every whispered word. Catherine would purposely keep her voice so low a dog would not hear her, but Dolly would catch every single word totally unaided. In exchange for the fruit and bread Catherine brought round, she would plead with Dolly to keep as clean a house as was possible, by not having the dung barrel inside the dwelling.

Lucy's father was the cripple, Daniel Hutchins, known to all as 'Old Sepoy'. This was due to Daniel having served as a young soldier in the East India Company. He had seen action in the first Anglo-Sikh war and during that campaign, had been severely wounded in the right leg, which led to amputation below the knee. He had carved himself a wooden leg of which he was fanatically proud, and this helped support his frame. However, although it was indeed the most beautifully carved wooden leg many had ever seen, it had been cut slightly too short and hence, he leaned to one side. This resulted in him walking along the street, looking as if he would topple over at any given stride.

Besides the eleven children they had successfully brought

into the world, there were five others that had not survived. According to Catherine, this haunted the indomitable Dolly more than the poverty she lived in. For all this, the Hutchins family seemed content with their lot.

Little Lucy was forever cheerful and never complained about the tasks given to her, however arduous. She had voted herself responsible for Beggar's welfare, although it was Lottie who dragged him out for the occasional and reluctant walk. It was an irony not lost on anyone that Lucy needed more looking after than the independent Beggar ever did.

Although lavender was harvested at different times of the summer, depending on what it was to be used for, the last crop of the year had been particularly good. July had produced nothing but sunshine which had extended the lavender year to much later than usual. Their work was normally completed before the August heat struck. Sarah stopped her work.

Her apron was starting to show the signs of her perspiration; damp patches slowly appearing on her dress and undergarments. It was not a pleasant feeling but one that was impossible to avoid in the extreme weather. She envisaged the scene that would no doubt play out later that day at the station. She was fortunate. She would not be outside the station with the crowds unprotected from the sun's rays, but on the platform beneath the shade of the vast canopy. Even there, in that cooler sanctuary, the heat would be close to unbearable and she knew it. Yet, she would not be deterred and she knew that no one else would be either. As the philosophical Lottie continued to announce, 'It isn't every day of the week that the Queen of England comes to visit.'

She turned to look at Lottie who was as usual still

working. Lottie's wrists and hands seemed as if they had been dipped into a bowl of incense and pearls of sweat fell occasionally from her cheeks and brow. Each time they dropped, Lottie instinctively, but too late, wiped her brow with the back of her arm, hoping to decrease the quantity that fell. A gang of tiny flies flitted around her face and Lottie waved her arm to send them scattering but to no avail. After several swipes, Lottie conceded defeat and carried on regardless, hoping the flies would eventually tire of annoying her and move on to somewhere else.

"Lottie?" said Sarah, searching for the damp cloth in her apron pocket. "Stop your work a few moments."

"But, miss…?"

"Do as I say, Lottie, you will take a break from working in this inferno and so will the girls and men in the yard. Please go and tell them."

"Yes, miss," answered Lottie, drying her hands as best she could on her clammy apron.

"See that they cool themselves down by washing their faces in the water trough."

"Yes, miss."

"And make sure they all drink, especially Lucy. Or she will surely shrivel and disappear altogether. Ten minutes for everyone, understand Lottie?"

Lottie allowed an obedient and grateful smile in response. Sarah watched her standing in the doorway still drying her hands and mopping her face, looking out into the yard. To Sarah's mind the sun shone so bright upon her that it made the shop look as if it were in complete darkness.

"Right you are, girls…" called out Lottie and she exited the shop to convey Sarah's instructions.

Sarah stood for a second, thinking how best to cool down. She then pulled a chair from the table over to where she had placed the finished trays of lavender. It was the coolest corner of the shop, unaffected by the windows or the sunlight spilling in through the door from the yard. It was the darkest area as well and consequently felt the most peaceful.

Outside, the chattering of the girls was quieter than usual, a consequence of the heat, Sarah surmised. This allowed her to close her eyes, to sit still and breathe in lightly. She concentrated on shutting out all the hubbub of an excited town and the sounds of constant horse and cart as they passed. Then, with the help of the lavender sprigs piled on the trays next to her, she allowed herself to be transported in her imagination back to her favourite world. Her favourite place and the font of all her most precious memories. The lavender fields. With John.

To the causal observer, Sarah would seem to be a lady at peace with the world. Her conversations or manner would not give the impression of anything otherwise. If you asked those that knew her well to describe her, they would not paint a picture of a woman desperately fighting an invisible enemy. A woman that had devised plans and strategies to block out truth and inevitability. A woman who walked a cliff path, oblivious to the fact that the cliff would eventually collapse, taking everything with it. The only way of avoiding death through falling was to step away from the edge before it was too late. But Sarah was not stepping away. Far from it.

Sarah Perks had a secret and a secret fear.

This secret could never be repeated to anyone. For if it were repeated, all those that learnt of it would condemn her as mad. None would understand or believe her. Since John's death, something had happened that even she could not explain. John had come back to her.

Not all the time and only at the fields, and then only late at night. This was not something she imagined, it was something real. When Sarah went to meet him, the John that greeted her was no figment of her imagination, no ghostly image. To Sarah's mind he was as real as he had been when alive. When they met, they would touch, embrace and when they kissed, it was the kiss she knew of old. His body was the same body she had lain with every night before his parting. The same muscles, flesh, limbs, tongue. This was no phantom touch; it was truly felt and tangible.

It was as if he had read her thoughts from the grave, knew what she had desired and had found or created a way of returning to her. With God's help? With the Devil's help? Whatever the freak of afterlife that had enabled such magic was, it had blessed them with not having to say the final goodbye. She did not deeply question the how or the why, she did not care about the reasoning. She was content that he had manged to defeat logic, nature, physics and the ways all men thought life and death worked.

There, each night, by the fields, they would re marry, renew their vows, she promising that there would never be anyone else, she would never seek another man, never be unfaithful and he in return would never leave her.

But Sarah feared that she was struggling to maintain the two worlds she now inhabited. The real world and her special world were beginning to clash. She had never doubted John but now she began to doubt herself. Her ability to hold on, to convince the real world that she was untroubled and in doing so preserve her special world.

The real world was full of characters and episodes that

gave her unexpected joy and happiness. Relationships were evolving that she seemed unable to resist or prevent. This real world was moving forward at a great speed with her trapped inside. Yet, for John Perks, the real world had ended and stood still the day he died.

For Sarah it continued to move, to create new chapters, to change. Her feelings towards people were strengthening, altering, developing. Her emotions and her faith were constantly being tested. She was finding it more and more difficult to stand still. Each day it became more difficult to resist its pull and she feared if she should succumb to its temptations, she would lose John. She worried that one day she would go late at night to the fields and he would not be there.

Late of an evening, when the weather was fair and all were abed, she would creep from the house and make her way along the lanes to the edge of the fields. John would be standing there patiently, waiting for her in their very special place. He would greet her with his loving, gentle smile and say. 'It fares well, Sarah. The weather, the crops, the family, it all fares well.' When alive he would say these exact same words in whatever situation they should find themselves. Whether in times of joy or sadness, rain or shine, good harvest or bad, as far as John Perks was concerned, it always fared well.

The last time she had visited was but the night before last. She had travelled the lanes guided by the bluish light of a poacher's moon. Bright and revealing upon the ground, where no tree or hedge obstructed its rays, but highlighting dark and forbidding places where it could not reach. Yet, Sarah felt no fear upon the journey, no trepidation as she strolled the familiar pathways. As she topped the hill's crest, there he was, as she knew he would be. His back towards her, humming the children's rhyme that they sang, perhaps content in the knowledge that she would not let him down.

She had walked up to him, tapped him on his shoulder and he had turned and greeted her. They had kissed, stood hand in hand, summer breeze caressing their faces. Then, in perfect unison, they had sung unashamedly, knowing no one else would hear their song, the song that the children sang at harvest time. Their marriage was alive, their wishes granted and… all fared well.

But that last night as their singing had drawn to an end, as the last verse faded effortlessly upon the midnight air, so had John. He had not bid her farewell as he usually did. He had left her standing troubled and alone, accompanied only by fears that he would not return. And with no hand in hers, no voice to accompany hers in song… she had wept.

She had sobbed the soaking tears of a broken heart that would not let go and because she would not let go… the torment would not leave.

Turning full circle until stopping with her back to the window

Chapter Five

The fly on her nose brought Sarah back to the real world. For a while she ignored it, whilst determining that she would endeavour to keep her two worlds apart. If others knew of her special world, they would think her sanity suspect; force her to let go and lock her away. She was adamant no one else would become aware or tempt her to think thoughts that were not of John.

But she could not stop questioning herself. And there were worrying, tell-tale signs emerging. She had felt more irritated by the people around her of late, not to the extent that she had snapped through shortage of temper, but she felt herself losing patience too easily. Her conversations with

Lottie, for instance, these she would find herself cutting short. Whereas previously she would let the debates draw to a natural conclusion. Her fears regarding John were creeping into her mind at inappropriate times. Yet, she knew that there was nothing she could do until her next visit to the fields, where she would explain to John her concerns.

Her strategy was to keep her mind busy. At night it was to dream of no-one but John. On occasion when she had dreamt of him before, he had visited her, when the stress of being alone and unloved had been too much for her to bear. When she had been desperately in need of his company. Of his strength. Of his touch. Of his love. Of his body upon hers. Then it had been nearly as real as when they were by the fields. But not quite the same. Because at night in her bed he was merely in her dreams, her fantasies. She knew that. At the fields he was real.

Sitting as she did in the darkest of corners, she thought herself too easily seduced by the smell of lavender. She must not allow thoughts of her special world to visit her mind in the light of day, lest she be discovered.

However, a new truth was battling to be heard. The other night he had left her early; something he had never done before.

Was it because of her encounter with the gypsy, Lazzy Smith, in the lane that evening? Where a desire most sinful had tempted her. Could John read her thoughts even when he did not stand beside her? Had he sensed her yearning, her wickedness? Did he feel betrayed? She could not countenance losing him, but this was the thought that now began to plague her. At their next meeting, she would convince him that she did not look to lose him. If he had detected her thoughts in the lane, she would assure him they were ugly bouts of frustration born out of her grief. The selfish longings of a woman whose husband no longer held her every single night in the privacy of their bed. She had little or no control over such things but would never let them take her completely. And William? What of William?

She shook herself from thoughts of William, shrugged off that transitional land that lay between her two worlds and opened her eyes.

All sense of time had been lost. Had Lottie come back in and seen her deep in thought and returned outside in order not to disturb her. Sarah decided this could not be the case, Lottie would surely have made her presence known. Then she thought 'Have I spoken aloud in my day-dreaming? Had Lottie heard and left, unsure what to make of what she had heard?' Sarah could feel the panic creeping back in, anxiety taking hold. She must not fall under her own interrogation.

A sudden urge to see her children, especially the frail little John, gripped her. Before she knew it, Sarah had stood, taken off her apron and laid it by the trays. She would have to make an excuse for her sudden exit, otherwise it might cast suspicion in Lottie's mind. Especially if Lottie had heard her speak out.

Sarah walked out into the sunlit yard and was scorched by the intensity. It was so thick that it stopped her in her tracks. Blinded by its direct assault upon her face, she was forced to lift her hand to her brow to create shade and enable sight. There in the far corner Lottie stood with her back to Sarah, talking to Annie.

"Lottie?" called out Sarah. Lottie did not hear her so Sarah called out again. "Lottie?" This time Lottie did hear and turned to face Sarah. But Sarah's shout had been so loud that others had looked her way as well and Sarah was conscious of the fact. "I need to go home for a few moments, Lottie, I won't be long. Please carry on with the sprigs and I shall return shortly."

"Yes, Miss Sarah." Lottie called back, walking towards her. Sarah tried hard to evaluate Lottie's expression, to see if there was any concern written on her face, any evidence in her manner that she had heard Sarah speak out. Cry out in anguish. But the glaring sun made this difficult and Sarah's anxiety increased.

"How many trays shall we do, miss?" But Sarah did not hear her for she had already turned and left the yard.

She had left at pace for she had a sudden fear that she had let slip her shield and that Lottie, or any of them, might suspect something. In truth, no one suspected Sarah of anything. Not Lottie, not Mister Davey, no one. None thought her behaviour odd or irrational, none questioned her right to come and go whenever she saw fit. She had not spoken out in her daydreaming. The only suspicion in the air was Sarah's. And it was unfounded.

As Sarah walked out into the street from the yard, she began to settle her thoughts and retake control. Her lapse, she assured herself, was merely temporary and she must not assume through paranoia that the walls of her mind had been breached. It was ridiculous to think that anyone could read her mind save God. But she had abandoned God, abandoned him in case what she and John enjoyed was deemed sinful. If God had not played a part in events, he might decree that holding to the memory was acceptable, but what they now enjoyed had been created by some unholy power.

Sarah knew she had much more than a memory, she had John alive. A 'memory' could not hold her hand at the edge of her sanctuary. A 'memory' could not kiss her in the evening breeze or touch her intimately. What Sarah had was much more than just a memory and she would not risk losing it because of God's judgment. She had not attended church for several weeks, excusing her absence with the workload of the business and that it was the only time for her to be with her children, which was true. Finally, she had let it be known that she prayed at home. "Hence," she had told everyone, "as I do not neglect my prayers, I know that God will understand and forgive my absence."

Whether God understood or not was still open to debate, but the family did. Sarah senior, Samuel, Catherine, her closest servants and most trusted employees, they all understood. They knew the pressures Sarah was under and had nothing but admiration for what she had taken on. Besides, these pressures would soon be removed. Her son Edward was but four and consequently far too young to inherit the business. Samuel and Catherine would assume control and Edward would join them when coming of age, as an equal partner. Sarah had politely rejected their offer to continue because she told them that she was tired. This was not true. At the time, Sarah had feared too many memories would haunt her working in the shop and John had yet to make his presence known. This decision she now regretted. She realised it would open the door to hours of unoccupied time and offer the real world's temptations easier access. But it was too late to reverse her decision.

She stood at the back door of No. 8, Cock Street and knocked. As she waited, she thought back to her exit from the yard. She vowed not to interpret innocent moments into signs of suspicion in future. None knew her secret and none would. They could not.

Having been given entrance into the house by the maid, she was shown into the drawing room where Sarah senior sat embroidering.

"Sarah? Can it be lunchtime already?" she asked, glancing up at Sarah but not stopping her work.

"No, no, it isn't, but I had some errands to run and thought to spend a minute or two with Anne." The older lady placed her embroidery work on the small card table in front of her and looked up at Sarah.

"She sleeps soundly, Sarah, and I would regret waking her."

"Sleeps?"

"Yes."

"Why? Is she taken ill?"

"Good Heavens, no! Merely tired, as we all are in this oppressive heat." Sarah didn't answer immediately so the kindly lady continued "I will of course wake her if you so wish. But I thought to let her sleep so that she was awake for you at lunchtime."

"Of course. No, you are right and there really is no need to wake her." Sarah stood for a moment. The old lady smiled a smile that was rarely seen. She sensed Sarah's stress, she could see it in her eyes, the occasional moments of silence before she spoke as if she were working hard to assimilate information.

The old lady thought she knew what Sarah was going through for she had seen similar grief before. In her mirror. During the years after she had lost her own husband. Many an evening she had studied the tell-tale lines under her eyes and the soulful sadness that those eyes harboured. Eyes that lost their sparkle and sank down to sit heavy upon the sockets. Eventually, as old Sarah well knew, there would be an easing of the pressure but there existed no cure. She could see her past grief now, in Sarah's eyes. But the old lady could not see the degree of pain building within Sarah's heart and could not guess at the agony Sarah was about to cause herself. Even one as observant and wise as old Sarah Perks, could not begin to guess how grief stalked Sarah's thoughts.

"Will you sit?"

"Sit?"

"For a while. You must be exhausted."

"Exhausted?" answered Sarah smiling back for the first time. "No, not exhausted. It is only ten in the morning, plenty of time before exhaustion sneaks its way in, I think." Sarah smiled but found herself unintentionally sitting as she spoke. "I do not necessarily refer to just today, Sarah. We all know how hard you work, and it will take its toll. You cannot do as you have done and there not be a toll to be paid." The old lady reached forward and gently placed her hand on Sarah's own hands which were nestled in her lap. And there the two of them sat with nothing being said. 'If I had not been made of sterner stuff' thought the younger Sarah to herself 'I would erupt and tell this beautiful old lady everything.'

The silence continued. Sarah thought about it, was sorely tempted. But before any surrender could take place, the old lady spoke again.

"Do you weep still, Sarah?"

Sarah thought hard how to answer the question. She was rallying mentally to defend the castle of her mind. Summoning the courage not to let this charitable woman scale her walls. See over the top of the ramparts and learn what lunacy and chaos lay within.

"It's fine to weep. You should weep. I weep even now."

Sarah did not speak, did not answer, frightened of what she might say. She suddenly energised and stood "This is very kind of you, really, but I'm fine absolutely fine." She looked at the old lady who said nothing, but just continued to look into Sarah's eyes. "I really must be back to my work. There is still so much to do before the great moment. I cannot wait, what a marvellous day for Hitchin, don't you agree? We will all be there, to greet her Majesty, I will be there…" she realised she was beginning to ramble and brought it all to an end with a question. "Will you be there? Later today, will you be there?"

Once again, the old lady smiled as she spoke, but this time she took her eyes from Sarah's, seeing that she was an unwanted intruder. "No Sarah, I will not. Far too hot for me to stand, even in the shade. Besides, I have agreed to take care of my grandchildren, remember?"

Sarah did remember.

"This afternoon," she continued, lifting up her embroidery from the table, "myself and Anne will come to your house and help Eliza with the looking after of Edward and little John."

"Of course, thank you."

"I understand little John makes good progress?"

"Yes."

"James told me that Doctor Hawkins is optimistic and that is good, because Doctor Hawkins is not an optimistic man."

"James?"

"Your James. He visits me most weeks and we talk, mostly of the old days. I say we talk but I talk, and James will occasionally contribute the odd pearl of wisdom." She stopped for a moment and glanced up at Sarah. "He's a good man and thinks the world of us all. Of you. Do not be afraid to share any worries with him."

"Yes, he and Eliza are both indispensable."

"Sharing concerns with trusted friends is a product of wisdom not weakness." said the elder Sarah looking back at her embroidery.

"Although in truth, little John has good days and bad." said Sarah, returning to the subject of little John's health, "At the moment he seems to be faring well."

The old lady paused in her work, without looking at Sarah as she heard those familiar two words, once so often spoken by her dead son.

"Then, that is good." the old lady looked up and smiled. "That is good that he is faring well."

"Yes." answered Sarah and turned to leave the old lady's drawing room.

"Sarah?"

Sarah stopped, nervous of what she might say, but she need not have been.

"Do not concern yourself with coming to see Anne at lunchtime. I will bring her down earlier than agreed and she can watch you ready yourself for this afternoon."

Sarah turned back to her. "That would be nice, thank you. Anne will enjoy that and so will I."

"It is but two weeks before Samuel and Catherine join you and then you can enjoy a long and well-deserved rest."

The two women smiled at each other and then Sarah turned and left.

A well-deserved rest, thought Sarah, as she walked down the Bancroft towards home. That was what all thought she desired and deserved, when in fact it was what frightened her most. In those idle hours what might sin set her to do? To abandon John? To abandon God, forever? To give herself to the evil which egged her on to debauched and debased thoughts? Desires that the Sarah of this world would condemn as abhorrent and vile, yet, the Sarah that trod the world in-between, found ashamedly tempting and seductive.

The street was becoming quieter as the heat became stronger. Less traffic of horses, fewer carts and barrows rattled and clattered along. Hence, the dust clouds were smaller and less obtrusive. The town was already stopping to prepare, with many already collected at the station, even though it was several hours before the appointed time of three o'clock. But it was such an historic event that most saw it as likened to a Sunday. A day to cleanse thoroughly, don one's best clothes and congregate in joyful and celebratory mood. Sarah hoped not too much drink would be consumed by those entering early into the spirit of the day and that all gathered would leave a good impression upon the Queen. The town had a strong Quaker community, but few others adhered to their strict code of alcoholic abstinence.

William did not drink, she thought as she walked. He did not dance nor sing. Yet, Sarah would enjoy the occasional madeira and had loved to dance. Her nature was a passionate one and this passion continued even now with John in their special world. When he had lived in the real world, they had both danced. Two-step, waltz, and both had been captivated by the recent craze for the polka. Sarah had loved this dance particularly and had insisted that the two of them dance it whenever they could. At arranged balls, festivals, garden parties and especially in private. In the privacy of their bedroom. Late at night before retiring to bed.

John had been shy and reserved when Sarah had first married him, but her natural sensuality and exuberance for life had washed the staidness from him. She had liberated him from stuffiness and formality, and he had surrendered willingly, because he loved her. In public they were perceived as respectable and proper, but in private they revelled in their waywardness and giggled at their improper antics like two wayward children. Not all their dancing had been so formal or regimented. On several occasions, John had invited Gypsy Draper to entertain in their garden of a summer's evening and they would step and clap along to the jigs, as if wild heathens.

After passing Samuel and Catherine's residence, Sarah found herself opposite the Ransom's farmhouse and thought of William. William Ransom. But only fleetingly, for she was all content and her mind at ease. Besides, she had promised not to countenance any unwanted thoughts, however tempting. The break from the yard was serving her well and giving her good reason to dwell on other concerns. She must not abandon this much sought-after tranquillity.

On reaching home, she was greeted by the sight of playful pleasure. Young Edward, dressed in play clothes and sailor's cap, stood by a giant half barrel, filled to the top with water and upon the water floated a ship of the high seas; no doubt recently launched in the great docks of Chatham and christened by the Queen herself, and now heading to the far Caribbean islands to capture pirates and the such like. To be more exact, it was a ship fashioned from an old wooden clog, with the side leather stripped away, two hazel twigs planted on its deck, serving as masts, with squares of old cloth attached as sails and all courtesy of James Smith. The same James that her mother in law had talked of earlier.

James Smith was now, as far as he could work out, sixty-three years of age. Possibly a couple of years younger, possibly several years older. He was a mountain of a man, who spoke little and said much. Easily thought of as a simple giant when first met, but that impression belied his incisive wisdom. When James did speak his pronouncements were astute and judicious. To such an extent that all that heard him were made to feel foolish and incompetent. His sage-like utterings were few and far between, and because of this many in the town thought him to be an unfortunate mute. Yet, those that had experienced his rare revelations, saw him as the oracle that dwelt at 62b, Bancroft.

He had no family that any knew of but had served the Perks family since a boy. He had worked the land under Edward Perks and then, for his loyalty, had been employed in the yard - when age rendered him unable to work long hours in the fields. Keeper of the yard, vegetable gardener, harvester of the orchard, journeyman, chief repairer of all things broken and enforcement officer when one was required! Usually of a Saturday evening when the last patrons of the town's fifty-one public houses were noisily walking along residential Bancroft. Even at sixty-three'ish, he was not a man to mess with or get on the wrong side of.

Outside the house, the walkway was elevated some three feet from the street. A sturdy but low wooden fence prevented people falling down the bank, hence, that side of the Bancroft was known as the bankside. James would lean on this fence, facing the house at the relevant hour, smoking his clay pipe with his mere presence quietening all that were rowdy. Voices that had been loud and raucous as they approached would fall gradually silent as they got nearer to James. They would pass him with surprisingly sober greetings, which James would acknowledge with a nod of his head, pipe still firmly gripped between his teeth. Once they had moved on far enough from James that they thought safe, they would allow their inebriation again to take hold and their raucous and untuneful singing to restart. He was also 'playmate in chief' to the Perks children, a role that James enjoyed immensely; an enjoyment that was only equalled by that of the Perks children.

Sarah immediately joined the spirit of the scene upon

which she stumbled, giving a performance of genuine excitement as she knelt on the cool cobbles, to be at a similar height as her eldest son.

"Ship, mama." Edward informed Sarah, holding the vessel, dripping wet, virtually under her nose. "It's a ship." he repeated in case she had not fully realised the nature of his new toy.

"It's the most wonderful ship I have ever seen, Edward." Now satisfied that his mother understood what it was he played with, he placed it back on the water in the barrel that was its ocean. "James makes it." added Edward, concentrating on steadying the ship to keep it upright.

"And has it a name, Edward?"

"Lavender."

"Lavender?"

But Edward was too busy to clarify. After a slight pause, the puzzled Sarah glanced towards James, who sat on his wooden stool. One that he had constructed himself to ensure it would take his weight, which was considerable. There was not an ounce of fat upon the man, but at six foot four, he possessed a frame that required sound wood and solid construction to avoid collapse. James looked at the questioning Sarah and momentarily took the pipe from his mouth.

"HMS Lavender." clarified James and he returned his pipe to its familiar setting.

"I see, HMS Lavender. And tell me, Edward, what cargo does HMS Lavender carry?"

Although Edward would not take his gaze from what he did, he was a little perplexed by his mother's question.

"Cargo?"

"Does it perhaps carry bottles of Perks lavender oil to the

Americas?"

"No, mama," he answered, finally looking back at his mother with HMS Lavender securely afloat. "Treasure, mama! It has treasure!" Edward's eyes widened to give emphasis to the magnitude of this information. He immediately turned to look at James, who was relaxed, leaning against the wall. The heat, as with most people, lay moist upon his weathered skin. His face, beard and shirt all consumed by the humidity. This despite the shade created by the wooden overhang above them.

"James?" asked Edward. James looked at him full in the eye, teasingly, and drew deeply upon his pipe. Edward waited patiently for James to answer and watched the aromatic smoke dissipate before repeating himself. "Please, James," pleaded Edward. "Show mama, please, James?" James at last smiled and taking his pipe from his mouth said, "Get ready then, Master Edward."

Edward, now as excited as any four-year old boy could be, leaned forward to the edge of the giant half barrel, eyes just peering over the edge of the wooden rim as if at sea level. On realising that his mother was still upright, Edward beckoned her to join him, which she did, although not sure what was expected of her. They both looked at HMS Lavender now on the far side of the barrel, pulled there by James. Then to Sarah's utter surprise, James too leant down so that he was at a similar level. They peered across at each other as if in hiding.

"Keep still, mama." instructed Edward, which confused Sarah as she had not actually moved. "Keep very still." repeated Edward, eyes fixed upon his prize ship, docked at the far side of the ocean. Then, Sarah and Edward watched James put pipe to mouth, draw heavily and then exhale the smoke in their direction, slowly across the surface of the water until they could not see him or the ship. But they did hear his voice. "Fog!" he boomed, as the smoke cloud drifted towards their noses and eventually engulfed them. "Wind!" exclaimed James. Sarah was conscious of his breath exhaling and after a couple of seconds, as if by magic, HMS Lavender appeared slowly from out of the smoke and floated gently on that single breath of air, until it arrived on their side of the barrel.

Edward was beside himself with joy and looked to Sarah as if to say, 'What do you think of that, then, mama?' Sarah too thought it impressive. She also thought that she was unbearably hot and the fresh water gently lapping at her nose looked enticingly cooling. She could not resist it. Without thinking, she placed both hands in the water and brought them out, dripping wet, to dab at her face. As she did so, she looked up to see Edward and James watching HMS Lavender in abject horror as it rocked wildly in the now disturbed waters. Finally, after struggling to remain upright, the ship could take no more and fell on to its side. They stared at the wrecked ship in disbelief. Sarah thought for a second and then as an apologetic consolation offered, "Storm?"

But neither seemed particularly impressed nor amused by her flippant excuse. So, with her naval experience now at an embarrassing end, Sarah decided it might be time to leave them to it. And so, she did.

Entering the house by the back door, Sarah heard for the first time the gentle sobbing of a baby. Her baby, little John. Upstairs in the room, she found Eliza rocking the cot. She was intent on calming the baby and she did not sense Sarah in the doorway.

Eliza Long was Sarah's housekeeper. Sarah had known

her as a child growing up across the county border in
Bedfordshire. As a local girl, she had been employed on the
Gurney's family farm for more years that Sarah could
remember. In fact, Sarah could not remember life before
Eliza. Sarah's mother Mary had been widowed early in life
but had continued to run the farm with Sarah's elder brothers
and younger sister. Reliable, loyal and loving, Eliza had
taken responsibility for young Sarah whilst Mary busied
herself about the farm.

Eliza always recounted on a winter's evening when the
fire roared at 62b, Bancroft and the cold wind raged
ferociously outside, that she was much amazed how well
little Sarah had turned out. According to Eliza, the little girl
that followed her around all day was a continual chatterbox
who never breathed between words and had more questions
than a London lawyer. She would retell embarrassing stories
of Sarah's youth, to the sighing of Sarah and the amusement
of John. They would listen politely to the stories that Eliza
had told so many times before.

'When a child' Eliza would commence, 'Miss Sarah
would follow me around like a bleating lost lamb, so she did.
Whether it was feeding the pigs and chickens, bringing home
the cows, mucking out the stables or doing the tidying of the
house. She was always there so close that if I turned too
quickly, she would get so wrapped up in my skirts that I
thought she'd gone and disappeared.' Eliza always laughed
at this story as if she had never told it before.

"And did I tells you the time we were a milking?" Eliza
would ask John and he would politely say, "No, Eliza, I
don't believe you have."

"Well, there I was, a-minding my own business, looking
after the cows early one morning, when Miss Sarah says to
me that she wished to do the milking. So as to stop all her

begging and her pleading, I gives up and shows her how to do it with old Bessie, the Gurney's best milking cow. And bless me, if she weren't halfway through a-teasing the milk from out of the teat, when she turns to me impatiently like and says 'How much longer, Eliza?' and no sooner had she asked the question than old Bessie gave a jerk and Miss Sarah's face was a-covered in milk! Bless me, the more Miss Sarah screamed out, the more Bessie lets her have it. She didn't have the sense to let go of the teat!"

Eliza would always roar at the end of the story, to the extent that she could not stop her laughter and tears of mirth cascaded down her weathered face. This would induce John into fits of uncontrollable laughter, laughing at Eliza's reaction rather than her story. Eventually, Sarah too joined in until all three of them sobbed and laughed until they ached. 'They were good times,' thought Sarah.

She had met John whilst she was staying for a short while with the Newton family in Bucklersbury, Hitchin. At the same time, Eliza had left the Gurney family and was also staying in Hitchin, taking care of an elder sister. Not long after John and Sarah's wedding and their moving into the house in Bancroft, Eliza's sister had died. Mary Gurney had a new housekeeper back in Henlow, and so Eliza was asked to come and work for the Perks, which she did.

Eliza turned to see Sarah in the doorway.
"Miss Sarah, now don't you start you're worrying, it ain't the illness, I'm certain of it." she assured Sarah as she approached the cot, "It's the heat and nothing else." Sarah moved past Eliza and to the side of the cot.
"How long has he been this way, Eliza?"
"No more than half the hour, Miss Sarah, I'm sure."
"Poor little man." whispered Sarah. Little John was lying on

his side, eyes closed tight, tiny red face buried into the damp pillow.

"I would have sent for you, if I thought it were anything serious." said Eliza, trying to squash any fears that Sarah might have. "You know I would."

Eliza believed in her heart that she nursed a dying child, but she would never tell that to Sarah. Even though she was the most honest and loyal of servants, she would not give voice to such thoughts. Like so many, she knew what Sarah was feeling with Mister John so recently buried. She could not bring herself to speak her heart and add heavier weight to Sarah's burden. Recently, when Sarah had asked her what she thought, she had lied to Sarah for the first time. 'What do you think, Eliza? Do you think little John will die too?' Eliza had summoned all her strength and as boldly as she could she had answered 'No.' But she had lied, lied with all the conviction of a guilty murderer in the dock. Yet, it was not so much a lie in Eliza's thinking, for had not Doctor Hawkins said he was seeing signs of recovery? That, in the good Doctor's words, 'He might well defy the odds and pull through yet.'

Eliza was a God-fearing woman and had immediately confessed her sin, repented to her maker for being of so false a tongue, and prayed for forgiveness and understanding.

"I'll take this bowl and refresh the water." informed Eliza, picking up the bowl and the soaking cloth with which she had dabbed at the child's cheeks and forehead.

"Thank you, Eliza."

"Right, miss."

Eliza stood for a moment, trying hard to think of something more comforting to say. But she could not. She had run out of comforting words to say and for Eliza Long, that was a very uncommon occurrence. "I'll be as swift as I can, miss" added Eliza and she left the room.

Little John was not so much crying as whimpering. 'Eliza might be right,' thought Sarah. 'This may simply be discomfort from the excessive heat.' Her hands were on the side of the cot, as if she were about to set the tiny bed in motion. But she instead looked across at the open window. The breeze that had blown into the house when she had first wakened was now almost gone. Almost. Sarah stared hard at the window and thought she could detect a miniscule of movement, the tails of the curtains moving gently to and fro. As if in slow motion, they lifted into the room and then subsided back to the window. Lifted. Subsided.

Sarah lifted her youngest child from the sodden bed, leaving his crocheted blanket in the cot, and rested his frail form against her shoulder. He did not increase his sad sounds of complaint, as if he sensed who she was. His tiny lungs, now tired of calling out, exhausted from his pleading, fell silent as she walked slowly over to the open window.

Outside she could see into the yard. Horses and carriage in the barn at the far end, with young Toby mucking out and his twin brother, Thomas, polishing brass carriage fittings until they gleamed. The boys did not live in but came each day, save Sundays, from their family home in St Andrew's Street. They were fourteen years of age and although hard working, they had the tendency to daydream. They would look off into space as if being called. No one knew what or who they listened to, but it would see them unintentionally pause their work. Though, only momentarily. For it would only be seconds before either Eliza would shout them from their daydreaming or James would tap them sharply on the back of their heads, usually with the bowl of his pipe.

Down in the cobbled courtyard, Sarah could see Eliza

working vigorously at the water pump as Lizzie Butler entered the yard. Pretty Lizzie was Eliza's help around the house. She was fifteen years of age and had been employed on a half day basis because much of Eliza's precious time was now taken up caring for little John. Besides being pretty, she was a pleasant, bright, cheerful girl, who would willingly work longer hours if they were offered. Which they might well be if little John should worsen.

After a few words with Eliza, Lizzie entered the house by the back door to start her assigned jobs. Eliza had resumed working the pump and at the same time was looking over her shoulder at Edward and James still at play on the High Seas. Sarah could just hear Edward asking, no, begging Eliza to stop her work and join them. No doubt desperate to have Eliza witness James Smith's wonderful magic of 'fog' and 'wind'. It was James that first spotted Sarah and little John at the open window and pointed, so that Edward and Eliza's eyes looked up too. They all waved and smiled, and Sarah gently waved and smiled back. Now, moving on the spot at such a slow rate that it was almost indiscernible, Sarah swayed backwards and forwards turning full circle until stopping with her back to the window. Little John's face was now bathed in the tiniest of breezes, a breeze that possessed just enough to play upon the child's cheeks and bring comfort and coolness to his tensed little brow.

Sarah could not see them below waving up at her son. Could not see Edward lifting HMS Lavender clear of the water, so that his baby brother could witness his pride and joy. Annoyingly for Edward, his little brother did not open his eyes, did not witness the great ship of the sea that he held up for him to admire. Instead, with his mother's gentle swaying and the soft murmuring of nature's breath upon his skin, he fell into a deep and contented sleep.

It was a sleep where, in an ideal world, babies dreamed of things to come. For little John it would be growing up to tease his sister Anne by pulling at her curls, to play and run with his elder brother, to sail the seas on ships constructed at the James Smith ship building yard. To hear tales of his mother as a child from the repetitive and loving Eliza, to walk the lavender fields at Gaping Hills, hand in hand with Sarah and hear tales of the father he never knew. To move into the family business, marry, bring into the world children like himself and give his mother grandchildren to spoil and dote upon. These are surely the type of things that babies dream of.

Sarah was aware of his stillness. She listened intently but did not halt her swaying.

His fragile torso, lifting and falling upon her shoulder as his breathing commanded, told Sarah that all was well. He was in the world that Sarah sought, a world at peace.

To just one side of the window was a chair. With her foot, Sarah carefully pulled the leg of the chair towards her, so that it was in front of the open window. She lowered herself gently into the chair, her back still to the outside and settled down with her son still in position and undisturbed. She allowed herself to think thoughts, but thoughts that were concerned with the real world. Not of herself, not of her husband and not of her sins. She thought of her children, of Lottie and those working at the yard, of her mother-in-law, Samuel, Catherine, Eliza and James. She thought of all those that she loved. For once she did not think of herself, she thought of others. Save William. She would not think of William Ransom, even though her heart and brain suggested that she should. She denied her thoughts access to him in case guilt should spoil her thinking. Gradually she thought less and the less she thought, the more she tired and as she tired, she slipped unknowingly into the kingdom of sleep.

Eliza, passing Lizzie sweeping the kitchen floor, climbed the stairs as quickly as possible without spilling the fresh water in the bowl and entered the bedroom. There she found them, both asleep in the chair. Quickly reasoning that the water was not needed at present, she placed it on a table close by, should they wake and require it. Having done so, Eliza tiptoed back across the floorboards to the open door, turned once more to check that they still slumbered, then left, silently closing the bedroom door behind her. She stood for a moment on the landing and, admonishing herself for shedding what she condemned as a 'silly tear', Eliza dried her eyes, straightened her apron, fanned her perspiring face with her hand and went to assist Lizzie downstairs with the household chores.

Whilst Sarah and little John slept, Lottie had almost finished the third tray of sprigs and began to wonder as to Sarah's whereabouts. It wasn't like her mistress to leave the shop mid-morning for any reason. But then Lottie remembered that, although the shop door was open, the closed sign hung in the window. On a normal day, they would be busy serving customers, but there wouldn't be many customers worth opening for on this momentous day. Because today was the day the Queen came to visit! Lottie was so thrilled that she had to force herself to show maturity and not exude too much excitement in front of the others. She took her position as head girl very seriously and the girls respected her for it. Annie, who was her closest friend and of a similar age, thought much of her. She had called Lottie the wisest friend a girl could ever have and was scheduled to be one of Lottie's bridesmaids, if Robert ever popped the question. The designation was mutual and Lottie, in time, would be bridesmaid at Annie's wedding. And because Lottie was so excited about the fact, Annie was now busy searching for a boyfriend and Lottie was helping.

Having placed the tray in the corner with the others, Lottie opened the shop door to look out on to the street. It was gradually emptying as the hours went past; the only businesses that were at all busy were the pubs. All putting up bunting and flags as if the Queen might be indulging in a pub crawl of some kind. Opposite the Pharmacy stood three pubs in a row. The Three Horseshoes, where her father was known to drink, then next door the White Horse, where her father was also known to drink and finally the Black Horse, where her father did not drink. He did not drink at the Black Horse because he was banned. Unfortunately, not all publicans and customers thought as kindly about Arthur Greenacre's sermons as Mister Davey and the clientele of the Three Horseshoes did.

As she stared across at the pubs, she spied someone waving to her. She realised, after squinting through the sun, that it was Robert's cousin, Albert Cummings. He worked for the Lucas Brewery in Sun Street and was delivering barrels of ale. Lottie waved back as he pushed his now empty sack barrow back down the street towards the Market Square and, most likely, towards the brewery. For the most part Albert was a charming, good looking lad a year older than Lottie. He had secured a good position at work and was set for a promotion to senior barrel boy. He was always whistling, whether at work or at play and because of that it would come as no surprise to anyone, that he was known to all as 'Whistler'. He was one of the few people that you would know was approaching before he was in sight. Lottie thought him to be growing into an extremely good-looking young man, strong build, with curly red hair and a mischievous grin. Cheeky, but likeable.

Suddenly, Lottie had a flash of ingenious thought. Quickly shutting the door to the shop, she crossed the shop floor and exited through the open doorway into the yard.

At one end she could see Annie working away, topping the lavender heads. She sat alone, as the other girls were helping Mister Davey and the men to prepare for the last cart to arrive.

Lottie walked straight up to Annie, stood in front of her, almost standing on her feet and said "Albert Cummings."

"No," answered the jovial Annie, "Annie Day. You should know that, Lottie, you're supposed to be my best friend." She chuckled, looking up at Lottie and giving her a wry smile.

"I knows I am your best friend, Annie, and that is why I say to you, Albert Cummings." replied Lottie staring at Annie with eyes that said, 'isn't that a good idea.'

"What about Albert Cummings?"

"For a husband, that's what I'm saying, Annie, what about Albert Cummings as your husband?"

"Albert?"

Because Annie paused to consider the suggestion, Lottie decided to provide more reason why Albert Cummings would make an excellent choice. "I mean, you're desperate on being married and I'm desperate on being your bridesmaid, right?"

"Albert Cummings…" mused Annie.

"And I mean, as you know, I'm also desperate to be married. But I reckon there's more chance of us finding you a beau, you walking out with him, him proposing, you accepting and you tying the knot with him, before my Robert even thinks about popping the question to me."

"You talk nonsense, Lottie Greenacre."

"I'd wager on it, Annie. My Robert and the words 'pop the question' seem to be averse to each other. No, I reckon putting both our energies into your marriage would be the better bet."

Lottie paused to give Annie a chance to answer but Annie didn't answer. She continued to think on the subject. But as far as Lottie was concerned, Annie had now had ample time to contemplate the virtues of marrying Albert Cummings and she needed to hear something more positive from Annie's lips besides his name repeated. "Well, what do you think, Annie?" urged Lottie. "Or should I say, Mrs Cummings?" she added with a knowing smile and a cheeky wink. Finally, Annie resumed her work and, without lifting her head said, "I'll think about it." as if Albert himself had proposed to her.

To say that Lottie was devastated would be undermining the truth, she was distraught. "Why on earth wouldn't you want to marry him, he's the perfect boy to wed!"

"Then you marry him."

"I can't marry him, I'm marrying Robert."

"Not according to you, you're not."

"What on earth is wrong with Albert Cummings?"

"I don't know, Lottie, you'll need to ask Doctor Hawkins, not me."

Lottie was quite taken aback by Annie's rejection and contemplated approaching the subject from another angle. One that may not seem so absurd to her best friend.

"He's Robert's cousin."

"I know." answered Annie, still not interested in discussing it.

"I'm sure he would put in a good word for you, Annie."
"Your Robert couldn't put in a good word for himself let
alone me." laughed Annie. Lottie was about to come to her
Robert's defence, but realising most of the information that
people possessed about Robert's incompetence had come
from her, she thought better of it. On the other hand, she
refused to give up so easily on persuading Annie to the value
of her nominee.
"What about the four of us walking out together one
evening?"
"Don't think so, thank you, Lottie."
"No? I thought that might be an ideal way of..." Lottie didn't
get to finish.
"Lottie? Please, it really is too hot for this."
"I can't see why you won't even consider him, that's all."
"Red hair." explained Annie. "He has red hair."
"I like red hair." commented Lottie.
"I know, but I don't. He has a nasty temper.".
"He's just emotional, I'd say."
"Emotional? Yes, so emotional that he has a nasty temper.
They say that his father is the same and he hits Albert's
mother." said Annie, determined to put a shot through
Lottie's sails.
"I never heard that." replied Lottie, now struggling to think
how she could possibly continue to support Albert's
suitability, having heard that. "I'm sure I would have heard
if that were true, Annie."
"He's Robert's cousin, ain't he Lottie?" asked Annie looking
up for the first time.
"Yes."
"Then that's why you probably ain't heard nothing. People
keep it from you out of respect knowing as you'll be
marrying into the family like."

Lottie saw the sense in this argument and determined to question Robert on the subject when she next saw him.

"I appreciate what you're suggesting, Lottie, I really do."

"In suggesting Albert?"

"No… not so much in suggesting Albert, but that you're concerned enough about me to suggest anyone. I appreciate it and knows it's because you has a big heart, Lottie Greenacre, and you're the best of friends." explained Annie to the somewhat deflated Lottie. "I just think that I has to find my man meself, that's all." Annie returned to her work.

"Suppose you're right, Annie."

Lottie had to concede defeat. After a moment's more thought, she moved away towards the door to the shop. There she turned and looked back in the yard. The men were standing under any shade they could find, whilst the girls had re-joined Annie to complete as much of the topping as possible. As they set to, one of the men purposely took a piece of bread out of his bread cloth in sight of Beggar. The dog looked as if fast asleep but, as always, he was alert to the prospect of any food and immediately launched into his familiar performance. Lottie watched for a while as they all did.

Lottie thought that her friend was most beautiful. Everyone said as much, one of the prettiest girls in the town some said. Lottie just could not understand why Annie could not find herself a man. She was always saying that she was desperate to marry and there was no lack of single boys that would willingly come to call on her. But she did nothing to encourage them. Nothing. Lottie could not understand it. 'If you're really desperate for something, you do something about don't you?' Lottie had asked herself. She was convinced that if she were in Annie's position, she would be doing everything she could to resolve the problem. But then, what about her own problem?

She suddenly thought about her issue with Robert being so backward in coming forward. She had to admit to herself that all she was really doing about her own problem, was waiting. Waiting for Robert to get his act together.

Could she be forcing something that was not meant to be. Robert professed all the time that he loved her, but did he really? She dreamed of a man of action, Robert was not that man and never would be. Lottie's ideal man would be exciting, ambitious, living on the edge. Robert was none of these things. Annie did not like red hair, but Lottie did. For the first time since her relationship had begun, Lottie posed the question to herself that she never ever dreamt that she would. Was Robert the right man? There was only one way to know for sure. There was only one person who would know the answer to such a baffling question. She would have to ask Miss Sarah when she returned.

Lottie quickly shook herself out of the temptation for Albert Cummings. She wanted many things from the man who would eventually be hers, but a beating wasn't one of them. Besides there were sprigs to be done and if she did not get on with her work, Miss Sarah would question what she had been doing, and that would never do.

She walked back into the shop and was immediately stopped in her tracks. Standing in the middle of the shop floor was a young girl. A scruffy girl of about fourteen. A gypsy girl.

Bancroft looking south

Chapter Six

"What are you doing in here?"

"Looking for the shura..." the girl replied. "The missy.... the shura, the boss woman."

"Well, the boss woman isn't here," answered Lottie and then hesitated, "I know you."

"And I knows you." retorted the Gypsy girl with a cheeky smile that made her even more familiar to Lottie.

"You're one of the gypsy girls who helped with the cropping in the fields."

"That's right, missy." she answered confidently, "When will the shura... the boss woman be back?"

Each year at harvest time, more hands were needed than at any other. Of the Perks workforce working in the yard, six of the girls and seven of the men were temporary seasonal workers who would be released after the harvest supper. There was never enough local labour willing or available to fill the huge vacancies, so it was not unusual to hire members of the travelling community. Whenever harvest time came about, it seemed to correspond with these travelling families turning up to camp nearby. This was an age-old ritual, where they moved around the country for work, either to sell their wares or hire out as manual labourers. It was what they did. Their nomadic lifestyle suited them and for the most part also suited the landowners and farmers.

"She won't be back, and you shouldn't be in here."

"Not doing nothing..."

"You're in here where you shouldn't be and I wouldn't call that doing nothing." As Lottie spoke, she could hear the aggression in the tone of her voice but could do nothing to suppress it. "The field jobs are all finished, the crops have been cut and you've been paid off."

The two of them eyed each other for a moment. The gypsy girl could feel Lottie's aggression. It was in her voice, her face, her eyes, her manner. The girl was used to it. It came with being a gypsy.

"I knows that." she replied, not willing to give ground. She needed to speak to the boss lady, the shura, not Lottie. Miss Sarah was familiar to her, for she had seen her many times before, though Miss Sarah may not remember her. As she had glanced into the yard the boss lady was nowhere to be seen. There had been no point in asking for her as she knew that those in the yard would simply tell her to move away.

"So, what are you doing here?"

"I wants a job, that's all…"

"I've just told you…" interrupted Lottie, but the girl could interrupt as well as Lottie could, and she did.

"Here." she said, "I was after a job here."

When she hadn't been able to see the shura, she had moved away from the yard entrance, to think of what she might do next. As she had stood considering this problem, she had seen Lottie open the door to the shop and stand on the step. She had watched her for several moments. Lottie's attention had seemed to have been grabbed by a boy who was calling out to her from the pub across the street. Once Lottie had left the shop doorway and returned inside, it was only a matter of seconds before she heard Lottie's voice in the yard. She had peeped round the gateway and seen her at the far end talking to one of the girls. The gypsy girl's powers of elimination had kicked in. If the door was unlocked which she was sure it must be, because she hadn't heard any lock turn or bolts being drawn, and if Lottie was in the yard, it must mean the shura was in the shop on her own!

"A job here?" asked Lottie, responding to the girl's stated purpose and much surprised that the girl would have the nerve to even ask such a thing.
"That's right, missy, I hears that you might be short-handed."
"Short-handed? We're not short-handed" Lottie instantly lied.
"Yes, you are." replied the gypsy girl with a broad smile spreading across her pixie face.
"No, we're not! And don't you dares argue with me." Lottie took a few threatening steps towards the girl. "Give me any more of your cheek, girl, and I'll have you beaten out of here. Do you hear me?!"
    The gypsy girl had not flinched or moved a muscle in response to Lottie's aggression, even though Lottie towered above her. To show weakness or step down was not the gypsy way. She had always been told that there were two peoples in the world, the Romany and all those that were not

Romany, and they were called 'gadjo'. The gadjo lived in houses, usually the same house all their lives and rarely moved to another house or saw another town.

They were made up of rich people who ate too much and poor people who didn't eat enough. A few of them lived in luxury and the rest of them lived in squalor. If the gadjo were hit by disease, they stayed where they were and watched their families die. If the Romany were hit by disease, they moved on to somewhere else. The gadjo lived with piles of excrement by their houses which stank and drew swarms of flies. The Romany left theirs in the hedgerows and woods where nature and weather would dispose of it. A Romany could not understand why any sensible human being would defecate in the same place as they ate, drank, and slept. They were a strange and unpredictable people, the gadjo, but if you didn't stand up to them, they would see that as a weakness, and they would walk all over you. With that in mind, the gypsy girl stood perfectly still, did not move and did not answer.

Lottie saw this silence as insolence.

"We don't employ you gypsies in the town, only in the fields!"

"I knows that," the girl finally answered in a calm and unflustered manner that infuriated Lottie even more. "But you're not usually short-handed like you is today. So, I thought I'd see if the boss woman wanted to hire me."

Lottie's attempt to control her emotions was failing miserably with every word the insolent girl spoke. "I've told you! We don't hire gypsies in the town..." but once again Lottie was rudely interrupted.

"Ah, but it's not down to you, is it? 'cause you're not the boss woman, is you?"

For a while, Lottie fell into a shocked silence. She now

remembered this gypsy girl particularly well. She had been the pick of the bunch. Hard working, cheerful, confident but never over-stepping the mark. Clever. Perhaps too clever.

"You do need extra hands, missy. I knows you do for a fact. You folk are all in a hurry cause of your Queen. She's coming to visit and you all wants to greet her. There's lots of the town already up at that railway station, standing about in the sun like raw meat cooking… you do need extra hands…."

Lottie opened her mouth to speak but before she could utter a word, the gypsy girl had flowed seamlessly into her next sentence.

"… But what you means to say is, that you don't want a gypsy."

There was a pause, a pause that Lottie was not in control of.

"Now that's nearer the truth, ain't it, missy?"

Lottie's silence continued and was only disturbed again by the triumphant gypsy girl.

"You're not wanting to hire me just cause I'm a gypsy... even 'tho I'm a hard worker too, and you knows I am, 'cause you sees me working the crops in the field, so you knows I'm a hard worker."

"It doesn't matter what I knows..." commented Lottie, at last finding her voice.

"And I knows you're short by at least two. I saw them sisters earlier, they was chatterin' on, heading for the station. You know, the ones that kept wandering off when they was supposed to be working in the fields with us. I did twice as much cropping as those two put together."

"Helen and Clara...?" asked Lottie, her voice untinged by any surprise.

"That's them. I saw them earlier and I thought, 'what are they doing in their Sunday best when they should be helping at the boss woman's shop, getting all that lavender topped in time for the stills?' And that's what makes it stranger than strange."

"Stranger than strange, what on earth are you talking about, girl?"

"What's stranger than strange is that you and the boss woman would rather hire those two lazy gadjo girls, who keeps wandering off all the time and letting you down, rather than a hard working honest, I says, honest, Romany girl." Once again Lottie was silent.

"So, what are you thinking, missy?"

"I'm thinking… I'm thinking, I'll give them two sisters a 'fever' like one they've never had before when I sees them next."

Lottie thought of the great pleasure she would gain later from passing on this information, this first-hand evidence, to Miss Sarah. Her eyes began to enlarge, and her face began to beam as she dwelt on the prospect. The gypsy could see that Lottie was now deep in thought, so decided to emphasise her point with more philosophical judgement.

"Stranger than strange, I thinks," she said. Then she breathed in deeply, quite dramatically in fact, before continuing with… "But I suppose it's down to what you gadjos think of us Romany and there's not much I can do to change that, is there? That's the way it is, that's the way it always was, right far back in 'istory, and I guess that's the way it will always be." At the end of her wise and profound analysis, she added a great sigh of despondency for added effect.

"Change what?"

"That you won't employ a hard-working girl like me just because of me being a Romany."

Lottie did not answer. Not because she would not and not

because she could not, but because she was thinking on the undeniable truth of the impertinent girl's words.

"Don't make no sense to me. Does it to you, missy?"

'No.' thought Lottie, in truth it did not make any sense. But she was damned if she was going to admit as much to this cocky little gypsy, whether she be hard working or not. But what to do?

Continuing this new climate of 'truth', they could, indeed, do with some help. But Miss Sarah was not present, this was also true. Lottie had no idea where she was or when she would be coming back, this was most definitely true. She decided to make at least one attempt to locate her, for if Miss Sarah had been held up anywhere, it would be at the house. She turned and went to the open doorway and shouted off into the yard.

"Lucy?!"

The gypsy girl heard Lucy's voice answer back from the yard.

"Yes, Miss Lottie?"

"Run to the big house and see if Miss Sarah is there... don't gawp at me girl, do as you're told, go on, run!"

"Very well, Miss Lottie!" answered Lucy as she exited the yard.

Lottie came back into the shop and leant against the table looking at the girl still standing in the centre of the shop floor. They looked at each other. Lottie, not certain if she had done the right thing and the gypsy convinced that she had.

"This is against my better judgement."

"Thanks, missy. You can get on with your work if you want, I'll wait in here till she comes."

Lottie could not help but smile at the girl's audacity.

"I'm sure you would, but I'm not leaving you in here on

your own. I'm not planning on being that charitable."

"Thinks I might steal something? I've never stolen anything in my life, God's truth."

"Don't take the Lord's name in vain, girl." scolded Lottie, convinced this could not possibly be true. Then she let her mind drift to where else Miss Sarah might be found if not at the house.

"I don't, it's the truth, I knows you think we all goes around stealing, but we don't. I don't anyhows. I don't need much in life, set of clothes, some food, a little coin. I'm real happy just a-wandering the lanes and countryside with me two dogs."

This last comment brought about Lottie's full attention.

"Two dogs?"

"That's right, missy, best friends I've ever had."

"How long have you had these dogs?"

"How long?" answered the puzzled girl, "since puppies, why?" But Lottie did not answer. "I calls them Fetch and Stay?"

"Fetch and Stay?"

"That's right, missy. Trouble is when I calls out 'Fetch and Stay', they're not sure if I'm talking to them or telling them what they has to do...so's they keep stopping and starting." said the girl with her cheeky smile growing and finally engulfing her entire face. She was fully enjoying her own joke, although, it was a joke that Lottie was struggling to appreciate. "Don't look so amazed, missy, I'm only jesting with you."

Lottie finally worked out the 'joke' content of what the girl had said but chose not to answer or to smile.

"I calls them Duke and Prince for real and they're the best rabbiting dogs ever. They're forever with me. Although not today, of course. I left them behinds today, as I feared the boss woman wouldn't give me no job if I had Duke and Prince with me."

Lottie had decided that it was best not to engage in conversation, as it might seem demeaning. If not to the girl, it would to herself. But the mischievous gypsy girl enjoyed chattering and was not going to be put off by a silent and sulking Lottie.

"Is that your dog? You knows, the one in the yard doing all the tricks?"

"Sort of. Why is it you want to know?"

"No reason, simply curious, like. I sees it out of the window from in that room." said the girl pointing to the office.

"You been in the office?" asked the alarmed Lottie.

"Is that what it is? I just went in to see if the shura was in there working. But she weren't. And as I was coming out, I looks out of the window and sees the dog doing all the tricks. Clever dog."

"You shouldn't have been in the office."

"Sorry, didn't do nothing. Like I was saying, I was just looking for the boss woman."

"Don't go in there again, do you hear me?"

"Sure." answered the girl. She thought about not speaking anymore until the boss woman arrived, but having thought about it, she decided that as it may be some time before she appeared, best to keep some sort of conversation going, even if it was just to pass the time.

"My father and uncles have dogs like that one you has, they teaches them all them tricks, and a few more. Clever dogs. They spend hours and hours teaching them. My father is well known for the teaching of the dogs. All round the country, he is."

Lottie thought for a while, hesitating until she found the

right question to ask. "Is he one of your father's dogs?"

"No. Why would you think he would be?"

"No reason. He turned up months ago, just wandered in the yard one day and never left. We didn't teach him the tricks. He already knew them."

"No, not one of my father's, but I knows the dog. I've seen him before."

"Where?"

This time it was the girl that did not want to speak. But after a while she realised that she would have to say something or there would be more questioning.

"Here and there, can't remember exactly, but I've definitely seen him before." she answered carefully, trying to make it sound unimportant. "Yep, of a normal day, Duke and Prince would be by my side."

"I'm really not interested in your dogs." snapped Lottie.

Even just standing still in the relative coolness of the shop, the heat was causing Lottie discomfort. The day was slowly moving on and it was only going to get hotter.

"I didn't bring them with me, it didn't make any sense to. I mean, I'm not going to get a job with two dogs with me, am I? Not unless I was after a job as a ratter."

Lottie had turned to her and took up her 'I am not interested' pose. But it did not stop the girl. "We gypsies makes all our decisions using our common sense, you see. Not like you, gadjos."

"Not like us. What do you mean, not like us?"

"What I says, missy, you're short-handed and desperate for extra hire. You'll hire lazy girls from the town, but won't have a Romany girl in your yard, even though you know her to be hard working. And then you sends one girl to get the boss woman, and then you has another stands guard over me in here. You ain't going to be short-handed the way you're going on. Oh no, missy, the way you're going on you're going be no-handed, let alone short-handed."

"I don't care! I'm not leaving you in here on your own!"

Silence.

"Don't trust me, eh?"

Lottie stared at the floor in front of her as if she were busy studying her shoes.

"Then takes me out there with you..." offered the girl with another bout of practical common sense.

"No." snapped Lottie and moved off the table to pace the floor. But the girl hadn't finished.

"... And then you can get on with your work whiles we wait."

Lottie was now close to boiling point, annoyed at being made to look illogical by this waif of a girl, to the extent that she now wished she had not sent Lucy to fetch Miss Sarah. "I said, no! Now, sit down and be quiet. Miss Sarah will be here in a minute or two."

"But if we went out in the yard, I could help you whiles we wait for her..." as the girl spoke, she had moved towards Lottie.

"Didn't you hear me? I said, no!" the gypsy froze still, stunned by the anger in Lottie's voice. "Now, sit down!" the girl looked round for a chair. "Over there!" ordered the angry Lottie pointing to the chair in the corner of the room where Sarah had sat earlier. The girl fearing that she might have exhausted Lottie's patience, walked over to the chair and obediently sat.

"And don't touch them sprigs, neither!" Lottie added. The girl looked at the sprigs piled on the trays appreciatively.

"Nice sprigs" said the girl, not meaning to sound sarcastic, but unfortunately that's exactly how Lottie took it and she threw the girl a warning glare that would have frightened the devil. But the gypsy wasn't the devil. She possessed far more gall than the devil and was unperturbed.

"So why don't you like me?"

There was a pause.

"I didn't say I didn't like you,"

"But you do. I can sees it. It's in your voice, in your eyes. You gives me those looks that says you do."

"I'll give you the back of my hand in a minute if you don't fall silent!"

"I hear tell the boss woman will be meeting the Queen." said the girl ignoring Lottie's instructions. "Is that true, missy?"

"Sort of, yes."

"She must be very important, must be royalty herself, I guess."

"That's a stupid thing to say. Miss Sarah ain't royalty... why do you say that?"

"Just thought she must be. Thought she must be a Duchess or a Counter, to meet the Queen…."

"A Counter?"

"Yeah, a Counter. You knows, what's married to a Count," clarified the girl indignantly." A Counter."

"Countess. A Countess is married to a Count not a Counter!" corrected Lottie patronisingly. "Miss Sarah ain't no Countess. Though in my opinion she's as good as and I'm not the only one round here that would say as much."

"So, she aint' no one royal, but she still gets to meet the Queen?"

"Yes, well, she'll be standing in the welcoming party on the station's platform. She won't actually be introduced to the Queen. Though I reckon she deserves to be."

There was a long pause whilst the girl tried to make sense of all that Lottie had told her. Knowing what she knew of protocol and royal meetings, it was her that should be meeting the Queen, she thought, not the shura. Having come to that conclusion, and not wanting to keep it to herself, she thought best that she should tell Lottie.

"By rights, I should be meeting the Queen today." stated the girl sitting up straight on her chair to look as regal as possible whilst still sitting in a dark corner of the room.

"The good Lord give me strength! And why, pray tell? Because I'm certain you will tell me whether I want you to or not. Why should you, a common little gypsy girl, hard working or otherwise, meet the Queen of England?"

"Because I'm a Princess, that's why."

"I think you must be suffering from the heat," said Lottie, thoroughly amused at the idea. "and I'm Victoria, the Princess Royal." And to prove the farcical point, Lottie moved around the shop floor like a Queen, waving as she went.

"Romany Princess, that's what I am."

"You're a raving lunatic, that's what you is!" retorted Lottie, abandoning her performance.

"I'm descended from the King of Gypsies. Henry Boswell, he was my great, great grandfather. And all the Romany knows that to be true."

"If you don't stay quiet, I'll have you restrained and gagged…and… put in the Tower of London." continued Lottie, but the girl was determined to finish her proclamation.

"When he died, all the gypsies throughout the land and Scotland and from across the seas in Ireland, came over for his funeral. It was the grandest funeral ever, grander than any that anyone could recall."

"Oh, yes? And where did this grand funeral take place, St Paul's Cathedral?"

"No. St Katherine's church."

"St Katherine's church? Where's that then, London?" jeered Lottie, unbecomingly.

"No… Ickleford."

"Ickleford? You mean, Ickleford as in the hamlet outside the town?"

"That's the one."

"You know what you are girl, you're raving mad, that's what you are! What sort of king gets buried in Ickleford?"

"A Romany king, and he was my great, great grandfather and I tells you that makes me a Princess, and so that's what I is."

Even though the girl's words were unbelievable, Lottie could see from her face that they were delivered with the forthrightness of one who totally believes in what she is saying.

"You ain't right in the head, that's what you is and I've got a good mind to send another girl to tell Lucy not to waste time fetching Miss Sarah, even if she finds her at the house."

There was a mutual beat as they both realised the magnitude of what Lottie had said. The girl was on it like a shot.

"Another girl? You'd send another girl?"

Lottie refused to answer because if she did, she ran the risk of compounding what she had already foolishly said.

"If you sent another girl there won't be anyone left to top the lavender! It's you that ain't right in the head, missy, not me!"

Lottie refused to respond and instead walked to the door and called outside. "Annie?!"

For one moment the gypsy thought she might have pushed the missy over the edge. She would only have herself to blame if Lottie called the girl back and told the boss woman not to bother.

"Any sign of Lucy or Miss Sarah?"

"Not yet, Lottie."

Lottie walked back in and the girl breathed a sigh of relief. Ignoring her completely Lottie went over to the shop door and opened it wide. Stepping down on to the step and then on to the pavement, she looked off down Cock Street towards Bancroft. Even in those few fleeting seconds, Lottie swore to herself that the sun burnt a hole in the top of her head and threw a bucket of hot, slimy sweat down her back. She could see no sign of either Lucy or Miss Sarah and so she gratefully went back into the shop. Returning to the table, she was aware that the gypsy girl's stare had not left her for a moment. For some reason, not particularly clear to Lottie, she found herself making a statement that was not entirely true but felt the right thing to say.

"I ain't got nothing against you for being a gypsy and that's the truth," Lottie found herself saying.

The girl was as surprised to hear this as Lottie had been in saying it. Using Lottie's statement as a boost to her confidence, she decided this might be a good time to restart the conversation again.

"Do you knows why I calls my dogs Duke and Prince?"

"No, and I don't want to know neither." answered Lottie petulantly.

"Cause to my mind, missy," answered the girl with her chin in the air and a haughtiness quite becoming of royalty, "A Princess has to move about in the right company, don't you think?"

Eliza listened carefully to Lucy's message, standing in the back doorway of 62b, Bancroft and then thought about what she had said. Having thought about it, she asked, "But is it important, child?"

"Don't know, missus." answered Lucy "She didn't say."

"If it's important then fair enough, but I don't want to disturb her if it's something that will wait."

"Lottie says to me, 'Lucy, run to the big house and see if Miss Sarah is there."

"And that's all?"

"Yes, missus, she didn't say it was important and she didn't say it wasn't important. Just for to come and see if she was here."

"And she didn't say anything else?"

"No missus, nothing else, just what I says." Lucy felt she was being forced to repeat herself a little. "I'd tell you more if there was more, missus, I really would."

"I know you would, child." answered Eliza, moving away deep in thought. "It would just be helpful if I knew why Lottie wanted to see her."

"Do you want me to go back and ask her?"

Eliza thought about it but then concluded that Lottie would not ask after Sarah for no reason. She was a more than capable girl and she surely would not want Miss Sarah back at the shop unless it was for good reason. She resolved that it was best to first establish whether Sarah was awake or still asleep in the chair. "No child, you wait here a moment."

"Right, missus." replied Lucy and as Eliza turned her back, she added "Is it alright if I stands just inside the doorway in the shade, whilst you're gone, missus?"

"Of course, child, of course."

Once Eliza had walked away and was out of sight, Lucy stepped inside the doorway, deep enough to catch some cooling shade but not so far that she would be trespassing in Miss Sarah's house. That would never do. Confident that she was standing no further in than necessary, she turned her back on the staircase, leant against the door frame and looked back into the yard.

She could see Miss Sarah's son, Edward, playing with some water in a barrel. Nearby she could see the giant form of Mr Smith, who her father, Old Sepoy, had said was the wisest man in Hitchin. There he sat on his stool, head leant back against the wall, his mouth wide open, snoring louder than a sty of pigs. If he was supposed to be looking after little Master Edward, he was not doing a good job, thought Lucy. 'Don't look like the actions of a wise man to me.' She came to this conclusion because Master Edward was splashing the water in the barrel and getting his clothes soaking wet. He had been trying to reach deep into the middle of the barrel of water but was now dragging over a wooden box to stand on, to aid his attempts in whatever it was he was attempting. Lucy could not work out what he was trying to do. But after a few moments she gave up wondering, because she could never understand why boys did what they did, whatever their age.

Upstairs on the landing, Eliza stood outside the bedroom door, listening. Listening for any sound that might indicate whether Miss Sarah was awake or not. She could hear nothing. Eliza sighed deeply, wiped her clammy and sweaty hands with her equally clammy and sweaty apron and, content that they were as dry as they possibly could be, slowly turned the doorknob. Opening the door as wide as possible, she saw Sarah exactly where she had left her, sitting in the chair with baby John drooped over her shoulder, both sound asleep.

Eliza looked at the peaceful duo and, though reluctant to disturb them, she knew it had to be done. She tip-toed over gently to them, and first prized little John carefully from Sarah's supporting hands. Once accomplished, she placed the slumbering child back into his cot. Thankfully, he did not wake. Eliza, when certain that he was not about to stir, pulled the crocheted blanket halfway up his tiny body and then allowed her attention to be drawn to his still sleeping mother.

Sarah should be allowed to sleep for a week, as far as Eliza was concerned. A month if she so wished. She had seen the woman she had known since a child work long hours into the night, organise the welfare of three young children, one of them teetering at death's door since his birth, and shoulder her husband's responsibility after his untimely death. In Eliza's opinion, Sarah had not been given the proper time to grieve and that was not right. Yet, Eliza noted, during that time Sarah had never lost her concern or kindness for others. She knew that her mistress had always been inclined this way and this was enhanced by her marriage to John Perks, the nicest, most caring of men. He had treated his staff and servants like family, with the same kindness given as if they were his own kin. It seemed to be a Perks trait, for was not young Mr Samuel of the same leaning? Eliza was not surprised that he had married a lady such as Miss Catherine. The Perks men seemed to naturally search for kind-hearted women to be their partners in life. James had told Eliza that Edward Perks had been just the same and she knew James had admired him greatly.

She had never known Edward Perks for he had died long before she came to the town. Death was a common thing of course, thought Eliza, but it was a sad truth that the good tended to die before the bad, and die young at that. Well, at least that seemed the way of the world to Eliza. James Smith's admission that he had greatly admired Edward Perks had made a weighty impression on Eliza, for she knew there would not have been many men in the world that James Smith would have spoken of in such glowing terms. Even to this day she knew that James visited old Mrs Perks most weeks to check on her well-being.

Eliza placed her hand gently on Sarah's shoulder, determined to wake her with softness. She would attempt this without too much fuss and at the same time allow the sleeping little John to continue at peace. "Miss Sarah?" she whispered.

There was no reaction from Sarah. Eliza looked at Sarah's face. Her eyes were heavy and her brow frowning as if she was in some great stress, as if some terrible shock had taken hold of her in her dreams. 'Whatever concerns Lottie had better be important,' thought Eliza, 'because I do this with great reluctance.' This time, Eliza gently shook Sarah's shoulder. "Miss Sarah, it's Eliza. I'm afraid you need to wake, miss." Sarah's body did not move as if it refused to shake itself and disturb the woman it served and housed. But as Eliza was about to call again, Sarah spoke.
"He's not there." spoke the sleeping Sarah. Her words spoken clearly but with hardly any movement from her lips. "Miss Sarah?" asked the puzzled Eliza, not sure if these words were spoken in her dream or not. "It's Eliza, miss, you need to wake." Suddenly, as if forced out of her dreamworld, Sarah sat upright staring out ahead of her. Her mouth gaped, her eyes although now wide open still stared within her dream.
"Miss Sarah?"
Sarah's mind was quickly rushing back from her dreaming to the real world. She fought hard not to wake, not to return, for there were still questions unanswered. But she had no power to stay and could not resist the pull of reality. She abandoned her attempt to remain and looked to where the voice had

come. Seeing Eliza confirmed for Sarah that the dream was done and there was nothing for it but to accept the fact, however reluctantly.

"Eliza?"

"Sorry to wake you so, Miss Sarah. But it seems that you're wanted at the shop."

"The shop?"

"Lottie sent Lucy to find you. The girl doesn't know why you're wanted, just that you are, miss."

Sarah stood up and straightened herself. Remembering that she had been holding John, she looked towards the cot. Eliza saw this and reassured her.

"He sleeps soundly, miss, more soundly than he has for the past week."

Having peered into the cot to confirm for herself what Eliza had said, she then began to wonder how long she had been away from the shop. "What time is it, Eliza?"

"Fifteen past eleven, miss." Eliza answered immediately for she had heard the quarter in the long case clock strike as she ascended the stairs.

"I should not have been away so long…. Lottie! I have left poor Lottie to manage, how selfish of me. Eliza?"

"Yes, miss?"

"Please send Lucy back to the yard to let Lottie know that I am on my way."

"Yes, miss." said Eliza hesitating, trying desperately to think of a good reason why her mistress need not hurry back…

"Quickly now, Eliza!"

"Yes, miss." Eliza said and obediently left the room to deliver the message.

Sarah moved to the open window which, although now completely absent of breeze, at least still welcomed in fresh air. Warm fresh air, but at least fresh. She breathed in deeply and closed her eyes gently as she slowly exhaled. Her forehead wet with the heat. The perspiration exasperated by the horror that had revealed itself during her slumber. Eliza had thought her to be just deep in mid-morning sleep, in some dream story that caused her to frown. But the frown belied the truth, the horror of what Sarah had witnessed in that sleepy passage of time. She knew that she should not hesitate but return to the waiting Lottie and whatever problem had manifested itself during her absence. But as always of late, she was torn between the solving of developing issues in both worlds. She must be strong. She must stay steadfast and avoid a collision of her two realms. If she failed in achieving this, she would surely be discovered and all would be stripped bare for the world to observe and judge. 'Surely,' thought Sarah, 'In that way madness lies.'

James awoke suddenly to the voice of Lucy shouting out "Mister Edward!" as she ran from her shade in the doorway to the barrel across the yard. Her warning voice was followed by a splash and the half-awake James being soaked upon his stool, as if a bucket of water had been poured over his head. His reactions, once sharp and impressive, had slowed with age, but his eyes still registered the need for concern as they alighted upon the feet of a small child. Upside down feet in the barrel of water. A small child's feet where a small child's head should normally be found. Two feet wriggling frantically in the air as when a small child wriggles to secure their first handstand. Before James had fully realised the significance of such a sight, Lucy, who was not that much taller than the barrel, had herself grabbed Edward's feet and tried to haul him back out. This she was never going to do and before she could call out and panic further, James had grabbed Edward by the ankles and lifted him from the watery depths.

Eliza arrived at that very moment, just in time to witness the unusual rescue. A sight that left her awestruck. She saw James standing by the barrel, holding the dripping Edward upside down above the surface of the water, as if he did not wish any of the falling water to hit the cobbles around the barrel. Edward, for his part, seemed quite unphased by the whole episode and unaware of the peril he had been in, had Lucy not been close by and watching. He was content. Unconcerned because although he remained still upside down, swaying in the air, he was clutching his precious HMS Lavender, which had recently sunk to the bottom of the barrel. It was a double rescue in truth and all were pleased at the successful outcome.

For Eliza, it was as if time had stood still, as if all were frozen by some magical hand, or all having to remain in a perfect pose for one of those new daguerreotype sessions that Thomas Latchmore kept lecturing on. Where a picture can be formed without canvas, paint, or brush. As her common sense returned, she sprang quickly into action with a clashing of orders.

"Bless my soul, what in Heaven's name…. James!?" she shouted. James looked her way without releasing his grip on Edwards's ankles. Edward was more concerned about the welfare of his two masts, which were now missing their sails, than the fact that he was hanging upside down over a barrel of water.

"Eliza?" replied the giant James.

"For mercy's sake, man, stand the boy the right way up!" exclaimed Eliza and as James did as he was asked, she turned and called for Lizzie. "Lizzie! Quickly, girl!" Lizzie appeared at the window to the drawing room. "Stops what you're doing, girl, do you hear me?"

"I hear you, missus." answered Lizzie, oblivious to what had taken place.

"Go quickly to Master Edward's bedroom and set out a complete set of clothes upon his bed.

"Complete set?"

"You heard me, girl, a complete set now, quickly!"

"Yes, missus!" replied the stunned Lizzie, disappearing to comply with Eliza's orders. In the meantime, Eliza strode over to the now upright but still dripping Edward and took him by the hand, turning to Lucy as she did so.

"Lucy?"

"Missus?"

"Run back to the shop and tell Lottie that Miss Sarah is on her way."

"Yes, missus." Lucy exited the yard, she knew not to linger or question when Eliza was in her General of the Army mood. As Eliza walked towards the door with the soaked Edward in hand, she was aware of the twins trying to smother their laughter.

"Thomas! Toby!"

"Yes, Miss Eliza?" they answered in unison, as all good twins should, but with their smiles disappearing as if swept away by a winter wind.

"Stop gawping and gets back to your work!"

"Yes, Miss Eliza!" and immediately they returned to their stable chores.

"Eliza?" asked Edward looking up at her.

"All's well now, Master Edward."

"But Eliza," repeated Edward, reluctant to leave the scene of the shipwreck and holding up HMS Lavender for Eliza to see, "Lavender. Lavender has lost her sails."

Eliza took the sail-less ship from him and handing it to James, replied "Don't you worry your little wet head about that, Master Edward, James will search for them. After all's said and done, if he'd been a watching you like he was supposed to be doing, you may not have gone for a dip." James took the ship from Eliza and walked back towards the barrel and, although chided by her remark, he did not let on that it had affected him in the least. James was always of the mind that if ever in doubt, the best way to respond to someone, was to not respond at all. He had followed this mantra many times and in part this had enhanced his reputation for wisdom. Eliza's withering stare had prompted him to adopt this sound policy of no response on this occasion as well.

As Eliza headed for the house, she was met by Sarah descending the stairs.

"Eliza, what on earth is all the fuss?" asked Sarah as her eyes came to rest upon the soaking Edward. "Edward!" she exclaimed but before Sarah could say more, Eliza spoke.

"There is no reason to be alarmed, Miss Sarah. Whilst playing with his ship, Master Edward has inadvertently gone for a morning swim."

"A swim?"

"Yes, miss, only he neglected to strip off his clothes first, miss."

With this cheerful comment from Eliza, Sarah at last became assured. "Oh Edward, honestly." admonished Sarah also now smiling at her bedraggled son.

"I'm taking him to change his clothes, miss. I've sent Lucy back with your message so Lottie will be expecting you." With that she led Edward back into the house. "Come on, Master Edward, let's see if we can't wring you out through the kitchen mangle."

Sarah stood recapturing her thoughts. After several moments, as if resolved, she exited through the coach drive to walk back along Bancroft to the shop.

James, having fished out the dislodged sails, watched her. He watched her as she stood and thought, and he watched her go. He may not, in truth, be the wisest man in the world like many people thought him to be, but he knew a troubled soul when he saw one. Although others were slowly starting to become aware as well, he had known all was not right with Miss Sarah for some months. He saw her in conversation with folks, chatty, laughing, considerate as always, appearing as right as the rain. But when she stood and thought, thinking no one observed her as she did, he saw her travel somewhere in her mind that caused her distress.

James lived on the premises but not in the house. He had a room alongside the stables. It was small, although any room would seem small to the giant James, but it was a comfortable room and served his needs. It was comprised of a bed, a cupboard, a table, and a comfortable chair. The room had one small window.

Sitting in his comfortable chair looking across his room, he could see through his window up to the window of Miss Sarah's room. Of a morning, often early before Eliza had risen or Lizzie had arrived, he would see Miss Sarah looking out of her window. Not into the yard it seemed to James, but further away towards the horizon or maybe the fields. Of what she thought, he had no idea. He could not read the minds of others, though many thought he could. Those that professed to have the ability of foretelling, such as mediums and fortune tellers and the like, just spoke the words people wanted to hear and then took their coin for the pleasure of it.

To be able to sense how people felt, well that was

different. God had bestowed that knack freely to all, so that people could keep an eye on each other whenever words were not forthcoming. To James' mind, some people used this inherent ability only occasionally, some selfish people seldom, if ever. And some such as James had appreciated this blessing and refined it. In truth, his usage of a few words was made up for by his being able to 'sense' rather than ask about the well-being of others. Sometimes this silent intrusion into people's minds provided more accurate information than any amount of chosen words could hope to produce.

He watched Miss Sarah often. He watched her because he was fond of her. He watched her too because he had made a promise to old Mister Edward Perks, days before he passed on.

For many years James had known little of his own background, believing that Edward's father Harry had found him abandoned on their doorstep and taken him to the parish workhouse. Every week Harry would visit him there, pay for his lodging and check on his health. Yet, Harry had not liked what he saw and when James was but a year old, he had been brought back to live in the Perks household. The Perks family gave him a home, they gave him work and they gave him access to a family that he had never had. As far as James was concerned, he owed the Perks family his life.

Because of their kindness, he had always kept a wary eye on the Perks brood and did so even now. All of them. And whenever it was within his power, he would see to it that they came to no harm. Miss Sarah had married into the family so was now as deserving of his watchful eye as any.

There were two important things that James knew about young Miss Sarah Perks. First, he knew her mind was troubled and not through the suffering of normal grief either. Something else, something even deeper played upon her mind. The second thing he knew was that late at night, when Sarah believed all others to be asleep, she would slip from the house and would not return until the hours just before daylight. James saw her leave and he saw her return.

Hitchin Railway Station

Chapter Seven

As Sarah crossed the road at the bottom of Brand Street, she forbade her mind to dwell on her dream. But she was struggling. It was just a dream she kept telling herself and dreams have their own reason for being. Dreams, she decided, came and went as they wished. they were not necessarily harbingering doom and should not be taken too seriously. But what if that were not the case? What if her special world and her dreams were somehow interlinked?

As she lingered in the fear that truth might lie in her dream, the great cart laden with the last of the lavender passed by, heading to the yard. The shires, Peggy and Polly, their coats matted from the heat, snippets of hedgerow clinging to their coarse hair and their sheen greyed by the dust, strode forward, unfaltering in their stride. Giles was at the reins and he waved to her as they passed, with Cedric and George sat on the tailgate.

"Morning, Miss Sarah." cried out Cedric over the rattling of the cart, "All done, miss!"

They tipped their caps smiling, pleased that the harvesting was at an end and relieved that they would be finished by mid-day. Sarah smiled back and used their friendly greeting as a means of dragging her thoughts firmly back to the present.

By the time she reached the coach drive, the cart was in the yard. Peggy and Polly had been released from their harness and were being led away to their stables and the unloading had already begun. The yard was alive with bustle and jostling, for there was still much to do if the bushels were to be unloaded and stored in good time.

Sarah walked past the busy, eager hands and into the shop via the back door. There she found Lottie leaning against the table looking at what Sarah could only describe as a cheeky face draped in rags.

"What is it, Lottie?"

"Sorry to bring you back, Miss Sarah..."

"I was looking to offer my services…" interjected the girl.

"Sorry to bring you back, Miss Sarah…" repeated Lottie.

"…seeing as you're so short-handed, missy…" continued the girl, completely ignoring Lottie.

"Be quiet!" shouted the furious Lottie.

"I was talking to the boss woman…"

"Well, don't speak until you're spoken to!" fumed Lottie, moving towards the insolent girl.

"It's alright, Lottie. Now girl, what's your name?"

"Rosa, missy. Rosa Boswell." answered the girl, bobbing the daintiest of curtseys. Sarah smiled as she did so and noticed that the girl seemed to be drowning in clothes that looked as if borrowed from a girl twice her size. Maybe in the forlorn hope that she would one day grow into them?

"She's one of the gypsy girls from the Little Spinney that we had working on the fields, miss." informed Lottie, at last beginning to calm.

"I knows you're short-handed, missy, so I thought you might hire me…" stated Rosa instead of asking and bobbed another curtsey Sarah's way, hoping her servility might help her cause.

"I see, but the fields are all done…"

"She means here, Miss Sarah, in the yard."

"I'm a hard worker missy, she'll tell you so…" said Rosa, eyeing Lottie to see if she would receive any help from that quarter.

"I have no doubt." replied Sarah kindly.

"Tells her how's I'm a hard worker." demanded Rosa, still looking for support.

"I'm sure Lottie wouldn't have sent for me if she had thought otherwise."

"I suppose she speaks true, Miss Sarah. Out of all the gypsy girls we hired this one was the most…" Lottie searched for a complicated word in the hope of impressing Sarah and to show Rosa how educated she was. "… the most conscious." said Lottie finally.

"I'm sure she is… conscientious, Lottie," answered Sarah, "…and having said that, I'm sure she remained awake throughout."

"It makes sense to me, missy…" interrupted Rosa fearing the conversation was moving away from her request. "as you need help and as I'm so hard working."

"And a Princess." laughed Lottie.

"A Princess? In what way a Princess?" but before Rosa could answer, Sarah had realised the significance of the girl's surname. "Rosa Boswell?"

"That's right, missy." answered Rosa, not sure if Sarah was going to mock her as Lottie had.

"Then you're a descendant of Henry Boswell, who was buried in the churchyard at Ickleford?"

"That's him!" replied the surprised Rosa. If Sarah had glanced sideways at that moment to where Lottie stood, she would have observed yet another surprised face.

"Yes, that's right, missy. He was hailed as King of the Gypsies all about the country and by my reckoning that makes me a Princess." Rosa once again lifted herself to her full five foot to regain her regal look.

"You mean…" said Lottie, not sure if to be flabbergasted or embarrassed, "…that there was such a person, Miss Sarah?"

"Oh, yes, Lottie, the most famous of gypsies was Henry Boswell."

"I told her so, but she don't believe it." said the triumphant Rosa pointing her finger at Lottie, "She don't believe a gypsy could be telling the truth even afore they even says anything."

But before Lottie could attempt to defend herself against this irrefutable truth, Sarah had entered the discussion on Lottie's behalf.

"I think that's a little harsh, Rosa," rebuked Sarah, "and there really is no need to point. I know of whom you speak and I am quite aware of Lottie's whereabouts in the room. I do not require you to point her out to me. Besides, I'm sure Lottie wouldn't be so presumptuous or unfair." Lottie decided that this might be a good moment to change subjects.

"She saw Helen and Clara on their way to the station, Miss Sarah. With a fever so high that they were joyfully dancing and singing their way up the road towards the railway station, would you believe?"

"That don't make any sense to me, missy, you giving thems any work."

"I might not after today,"

"Then you can give me their work instead and I'll do all of it on my own."

"Don't be so forward, girl!" reprimanded Lottie, even though the girl had been confirmed as a Princess, which was something Lottie was finding hard to swallow. However, if Miss Sarah said it was so, then it must be so and Lottie would just have to accept it.

"And then you'll just be paying one wage instead of two." said Rosa, continuing to make her case.

Sarah was not sure what to make of Rosa but could not deny that she was intrigued by the impish gypsy girl descended from Henry Boswell, King of the Gypsies. She could not reason any logic behind this inquisitive urge that consumed her, but she felt compelled to find out more.

"Lottie, will you kindly go and check on the girls for me?" asked Sarah. "If you will, Lottie, thank you. Otherwise they may slow in their work due to discussing what might be taking place in here."

"Of course, Miss Sarah." answered Lottie and without further questioning of her mistress, she went out to the yard.

"That your name, missy? Sarah?" asked Rosa eyes shining bright and cheeks rosy-reddened by fourteen summers.

"Yes."

"Nice name and you're more clever than most…you knew about old King Henry."

"Yes. I knew because I have seen his grave in St Katherine's churchyard. Now, let us see if we can make your audacious proposal of employment work for both parties."

"Miss?" queried Rosa, thrown by Sarah's use of two quite complicated words. This was something Rosa knew the gadjos often did to sound superior. But this lady wasn't coming over superior. There was something different about this lady...

"I am indeed short-handed, and you obviously need the money, so…" But before Sarah could complete her sentence, Rosa had once again interrupted. The little girl had no learning or understanding of dialogue etiquette and when she felt she had something to say she just said it.

"I do missy, but that's not the only reason. The money is always needed, missy, it would be a false take if I said otherwise, but that ain't the only reason why I wants to continue working." As Rosa looked to explain more and without knowing it, she had excitedly moved towards Sarah sitting at the table. She was standing almost in front of Sarah, her eyes gleaming, wide open as if they would drop from their sockets with excitement. Her whole face now imbued with the endearing anticipation of a young child on Christmas morning.

"The smell, missy."

"Smell?"

"Of the lavender, missy. It's the smell of lavender."

There was a silence. Sarah stared at little Rosa, trying hard to judge whether the girl mocked her or looked to jest, and Rosa stared back at Sarah looking to see if this lady understood her or not.

"For to my mind, it's the smell to beat all others."

"In truth?"

"In truth, missy."

Sarah stood, amazed, and moved away from the table to collect her thoughts.

"That's why I loved picking it, see? That's why I rushes up to be the first in the line to get taken on each year. When I smells the lavender, I'm as happy as a lamb in springtime, nothing else in this whole life makes me so content. When it comes into bloom, I loves it. With lavender in me nostrils, missy, I feel the world belongs to me, as if I has the countryside inside my head."

"What a poetical young lady you are, Rosa Boswell."

"I'm not telling you no falsehood, missy and you may think me divvy."

"Divvy?" asked the perplexed Sarah.

"Crazy, missy," answered Rosa, feeling important that she had used a word that a gadjo hadn't understood.

"Not at all. I don't think you at all… divvy."

"My folks do. They think the smell has turned my head to being more silly than sensible. They laughs at me mostly."

"Because you love the smell of lavender?"

"No, missy, because I lay in it. All night sometimes. You won't be angry, will you?" asked Rosa plaintively, "But I does it on your property."

"You do what on my property?"

"I takes my blanket and lays it between the furrows on your fields off Grays Lane and then I sleep in the field all night. Me, the stars, sometimes the moon and the lavender. I lays there and let the stalks breeze through between my fingers and as I does this, the whole night-time smells of lavender. I reckons it's stronger when you can't see it, 'cause your eyes don't get in the way. Your eyes stop you getting the full scent and when it's dark and there's nothing to see, you can lose your mind just to the smell. Supposing you could just shut your eyes but it ain't the same, missy, just ain't the same."

Rosa wasn't sure if Sarah's facial expression was one of bewilderment or curiosity, "You understand, missy?"

"I understand completely, Rosa."

"You do?"

"Yes." answered Sarah and she beamed a smile that had not been glimpsed by the world since her John was alive.

"Is that because you've done it?".

"What, lain in the fields at night? Heavens above, no!"

"Perhaps you should, I mean, they're your fields, ain't they?"

"Well, yes, I suppose they are..."

For some reason that Sarah could not explain, she felt completely at ease with this exceptional young girl. For months now, Sarah had always been selective in what she allowed people to see and hear; staying completely in control of everything she said or did. The stress of living in this way, day upon day, had been wearing her down. The pressure of being constantly on guard had begun to gnaw at her nerve ends but now... she felt free to speak her mind. How could she be so sure that her words were safe in the hands of this chattering girl. She could not be, but she did not care.

"I will tell you a secret, Rosa Boswell." said Sarah coming to sit on the edge of the table.

"You don't have to, missy. Secrets ain't no secrets once they're shared."

"That is true. But I wish to be as honest with you as you have been with me, Rosa." smiled Sarah reassuringly. "I have not lain in the fields at night as you have done, but there are many occasions when I have wandered up, late into the evening, especially when a summer breeze is blowing gently and warmly and..."

Sarah paused, realising the seriousness of what she planned to say. Suddenly, she was gripped by fear that in so doing, it might have a negative impact upon her special world and she struggled to stop herself.

"And, missy? And what?" she heard Rosa ask.

"And... and on such an evening, I have stood at the fields edge and been thankful for God's bounty."

This was true, but it was not all Sarah wished to tell.

"I believe you, missy. I know that to be true, because I have seen you."

Sarah's panic took her from the table's edge towards the corner where the trays of lavender stood.

"You have?" asked the frightened Sarah, keeping her back to her urchin inquisitor.

"Once or twice."

"In truth?" asked Sarah.

"In truth right enough, missy. I knows something else that's in truth that you haven't said." Rosa paused and then added, "You sings."

Sarah did not respond but waited for Rosa to continue.

"I've heard you, missy. Standing by the edge of the fields, you sing. A couple of nights ago, I was laying in the field not more than a few yards away. I heard you. I lay there listening. After a while you stopped singing and walked back the ways you came."

Rosa paused to see if Sarah would speak.

"Nothing wrong with it, missy. If the fields were mine, I'd stand there and sing and I wouldn't care who knew. And I knows the song you sing's too, and I knows it off by heart. It's a beautiful song, missy, and I reckons the lavender loves your singing of it just as much as I does."

Sarah convinced herself that these truths were in safe hands, regathered her composure and turned once again to face Rosa.

"Let me see now, Rosa Boswell. I will promise never to tell the owner of the lavender fields that you trespass by lying in her furrows, if you promise not to tell a soul that Sarah Perks stands by the edge of her fields at night and sings. Are we agreed?" "

"Don't see how it's anything to be ashamed of, missy…"

"Agreed?" interrupted Sarah repeating her offer more firmly. "If you wants?"

"I do wants. And you must not think this lady gadjo to be divvy." requested Sarah, believing she was striking a bargain in fluent Romany."

"A lady gadjo's a gadji, missy, but I agrees." said Rosa, spitting enthusiastically on the palm of her hand and offering it to Sarah to cement their agreement.

Sarah followed suit and spat delicately on to her own before clasping Rosa's in hers. The spirited and delighted Rosa then proceeded to shake her hand so vigorously that Sarah thought her wrist might break.

"What an unusual girl you are."

"I knows and I'm sorry for that, missy, I'm something silly for lavender…but if you gives me a job helping you here, I gets to smell it a little bit longer. It can be a short season that the lavender has and it's a long-time round to the next summer." chatted the irrepressible Rosa.

"You could place cut sprigs in your caravan."

"We does that, our vardo is full of it, but it ain't the same." answered Rosa. "Dried ain't the same as when it's sprouting fresh from the earth, missy."

"No, no, I suppose not. Very well, Rosa Boswell, Princess of the Gypsies, I think you are the most charming young lady I have ever had the good fortune to meet and I am glad you have accepted the offer. You do really want it?"

"I do really wants it, missy, I rightly do!"

"Then, that is good." There was a split-second pause before Sarah continued with a little more gravity "And Rosa, you will work as hard as you say you can and you will not let me down."

"I won't let you down, missy, no fear of that. I keeps my word, all that knows me knows that and do you know why you can be certain of that, missy?"

"I trust your word, Rosa."

"But you have more than my words, missy, you have the speaking of Old Jinnepen."

"Old Jinnepen?"

"She's the wise woman... Do you mean, missy, that you've heard of Henry Boswell but not Old Jinnepen?"

"I'm sorry Rosa, is this a fortune teller or a medium of some kind?"

"Old Jinnepen ain't no false fortune teller, missy, stretch me she ain't. When I was born, she takes my hand in hers and says to my folk, this girl will never lie, that's what she told them and I never do."

"That's very admirable, Rosa." answered Sarah, moving towards the open door. "Lottie!?"

"I sometimes avoid the telling of the truth like, missy, but I never lies." said the earnest Rosa, "But believe me, Old Jinnepen is wiser than anyone that walks the earth. She tells you something and you better believe it's true because it always is. And she don't use no crystal ball, neither, or cards or tea leaves or anything, she don't need none of that."

"I see."

"Don't doubt her, missy, she just takes your hand, like this…" and as Rosa spoke, she took Sarah's hand in hers. "… and you sits with her for a while, no one speaking..." and to emphasise the point, Rosa closed her eyes, still holding Sarah's hand and paused. "Then when she's ready she tells you what is what."

"She sounds a very gifted lady" said Sarah, regaining her hand and becoming aware of Lottie standing just inside the doorway. "Lottie, please set Rosa to work with Lucy and then tomorrow she can sit with Annie and learn what's to be done after the stilling."

"Yes, Miss Sarah."

"And Lottie, see that Rosa is treated in exactly the same way as the other girls, you understand?"

"Yes, Miss Sarah." answered Lottie and then turned to Rosa "Right, out you go your majesty and we'll shows you what's happening today."

Rosa exited into the yard and Lottie paused at the door as she went to follow her.

"What's your opinion on what she was just saying, Miss Sarah?"

"In what way, Lottie?"

"Her old Jiminepegs, or whatever her name was," asked Lottie realising that she had probably mispronounced the name. "Do you hold with such things, miss?"

"No, Lottie, I do not hold with such things, yet, neither do I condemn those that do. It is quite natural for people wanting to know what tomorrow might bring..." Sarah hesitated for a moment.

"But I do not believe any person, however well-meaning, can predict the right course to follow or what path should be taken to guarantee one's happiness. Things just… happen."

"That's a shame, miss, for if it were true, I might seek this old woman out myself."

"Oh?" said Sarah but she was not really paying attention to Lottie. Her mind was elsewhere.

"Yes, miss, to see if she might know when my Robert might get around to proposing and whether it was worth pursuing my love matching between Annie and Albert." Lottie waited for Sarah to comment, but Sarah was still not listening. "Oh well, miss, what will be will be, I suppose."

Sarah did not see Lottie exit and had involuntarily sat in the chair by the trays of lavender, thinking on what Rosa had told her. She had been seen or at least heard, at the field's edge, singing. But had she heard them both singing? Rosa had not said so and would surely have said if she had heard two voices. Was it possible that although Sarah knew John's presence to be real, did he only appear to her?

Sarah's thoughts converged upon this fact and she began to recall the dream that had frightened her so much earlier. In her dream, it was night-time, and she was walking as she always did along the over-grown lanes towards the fields. She was full of her usual joy, knowing that she was going to see her John, be held by him, kissed by him, it would be as it had always been. As she had walked, she had come upon the place where she had been accosted by Lazzy Smith. She stopped involuntarily and no matter how much she tried; she could not move from that spot. In her dream, she had tried not to remember what had happened there, what sinful thoughts had taken her prisoner and how she had regretted them ever since. The darkened hedgerow suddenly became bathed in light. Looking up she could see that the one cloud travelling the sky, that had obscured the three-quarter moon, had slipped on, and allowed the moonlight to escape its clutches. It lit up the branches, the very branches that she had been trapped in on that harrowing night. There she spied, caught upon a branch, a button. A bright button hanging. She recognised the button and reached to take it from its perch. She could see that it was hers, ripped from her dress sleeve. She glanced at her sleeve and there was the empty place that had once housed the missing button, a wisp of cotton dangling, a single strand of cotton that had once secured the button in place.

In her dream, as she had stood wondering, not being able

to walk on, the moonlight had shone deeper into the thicket. There, glinting, fixed upon her, she saw eyes. Two eyes. Not moving, not blinking, just staring out at her. Then suddenly, a manic commotion and the bird, for that was what it was, ferociously flapped its wings and flew at her! Sarah ducked as the angry bird passed her head, squawking as it flew out into the night sky. Still lunar lit, Sarah could make out the undoubted outline and colouring of a magpie. One magpie. Alone. One for sorrow.

She found herself backing away from that unsavoury spot, but still watching the magpie that now sat low on the branch of a nearby tree. Then, Sarah had realised its significance. She was not prone to superstition as she had told Lottie and in normal times would chide all those that were so inclined. She looked up the lane towards the field and then walked in that direction. She walked fast, almost running, until her panic brought her to the spot where he would always be waiting. She stopped, frozen in her tracks, standing where she always stood, where she would watch him for a few seconds before walking up and joining him. But he was not there.

"He's not there." said Sarah, allowing her memory to form the words aloud, thinking she was alone with her nightmare.

"Miss Sarah?"

The voice startled Sarah and she turned suddenly to face Lottie.

"Are you alright, Miss Sarah?" asked Lottie, worried because she could see the pain in Sarah's face and what Lottie thought to be tears in her eyes. Lottie had never seen tears in Sarah's eyes. She had always thought Miss Sarah to be too strong a creature for such undignified things as tears.

"Lottie," answered Sarah, recovering her composure with great speed. "I didn't hear you come in."

"Does something trouble you, Miss Sarah?"

"Good heaven's no…" exclaimed Sarah, but realising that this reaction would not suffice, "Well, yes there is Lottie, in truth. I think something has gone into my eye, a piece of dust or the like, or one of these countless midges plaguing the air," she lied and walked towards Lottie. "Dear Lottie, can you see if you can detect anything?"

Sarah opened her eyes wide and Lottie obediently looked closely to see if she could see anything. "Whatever it is, it has annoyingly made my eyes water."

"I can't see anything, Miss Sarah,"

Sarah moved away from her, reaching for the damp cloth in her apron but, realising that she was not wearing her apron, she turned her back on Lottie and dabbed convincingly at her eyes with the end of her sleeve. As she did so Sarah noticed the button that had featured so heavily in her dream was still attached.

"There!" exclaimed Sarah, nearing the end of her performance of deceit. "Whatever it was has most definitely gone now and I will just have to resist the temptation to rub my eyes."

Lottie was virtually convinced and, with her unease subsiding fast, smiled back at the seemingly cheerful Sarah.

"How does our new recruit?" enquired Sarah.

"Well enough, Miss Sarah. Some of the girl's faces were a picture, miss, a little resentful, I think. But Rosa seems oblivious and besides, they're all too busy to be dwelling upon it."

"How fares the unloading?"

"Almost done, miss. Mister Davey says all will be stored in plenty of time, although unlikely the topping will be completed, despite the extra pair of hands from the royal palace." teased Lottie.

"Lottie." chided Sarah.

"Sorry miss. I know what you're a-thinking, miss. You're a-thinking, be charitable, Lottie, be charitable."

"You were right to send for me. I know what you think about the gypsies, but the good news is we don't have any dogs and we definitely don't have a kennel."

"We have Beggar, miss. She says she knows Beggar and she says her father and her uncles train their dogs to do such tricks."

"You think Beggar may be one of their dogs?"

"No, Miss Sarah, although she does have dogs of her own. Told me that they were called Fetch and Stay."

"Fetch and Stay?"

"And I believed her, miss, just for a second, mind... she likes to jest, I think." added Lottie, a little embarrassed at her own foolishness.

"Lottie, in all honesty, do you think she would have told you she had two dogs if she knew two dogs had recently been stolen locally?

"No, miss. No, I don't."

"Good," replied Sarah, pleased that Lottie could see the flaws in her prejudiced thinking, "and did she say how she knew Beggar?"

"No, miss, but she definitely said she knows of him."

There was a knock at the open door and Mister Davey stepped in.

"Begging your pardon, Miss Sarah, but all is unloaded. Miss Lottie's girls are storing the last of the bushels in the second barn and Silas and Bartholomew have stabled Peggy and Polly."

"And all done in good time." congratulated Sarah.

"Yes, miss."

"Well now, what is the time, Lottie?"

Lottie walked over to the office door and, peering in, saw the wall clock indicating noon.

"Exactly midday, Miss Sarah." answered Lottie, returning even as the clock struck the hour.

"Then I suggest we begin tidying and locking away. Whichever happens first, the tidying completed or the clock striking one, will be the time to go to our homes and prepare for the Queen!" affirmed Sarah looking across at the happy pair. "Agreed?"

"Agreed, Miss Sarah." replied the more than content Lottie and Davey.

"Then don't just stand there, let's be about it!" and with those encouraging words, Lottie and Davey left the shop to spread the good news to everyone else.

Sarah's cheerful exterior belied her inner torment. If they had been able to remain in the room unseen, they would have witnessed Sarah's expression change from joy to anguish. Her perceived cheerful disposition over-run by fear in a frightening instant; the nagging thought that her dream may be an omen, even though she chastised herself for entertaining such a ridiculous notion.

And yet, it would be easy enough to assuage her troubled mind and to do so she would need no spiritual help, no deck of cards or dispersed tealeaves at the bottom of a cup. She became resolved. She would go to the fields that night.

An evening had been arranged by Samuel and Catherine to be held at their house. An opportunity for the Perks family and close friends to discuss the day's events. She would attend that, but if it should run late into the night, she would feign a headache, return home and then, unseen, walk to the fields. 'Yes' thought Sarah, 'That is what I shall do.' There she would surely find John, as always, and put all niggling doubts to bed.

It was time to lock up. Going to the shop door, she placed the bolts across and then turned the key in its lock. She then lifted the trays that were full of sprigs and took them out into the yard.

"Annie!?" called Sarah. Annie stopped her stacking of the bushels and came obediently to Sarah. "I have an errand for you, but it will not delay your finishing on time. I would like you to take these trays to Mrs Doogan in the church yard and say that I would appreciate it if these were handed out to the ladies of our group and anyone else that she feels to be deserving."

"Yes, miss."

"Just take the bottom two trays if you will." Sarah instructed and as Annie left the yard, Sarah sought out Lucy. She finally found her high up in the loft of the top barn "Lucy?" Lucy came to the edge of the open loft and peered down at Sarah.

"Miss Sarah?"

"Here are some sprigs for you to sell outside the station. Share them out with any of the other girls that would have some and you may all keep the money you take."

"Oh, thank you, Miss Sarah! I really appreciate it, miss."

Sarah returned to the shop and surveyed what else she needed to do. After glancing around at the orderly room, she came to the decision that nothing else was required. The table needed to be cleaned from the debris of sprig making and the remaining bushels taken back outside, but they could wait. One of the girls could be assigned that chore first thing in the morning.

Sarah considered herself ready to return to the house and prepare for the afternoon. No doubt Mrs Parker was already making her way there… at the thought of Mrs Parker, Sarah suddenly remembered her new brooch and entered the office to fetch it.

Sarah could see instantly that the brooch was not where she had thought to find it. She searched everywhere, in between the books and registers that stood towards the back of the counter, even in the cash box in case she had put it there for safe keeping. She looked on the shelf above, the floor beneath the counter and every conceivable place she could think of, but to no avail.

She had brought Mrs Parker into the office to show her the brooch. Then, Lottie had entered to save her from the pain of never-ending conversation, by inventing the imaginary rat. A rat the size of a dog. A ruse that had seen Mrs Parker exit the premises faster than the Queen's train.

But what had she done with it after that? Had she returned to the office and stowed the brooch away? Is it possible she took it home when escaping from the shop earlier? Perhaps she had put it down in her mother in law's house? Had she taken it out of the office and into the shop when she had bound the sprigs with Lottie? She could not recall doing any of these things. She left the office and returned to the shop. After several minutes searching and despite knowing that her head had been much troubled earlier, she concluded that the brooch was gone.

Sarah stood, staring at the table, aghast. She was thinking the worst, that it might have been stolen, when her thoughts were abruptly shattered by a loud scream from the yard. A girl's scream. Before she could move to investigate, she heard Lottie's voice.

"You'll be fine, so stop your weeping and hollering. Now, in here with you."

Lottie entered, supporting the distraught Rosa, who was

holding her wrist as if in great pain.

"Sorry, missy… sorry..." apologised Rosa, her face full of anguish as if she were bearing the most indescribable agony. "No sooner does she start topping, miss, than she gets a bee sting."

"I'm sorry, missy, but I suffer with them bee stings."

"You're not the first girl to get a bee sting, girl," continued Lottie, "never known such a fuss."

"I know, but I suffer greatly, missy… honest I do… honest."

"Shall I take her back outside, miss?" Then, as Lottie was speaking, Sarah saw Rosa's eyes struggle to focus.

"I really is sorry, missy, I really is…" and before Rosa could finish her sentence, she began to lose her balance.

"Lottie!"

Lottie turned sharply to look at Rosa and managed to catch the swooning girl, just before she hit the floor.

"Well done, Lottie, bring her over here." commanded Sarah, pulling out the wooden armchair in the shady corner of the room.

Rosa, not yet completely unconscious, began to mumble, trying to convey as much information as she could to the attending Sarah and Lottie. "They don't like me, I think, missy, and they use more venom on me than on most other people…"

"She's very pale, Miss Sarah. I never see anyone react so before."

"I have once before, Lottie. Whereabouts is the sting?"

"On her hand, I think," Sarah searched for the point of injury. "She had just about started topping, when suddenly she screams out and jumps up like she'd been bitten by the devil."

"Lottie, go to the vegetable store, take a large onion out, cut it in half and bring both halves here."

"Yes, Miss Sarah,"

Sarah knelt by the chair, arm around the near delirious Rosa, supporting her.

"I feel as if the world is spinning…" murmured Rosa.

"You'll be fine… Just sit still and rest on me…" Sarah felt Rosa's forehead and immediately changed her diagnosis, deciding that young Rosa was far from fine. The girl's forehead was on fire, the consequence of a burning temperature.

"I suffer more than most, missy…" repeated Rosa, eyes closed, head swaying gently, "My father says I must have killed a big old queen bee when a small child and this is her vengeance."

"You need to stop talking and save your energy, child." Whether Rosa could not hear Sarah or was just refusing to obey was hard to tell, either way she continued to mumble. "I'll be alright soon, missy… and then I can top them lavender stalks for you."

Lottie re-entered the room with the requested onion cut in half.

"Well done, Lottie, now go and fetch a bowl of cold water from the pump, a cloth and also a blanket."

"Shall I go and fetch the doctor as well?" suggested Lottie, trying to make up for her lack of concern at the beginning.

"Lottie, please just do as I say and quickly!" Lottie turned and ran out to complete her second task.

Sarah took one half of the dissected onion and placed it on to the girl's sting. She could not see the sting still imbedded which was a good thing, but Rosa's lower arm was swelling and reddening. Sarah contemplated what best to do. She could send for Doctor Hawkins, but it was most unlikely he would come. At this moment, he would be dressed in his most splendid finery and heading for the railway station. If

Rosa's case proved an emergency, would that make any difference, pondered Sarah. Probably not, especially when it became evident that the patient was a mere gypsy. Or was she being too harsh on the distinguished surgeon? It was hard to gauge. In the meantime, should she let Rosa sleep undisturbed or try to keep her conscious?

"Rosa?" whispered Sarah, on deciding the latter. "Did you say you have suffered like this before?"

Rosa murmured something but it was inaudible. Sarah tried again. "Rosa, stay awake if you can."

Sarah waited for an answer. "How long did you suffer last time?"

"Not long, missy," answered Rosa, her volume now only that of a hushed whisper. "I keeps wanting to sleep you see, that's all… I just has to sleep… that's all…"

"I'm not sure if that's a good thing… Rosa?"

At that moment, Lottie returned with the bowl of water, the cloth and blanket.

"Here we are, miss." Lottie immediately placed the blanket around Rosa's shoulders.

"Now sit here, Lottie, and press this onion on to the sting." Sarah went to a locked cabinet in the office to fetch a medicinal bottle, which she thought might help. As she did so, Lottie continued to press the onion hard on to the girl's wrist just as instructed. She looked at Rosa, who was half awake, clearly in pain and Lottie felt sincerely sorry for her.

"Heavens, girl, you is suffering." she said aloud to herself.

"Sing it missy…" murmured Rosa.

"Lay still now."

"Sing that song, missy."

"Miss Sarah, ain't here. It's me, Lottie."

"Sing it missy... sing the song…"

"Sing what song, Rosa?"

Sarah returned with the bottle of oil tincture and, tipping it upside down on to the cloth, moved to swap places with Lottie, who instinctively knew what was required of her. Lottie moved the table closer to the chair and placing the bowl of water on to it, soaked the cloth in the cold water and applied it to Rosa's forehead. Sarah threw away the half onion and pressed the cloth soaked in oil on to Rosa's swollen wrist.

"This is more likely to help."

"Look at her hand, Miss Sarah,"

"This is far more likely to reduce the swelling. The onion will bring out the sting of course, but it won't reduce the swelling as well as this."

Neither spoke for a while and Rosa seemed to have finished her mumbling request for a song. Lottie feared she might have died and Sarah, sensing Lottie's worry, reassured her otherwise.

"Sleeping, Lottie, that is all." smiled Sarah. "At least she is breathing more easily now."

Sarah stood and looked down at Rosa, neatly wedged into the wooden armchair, now fast asleep.

"That will do for now, Lottie, we'll let her sleep, I think," and placing the soaked rag on to the table, she moved away slightly and watched Lottie continue to dab the cloth on to Rosa's brow. Then, after a final application, Lottie dropped the cloth into the bowl and joined Sarah.

They paused for a moment, both focused on the sleeping girl, Sarah with affection and Lottie with a certain amount of guilt for her earlier attitude.

"Will she be alright, miss?"

"Hopefully."

"Her hand's twice the size… I've never seen anything like it, miss."

"I have." said Sarah, remembering a previous incident. "Once before, when I was first courting Mr John, I saw a young girl, younger than Rosa, react in a similar way. Some people react quite badly to the bee's sting."

"Did she recover, miss? The young girl?"

Sarah paused before answering. "No, Lottie, I'm afraid she didn't."

Silence.

"Earlier, Miss Sarah, when I was sitting with her and you were fetching the tincture, I think she thought I was you, miss."

Sarah looked at Lottie.

"Asked if I'd sing the song again."

"Did she?" answered Sarah, knowing that she would never be able to explain this to Lottie.

As Sarah was not forthcoming, the inquisitive Lottie asked, "What song would that be, miss?"

"I think she is somewhat confused by her fever, Lottie." replied Sarah, brushing it off and then, becoming aware that she could hardly hear a sound from the yard, "Is all finished?"

"Yes, miss, all done and more topping than we thought possible got finished."

"That's good."

"And I don't know whether this was right or not, miss, but because everything was done, I told them all to go. Begging your pardon, miss, bit of a liberty, I know."

"It wasn't a liberty, Lottie. It was exactly what I'd expect from my head girl."

After a while they heard the wall clock in the office strike the hour. It was one o'clock.

"You should be going, miss."

"I can't find my brooch, Lottie." said Sarah, not taking her eyes from the sleeping Rosa.

"The one you showed Mrs Parker?"

"Yes. I thought I'd left it in the office, but I've searched both the office and the shop and it's not to be found anywhere."

"Is it at the house?"

"No. I'm convinced I left it here. Here in the office." informed Sarah, still looking at the sleeping Rosa.

Suddenly, a thought occurred to Lottie and she moved away from Sarah, quickly running earlier events through her mind.

"She'd been in the office, miss." Lottie spoke softly so that only Sarah would hear.

"I was frightened you might say that, Lottie. Did you see her in there?"

"No, miss, but she told me she'd been in there. Told me she'd gone in there to look for you and then she'd watched Beggar performing his tricks in the yard from the office window."

Sarah did not reply or comment.

"That was what she told me, miss." Lottie felt nearly as deflated as Sarah. They both stood in silence, both trying to deny their thoughts from the most likely answer.

"Begging your pardon, miss, but if you're definite that you left it here and not at the house and it cannot be found… well, to my mind miss, it can only have been stolen."

"Didn't you say that young Thomas Royce was around here earlier?" Sarah was desperate to find some other possible explanation. "You said yourself that you had to chase him off."

"Yes, miss, I did, but he was only in the yard, he never came in here. It was the crack of dawn and I don't think we'd even unlocked the door to the shop by then."

"Oh Lottie," Sarah was beginning to lose faith in the power

of charity. "if it's true, I am so, so bitterly disappointed."

"I don't know what other answer it could be, miss. I knows she's a character but she's a still a gypsy. It's in their nature."

"Not all of them, Lottie." answered Sarah, still looking to defend. "Oh, and I thought I was a good judge of character."

"You are, miss, an excellent judge, but I think the gypsy charm got the better of you."

"Am I so easily fooled, Lottie?"

"I reckons you're always looking for the good in people and although that's a fine thing, sometimes, just sometimes…"

Lottie didn't have to say what she had intended to say.

"I am too easily, deceived? Perhaps I am. Oh dear, I'm not just disappointed, it's worse than that, I'm angry. Angry with myself for being so taken in. I fell for her sweet nature and what I thought to be her refreshing innocence. It is a hard lesson to learn, Lottie. That even in such a short time, trust can be so easily broken and charitable goodwill repaid with contempt. All that may be said in her defence, is that she had stolen the brooch before we had met and conversed. I must believe it would not have been the case if the temptation had been put before her after our conversation.

Lottie did not know what to say. She thought Sarah was clutching at straws and felt heartbroken for her. Sarah, for her part, was now wandering around the room looking for something to focus on, brushing the unwanted pieces of cut lavender from the table on to the floor. Unthinking, she picked up her discarded apron from earlier and looked back at Rosa.

"Don't worry about her, miss, I'll sit with her."

"Lottie?"

"Don't worry, miss, I know I'd miss the Queen and all the cheering but, well to be totally honest, Miss Sarah, I'm not that keen on the station. Dirty, smelly building. I'm sure I would choke and be ill upon the fumes if I went, miss."

Sarah was about to speak but Lottie's mind was made up. "If I don't go, I won't be disappointed when Robert doesn't use it as an opportunity to propose. And I would find it difficult to stop myself from strangling those two Royce sisters, so best I not be put in temptation's way."

Sarah looked at Lottie. "Honestly miss, you get along. If I went, I'd only be at the back of the crowd and probably wouldn't see the Queen anyhows."

"That's very kind of you, Lottie," answered Sarah, with her faith in the worth of charity restored.

"Nonsense miss... and if she recovers whilst you're gone, I'll search her, recover your brooch, clip her ear and send her on her way. Do you want me to report it to the constable?"

"Perhaps I should, if she is taken to task for her crime, it may make her think twice in the future. I will think on it, perhaps a severe reprimand will suffice."

Lottie picked up one of the wooden chairs next to the table and moved it nearer the sleeping Rosa. Sarah dropped her apron on to the table and heard a noise on contact that bore no resemblance to cloth on wood. Lottie turned and saw Sarah staring at the table.

"Miss Sarah?"

Sarah did not answer her, but picked up the apron from the table and, having put her hand into the apron pocket... she pulled out the damp cloth and from beneath that, the missing brooch.

Lottie was unsure what to say, so chose to say nothing. Sarah remembered placing the brooch in her apron for safe keeping. She looked at Lottie and then at Rosa.

"I believed she had done it, Lottie... for a while there, I quite despised the child for something she had not done."

"It was an honest mistake, miss." said Lottie, trying to lessen

Sarah's heavy feeling of guilt.

"It was anything but honest, it was a terrible mistake, Lottie! Think what might have come of it if I had not rediscovered the brooch. She may have been hauled off to the police station and put in a cell, even stood up before the magistrates. It was a wicked thing that I thought and I am greatly ashamed."

"Nothing need come of it, miss, only you and I need know." Lottie was desperate to help but her suggestion only made Sarah feel worse.

"But I do know, Lottie. I judged her unfairly and on no evidence, mind! I did not even take the trouble to search her clothes before condemning her." Lottie went to speak again but Sarah stopped her in her tracks. "You must stop making excuses for me, Lottie!"

Lottie fell silent.

"I know you do it through good intention, I know that." Sarah paused and then added, "I feel like Hilda."

"Miss?"

"How you said Hilda had felt about blaming her aunt for something she hadn't been guilty of."

Sarah placed the apron back on to the table and placed the brooch on top.

"You go, Lottie. Please, I have no appetite for it now. Kindly stop in at the house and let Eliza know what has happened and ask her to relate the same to Mr Samuel and Miss Catherine. I will explain fully to them when I see them this evening and if not then, I will do so in the morning."

Lottie moved towards the open door but hesitated. She looked back to see Sarah looking at Rosa.

"If she makes some recovery, I will make her a bed in the back room, and she may stay the night there. She seems to breathe more evenly now. I'm sure she will be fully recovered by the morning."

Sarah looked at Lottie standing at the door, reluctant to leave her mistress in such circumstances.

"Go Lottie, or you will surely be missed."

"Me, miss?"

"By your father, Lottie, I'm sure it would make him a proud man to have his wonderful daughter standing by his side the day that the Queen of England came to Hitchin. And who knows what devil may get into Robert on this special day."

Lottie smiled Sarah a smile of gratitude, a smile that Sarah fully understood.

"If Hilda can sacrifice the day to make amends, then surely, so can I." said Sarah, looking back to Rosa. As there was no more to be said, Lottie Greenacre left to see the Queen.

As Sarah watched the sleeping Rosa, she listened. From outside she could hear no noise, no chattering, no cart, no neighing horse nor barking dog. The town was absent, gone off to the station and everything at Perks Pharmacy was silent.

And in that silence, a voice was heard. A voice singing. It was Sarah's voice and her voice sang....

Lavender's blue, dilly, dilly, lavender's green,
When I am King, dilly, dilly, you shall be Queen.

Who told you so, dilly, dilly, who told you so?
T'was my own heart, dilly, dilly, that told me so.

Call up your men, dilly, dilly, set them to work,
Some to the plough, dilly, dilly, some to the fork.
Some to make hay, dilly, dilly, some to cut corn,

While you and I, dilly, dilly, keep ourselves warm.

Lavender's green, dilly, dilly, lavender's blue,
If you love me, dilly, dilly, I will love you.

But that night... he was not there

Chapter Eight

At ten minutes after three, the scenes at Hitchin railway
station and at the Pharmacy at No. 9, Cock Street could not
have been more different. One was a cacophony of sound
with cheering, clapping and bands blasting, whilst the other
had the quiet of an unattended wake. The bunting hanging at
the station, drooping in the breathless air, witnessed the
Queen's stay of eight minutes and at the same time the glass
cabinets holding oils and tinctures were the only audience to
observe Sarah's attendance upon Rosa.

There were two similarities though. Firstly, the singing. The
ecstatic Hitchin crowd's rendering of 'God Save the Queen'
roared out with gusto, as Sarah's sweet and melodic voice
purveyed the air with her rendition of 'Lavender's Blue'.
Secondly, the Royal families. Alexandrina Victoria Hanover,
niece to the late William IV, stood at Hitchin station and less

than a mile away, Rosa Boswell, great, great granddaughter to Henry Boswell, King of the Gypsies, sat asleep in the Perk's shop.
As the young Mary Exton curtseyed and presented the earlier-described gifts to Victoria, Sarah dabbed a cool, wet cloth on to Rosa's forehead.

Around five o'clock, Rosa awoke, still reeling from the bee's venom but with strength enough to speak and to transfer on to a rough bed in the backroom. After a few instructions, including where to find bread and apples if she awoke hungry, Sarah left promising to return first thing in the morning. Convinced that Rosa was over the worse and leaving Beggar to stand guard or rather lay on guard in the yard, Sarah locked the wicket door in the large gates and walked home.

She arrived to find the house and yard all a bustle. Sarah senior was sat in the drawing room, fan in hand, talking to Eliza, whilst outside in the yard the amiable James was entertaining both Edward and his sister Anne. A second ship had been quickly fashioned and the barrelled ocean was now home to a conflict between a Royal Navy frigate and HMS Lavender, which had recently converted to a pirate ship complete with skull and crossbones. Thomas and Toby were busy at their unfinished stable chores; unfinished because they had been allowed time to go to the station to witness the great event. Toby was working his way across the yard to be as near to pretty Lizzie Butler as possible. They were swapping stories of the great event and at the same time giving breath to a fledgling romance. The relationship was at an early stage and had still to progress to the 'holding of hands' stage let alone the 'late evening spooning' stage.

However, this had not gone unnoticed by the household and had prompted some serious teasing from Eliza and Toby's twin brother, Thomas.

Sarah explained in as few sentences as possible what had transpired at the shop and why she had been unable to attend the Queen's visit. She made heavy play regarding her feeling of guilt, having suspected Rosa of a crime she had not committed, so that her decision to miss the great event made more sense.

All through the explanation, Eliza and Sarah senior listened carefully, too carefully for Sarah's liking, as if they did not fully believe everything she had said. But once again Sarah's suspicions were unfounded. Eliza's close attentiveness was because of her pride in her mistress's actions. It was the sort of moral honour that she knew her Miss Sarah valued and lived by. 'There are not many' thought Eliza 'who would have done as Miss Sarah had.'

For Sarah senior, however, it was a different thought that kept her listening intently. She found Sarah's decision to miss out irrational, taken too quickly and not with the bigger picture in mind. If the gypsy girl was sleeping, then she would have slept quite safely whilst Sarah attended the station. To the old lady, Sarah's story and excuse did not lack truth, just logic. She knew for a fact that her daughter in law had been most excited about the visit and, in her opinion, it was essential that the Perks family were in attendance on such an important day. It was not enough that Samuel and Catherine had been present. They had yet to take up their roles in the company. Also, there was something else that should have been given serious consideration. Sarah's absence may have been mistakenly interpreted as sour grapes on her part for not being asked to make the presentation. The old lady knew that this was not the case but was concerned that Sarah's usual common sense and astuteness had not spotted this possibility. It was all just another sign to the old lady that her daughter in law was struggling. To her mind, grief was not a complaint that could be seen out and endured completely alone.

Eliza had informed her that Sarah never showed her feelings to anyone but carried on as if nothing had happened. Sometimes, as if John had never died. Eliza had seen this attitude as a reason to be impressed but Sarah senior saw it as another cause to be worried. Her daughter in law had loved her son, she knew that, and that love had been reciprocated. They had been inseparable, doting, deeply in love. Sarah's actions were not consistent with a widow dealing successfully with the burden of grief. Pretending that it had never happened was a slippery path to an unbearable pain that would never go away, or ease.

She had spoken to James, as she always did. In his opinion, which the old lady valued above all others, he thought Sarah to be possibly in some state of denial. However, during their meetings, James had not seen fit to tell the old lady about Sarah's absences from the house at night. For now, he would keep that knowledge to himself. "Are you sure this girl can be trusted in the shop?" asked Sarah senior.
"Yes. I have no fear of that, the girl is as honest as the day."
"Let us hope you are right, Sarah."
"I feel I have made the right decision. I really do. The only decision I could have made under the circumstances."
The old lady did not reply. Sarah did not add to her statement and Eliza, who would not speak unless spoken to, sipped her tea. All three sat in silence, sipping tea.
Sarah felt the two pairs of eyes upon her.

"Well, I'm sure that this evening we will be well informed of all that took place this afternoon. Samuel and Catherine will have much to tell us."

"Eliza?" said the old lady, turning her attention to Sarah's unusually silent housekeeper.

"Ma'am?"

"Have you heard any news?"

Eliza always found Sarah senior quite daunting. Intimidating, to be truthful, as many did. Sarah senior was revered in the town, much respected by all and known not to suffer fools gladly. Unfortunately, Eliza always felt foolish when talking to the old lady. The Perks family had a reputation for being open and inclusive with their servants. Engaging staff in conversation and asking them their views on various subjects and current topics was normal for them. Although Eliza was quite at ease with Miss Sarah and had been with Mister John, it was not a situation she enjoyed with Miss Sarah's mother in law. She knew she must think of something that was well worth speaking of and would not leave her sounding ridiculous.

"Well ma'am," began Eliza, having decided on a piece of gossip that she knew to be totally credible and unlikely to let her down. "I hears, ma'am, on good authority, that Matilda Dawes is pregnant and four months pregnant at that, which is a surprise to everyone, and I hears she don't deny it. Not that she can deny it with a bump as big as a baker's oven leading her around everywhere. Now, what's wrong with Matilda Dawes being four months pregnant, I hears you thinking, ma'am? But when I tells you that her husband has only recently returned home, and no more than three weeks ago, from serving two years hard labour in Bedford prison, well, that might make you think different. Now, I'm no good at all with all them mather-amatics, ma'am, but even I can work out on the fingers of me two 'ands that that doesn't add up. So, ma'am, on hearing that, I should imagine you'll agree with me, that her husband is most unlikely to be the father of her expected child."

There was a very slight pause before the old lady spoke.

"I was referring to the Queen's visit, Eliza."

Eliza's heart sunk.

"I wondered whether you had heard any news on the Queen's visit."

The old lady thought Eliza foolish, Eliza thought the world had ended and Sarah wished the evening would start and pass as quickly as possible so that she could go to the fields.

The hours passed slowly. Although all were cheerful and of the view that the Queen's visit had been a great success, the evening dragged unbearably for Sarah. She was fighting hard to seem genuinely concerned about having missed the event and sincerely glad that all had passed smoothly. Samuel and Catherine were quite at home hosting; their first opportunity since returning to Hitchin and the gathered were made up of some of the most influential members of the town's community.

As she looked across the room, she could see Samuel in jovial mood with Joseph Sharples and the young Frederick Seebohm. Close by, Catherine was holding court with Samuel Lucas, William Hawkins and the irrepressible Septimus Wright, who were informing her of their plans to open a bank for the poor. It would be called the Hitchin Penny bank.

"It is a ground-breaking idea, we think, with the building hopefully being situated within the precincts of the poorest area of Hitchin. Somewhere close to Dead Street or Back Street, there is a plot in St Andrews Street that we are seriously considering. A Penny Bank, Catherine, that will enable the most disenfranchised of the community to save and prosper with financial security." Sarah could hear Septimus explaining to Catherine, who was obviously most impressed by the idea and was listening intently.

"It sounds a wonderful opportunity, Septimus, and I will tell everyone of the good news on my visits to the area. Even Dolly Hutchins shall hear of it.

"Dolly Hutchins hear of it?" asked the surprised Frederick Seebohm, "But I understood the woman to be stone deaf?"

"It is a new hearing disorder that Dolly suffers from, Frederick, called 'severe selective hearing loss.' This complicated infliction allows one to hear only that which one wishes to hear."

General laughter ensued amongst Catherine's audience, as all were aware of Dolly's infliction, save Frederick Seebohm who was not.

"Then Dolly is just the person to be aware of our venture," commented Septimus, "for we are proposing that even women and children will be allowed to open accounts and in their own names. Ground-breaking I tell you, Catherine, and it will enhance Hitchin's growing reputation in the world of commerce."

Septimus was a keen and active player in the town's growth and was a trustee of the Hitchin Benevolent Building Society, along with Jeffrey Lucas and William Bentley, amongst others. This financial organisation had achieved mixed results, as several of the banks in Hitchin had. For the most part, they had either not got off the ground; failed, merged or both. Despite this, the optimism and determination of Septimus and his associates to succeed had to be admired. They were young, enthusiastic, and looking to see the town thrive.

There had been countless plans and proposals since the railway had arrived at Hitchin the previous year, but the Queen's visit seemed to have given all projects an added stimulus. The young and entrepreneurial saw opportunities to improve the lot of the people and at the same time make substantial amounts of money. Market forces at work in a market town. To the minds of the business fraternity, it was a simple fact that the more the wealthy investors prospered, the more the ordinary citizens would benefit.

Sarah was pleased for their exuberance and understood that these were fast changing times, but her heart was not fully engaged. She wished that time were a static force and would stand still. For if time was unmoving, she posed, then her special world with John would remain unaltered. It would gain an immunity from destruction and she would not fall victim to the slings and arrows of outrageous fortune.

"Good evening," a voice from behind brought her mind back to the present, for she recognised it immediately. She turned to face him.

"William."

"Sarah. You were much missed today."

"Thank you, I greatly regret not having been able to attend. But for circumstances, I would have been there."

"I have heard your reason, Sarah, and it is quite admirable. In truth, it has been the main topic of conversation, after what jewels the Queen was wearing, of course."

William smiled. Sarah smiled back. She could not stop herself.

"But you were missed, none the less."

"Thank you."

"And how is the young girl?"

"Well enough now, I think. She sleeps."

"That is good. That she sleeps."

"Yes, it is" Their conversation was running its familiar course of hesitancy, where neither party found the right words that would put the other party at ease.

"A shame though that you were not able to attend…"

"I could not assign the job to anyone else. It was also the only way I could think of allaying my guilt, other than crawling to Canterbury on my hands and knees dressed in nought but a sackcloth."

"I understand completely." smiled William.

Although initial conversation was always somewhat stilted, she felt comfortable in William's company. The attraction was undeniable and reciprocated. Despite all her reservations and vows, her resistance and fears, she felt as comfortable with him as she did with… John.

"Hopefully, you will not need to cancel our trip?"

"Trip?"

"To Wilbury Hills. I take it Samuel remembered to ask you?"

'Of course, Wilbury Hills. Yes, he did mention it."

"And it suits?"

"Yes, yes, it suits. Thank you. I look forward to it."

"We are discovering much there, each day something of interest comes out of the ground. Coins."

"Coins?"

"More Roman coins than I have ever seen in any museum. Although it is far from a hoard, hardly that."

"I see."

"But a substantial amount, none the less. Interestingly, there is the possibility of some irony involved regarding the excavations."

"There is?"

"It may be that some careless overseer had dropped these coins which were meant as payment to different tradesmen during the development of the Icknield Way. Ironically, they are being unearthed during the building of the Great Northern railway, do you see, Sarah?"

"Yes, yes, I see."

"One has to be alert though as if unwatched, the navvies are likely to throw objects of great historical value away, considering them to be of no particular interest."

"Navvies?"

"The workmen. I understand it is taken from the word navigator. Although, they do not navigate, they dig, usually whilst under the influence of alcohol. For the most part they are Irish."

Sarah was finding it hard to concentrate on what William was saying and interjected short comments that she thought to be apt.

"I see."

"They have suffered greatly in recent years, the Irish," continued William, "Because of the horrors caused by that foul famine and their suffering compounded by heartless landlords, few have remained in Ireland. Those families that have not emigrated to the Americas, have come to England to work upon the railways."

Sarah did not comment. William looked long and hard into her eyes.

"You are sure, Sarah? I do not press you unfairly?"

"Regarding what?"

"The trip to the Wilbury Hills? I say, I hope I do not press you unfairly?"

Her heart was saying 'No', but it was conflicting with her head which was struggling to mouth anything.

"Sarah?" he sensed her reservation.

"No, you do not pressure me at all, William, I look forward to the trip and depending on little John faring well at the time, I will not look to cancel. Thank you."

"That is good then."

'Yes."

"You seem occupied, Sarah, is there something that worries you?"

Sarah opened her mouth and once again she struggled but nothing came out, neither denial nor admittance.

"Is it perhaps the business?"

"Business?"

"Yes. I hope you do not have concerns regarding mine and Samuel's discussions concerning the stilling of your lavender…?"

"Concerns?" flustered Sarah. She was finding it increasingly difficult to keep her impatience in check. It was so difficult when all the time she secretly wished to be elsewhere. "No, not at all…"

"For if you do have any concerns…"

"William? I will be honest with you, I suffer a little from a headache, I think. Nothing too distressful, you understand, but with all that has happened today and the heat, this accursed heat… and everything"

"Of course, I fully understand… Can I fetch you some water?"

"No thank you…" Sarah decided it was time to make her leave. She was striving not to bring suspicion upon herself. "If you'll excuse me, William, I'll explain to Samuel and Catherine… yes, I think that will be for the best."

Before William could offer his sympathy or wish her a goodnight, Sarah had moved away from him towards Samuel. In her hurry, she knocked into Doctor Hawkins, spilling his drink.

"I'm sorry, so sorry…"

"Not at all, Sarah, no harm done. I was not looking and it

was entirely my fault…" But before he could finish what he was saying, she had left him and now stood at Samuel's arm. "Samuel? I'm so sorry, but I have the vilest of headaches." Samuel's face changed instantly from that of a man enjoying drink and humorous conversation, to one of concern.

"Poor Sarah… is there anything I can get you…?" again she interrupted someone who was genuinely perturbed by her suffering.

"I think I just need to rest, that is all."

"Of course, I understand, shall I see you home?

"Honestly, Samuel, I shall be fine, I live virtually next door and am not in need of an escort. Thank you for this evening…"

"If you're sure…?"

'I am positive…" Sarah could feel anger welling up inside, a ridiculous anger. It was anger at herself for lying. Yet, she was trying to deflect this anger away from herself and on to innocent bystanders. She was telling falsehoods and becoming constantly annoyed with those that loved her and were concerned for her well-being. Becoming annoyed and angry at people who were simply being sympathetic regarding her headache. A headache that she did not have. All she had was a burning desire to leave the party and make her way as quickly as possible to the fields to see if John would be there.

Having passed several people, smiling and acknowledging them politely as she crossed the crowded room, she made for the open door that gave her hope of escape. As she reached it, her arm was pulled back, gently but firmly, which caused her to turn and see who it was that had stopped her escaping. It was Catherine.

"Come with me."

Sarah tried to make an excuse, but Catherine was already

leading her by the hand along the corridor, away from the party. At the far end, she opened the door to the study and, before Sarah could protest, they had entered the room and Catherine had closed the door behind them.

In an instant, the noises and voices in the drawing room became muffled, to such an extent that they became barely audible. The room was relatively cool, and Sarah felt her inner turmoil cool likewise and begin to soften. Catherine had her back against the door as if to prevent anyone else entering.

"Catherine, I'm so sorry but I seemed to have developed the most horrendous headache."

"I know. Samuel told me."

Catherine stepped forward and gently took Sarah's hands in hers.

"I will not detain you more than a minute. I just want you to know, that although we are sisters in law, I would like it that we were much more than that."

For a moment Sarah was not sure what to say or, indeed, what Catherine was trying to say.

"Since I have arrived you have been so kind and generous, and I want to repay you however I can. I know you talk to our mother in law, but I would… well, I would like you to think that you can talk to me as well, if the occasion should ever arise. I know you are a woman of great strength and determination, but if you should need a friend of similar age to speak to or even a shoulder to cry upon…"

"Catherine…"

'You really don't need to answer me, Sarah. I just want to repay some of the kindness that you have shown to me."

Sarah paused, thinking on what Catherine was saying. This woman, whose heart was made from all things charitable, was reaching out to her. Sarah loved the woman for what she said. Her kindness stunned Sarah out of her melancholy and straightened her mind, for a second. Only a second.

"Catherine, that is extremely kind and I am so grateful. I know your offer is made with the utmost sincerity and whenever I should find myself in need of support, advice or, as you say, a shoulder to cry upon… you, dear sister, will be my first port of call. Thank you, with all my heart."

Sarah, unprompted and without design, leant forward and kissed Catherine sisterly upon the cheek. Catherine in turn wrapped her arms around Sarah and squeezed her so tightly that Sarah feared her lungs would be forced to gasp for air.

The hug was glorious to Sarah's mind. A strength she could not give herself. It took all her might not to give in to its charms and persuasions, and as her desire to keep all things secret began to crumble and her unconscious need for an ally began to scream, Catherine released her.
She had almost succumbed to her offer of comfort, just as she had earlier to her mother in law's. But she would not. Dare not.

Standing back Sarah could see tears in Catherine's eyes, tears because Sarah had simply acquiesced to her thoughtful proposal. Tears, because Sarah had accepted that her shoulder would be her future place of comfort.

Sarah thought herself to be an intelligent woman. But here she stood for the second time, trying hard to make herself distant from someone whose only crime was charity. It was Sarah's defence, a barricade put up to prevent kindness from overcoming her. If she should ever be tempted to 'open up' to those that cared for her, who knows what she might say or tell.

"But I keep you unfairly when you feel as you do." apologised Catherine, opening the door of the study and leading Sarah back into the corridor. "It is no doubt caused by this oppressive heat, but I'm sure a good night's rest will soon rid you of your annoying affliction."

"Yes, I'm sure it will."

At the front door, Catherine spoke once more.

"I wish for rain, Sarah, but will no doubt regret it when it finally falls. One day I wish for rain and whenever it comes, I wish for the sun. Sometimes it is best that we do not wish for things, I think, but best to accept what we have. I imagine God knows what we are deserving of, don't you think?"

The question was undoubtedly rhetorical, but for a second Sarah thought Catherine's gaze to be searching, looking for any clue to... whatever it was she might suspect.

'No,' thought Sarah to herself. 'This is just Catherine's natural kindness coming to the fore. It is folly to think otherwise.'

"Good night, Catherine and thank you."

"Good night to you, sweet Sarah," and as Sarah walked away, Catherine added "Sleep peacefully if you can." But Sarah did not hear.

Once in the yard, she could see the window to James' room unlit, with the candle snuffed and no doubt the gentle giant asleep. She found Eliza in the pantry, sitting in her rocking chair, snoring. According to Eliza, she did not snore and it was just a terrible rumour invented by Master Edward and Miss Anne to embarrass her. The fact that the two children said they had sat by Eliza and watched her torrents of snore break the air and disturb the horses, was another unforgivable white lie. Eliza had chided them and warned them that they would never go to heaven for spreading such falsehoods.

Sarah did not wake Eliza but placed her shawl upon the table next to her, so that she would know her mistress was home. Eliza always found it difficult to retire before Sarah was abed.

She took a lit candle and, whilst protecting the flame with her cupped hand, she climbed the stairs to her room. All was silent from little John's room. All was content with Edward. He always slept soundly, worn out no doubt by all the adventures on the high seas that had been instigated by James. Sitting on the edge of her bed she could see out of her window towards the fields. The sun had set, and the last light was fading fast. A half-moon ruled the sky unchallenged, for no cloud had managed to drift close and mask it from earth's view. She sat and waited.

She waited for the last of the guests at 27, Bancroft to make their way home. Waited for Eliza to wake, see her mistress' shawl and, being content, make her own way to bed. She waited.

Eventually, time saw that these things happened.

The happy voices from the party ceased and the revelling came to an end. Eliza noisily made her way to bed. The streets became clear of life, bar a single dog howling in the street. No one responded to the dog's howls. No human, no other dog. Bored of being ignored, the lone hound wandered off to find a better place, where his howling might cause others to join him in song.

Still Sarah waited to be certain that the world slept.

At last it was time. Enough minutes had elapsed to ensure journeying safely. She went to stand but found she could not rise from her sitting position. The moment she had been waiting for had arrived but now she was gripped by the fear that had dogged her throughout the day. What if when she got there, John was not waiting for her? Should she wait for another day? She could not wait, for the delay would destroy her. The irrationality of her thinking jarred and made no sense. She feared finding him not to be there and she hesitated. But if she did not go, she would never know? Which was worse to her mind, not to go or to go and find he had gone?

Silence.

An hour came and went.

Another hour. It was now one o'clock in the morning. One thirty.

After extinguishing the candle in her room, Sarah closed the bedroom door silently behind her and crept down the wooden stairs, avoiding where she knew the creaks to live. Taking her summer shawl from the pantry table, she cautiously opened the back door and left the house. Stepping out into the yard, as always tiptoeing so she would not raise a clatter upon the cobbles, she crossed the yard and started her familiar walk to the fields, almost unseen.

Her walk was like no other she had made since John's reappearance. Always before, she had been full of the joys of life, as a fiancé meeting her betrothed in the early hours of their romance. When nothing mattered and the exhilarating world and all its promises still lay before them. To outside eyes, their meeting at the fields might seem ghoulish, unsavoury, even demonic. But to Sarah and John, it was as if nothing had changed. They had defied God and Satan in their victory over mourning and the untimely demise of a loved one. But this was not one of those previous nights.

Despite her determination to be steadfast in her purpose to John, she was no longer in control. The reins that steered her thoughts and feelings had been ripped from her hands. Her ability to keep doubt at the door was crumbling, shattering with every waking day.

Things had changed in the real world, they had grabbed at her, collided with her intent, tossed her like a rag doll in a turbulent wind at sea.

She saw herself now as a lone hand on one of Edwards's imaginary ships, with John in another ship alongside. Once upon a time the two of them had happily charted peaceful waters, moving gracefully from one fantastical island to another. But now a storm raged, a tempest whipped the waves and the once happy pair were being torn apart. They had come upon that watery expanse in paradise where two oceans meet, and no matter how hard the two try, neither will be reconciled with the other. Every day saw her being drawn further away towards new and fresh horizons with him being left on seas already travelled.

Once upon a time, his great craft had been securely tied to hers, but the rope that bound them together had slipped its loving hold and now trailed in the water behind, untethered. She was being pulled far ahead by the winds and currents, whilst he sat motionless and becalmed on millpond waters. She could see him in the distance, withering upon the horizon, moving from a hopeless speck, until finally disappearing altogether. Left alone. Becalmed and abandoned.

She must seize this opportunity to meet with him and explain her dilemma and he would resolve the problem as he always had. As he always did. Nothing was beyond him. For whatever befell them, John would always find an answer and see to it that all… 'fared well'.

She walked up the last lane, her pace quickening with every

step until she turned the penultimate corner. It was the spot where Lazzy had appeared to her from out of the hedge like some wild animal trapping its prey. But unlike in her dream, she did not stop, she would not stop. She would not dally to question what she had thought there and what she had wished for. She would not delay. On she ran, up the hill, heart beating, lungs pumping. Fear and longing battling for supremacy.

In a moment she would be able to see him, standing, waiting. As she was turning the last bend, taking the last steps, she closed her eyes and then... she stopped.

She could not bring herself to look.

She was fearful that her wretched dream had forecast the truth and his absence was about to be confirmed. Her heartbeat raced, her anxiety thrashed, and her stomach grew sick with the unthinkable thought. Still she stood, eyes closed. She knew she must open them and see, or else turn away. Walk away and never know whether he stood there to meet her or not.

Her eyes were shut tight. So tight that they hurt. Then slowly, very, very slowly, she opened them.

The view that met her eyes was now better lit for the shutting of them. She could quite clearly see the fields ripped of their crops. The light beige of the earth, the yellowy green of the bleached grass in front of her. On the far side, the tree lined horizon stood static, silhouetted, and the half-moon bathed the spot where he would always be.

But that night... he was not there.

Her terror was realised, and her horror gave birth to a scream that came from the pit of her stomach and broke the still air like a crack of thunder.

She could not stop herself, could not find the will to muffle its escape and as it left her body, it took with it every ounce of her remaining sanity. She fell to the ground and sobbed uncontrollably. But this was not the wailing of a woman who feared her love might leave her. This was the distraught rantings of a woman who knew he had left and was unlikely to ever return.

Long into the dry night, Sarah cried until her face was soaked and every muscle ached from the effort. The hours passed and the crying never ceased. Throughout, she searched the skyline for a sign that he may still be coming, or any sign that he had been there. She looked for anything that would give her hope. Her glazed eyes searched the far trees to see if he stood there between the shadowy trunks watching her from a distance. Disappointed, annoyed, angry with her for thinking to leave him for someone else. That was how Sarah perceived things, rightly or wrongly. She was to blame.

Eventually, when all strength and reason had been syphoned, she fell forward to the ground and lay there unable to move. Unwilling to move. One side of her face pressed into the earth, ear to the ground as if listening for John's footsteps. Her cheek, damp from constant weeping, collected a layer of dust from the scorched earth. Caked with soil and guilt, she thought how helpless all now seemed.
All her plans to keep herself isolated from those that cared for her, were forgotten and forsaken.

If anyone should happen upon her now and witness her distress, she would not care. She would have no will to hide. But she knew she was alone because she felt alone. Unseen.

Unheard by all, including John. She remained lying there though, just in case he should come looking for her. If she stayed long enough, he may see her, pity her, come back to her, forgive her and take her once again in his arms and love her. She would promise again never to leave him. In thought or in body.

To Sarah, his absence could only mean one thing. John had read her thoughts from afar, felt her slipping away from him. Whether it was her sin-stained meeting with Lazzy or her irresistible attraction to William, John knew all these things and saw no reason to return to meet with her.

She determined not to move, to lay there and die there. For that was the only way she could imagine ever seeing him again. But once more, horror struck at her as she remembered that access to the gates of Heaven were sanctioned through the will of God and she had abandoned God. No amount of repentance may ever see him accept her back into the fold.

As the night moved closer and closer to daylight, her crying began to subside. Not because she had no more tears to shed, but because her body lacked the strength to bring them to the surface. There, prone upon the ground, as if in distraught supplication at the foot of some great altar… she fell asleep.
A deep sleep, where no dream would disturb her and no change of weather would wake her. Exhausted.

The night continued its journey, it would not stop because of Sarah's anguish and so time moved on. If some great bird had flown above at that moment, it would have gazed down and, upon seeing her motionless body below, would have believed her to be dead.

The sun could not be detected yet, but its rays were just

starting to light the eastern horizon. Fingers of light were slipping through the trees as if to prod her awake. The forlorn Sarah had slept deeply but for no more than an hour at most. Her mind came to first, and she thought herself in bed.

After a moment of her brain readjusting, all came trickling back. The memories resurfaced and collaborated until she recalled all that had brought her to that place. She opened her eyes. She saw stones, dust and tufts of stubble from recently cropped lavender. Pushing herself up by her arms, she assumed a kneeling position and looked around. Having slept, despite it being a short sleep, she began to regain her reasoning and her sanity.

Once again, she was concerned that someone might see her. Her self-respect had returned as had her desire for secrecy. She would need to think what was to be done. She needed time. She was cast adrift from John with no obvious way of finding her way back to him and she needed to think of what was to be done. What could be done? She stood up and looked at her dress, all coated in soil and cemented on to her clothes by the dew. She brushed at herself, but to no avail. Having turned slowly full circle and confident that no one was in sight, she decided on returning to the shop and cleaning herself before heading home. In the small side-pocket of her dress she kept a key to the wicket gate at the yard. That would be her first port of call.

The whole walk home she passed no one. The sun had yet to show its face and, as she entered the town via Brand Street, still not a soul was to be seen. Most were still languishing abed after the celebrations of the previous night. Turning into Cock Street, she came upon an absence of people, which she was thankful for. Sarah prayed that she would reach the yard before she met any early riser, she did not want anyone to see her in such a dishevelled state. Her hair was matted and her face a mask of light mud, as if she had burrowed into a rabbit hole for the night. She had not yet thought of a worthy enough explanation for the sight she would present, and only the sanctuary of the yard would guarantee safety and time to think. The workforce was not called until mid-day as promised, so all bode well.

Sarah opened the wicket gate, looked both ways along the street, then entered the yard locking the door behind her.

Most of the yard was still in shade and the air was cooler than the previous morning, although the breeze remained asleep and somewhere hidden. Having pumped fresh water into a bucket from the pump, she cleaned her face and wiped down the front of her dress as best she could. The cold water washed away the sleep and allowed the mind to think more clearly. Despite this she felt weakened, exhausted, drained. She needed to sleep properly and would have to be quick if she hoped to return to her room before Eliza awoke. It would be best if no one knew that she had been absent all night. As she wiped her face, pleased that the first phase of her plan had been accomplished without witnesses, a voice spoke. "Morning, missy."
Sarah swung round to see, standing in the doorway to the shop, half eaten apple in hand, an even more unkempt Rosa than the one she had left asleep the day before.
"Rosa?"
"Didn't mean to frighten you none."
'You didn't, I just forgot for a moment that you were here. How do you feel?"
"Bit drowsy, missy, but I'm recovered."
Colour had returned to the girl's cheeks and the swelling in

her wrist had all but disappeared. Sarah's eyes dropped to the ground beside Rosa, as for the first time she realised that she was not alone. Laying at her feet was an obedient Beggar. Rosa had spotted Sarah's gaze.

"Early hours I awoke and opened the door for some air, missy, and he came to inspect me and somehow followed me inside."

"So, you had some company?"

"Yes, missy."

As always, once Sarah became engaged in conversation, her mind returned to the real world, which was good. In that vein of mind her thoughts were less likely to wander inconveniently. As Rosa spoke, Beggar lifted his head to look up at her. There was a familiarity there that prompted Sarah to remember something Lottie had said.

"Tell me Rosa, have you met Beggar before?"

'Beggar, missy?"

"The dog."

Rosa did not answer immediately.

"I've seen him before, yes, missy. But he ain't one of ours."

Sarah could sense the hesitancy and was curious.

"He's not?"

"No, missy."

"Is he a gypsy dog?"

"Was, missy."

Rosa could see that Sarah was going to enquire further.

"He's at a better home now, missy. The owner won't be coming back for him."

"He won't?"

"Unlikely, missy." assured Rosa and before Sarah could ask more, "Now I should be off."

Rosa bent and ruffled Beggar's ruff. "Now, you be a good dog for missy, do you hear?"

Beggar glanced up at Rosa as if he understood and, as she moved away towards the gate, he followed her, thinking he might be going somewhere.

"I want's to thank you, Missy Sarah, for looking after me."

"You're going?"

"I think it's best."

"But why? I've offered you work, Rosa. We will start again at noon. Is it really worth your going and then coming all the way back again?"

"I'm not coming back, missy," replied Rosa. "I'm really grateful, but it wouldn't be no enjoyment in it, methinks."

'I don't understand. The job was offered in good faith…" But Sarah couldn't finish.

"I knows it was," As she spoke, Rosa came back to Sarah with Beggar at her side, "and for that I will ever be grateful, missy, but it wouldn't work. I knows that now. I thought that working for you would be straight forward, like in the fields, but it wouldn't be."

"I don't understand, why ever not?"

Rosa considered whether to explain or not and decided that she owed it to Sarah to be honest.

"'Cause though they don't say nothing, missy, I can hears them. The other girls. They resents me and it won't matter what you say to them, missy, they'll still resent me. Won't be nice me being here, for me or for them and in fact, not for you neither. But I is grateful, missy, honest I is." Rosa smiled her 'thanks' and once more ruffled Beggar's neck.

"Bye, Beggar boy, thanks for keeping me company." Beggar didn't follow her this time, as if he knew she was leaving alone. Sarah took the key from her pocket, unlocked the wicket gate and Rosa stepped outside into the street.

"I'm sorry you've decided not to stay, Rosa. I'm sure the girls would have come round in the end."

Rosa did not answer this, as her mind was made up and she was not going to change it. She knew that sometimes you just know when you have made the right decision and this was for the good.

"And if you ever be needing some help, missy, you know odd jobs and the like, and not necessarily in the yard here, but up at the field or somewheres, then you can find me at the Little Spinney."

"The Little Spinney. I will definitely keep you in mind, Rosa."

Rosa began to move away and then remembered.

'Tell me, missy, did you get to see your Queen?"

'No. No, I didn't."

"I'm sorry for that, truly I am. But I suppose at least you got to be with a Princess, eh, missy?" Rosa grinned her huge, mischievous grin, a grin that encompassed all her facial features from the top of her forehead to the dimple on her chin and from one petite ear to the other.

'Rosa?"

"Missy?"

"You are the most remarkable young lady."

"Yes missy, I knows. But only 'cause my folks is for ever saying so, you understand? Although the difference is, you seems to find it a good thing whereas they tends to find it 'irritatin."

"Well," Sarah smiled, not knowing what else to say. In Sarah's judgment, Rosa's confidence, which truly did border on cockiness, was totally endearing and seemed more of a virtue than a flaw.

"Mind you, missy, I tries not to let it go to my head too much, otherwise some people will think I'm too full of myself and that I need taking down a peg or two… like your Miss Lottie."

"Lottie is a good girl at heart."

"I knows that, missy."

"Strong willed, out-spoken and determined, but very loyal. Not unlike yourself, Rosa. In truth you two are more alike than you would think."

"I tell you what I thinks, missy," replied Rosa, her kindly smile of cheekiness turning to one of true concern. "I thinks that I don't know where you've been, or what works you been doing, but you look as if you ain't had no sleep and are fit to drop."

As if on cue to Rosa's words, Sarah began to feel the tiredness that up to know she had unconsciously kept at bay. For a moment only, Sarah considered Rosa's comment might be prompted by first-hand knowledge, as if she had been in the fields again that night. But she realised that could not be possible, as Rosa had been locked in all night.

Without waiting for Sarah to reply, Rosa turned and walked back to her folk's encampment at the Little Spinney. As she walked, she thought that Sarah may have been back to her fields singing to the lavender all night. But she dismissed this, as the lavender was all cut and gone. 'No,' thought Rosa, 'She couldn't have been at the fields, as now she has no reason to be there'.

Sarah went back to the bucket of water from which she had refreshed herself earlier and repeated the process. If she were quick and if luck should be on her side, she may still be able to creep into the house without James or Eliza seeing her. She had not eaten since yesterday's breakfast and now she was feeling the effects. The night in the open and the trauma that had engaged and sapped every ounce of her energy, had taken its toll. She must return home as quickly as possible and then sleep for as long as possible.

She left the yard and began the walk home. There were still very few people about, but it was close to five-thirty and the day was beginning before Sarah was ready for it. She quickened her pace, but the more she tried to hurry, the less distance she seemed to cover. The odd person that she passed or saw across the street, seemed to be clothed in a haze that she foolishly put down to an illusion created by the heat. A passer-by bid her good morning, but their voice sounded distant as if spoken from the other side of a wall, sounding as a voice does when calling you from a sleep. Her legs still carried her, but they were not hers, they were legs borrowed from someone else that had not been attached to her correctly. She knew this feeling and knew that she must reach her home, her room and safety before it prevailed upon her. She could see the house, but the more she walked, the further away it seemed.

She heard a voice, someone calling her name. She tried to look as she walked, tried to ascertain who it was? Someone across the street. She decided to ignore the call and push on for home. But then, her legs stopped of their own accord. She tried to move them on but to no avail. Her head became heavy and, in a desperate attempt to stop it dropping like some great dead weight and falling off completely, she strived to look up. She succeeded. For a moment only, she regained control of her neck muscles and forced her belligerent head to stare up into the sky, the blue sky. A pale blue bright sky that inexplicably began to darken. The blue descending rapidly through its repertoire of shades from sky to cornflower, cobalt, navy, royal then the darkest blue of outer space. There, as she tried to desperately recapture the original sky, her borrowed legs abandoned her completely. The rod that had kept her steadfast and standing for so long, finally evaporated into bone dust and Sarah fell to the ground.

All was dark. No strength. No dreams. Just darkness.

"One of the best and longest harvests in living memory"

Chapter Nine

Familiar smells. The ceiling she was staring at as she opened her eyes, she knew well. Her left elbow ached and the back of her head was sore. Painfully sore. She took her hand from under the blanket to feel a large egg-shaped bump on the back of her skull. It was sore to touch so she decided best not to. She thought for a moment, tried to remember.

Lifting herself up, first with her left elbow but because that caused her so much pain, she shifted her weight to the right elbow, sat up and looked around. In seconds, her suspicions were confirmed. She was in her bedroom at 62b, Bancroft. But how? The bedroom door opened and Eliza entered.

"Lord have mercy, you're awake!"

"Eliza?"

'Thank heavens for that, Miss Sarah, and just in time, for hasn't Doctor Hawkins just returned to check on you."

"Eliza?"

"Now you stay there, Miss Sarah, and I'll bring him straight up." Before Sarah could ask any questions, Eliza left the room. The door was slightly a jar and she could hear Eliza calling as she went down the stairs. "Doctor? Doctor? Bless my soul if Miss Sarah isn't awake and sitting up in bed!"

Sarah struggled to sit more upright. She was in her nightgown but could not remember putting it on. She could not remember reaching home. There was hardly time to gather her thoughts before the door opened again and the short stocky figure of Doctor Hawkins entered the room. "I see that Eliza is quite correct in her diagnosis, you are most definitely awake."

"I am, but I'm not sure what happened to me."

'You fainted, banged your head on the cobbles and have been suffering from the effects for the best part of two days." As Doctor Hawkins explained, more memories returned. She now recalled feeling dizzy and unwell as she had neared the house. She vaguely remembered a voice calling her and then…

"What day is it?"

"Saturday."

"Saturday?"

"Lean forward, Sarah, if you will?"

Sarah did as she was asked and he felt the back of her head. As he pressed her egg-shaped bump, she flinched and winced in unison with his asking "Does that hurt?"

"Very much."

He released his hands from the back of her head.

"But only when you press it as you just did."

He pushed up her pillows and helped her to move back into a more comfortable sitting position.

"It is good that you feel the pain, it would be disconcerting if you felt nothing."

"I suppose I fainted from the heat."

"Possibly."

"Possibly, but what other cause could there have been? Whatever it was, I'm sure I'll be fine."

"Let us agree on something before we continue further, Sarah. You will assume the part of the patient and I will pretend to be the doctor. Agreed?"

"Agreed… but all I suggest…"

"You suggest nothing, I will tell you."

There was a pause. She fell silent as instructed and his face took on a more serious expression.

"As I said, you fainted, knocked your head severely and have slept for longer than is natural. Concussion is the medical term and it can be straight forward and the recovery fairly quick, but on other occasions it can linger for weeks or even cease and then return."

She listened but offered no comment.

"In my opinion, as your pretend doctor," his expression relaxed and his congenial smile returned, "You are suffering from exhaustion. You have been doing too much, Sarah, and you need to rest."

"Rest? But I can't rest…"

"You must rest, Sarah. You cannot continue as you have, it is too much." He walked towards the bedroom door, "I will leave some medicinal powders with Eliza which will help you to sleep. I say 'sleep' as in a sleep of rest rather than an enforced slumber caused by your injury." At the door he turned back to look at her. "Rest, Sarah, and I will return tomorrow."

"But I cannot lay here any longer."

"You can and you will, or I will not be held responsible."

"But what of the Pharmacy?"

"I understand that has all been taken care of." With those brief and ambiguous words, he left the room.

Sarah slumped back into the pillows and felt helpless. Not because of her injuries, but because she had lost two days of valuable time. Time that should have been spent on planning how to reach out to John. She would not give up on achieving his return and the onus was on her. She was the one at fault and it was up to her to make amends. He was sure to be looking on, so she must prove to him that she was truly repentant and show that she was doing everything within her power to put things back as they were.

"May I come in?" asked Sarah senior, half in the room.

"Of course, please."

Sarah sat upright again as best she could and the old lady sat on the chair next to her bed.

"How do you feel?"

"Fine."

Sarah could see that she was not believed and it would be pointless in her maintaining such an obvious falsehood.

"Tired and a little sore, but I will be fine, I'm sure. Doctor Hawkins thinks I will be up and about by the evening."

"That's strange," answered the old lady, raising her eyebrows in mock confusion, "He just said exactly the opposite to myself and Eliza."

"Oh." Sarah realised the lies, however small, were coming too readily to her lips and she must resist the temptation. She knew all too well that once a lie became a first line of defence, it was a slippery path to eventual discovery. So far, she had prided herself in not lying but in simply avoiding having to tell the truth. There was a subtle but important difference.

"But I cannot lie here indefinitely… what of the business?"

"That has all been taken care of."

"It has?" asked the bewildered Sarah, "How do you mean, taken care of?"

"There has been no great difficulty in achieving this. Samuel and Catherine were due to join you within the next week, so they have simply started now instead of waiting. Yesterday, they spent the day with Lottie and Mister Davey, who went through as many things as they needed to know."

"But that is unfair on Samuel and Catherine."

"It was Catherine's idea and a sound one to my mind. The girl is smart and will do well with Samuel. As she herself said, waiting another week would make no real difference to the amount of preparation they had planned. They have employed a governess a week earlier than originally planned, which also proved no great difficulty. All is taken care of."

"I see." answered Sarah, not sure if this was for the better or not.

"I have also taken the liberty of making a few changes here at your house."

"Changes? In what way?"

"Lizzie has moved into the top room on a semi-permanent basis. She will be able to help Eliza more readily if she is on the premises all the time. I understand her cooking is better than her cleaning so she will be a great asset. In addition, I have also instructed one of my maids, Meg, to attend here as well on a part time basis. She is a hard worker and will not let you down. I have told her to come each morning for a few hours to generally clean and tidy. Once you are fully recovered you can, of course, reverse these changes as you see fit."

"Thank you, but there really is no need."

"Sarah," The old lady looked at her sternly. "You have taken a nasty knock to your head. Let that knock also serve to

bring you to heel and remind you of your own fragility. You cannot continue as you have. It would stretch the stamina and will power of any woman, let alone one who has so recently suffered bereavement. No, it is time that you let your abundance of common-sense return and help you in making more practical decisions. I speak of the common-sense that I knew you to have when John was alive. In my opinion it has been absent from your thinking for too long."
Sarah said nothing. She did not know what to say.

"You may think me interfering Sarah, but truly, I have made these decisions on your behalf only through sincere concern for you and your family. My family. You are my daughter in law, your children are my grandchildren. You have pushed yourself too far and now you must rest."
The old lady stood and moved to look out of the window. Outside she could see James leaning against the wall to his dwelling, looking up at the window. When he saw the old lady looking down, he looked away as if he had not seen her.
"It is another warm day. Not as hot as before, but still warm."
Sarah did not reply.
"The harvest has finished. One of the best and longest harvests in living memory. The hardest and busiest time of our year is over. An ideal time for Samuel and Catherine to start, I think. Don't you agree?"
The old lady did not look back as Sarah answered.
"Yes, ideal."
"Starting one week earlier than planned makes no difference to them. They have already struck up a good working relationship with all at the yard. It is not as if Samuel is not known to them all and he is as excited as a child in a sweetshop to get started. He has studied well in his

apprenticeship in London and qualified impressively. His brother and father would have been most proud of him." The old lady paused before adding.
"God willing, are proud of him."

Now she too fell silent. Staring out of the window as Sarah often did, maybe she too looked towards the fields at the top of Gray's Lane. Fields first furrowed and sown by her husband Edward when they were first wed. Perhaps she thought of him, now long gone.

Sarah resigned herself to the change. There was no sensible reason to question it. Although at first, she had thought it ill news, she realised that it was inevitable. It might also work to her advantage. Sharing her time between work, children and John was proving difficult and had begun to cause her great stress.
"As you say, perhaps it is for the best."
The old lady looked towards Sarah, pleased to hear her admit the sense in what had been decided. Relieved, she looked back out of the window and without thinking, found herself saying more.
"Now you will have time for yourself, Sarah."
"Time?"
It was something she had wanted to say for a while, but the time was never right. It was right now.
"Yes, time, Sarah. Time to grieve."
The old lady broke her gaze out of the window and moved towards the bedroom door.
"Now rest. We have told the children that they may come in to see you later today if you are recovered sufficiently. Perhaps this afternoon you will feel up to it."
"Yes, I would like that."
The old lady opened the door to exit and was stopped by Sarah calling her.

"Mother?"

She looked back at Sarah.

"Thank you."

The old lady smiled. It was the first time Sarah had called her 'mother' since John had died. 'Perhaps,' thought the wise old matriarch, 'just perhaps, this might be a sign that things are about to take a turn for the better. Perhaps.'

Not long after Sarah senior had left the room, Sarah dozed despite herself and finally drifted into another needed sleep. But this sleep did not last two days nor even a day; two or three hours at most.

She awoke to find Anne and Edward by her bedside, with Eliza standing guard behind them. They had been told that their mother was suffering a little through the heat and hard work, but there was nothing to worry about. Consequently, they bombarded her with their own news. It seemed that neither child would wait for the other to finish their story, so they managed, without intention, to alternate.

"Mama, Grandma has taught me how to make plum duff pudding."

"Well done, Anne."

"Mama, James has given me a catapult with a rubber band."

"What on earth is a rubber band, Edward?"

"And did you know, mama, that plum duff doesn't have any plums in it?"

"I didn't know that, Anne, no. How strange."

"James says it's a new thing called elastic."

"Well, I'm sure James would know."

"Just dried fruit, eggs and suet."

"How wonderful, Anne."

"Mister Perry made it."

"Mister Perry, I thought you said James made it, Edward?"

"We've placed it in the coolest part of the pantry, mama."

"That's very clever of you, Anne, and very wise."

"Mister Perry made the rubber band, mama…"

"I see…"

"We're all going to eat it at Christmas."

"I can't wait."

"… and James made the catapult."

"Of course, he did… Well, you two seem to be having the most wonderful time."

"Will you be better again soon, mama?"

"Yes Anne, I'm feeling much recovered already."

Eliza decided enough was enough.

"Miss Anne, Master Edward, if yous two go down to the kitchen, I thinks you'll be finding Lizzie there has some twisted barley sugars."

This well-chosen statement brought the two children to a sudden silence.

"And I thinks she's a planning on throwing them aways, because she can't find no young children to give them to."

They needed no further encouragement. Before Eliza could utter another word, they had bid Sarah goodbye and rushed out of the bedroom to the kitchen, where they pounced on the unsuspecting Lizzie.

Eliza poured some water from the crystal jug into the glass.

"Eliza?"

"Miss Sarah?"

"What would I do without you?"

"You'd probably gets someone younger and not as talkative, I guess, miss."

"I wouldn't swap you for the world."

Then you'd be nearly as silly as I think you to be."

Eliza, partly through embarrassment and partly through necessity, set about tidying the blankets covering Sarah.

"And little John, Eliza, how is he?"

Eliza answered without stopping her chosen task.

"He had not such a good day yesterday, miss, but today he seems much brighter. Doctor Hawkins has been checking on him as well as you and he says, that to his thinking, the little man is making sound progress."

"He does?"

"'He's making sound progress, Eliza,' he says to me, and I have no reason to doubt such a learned doctor as Mister Hawkins is." lied Eliza, avoiding Sarah's gaze at all times.

"And you believe him, Eliza? He does not say these things only to be kind?"

"He's a doctor, Miss Sarah, doctors don't tell lies." answered Eliza, now re-tucking all the blankets for a second time. She found it best to keep herself busy when disguising the truth about little John with false words. "Them doctors tells you if you're well or if you're unwell and if you're neither they tend to say nothing. I'm a guessing their fee doesn't go up and down either way. It's only ordinary folk that lies, miss, not learned doctors."

Sarah was not sure if this assured her not, but she was too tired to question Eliza further.

Eliza finished what she had been doing for the second time and looked at Sarah from the end of the bed. She placed her hands on her hips as she was in the habit of doing and thought for a second before speaking.

"I think he's sleeping, miss, but if he's awake I could bring him through to you?"

"No, don't disturb him. I just worry that his whole life is either one of crying or one of sleep. I would that he would recover soon, Eliza."

"Yes, Miss Sarah, as we do all."

'Crying and sleeping,' thought Sarah to herself as she let her head flop to one side on her pillow, 'How familiar those two states are to me at present.' She noticed the curtains at the window lifting and dropping.

"Is there a breeze, Eliza?"

"Yes miss, a slight one. Just enough to stop the world from frying and enough to guarantee a restful night." Eliza had walked towards the window now, as had Sarah senior earlier and gazed out as if the answers to all problems lay outside. It is common knowledge that when people are deep in thought, confused or troubled, standing at an open window will induce calm, if not the answer sought. "How's your head, miss?"

"Sore."

"Not surprised, miss. When he brought you in and laid you down, I felt it and for a moment I thought you had grown a second head."

"It feels as if someone has tried to cut off the first one."

"You did frit me for a while, miss, honest you did. What with you sleeping for so long and no amount of smelling salts able to bring you round."

"Where did he find me?"

"About twenty yards back up the street, miss. And lucky he did. There weren't many up and about at that time of day, what with the celebrations the night before."

"I'm lucky to have him, I know."

"Lucky, miss?"

'And you of course, Eliza, I'm lucky to have you both."

"Sorry, miss, but I don't follow?"

"I say, I'm lucky. Lucky to have you and James."

"James?"

"Yes."

"Bless me, it weren't James that found you, miss."

"It wasn't?"

"No, Miss Sarah, it was Mr Ransom."

"Mr Ransom?"

"Young William Ransom, miss. Seems he was up early fiddling around with one of his new-fangled agricoltured…. agri…. farming machines, miss. Lucky he was a-fiddling, miss, otherwise who knows how long you would have lain there. It seems he saw you fall and was straight over. He carried you into the back hallway asking which way to your room, miss. No sooner had I said where it was, than he was up them there stairs with you in his arms before I could even ask what had happened."

Eliza was not looking at Sarah, she was still looking out of the window. But if she had been, she would have seen Sarah's face take on the strangest of expressions.

"I know it's not my place to be saying such things, miss, but I reckon that young William Ransom has a soft spot for you."

Sarah said nothing and so Eliza said more. "He came a calling yesterday, to see if you were well enough for visitors. Twice."

Sarah continued her enforced silence.

"He was here earlier, but when I comes to check on you, miss, you seemed asleep."

Sarah had not been asleep. She had heard William's voice downstairs but had decided it was for the better if she did not speak to him. He was kind and considerate and she wanted to speak to him, but she could not afford to let him into her heart anymore than she already had. It was too dangerous.

"It was just before you saw the children. As I say I did check on you, but you seemed deep in sleep, so's I didn't think it right to disturb you."

Eliza ran her hands down either side of the curtains to ensure they contained no creases. Then, as it seemed Sarah was not going to be forthcoming with a comment that Eliza could interpret one way or the other, she gave up and moved towards the door.

"I'll come back every hour to sees you're alright, miss, but if you require anything, there's a bell there on your side table, by your water. Just rings it and I'll comes a running, miss."

"Thank you."

Eliza left, closing the door behind her.

'William,' thought Sarah. It was William that had found her like some damsel in distress, scooped her up and carried her into the house. A knight in shining armour. A dashing hero that in any other life would have captured Sarah's heart completely and won her hand by now. But not in this life. There was no place for another man in this life.

Any sane person would think this a good time to come to terms with life and death. That the time to end the struggle to understand and accept both for what they are, was now. With all the changes and her exhaustion, now was the perfect opportunity to start again. In normal circumstances Sarah would have agreed.

Earlier, before the children had been admitted, she had slept a short sleep. But a sleep long enough in which to dream and in her dream, John had forgiven her and now called out for her. He was looking for her. She saw him wandering nowhere in particular, in fields that she did not recognise, across a landscape that was foreign to her. It was as if he were lost. She could see him, but he could not see her, even when looking directly at her. It was as if she were invisible to him. When she called out to him, he moved on, oblivious, as if he had not heard her call. In her dream, she reasoned that she must try harder, shout louder, look longer, until she found him and they were reunited.

Three days passed and Sarah was close to full recovery, from the injuries sustained in her fall that is. The determination to pursue her chosen course remained unchanged. If Sarah senior could have known Sarah's thoughts, she would have judged her daughter in law's common sense still disappointingly absent.

During her convalescence, she had heard William's voice on several occasions, downstairs in the hallway. Each time she had found an excuse not to see him and once had again feigned sleep when Eliza came to check on her. It was a move that had made sense to Sarah at the time, but in retrospect was bound to have incited suspicion in Eliza's sharp mind. She was bound to question why Sarah had felt well enough to receive other well-wishers but not William. Her saviour. The man who had plucked her from the pavement and strode heroically with her from danger to safety.

In the space of the days that she rested, she had thought long and hard about what was to be done. She knew waiting at the fields would now not suffice and if John were unable to return of his own accord, or unwilling to return, she would have to make it possible. Only in that way would she be able to reaffirm her love and faithfulness. But how?

Back in November the previous year, but a few days after John's passing, she was no different than any other widow. Her world had been ripped asunder and her heart split in two. To Sarah's mind, the envious grim reaper had chosen her husband randomly, for no better reason than that she loved him with all her being. The old were easily taken because their ability to fight was reduced from long years of living. The young were also often taken, because they had not been allowed enough years to grow strong. But John had been in neither of these categories. Suddenly struck with an unnamed illness that debilitated a healthy, passionate, loving young man within a week. Initial shock was followed by disbelief and then quickly overtaken by fear and dread, and before she could prepare herself mentally, he died. It was a mere six days from the illness taking hold to the grave accepting him. She had begged God not to take him, pleaded that she should not be robbed of her reason for living, but her pleas fell upon unsympathetic ears.

Slowly she was coming to terms with his passing. Her original disbelief was reluctantly turning into acknowledgement and she was almost reconciled to the fact that he was gone. Virtually ready, as all dutiful widows, to privately beat her chest and wail inwardly for her tragic loss.

Then one evening whilst standing at the fields edge, wishing he were still there with her, a miracle occurred. Through some mystical connivance, that he never explained and she never understood or questioned, he appeared to her like some risen Christ. Standing right beside her as if all had been a cruel nightmare.

In awe and wonder, she had stood still and would not let herself believe. He must have sensed this.
To prove it was no idle fantasy, he had taken her in his arms and kissed her. Long and meaningful, and it was just as before. She knew it was no trick of her mind because she had touched him and she had felt him. The mind can lie, she knew that, but the sense of touch does not, it transmits the truth only. It was him, back with her. On that first night of their special world, they had made love by the lavender fields. With the same passion, the same eruption of desire, the same tender caring as before. It was just as she had remembered and she gave herself, knowing it was true.

He had told her not to ask how, or reason why. They would simply accept that it was, and let it take them where it will. They would journey into their special world, a world of unchartered waters, with no preconceptions or regrets.

But now she had foolishly given him just cause to leave and she wanted him back. Whatever it took.
All that she had thought right and proper now had no bearing upon her. There did not exist good nor evil and hence there was no God or Satan to fear. Whoever or whatever assisted her and whichever demons she needed to approach to succeed, she would. Accepting whatever the price demanded may be, without hesitation. Just as he must have done to be with her.

Thinking these thoughts, she found herself looking at the bedroom door. There, hanging on a hook, was her everyday parasol. A grubby, slightly battered white parasol devoid of any tassels. At least she had avoided the ignominy of attending the station with that as her protection.

Eliza met her coming down the stairs, parasol in hand.
"Miss Sarah?"
"Before you object or make a fuss, Eliza, I am going to walk."
"Walk, miss?"
"Yes, walk, Eliza, as recommended by Doctor Hawkins. He tells me the air will do me good and as you said yourself, doctors never lie."
"Very well, miss, do you want James to accompany you?"
"No, I don't need company, just the air. But to avoid you worrying unnecessarily, I will first visit the Pharmacy to speak with Samuel and Catherine. I will make them aware I am alive, well and much recovered. Then, if that short

excursion has not exhausted me too much, I shall walk the lanes to the fields."

"Is that wise, Miss Sarah?"

"It is very wise; Eliza and it is what I wish."

"Very well, miss."

"Don't fret, Eliza, I promise I shall be sensible at all times and if I should feel any fatigue setting in, I shall return straight away."

"Yes, miss."

Sarah left the house and walked into the yard to be met by James.

"You look much recovered, Miss Sarah."

"Thank you, James, I'm glad you think as much. My housekeeper, Eliza the worrier, believes a walk not to be consistent with the doctor's orders."

"The air will do you no harm, miss."

"And that is what I seek, James. A walk will heed my recovery rather than inhibit it, wouldn't you agree?" she asked rhetorically, walking towards the open gate.

"As long as the walk doesn't take you too far, miss, or in the wrong direction."

Sarah heard James's last comment but ignored it and walked out into the Bancroft for the first time since her collapse. She was putting her plan into operation. It would require guile and courage, but first she must put all those that might be concerned about her, at ease. Let them all know that she was at peace with herself and all stress had vanished.

Everyone at the shop was pleased to see Sarah and a great fuss was made of her. Catherine insisted on sharing tea and scones and Samuel continually praised the proud Lottie for the excellent training she had provided. He felt he had learnt more about the actual running of the business in the last week, than he had ever thought possible. He then proceeded to bore her with his infamous plans once again before Catherine finally came to her rescue.

"Samuel, you have plagued poor Sarah with your plans since we returned to Hitchin."

"I have?"

"You have. Sarah probably knows them better than you do, so pray let her be. She is supposed to be free of all pressures."

"I'm sorry, Sarah, I forget myself at times, but please believe it is only through enthusiasm that I repeat them to everyone I see."

"I know it is, Samuel."

Catherine saw fit to change the subject.

"Sarah, you will be pleased to know that we postponed our outing with William."

"Outing?"

"To Wilbury Hills. We were both quite happy to wait until another time so that you did not miss out on the excursion."

'Of course, I had forgotten, when was it we were supposed to go?"

"Yesterday," answered Samuel, "but it matters not."

"I believe William called to see if you knew when you might feel well enough." continued Catherine, looking carefully at Sarah to see if there was any visible reaction to William's name.

"Yes… well, soon, very soon I'm sure."

"An opportunity that should be pounced upon if possible, don't you think?" Catherine was probing. "Especially with your passion for local history."

"It should indeed, yes." Sarah was giving nothing away, one way or the other and so Catherine refrained from talking further on the subject.

"Samuel, let us see to the securing of the shop, it is almost closing time."

"Of course, Catherine."

"And whilst we do that, Sarah can have a few moments of conversation with Lottie. I'm sure the two of them have much to catch up on."

"Thank you, Catherine, I would appreciate that."

As Catherine and Samuel set about the age-old ritual of closing the shop at the end of the working day, a ritual Sarah knew only too well, she went out into the yard to find Lottie.

She found her speaking to Annie outside the top barn where they seemed to be involved in the most earnest of conversations. Everyone else had left for home, so she sat on a wooden box in the evening sunshine and waited to be noticed. Eventually, their conversation seemed to reach a lighter conclusion, as still not noticing that Sarah was present, they hugged, kissed and walked arm in arm before realising.

"Miss Sarah?"

"Annie."

"I'm glad you're recovered, miss."

"Thank you, Annie."

"But in truth, miss, sad that you're not coming back."

"Why is that? Do Samuel and Catherine beat you?"

"No miss," chuckled Annie, "they are as sweet as pie."

"Perhaps I shall return one day, Annie, who knows? Besides, there may be times when I am needed to help in the yard. Between you and me, it will not be too many months before our happy pair contemplate a family and maybe then I will be called upon."

"That would be nice, miss, on both accounts"

"You are not completely rid of me yet, I think. In the meantime, I shall look to visit most days to check that you are all behaving yourselves."

"It will be good to see you, miss, honest it will. Well, I needs be off. Night miss, night Lottie."

"See you bright and early in the morning, Annie."

"You will."

As Annie left, Lottie watched her go with what can only be described as a huge smile of satisfaction covering her face. Finally, she sat on a box next to Sarah.

"Me too, Miss Sarah."

"You too what, Lottie?"

"Glad that you're recovered, miss."

A warm smile covered both faces as they remembered how much they meant to each other and both regretted that things would never be quite the same. It was another sad case of moving on to newer pastures and inevitably leaving something precious behind. Sometimes, that which is unavoidably abandoned, is so precious that it renders itself irreplaceable.

"I have missed your gossip, Lottie."

"That's an awful thing to say, Miss Sarah."

"I know it is, Lottie, but it's true. Now tell me, did your father enjoy the day, despite the smelly station?"

"He loved it, miss, we all did. And we caughts a sight of her Majesty over the tops of the crowd. I thought father was going to have himself a heart attack. There we was, Miss Sarah, with all the town crushed together and straining to catch a glimpse, when father shouts out at the top of his voice, 'I can see the top of her 'ead!' As he says it, he points violently, knocks off Mrs Parker's large feather hat, which was proving an unfair obstruction anyways, and causes it to land on the ground in front of her."

"Oh dear."

"Oh dear is right, miss, but it gets worse. Having heard

father shout out, the whole crowd moves forward craning their necks to see the Queen's 'ead, so that Mrs Parker, who has bent over to pick up her hat, is knocked forward on to the floor and almost crushed in the stampede!"

"Heavens Lottie! Was she injured?"

"Only her pride, miss. She was able to crawl forward on her hands and knees, with her hat between her teeth and get out under a barrier to safety."

"Poor Mrs Parker."

"It couldn't have happened to a better person, miss."

'Lottie, that is most unfair."

'Maybe miss, but it's the way I feels so I can't say otherwise 'cause that would be telling lies."

'And what about Robert?"

"Robert?"

"Did he take the opportunity to propose?"

"No miss, he didn't."

"Oh dear, I'm sorry, Lottie."

"No need to be sorry, miss. He didn't take the opportunity to propose, but I did take the opportunity to send him on his way."

"Lottie!? Whatever for?"

"I realised that despite all our long walkings out together, he wasn't the man for me. Too tame, miss. Too proper. I was the one wearing the trousers, miss, and that ain't right to my mind. Our relationship would only have made sense if we'd swapped clothes, miss."

"Are you sure you won't come to regret it, Lottie?"

"Not a chance, miss."

"It will seem strange, Lottie, won't it? No young man to walk out with of an evening?"

"No, miss, because I has a young man to walk out with of an evening. Albert Cummings!"

"Albert?

"Yes miss, Albert. I had him all lined up for Annie, you sees, but the more she weren't interested, the more I was. The only thing was though, rumour had it his father beat his mother and you know what they say, miss, like father like son. So I says to him, on our very first evening, 'Albert Cummings, if you're walking out with me, you must know something. You so much as raise your hand without my saying so and I'll cut your balls off with Mister Davey's blunt scythe and throw them in the fire, so help me, God. Excuse my language, miss."

"Lottie! That's an awful thing to say!"

"I know, but it's something that had to be said, miss."

"What did he say?"

"Well, he looks at me all surprised like. So's when I'd explained what I'd heard, he right roars with laughter and says it's more like his mother beats his father, not the other way round. And I'm tending to believe him, miss. On accounting that his mother is taller than me, and his father makes you look like some giant!"

"Lottie, you are totally…"

"Now, miss Sarah, no great big words that I don't know the meaning of, if you please."

"You are so brash... and confident."

"I don't know about the 'brash' bit, miss, but you have to be confident when you're planning on a wedding. He's strong of body and strong of mind and though I chalked down a line that he couldn't cross, he definitely wears the trousers and that's the way it should be."

"You're very forward, Lottie, but I do admire your determination."

"Within five minutes of me a fluttering my eyelids at him, miss, he'd strolled across to me, asked me out and when's I says 'yes', he kisses me on the cheek and says that he'll call for me at seven and that I best be ready cause he don't like to be kept waiting."

"Did he, indeed?"

"Indeed, he did miss, but I likes a man that knows his mind and Albert definitely knows his."

"Well, I'm pleased for you, Lottie."

"You have to be quick, miss, otherwise you can end up on the shelf with no one to walk out with."

"Like poor Annie."

"She ain't poor Annie anymore, miss. Oh, no, because I gave her my Robert."

"You gave Robert to Annie?!"

"Don't fret miss, Annie's over the moon. Seems that she has always had a soft spot for my Robert. Only, because I was a-walking out with him, she didn't want to spoil our friendship by letting her fancying of him be known."

"But I thought she ribbed you constantly about Robert?"

"I suppose that was just her way of dealing with it. Knowing there was someone out there that she really wanted, but couldn't have, she had to pretend to everyone else that there weren't no problem."

"I see," replied Sarah, finding the comment too close to home.

"Women, eh miss?"

Lottie continued to relay more whilst Sarah half listened.

"Father is now the best of friends with Mister Davey since their falling out and theys often go fishing together down at the Oughton River. Oh, and little Lucy Hutchins' mother, Dolly, has finally had all her rotten teeth extracted. But she ain't all gums, miss, oh no. Old Sepoy has been and carved her a set of new teeth out of wood, something he learnt from a Japanese man. And so's that they looks real, he's whitewashed them first. According to Lucy, if the youngsters are misbehaving when's they should be a sleepin', Dolly creeps up to them at night and when there's a little moonshine, she snarls like a wolf, and her new whitewashed teeth glows in the dark. Near frits the kids half to death!"

Sarah's eyes travelled round the yard as Lottie continued to relate all the latest gossip. The yard looked extremely tidy, everything in its place. Boxes were stacked neatly, stills swept with ashes emptied and no unsightly droppings outside the stable doors. But there was something missing. She tried hard to think of what of it was and then the answer came to her.

"Beggar," interrupted Sarah, whilst Lottie was still in full flow, "where's Beggar?"

Lottie paused for a moment, allowing the enthusiasm for her previous story to subside. "We don't know, miss."

"Has he wandered off?"

"Sort of, miss. The day after the Queen, I had to take some apples to my cousin in Walsworth and as I'd decided Beggar was looking more and more like an overweight butcher's dog, I thought to take him with me for the exercise, like. Anyhows, my cousin lives on the far side of Walsworth, in one of them cottages on the Willian road. I'd dropped off the apples and as a treat for my cousin's kids, we gets out some bread, and Beggar does his performance. Well, all was good when we got up to leave, but stepping outside their gate to come home, he suddenly turns. He looks up the Willian Road and starts his snarling. Before I could do anything, he's off like he's smelt a rabbit and out of sight through the hedgerows. I looked around for him for a bit, but remembering he always makes his own way home, I leaves him to it and comes back by meself. We ain't seen hide nor hair of him since."

"That is strange."

"Very strange, miss. We've asked about, being as he's so well known in the area, but no one's spotted him yet."

"It won't seem the same without Beggar."

"No miss. No entertainment in the bread breaks makes it a solemn affair compared."

"He might wander back, I suppose, he does tend to do as he pleases. After all, it was him that found us, Lottie, not the other way round, remember?"

"Poor little Lucy misses him something terrible an' all."

Their conversation was abruptly halted by Samuel stepping out into the yard.

"Well, all done. Lottie, time for home and supper I think."

"Yes, Mister Samuel." Lottie and Sarah stood up from their boxes as Catherine locked the back door to the shop and joined them.

"Lottie, give me a hand with the gates if you will?"

Sarah asked to borrow a small wicker basket, as she might wish to pick fruit from the hedgerows and trees. As Catherine obliged her, Samuel and Lottie closed the big gates and unlocked the wicket gate. Stepping outside, the sun's warmth was waning and Sarah judged around two hours left to sunset.

"Goodnight, Miss Sarah. I really enjoyed our chat and I'm glad you're recovering so well."

"Goodnight, Lottie, I'm sure we will be able to catch up again very soon."

After bidding goodnight to Samuel and Catherine, Lottie left them for home, there to ready herself for walking out with her new man. A man that wore the trousers.

"Are you sure you will not walk with us, Sarah?"

"Thank you, Catherine, but no. I am determined to take a lengthy stroll as recommended by Doctor Hawkins and as I have spent most of the time sitting in the yard talking to Lottie, I shall not return home yet, I think."

"Do you want me to accompany you?"

"That is kind of you Samuel, but you and Catherine should make your way home. I know what a long day the Perks Yard demands of one. You go and I will see you both at some time tomorrow."

"Very well but promise you won't overdo things and that you will head home as soon as you feel yourself tiring."

"I will, Catherine, I promise. There is still plenty of light left for a short walk in the evening sun."

Catherine raised her parasol with tassels and Sarah raised her grubby white one which had never had tassels.

"If he should call again, Sarah, see if you cannot arrange a new day for our trip with William. Another Sunday would be best for us."

"Or any Sunday… after church, of course." added Samuel.

"Or if a Sunday doesn't suit, you and William could go alone, perhaps." With that sly and suggestive remark left hanging in the air, Catherine turned and headed for home calling the perplexed Samuel as she went. "Samuel."

"Catherine often leaves like that and calls me as if I was a disobedient pet. Most undignified. I think I might suggest that in future she calls out 'Spaniel' instead of 'Samuel'. What do you think?"

"I think you'd better hurry before she feels obliged to call again."

"Yes, I suppose that might prove wise. Goodnight, Sarah."

"Goodnight, Spaniel."

With a school-boyish laugh at Sarah's farewell, Samuel turned and sped after Catherine.

Some twenty minutes later, Sarah arrived at the field's edge and stood for a while. She had passed quickly along the lanes, not hesitating at Lazzy's bend, nor waiting a moment before rounding the last turn in the lane in the hope that John might be there, standing, waiting. But she knew he would not be. Could not be there. Not yet.

Despite this, she suddenly felt as if… She turned to look behind her, but there was no one there. Yet, she felt that someone was there. Watching her. Was it John, urging her to carry on? Encouraging her not to falter? She looked up in case she would see his smiling face looking down at her. But the skies were clear of such imagery.

Shrugging off her subconscious wishful thinking, she looked ahead, reminding herself that she had not come to visit the fields, or to ponder on what had passed. Her destination lay beyond and she must now focus on what was to be done to regain her special world.

Across the fields, through the far trees and down the seldom used lane that led to the Little Spinney. This night, she had no desire to stand at the edge of the fields. She had a plan and for that plan to succeed, she must first gain certain information. In the far copse that she would need to traverse on route, were several apple trees. Apple trees that drooped their harvest in easy reach of the shortest of gatherers. The rosiest, red-ripened of apples, that would have tempted even the most reluctant inhabitants of Eden. Sarah would linger there, picking and filling her basket and so arrive at her destination bearing succulent gifts. An offering.

Outside the nearest vardo to where she stood, a fire burned and crackled

Chapter Ten

By the time Sarah reached the Little Spinney, the sun was beginning to sink into our sunset and becoming someone else's sunrise. Bringing closure to a day that she had known whilst at the same time waking the people of some far away foreign land. She stood for a moment between the trees. She could see several vardos spaced apart, settled within the tiny copse known by all as Little Spinney. This small wooded area lay five hundred yards from the river's edge, close enough to collect water but not so near that one would be disturbed by local people strolling the riverbank. Outside the nearest vardo to where she stood, a fire burned and crackled, with a cooking pot hanging precariously above. The smoke rising peacefully into the trees that sheltered the scene, gave emphasis to the tranquillity of the natural surroundings. She could see three people around the fire, two adults and one young girl. Rosa.

Rosa's mother Nina, rotund, severe and wearing a head scarf that failed to keep her mop of ginger hair in check, saw Sarah heading towards them first.

"Who's that? A gadji?"

Her husband Nick, wiry, weather tanned and sporting slick, black hair, stood up from stoking the fire and looked where his wife was pointing. He did not speak. Neither spoke. They stood perfectly still watching the advancing Sarah draw ever closer.

Rosa sitting on the wooden steps of the vardo, noticed their stillness.

"What are you two at, standing there like something frozen?" They did not answer or take their eyes off Sarah and for the first time, Rosa looked her way as well.

"It's the missy!"

Nick looked at his daughter. "What missy?"

"The missy I tells you all about. The missy what offered me the job and looks after me when the bee stabs me."

Rosa moved quickly towards Sarah. Two dogs looked to follow her, but Nick raised his hand and spoke firmly.

"Duke… Prince… stay." The dogs immediately settled down at his feet and did not even whimper, let alone bark at the approaching stranger.

"Missy Sarah?"

"Good evening, Rosa. I come bearing gifts."

"That's kind of you, missy, but no needs to be bearing any gifts."

"Well, I know how fond of apples you are."

Rosa took the basket from Sarah and placing it on the ground, dragged Sarah by the hand to meet her parents.

"This is my father, who be called Nick,"

"Pleased to meet you, missy," greeted Nick enthusiastically, shaking Sarah's hand.

"And this is my mother, she's being called Nina."

Sarah smiled and stretched out a hand of greeting to her as well, but it was politely ignored. Nina just nodded and picking up the basket of apples, took them inside the vardo.

"Don't pay no heed, missy," apologised Rosa, "she don't speak much and she's not that fond of gadjos neither."

"Come sit down 'ere missy and we'll get you something to eat," said the more talkative Nick. "so's you really exist?"

"Sorry?"

"Don't worry, missy, I told them everything that happened at your yard and they weren't willing to believe me."

"Couldn't get my head round a Romany being offered work in town, that's all missy."

"Well, I can assure you, Mr…?"

"Nick."

"Mr Nick…"

"No, missy, just call him Nick, no mister." corrected Rosa.

"I see. Well, Nick, I can assure you and your good wife that it is true. I did offer Rosa work and I am extremely disappointed that she could not bring herself to accept the offer. It was sincerely meant."

"Best thing really, missy. Truly kind of you and all, but best she didn't. Wouldn't work, you see?"

"I understand your meaning, Nick, but with time I am convinced…"

"Not enough time left in the world for it to become any different, missy. Feelings is too strong on both sides of the fence, to my thinking. But I'm thanking you for your kindness to the little'un."

As they spoke, Nina came back out of the vardo with a small piece of bread and one of the apples sliced up on a plate. She stood by Sarah and held it out for her to take.

"For me? Thank you but I…"

"Best you take it missy, it's the way of things. You'll upset her if you don't."

'I see. Well, thank you Nina, thank you kindly."

Sarah was not particularly hungry but thought it best to eat as she did not want to give any offence. They did not speak as she ate, but just watched her intently, not eating themselves. It was strange. As if they were sitting in judgment upon the quality of her ability to consume food. After a few mouthfuls had been digested, Sarah put the plate down on the ground, over-smiling to show her gratitude.

"It was kind of yer, missy, to nurse our Rosa and her sting."

"Nonsense, it was only right that I should. After all, it was one of my bees that stung her."

"Bees has always had a liking for our Rosa, but herself reacts badly to 'em."

"Yes. Although I assume not so much to bees themselves as much as their stings."

Another of Sarah's attempts at humour that faltered even before it hit the stony ground. But Nick and Rosa smiled politely despite their puzzlement.

A stilted pause ensued as all waited to see who wished to speak next.

Sarah knew what she wanted to ask and was digging deep to find the courage to voice it. Rosa was still surprised that Sarah had walked out to the encampment, just to bring some apples. She was thinking there must be another reason. Nick thought Sarah was a good-looking woman and hoped Nina did not realise what he was thinking. But he need not have worried. His secret was safe, as Nina was not thinking about much at all. She was suspicious of the non-Romanies and, although she was grateful in her heart for what this woman had done for her daughter, Sarah was still a non-Romany. She was a gadji and Nina's experiences over the years had taught her not to trust them. Any of them.

After several minutes of people smiling at each other and looking into the flickering flames of the campfire, Rosa decided to break the deadlock.

"How's that dog, Beggar, missy? Still up to his tricks, is he? Still dancing, is he?"

"No Rosa, I'm afraid he isn't. We seem to have lost him, or rather he has perhaps tired of us and moved on to pastures new."

"That's surprising missy, he seemed happy."

"Yes, he did. But unfortunately, he is no longer with us. Lottie tells me that she took him for a walk to Walsworth and unfortunately lost him somewhere along the Willian road."

"Lost him?" asked Nick.

"Well, from what I understand from Lottie, he started snarling for no obvious reason and then ran off up the road before disappearing into the hedgerow."

Sarah smiled as if to say, 'would you believe it?'

"Lottie thinks he most likely caught the scent of a rabbit, or a small deer, possibly."

Nick, who had been stoking the fire, stopped what he was doing for a second and then continued at a much slower pace. Rosa and Nina looked at Sarah and Sarah sensed the change in atmosphere.

"Have I said something?"

"No missy, not at all." replied Nick, taking out his pipe and lighting it with a thin stick from the base of the fire. "Does he usually comes back to you missy, this dog?"

"Yes, usually. Why do you ask?"

Nick did not answer. Sarah guessed at their hesitancy and turned to Rosa.

"You know whose dog it is, don't you? Has he run back to

his master?"

Before Rosa could answer, Nick spoke.

"I'd say that'd be very unlikely missy, very unlikely he'd be doing that."

Nick felt Sarah's eyes on him, wanting him to say more.

"Well, are you goin' to tell the missy or not?" snapped Rosa impatiently.

"You knows it's not a story we likes to tell, Rosa. Too much embarrassment, to my mind."

Nick, still with his attention on the fire, moved a few logs around, not because they needed to be moved, but because he was still deciding whether to continue or not. Eventually he decided that he would.

"We teach the dogs the tricks, missy, our family is well known for it. All round the country the Romany knows we be the best teachers around, everyone's a knowing that as a fact. But there's a way to teach them and there's a way not to teach them. We teach them with kindness."

Nick gestured to the two dogs lying in the grass to one side, peacefully, eyes almost shut but not quite.

"Does them two look all content to you, missy?"

"Yes, yes, they do."

"And that's because they is. They is content, missy, because we don't beat them."

"Beat them?"

"That's right, missy Sarah," affirmed Rosa. "they get treats all the time, you see. Father keeps getting the dogs doing their tricks, over and over and every time they gets it right, missy, they gets another treat. If they don't get it right, they don't gets a treat. So, the dog learns, get it right, get a treat."

"That sounds reasonable, Rosa."

"There's one person we knows," continued Nick, "who don't believe in giving them treats. This person teaches the dogs differently to hows we do it. If they don't get it right with this 'ere other person, the dog gets beaten. Sometimes badly."

"But that's terribly cruel."

"Yes, missy, very cruel. That way the dog learns to fear you. He does the tricks, not because he loves doin' the tricks, missy, but because he's frit that he'll get beaten if he doesn't."

"And Beggar was taught this way?"

"Yes, missy."

"You're saying that Beggar belonged to this other man?"

"He did, once."

"So, he escaped from this man and came to us at the yard?"

"Reckon so, missy. I hates to say it but this man is a cousin, yet, not a cousin we likes, as he brings shame on us all with his ways and his doings."

"He's a wicked man, missy," said Rosa and from the tone of her voice it was obvious that there was no love lost.

"And this man, your cousin, does he live locally?"

Nick stood up and leant back against the rear wheel of the vardo, breathed in deeply on his pipe and watched the smoke mix with that of the fire.

"Used to. Used to be one of us here, missy. But he was told to go. None of us here had time for such as him. Brought too much shame on us, so all the camp tells him to go. His family are dead, save a sister, and she'd had enough of his ways too."

"And this man, this cousin… What was his name?"

Nick took his pipe from his mouth and looked Sarah in the eye.

"I think's you know who he is, missy. Lazarus is his name, but you knows him as Lazzy Smith."

Sarah did not speak.

Beggar's attitude whenever Lazzy came calling made sense now. The despised master. Beggar had somehow gained the courage to turn on him. The way he chased after Lazzy that night in the lane, when Lottie had come looking for her. It all made sense.

"Lazzy comes into your shop, times, I'm thinking. Does he play all friendly and polite with you, missy?"

"Yes, to a certain extent. Yet, now that I know that he treats innocent dogs in such a cruel and heartless way, I will see to it that he is not allowed on the premises in the future."

"He's not to be trusted, missy, not to be trusted at all."

"I know."

Silence.

It was obvious that Nick wanted to say more on the subject. Normally he would not have concerned himself so, especially for a gadji, but this was no ordinary gadji, this woman probably saved his daughter's life.

"There's something I needs to say."

Sarah looked at him.

"Before he was sent away, he spoke things that we don't believe are true, but he spoke them missy and you should know of them."

"I don't understand."

"He boasted that the lady at the lavender shop, has…" Nick hesitated.

"Has what?"

"No one believes him missy, but he says that you has… 'feelings' for him."

"Feelings?"

"Lazzy's mouth is as big and harsh as his training missy and he's not believed by no one. But I thinks you should know what he says."

Sarah was taken aback and her voice muted by the horror of Nick's words. She did not respond. She did not know how to respond.

"I owes it to tell you, missy."

Still Sarah sat silent.

"For Rosa, I owes it to you for Rosa, you see."

"Thank you, Nick," she said at last. "I appreciate you telling me of his uncouth and unfounded boasting."

She smiled and mustered all her energy to say, "I can assure you that I do not have and I have never had any 'feelings' for that dreadful and… vile man." she lied.

Rosa felt obliged to add her voice.

"No one thinks it to be true, Missy Sarah, but we thinks you should know he says it."

'Thank you, Rosa. Nick. Thank you for telling me, I'm obliged to you."

No one spoke.

To change the subject, a subject that she found distasteful because of her guilt, because she was now lying and denying feelings that she knew she had experienced even though only fleetingly, she asked what seemed a random question. But one that had much more to do with her reason for being there.

"All these beautiful vardos, who lives in them?"

"Family mostly, missy. Rosa's elder brothers and sisters, cousins with their partners and children. It's quiet now, as it 'appens they're all at the river."

"Swimming?" asked Sarah.

"Fishing." replied Nick.

"So, everyone living here is a relation?"

"As good as."

"And what of Old Jinnepen? Is she related to you?"

"Lord no, missy."

"So, she lives somewhere else?"

"Why do you ask, Missy Sarah?" interjected a curious Rosa.

"No reason, no real reason…"

'You wanting to ask her a question?"

"Not necessarily, Nick. I was just intrigued. Rosa told me about her and I thought she sounded a fascinating woman... I was intrigued, that is all."

"She's a strange woman missy, wise and gifted, but strange, with a dark past. Thems with a dark past are always grasping something beyond the rest of us."

"You believe her to have powers, Nick?"

"I do believe, for I knows she has."

"In what way? Do you mean, as in fortune telling?"

"More than that missy. Old Jinnepen has powers not understood by no one."

As Nick poked the fire, Rosa watched Sarah. She seemed to hang upon Nick's every word. This was not the Miss Sarah she had known at the yard, or even the one that arrived carrying a basket brimming with apples. The more Nick talked about Old Jinnepen, the more this lovely lady, who had offered her work and nursed her when ill, changed. Visibly changed. As Nick told the tale of Old Jinnepen, Sarah's eyes widened as she listened, her lips parted and her breathing seemed to intensify through suppressed excitement.

"You has to understand missy, that Old Jinnepen is a hundred years and more." continued Nick. "None I knows of remembers all the happening of it, as we was too young or not yet born. Besides, she's not from these parts, she was part of a family up north. So, most of what I'll say is through hearing the telling of, rather than the knowing. They reckons she was a lone child, sort of secretive and didn't mix with no one, but they says she was a rare beauty missy, blessed with looks to turn any man's head. Anyhows, when she was no older than my Rosa here, she was taken without her say so. This man what takes her, found her a-picking the blackberries in the woods and he grabbed her and took her violently against her will. She was such a beauty, see, not that she flirted or teased the boys with her beauty, missy, because she kept herself to herself. But this man, a much older man and a man known to be no good, takes her despite her screams and her rantings. People hears her screams and come a running.

They finds her standing in the woods, her cloths all ripped from her and scattered and she is standing and pointing the way the man has run off. No doubting who he was, because she knew him and she's a screaming his name and a cursing his family and his children and any children they might one day have. He's found, but before they can gets him in front of a Kris, a council court, that would have expelled him, her father walks up behind him, pulls back the man's head and with one stroke of his knife, cuts his throat. Just as if he were a lamb to be butchered. Saying nothing, he then packs his vardo and moves down this way. Their story has gone before them you see and they has the sympathy of the community down this way and so they're allowed to camp in the area."

Rosa's eyes were still on Sarah. Sarah's eyes were still wide open, unblinking, absorbed by Nick's account.

"On the face of it, missy, justice was done. But though the girl cursed the villain and his kin, she's been cursed as well, for she's a-carrying his child. That's something the family couldn't hide. So come nearer her time, they moves off to have the child. No one knows where. Weren't too far away, mind, for they were back with the community within a couple of days. But though they was back, missy, there was no baby with them."

Nick paused and, taking his time, inhaled deeply on his pipe. Sarah did not move. She did not take her eyes from Nick.

"What happened to the child?" Rosa asked on Sarah's behalf.

"No one's knows. None are certain. Some says when the child was born, her father drowned it, some say the girl herself drowned it, no one knows for sure. But one thing was certain, she didn't keep it."

The story over, Nick threw more logs on to the cooking fire and for the first time, Rosa saw Sarah take her eyes from Nick as she spoke.

"Poor girl."

"Yes, missy Sarah, it's not a nice tale to my mind, neither." agreed Rosa, still looking at Sarah.

"That poor wretch has had to live her long life with that terrible burden. It must have always preyed upon her mind."

With those words from Sarah, all fell silent, thinking on the tale and the horror suffered by Old Jinnepen as a young girl. The savagery of the loss of her virtue and her inability to look her child in the face, must have scarred her with an unhealable wound.

"Every day of her life, she must have wished she could turn time back, I reckons. Turn time back to just afore she went into those woods and have time stand still if that were doable." said Nick, philosophically.

"Is it?"

Nick looked at Sarah.

"Is it possible to turn time back and have it stand still?"

Nick hesitated for a moment before answering, thinking to himself that this kind lady from the town was a strange one to figure on all accounts.

"I don't know, missy, that's past my knowing."

"Would Old Jinnepen know?"

To Nick, Rosa and even Nina, Sarah's questions and presence were now causing puzzlement. There was obviously a reason for such questions, but none of them knew what it was, or could even begin to guess at it.

"Possibly, missy, she's the wisest I know."

Sarah considered his answer. In the quiet of her contemplation, Rosa spoke up.

"Has you got a question that you wants answering then, Missy Sarah?"

Sarah did not reply, as if she had not heard. Rosa waited a while before repeating her question.

"Missy?"

"I'm sorry Rosa, you were saying?"

"I says, missy, has you a question for Old Jinnepen?"

"No. Well... possibly. It's not important, really." lied Sarah.

For the first time, Nina, who up to that moment had seemed happy to listen and watch, spoke.

"If you has a question for her, lady, better be quick."

Sarah looked at her searchingly.

"As I hears it from folks, Old Jinnepen is being closer to death every day."

On a single beat, Sarah's heart quickened.

"She's ancient, lady, not even Old Jinnepen can live for ever," and then as an instinctive afterthought Nina added, "none of us can, lady."

A moment's hesitation before Sarah answered. "No. No, of course not."

Sarah energised, fearing that her guard had possibly been down and her mind may have been too open to these kind people. She stood and brushed down her skirt to show that she was ready to leave.

"Thank you for your hospitality, you have all been most

kind. Thank you, Nina, for the food."

"You brought it, lady."

"Yes, yes, I did, didn't I? But thank you, anyhow, for sharing it. I really have kept you for too long and I must be home. Eliza will start to worry." Sarah suddenly realised that they would have no idea who Eliza was and that she was now speaking simply for the sake of speaking. It was time that she was gone.

"Goodbye Rosa and if you should change your mind about the work…"

"Thank you kindly, missy Sarah, but I won't be changing it anytime soon."

"No, and understandably. Well… goodnight to you all." Sarah turned to go, the dogs lifted their heads with their dozing disturbed and she had not got more than three steps, when Nick spoke after her.

"I can tells you where she can be found, missy, if you wants to know?"

Sarah did not turn to look back but neither did she continue to move. She waited.

"She be camped on mad Alington's land, up at the big house on the Willian road."

"Thank you." whispered Sarah, not looking back as she walked on…

"Somewhere in the mad Lord's woods, I hears tell. Be careful, missy, they're a crazy people that he keeps around him. Good luck go with yer!"

Sarah walked on through the copse never looking back and not knowing that the three of them stood still, watching her go until she was out of sight. They were instinctive people and instinct had told them that all was not right with this polite and proper lady.

"Rosa?"

Rosa turned to look at her mother.

"That one is troubled, daughter." With that, Nina picked up Sarah's plate and finished off her apple and bread as she returned inside their vardo.

Sarah made her way home, her mind refusing to listen to the warning notes repeating their alarms in her head. Many of the self-made rules that had got her this far were crumbling within her. Her ability to keep the two worlds apart was no longer feasible. She had resorted to telling lies to cover the truth. She had lost control and she knew it. She was no longer making the decisions, something that lingered within her was making them for her. She knew she was following a course that the old Sarah would never have travelled.

She also knew that when John were alive, if she had told him what she was planning, he would have called for Doctor Hawkins or talked her out of such an un-Christian course. But she was not in control, John was no longer around and there was nothing to stop her following her obsession to reach out. Nothing. Whatever the cost to herself, her soul or her life.

She arrived home just as the last rays of light were fading from the horizon. Eliza was at the back door of the house, waiting.

"Miss Sarah, at last. I was just starting to worry, miss."

Sarah brightened and smiled effusively.

"Dear Eliza, there really was no cause for alarm, I am quite safe. I am much better for my walk and I am home before darkness, am I not?"

"Yes, but I did start to worry, miss…"

"There was no need, as you can see."

"… and I was going to send James to see if he could look for you, but I could not find him, neither."

Before Eliza's sentence was completed, James strode into the yard from the street.

"There you are!"

"Yes, here I am, Eliza."

"I was looking for you."

"And now you have found me, woman."

"But where have you been, man?"

Sarah chose this conversation between her most loyal servants to be the moment to bid goodnight.

"Eliza, I am to bed and I suggest you do the same and not berate poor James so much."

"But Miss Sarah, if you had fainted again…"

"But I did not."

James saw this as his opportunity to retreat from Eliza's questioning and he disappeared quietly into his room unnoticed.

"Look at me, Eliza. Tell me, truthfully, do I not look well? Do I not look as if I have benefited greatly from my walk in the countryside and have gained much goodness from the fresh air?"

Eliza did as she was instructed and looked at her mistress. She had to admit, there was a redness to Sarah's cheeks and her once tired face now radiated with a smile that was wide and sang of elation. There was also an energy evident in Sarah's voice and actions that had been missing before. Although these things were more undeniable rather than familiar, it was not a smile or energy that Eliza fully recognised. More like that born of effort, rather than a result of true feelings.

"Well?" encouraged Sarah.

"Well, yes miss, but what with you only so recently been ill."

Sarah stepped forward to Eliza and held her by both arms as if she were about to shake her. "Eliza, I am fine and I am returned without any sign of relapse. To such an extent that I shall walk again tomorrow and you will promise me tomorrow that you will not worry."

"Yes miss, but…"

"Promise."

"I promise, miss."

"You promise what, Eliza?"

"I promise I won't worry, miss."

"That is good, sweet Eliza and now I am to bed, for the evening grows late and tomorrow is another day to be enjoyed." Sarah turned and climbed the stairs to her room leaving Eliza, standing transfixed in the hallway. It was Miss Sarah and she was home and safe and seemingly well. But it was not the Miss Sarah she recognised. It was as if one Sarah had left the house and a completely different one had returned. Same face, features, body, but not the same person.

Sarah had never been to Letchworth Hall before. She had seen it several times from a distance but had never been inside its ancient stone walls. Now she found herself standing outside the front door, waiting to see if anyone would answer the doorbell. Inside she could hear singing, laughter, and the raucous sound of revellers. She knew well the stories of this debauched house, but she sought Old Jinnepen, who she knew lived somewhere within the grounds. This would unfortunately mean first speaking to Alington. On the other hand, if luck played its part well, she might avoid speaking to him in person and gain the required information from one of his workers.

The sounds from inside continued unabated; if anything, they grew louder and even more wild. Undaunted, she pulled the large bell lever a second time. She looked back over her shoulder to see if anyone was about within the grounds. Standing there, she became aware of a cold chill that spilt from the nape of her neck and flowed down the length of her spine, like near freezing water overflowing its receptacle. She had not heard the door open but knew someone now stood behind her. She turned to face the door and the familiar face of Lazzy Smith, sleering.

"Why, Mrs Perks. What brings you a-calling to Letchworth Hall or needs I not ask such a question?" His sleer widened into a grin, his yellow, and in places blackened, teeth were purposely exposed as if he were proud of them. Sarah's first thought was to turn and leave but that would achieve nothing. She would be strong and undaunted for she needed to speak to Alington. She would not be put off course by this abhorrent and corruptive creature.

"I wish to speak with your master."

His grin instantly disappeared as if grossly offended. "I'm a-thinking I have told you afore, Mrs Perks, I has no master save Lazarus Smith." He did not look to move, as he had not done during their altercation in the lane. His glare bore through her with an icy viciousness that froze her senses. But she was resolved.

"Please be good enough to inform the Reverend Alington, that Mrs Perks would like a brief word."

Lazzy still did not move and his expression remained as before, but now framed with contempt. Contempt, thought Sarah, because he thought she had made a promise to him and then reneged on that promise.

"I will not keep him long."

It seemed that he was cemented to the spot like some hideous dungeon victim in Madame Tussaud's Baker Street museum. He continued to stare into her eyes as if attempting to trespass further and sear her brain with his loathing. As she went to speak, his whole vista suddenly relaxed back into the smarmy sleer that was his trait.

"I would you come in, Mrs Perks, I really does, but the goings on that are filling this place now, would cause you much alarm and disgust, I'm thinking."

"I only wish to ask…"

"It's sinful people in here, Mrs Perks, sinful. I'm a thinking that the goings on and the nakedness would shock you unfairly. For the wicked people in here is having no care of what they says or what they does. It's the devil at play in here, Mrs Perks and would not be to your liking, I'm thinking."

He paused deliberately.

"Or might I be mistaken?"

He waited to see if Sarah wished to answer but she did not.

"Am I wrong, Mrs Perks? Is it perhaps, in truth, being exactly why you is here?"

Sarah found herself beginning to battle for her dignity against the sensual demons that lurked within her, just as she had that fearful night in the lane. It was a battle that had to be won or otherwise it would divert her from her true purpose. A purpose that, with every second, she was struggling to recall.

"Please?" as she spoke the word, she could not disguise the desperation she felt, and her 'please' was nothing but ambiguous. Whether it was begging to speak to Alington or begging to be let in, Lazzy was not sure and nor was Sarah.

Slowly, as if in some great tragic stage play, he stepped back for her to see, opening the door wider and wider as he did so. The door seeming to assume greater proportions than were realistically possible. Still he pulled back the giant door, a door now that must have filled the wall. Further and further the vast door opened so that at last all those inside the great hall were revealed.

Her gaze was confronted by a tableau of depravity. Wild fiddlers burned their bows across strings of cattle gut, frantically encouraging the gathered to indulge in unspeakable outrage. Near naked girls danced between writhing bodies upon the floor, unfettered; touched and caressed by uncompromising hands and fingers that were never brushed away. Supported by medieval furniture that creaked under the strain, couples fornicated and revelled in the encouragement of drunken voyeurs. Groups twisted grotesquely together, forming an unrestrained mould of limbs, each seeking favour in sanctuaries unholy. Sweat poured and lubricated, enforcing welcoming bodies to slither like Satan's snakes, seeking souls to suck dry. The sights that played out in front of Sarah's eyes held her transfixed, torn between looking away and indulging her own suppressed frustrations. Like some great canvass daubed by Blake, Hogarth, Bosch or the contorted images of Bruegel's hell. It spread out in front of her, hiding nothing, revealing all. There was no pain or regret written upon the faces of the willing participants, just the joy and ecstasy of constant sexual release.

Through the noise and debauchery, at the far side of the hall sat the figure of a satisfied orchestrator on a great throne-like chair. It was Alington. Sarah knew it to be him despite his semi nakedness and crown of thorns lopsided upon his head, stolen from the sacrificed Christ. He slouched, surveying his carnival of immorality, conjured from his darkest demons, directing and instigating scenarios that took his sordid fancy. He was master of all he saw, triumphant in his own handiwork, visually engaged and unashamedly proud of his decadent creation.

On seeing Sarah, he beckoned her to him. She did not consciously move but move she did. Nearer to him she went as if she had been summoned and all resistance was futile. She stood just in front of him, like a beckoned slave. Now the centre piece in a melee of bacchanalia, she felt hands brushing her cheeks, her thighs, her breasts, for now she too stood unashamedly naked. How and when she had disrobed, she knew not. She remembered not and she cared not. Alington lifted his thin and scrawny arm and pointed to the great fire that burned at one end of the hall. With the brash gaiety of demonic music screeching in her ears, she looked in the direction he had silently commanded.

There she saw another naked girl, this one as beautiful as any Helen of Troy, skin gently suntanned with tints of olive, jet black hair long and fanned out across her shoulders. On the floor in front of the fire, she sat astride a torso, in a position from which no misinterpretation could be made. This exquisite icon of femininity rocked slowly backwards and forwards upon the groin beneath her, whilst looking down at the recipient's unseen face. A face that remained hidden from Sarah, being masked by furniture and others engrossed in similar shaping. Silhouetted by the roaring fire, the light from its flames licked and flickered down the girl's bear arms, body and breasts. With her arms outstretched she suddenly braced herself, her hands upon the man's chest, her neck now strained and stretching skywards as she approached the desired moment and with a jolt and prolonged scream that signalled the conclusion of their coupling, she collapsed down upon his chest.

Sarah looked back at Alington who was watching her carefully. Once more he pointed and ushered her to go nearer to the couple. The girl had stood up from her partner, looking seductively down at him, smiling from her satisfaction and for his. He had lifted himself up on to his elbows and gazed back at her, watching her. She gently wrapped a sheer garment around herself, that clung to her nakedness with the moistness of her skin, hiding few secrets. Then the girl looked towards the approaching Sarah, her knowing smile never leaving her face. Turning away, the girl walked to another man and began her sacred ritual over again, like some temple Priestess, invoking the favour of Bacchus and Dionysus. The man on the floor was also watching her, content.

All Sarah could see was the back of his head. She drew nearer and to one side that she might catch a glimpse of his features. He sensed her stare and began to turn his head slowly from the girl to look at Sarah. At last they looked each other square in the face. His broad grin and laughing eyes roared to decibels that shut out the sounds of the orgy that surrounded them. Sarah's shock was only matched by her abject horror as she realised it was John.
As Sarah screamed her 'No!' of painful disbelief... she awoke.

Had she screamed only in her sleep or out loud and, in doing so, woken the house? She could hear Edward outside chattering to someone. She could hear Thomas teasing Toby over his affections for pretty Lizzie and she could hear Eliza talking to someone in the hallway. Satisfied her scream had been dreamt and none had heard, she rose from her bed to dress. She chose carefully from her wardrobe, thinking of the day that lay ahead. She paid little heed to her nightmare. It was a dream after all, and she would not be deterred because of its uncomfortable nature. Not all dreams were portents of things to come, Sarah reminded herself, and they should be treated purely for what they were. Today she would go to the hall and find Old Jinnepen. If there was a way of reaching John, the wise old woman would surely know of it. That was her chosen course of action and there was no way on earth she would not pursue it now.

Standing in front of her mirror, she considered the dress she had chosen. It was a shade of shimmering olive green, one that John had admired and, although not particularly foppish, it had more lace on the cuffs and neck than she would usually have worn. The buttons at the top could be left undone and in doing so expose more neckline. Alington was not fond of Hitchin folk and because of this, she was unsure of the welcome she may receive. But she desperately needed to step on to his land and she would require his permission to do so. If she needed to flatter, then she would. As she unconsciously put her hand to her face, she thought on what she saw. A woman not yet thirty years of age, her complexion still fair, freckle dashed, yet, with no lines or wrinkles to lessen her appeal. She dropped her hand to the top of her dress, pushing the lace to either side and in doing so revealed more of her throat. As she contemplated what lay ahead, there was knock at her door.

"Miss Sarah? Miss Sarah, are you awake yet?"

"Come in, Eliza, I am awake and dressed."

Eliza entered the bedroom as she spoke "I didn't wake you miss, for I feared you may have been tired from your walk…" as Eliza spied the dress that Sarah had chosen for the day, she thought Sarah may have an idea why she had come to her room. "I don't knows if you know or not," continued Eliza, "but you has a visitor, miss."

"A visitor?"

"He came round earlier, asking after you, miss. I don't know if you might have heard him or not?" asked Eliza looking at

Sarah's dress and seeing that Sarah seemed to be paying particular attention to herself in her mirror. "But I says to him you was asleep and he says, I'll return later, and I says that would be more convenient, and he says, then I will. And now he has been and done as he said, and he is here again." Sarah, finally realising that Eliza was being unusually enthusiastic about announcing a visitor, turned to her for clarification.

"Who is it, Eliza?"

"Young Mister Ransom, miss." Eliza beamed with a smile that hid little of her opinion. "He's downstairs in the drawing room. I tooks the liberty of putting him there."

"Thank you, Eliza," replied Sarah, trying to sound as unflustered as possible. "Please tell him I'll be straight down."

"Yes, miss."

As Eliza opened the door, she paused for a moment to add "I like your choice of dress today miss, I must say. Very fetching." Eliza shut the door behind her and, after grinning to herself on the landing, left to relay the message to William.

It was obvious that Eliza had misinterpreted the choice for her chosen dress, but it mattered not. William had probably called to arrange a new date for their trip to Wilbury Hills. His visit would not delay her unnecessarily and then she could begin her walk to Letchworth Hall. Moving away from the mirror, she glanced out of her bedroom window and noticed a dramatic change in the colouring of the sky. It was still warm, humid in fact, but the sky had lost its bright azure and had instead adopted a darkish grey hue. Overcast and foreboding, it might herald change in the weather and a storm may well be in the offing. She must not waste too much time in conversation with William. If the skies forewarned rain, she would need to start her walk sooner rather than later. Her excuse for knocking at Alington's door was to be that she had been strolling, inadvertently lost her way and, because of her prolonged outing was in sore need of water. Just enough of an excuse to engage in conversation with him and then slip in a question regarding the whereabouts of Old Jinnepen.

William sat patiently, waiting. After several minutes, the drawing room door opened and to his mind a woman of great beauty entered.

"William."

"Sarah."

"Good morning, William, this is a pleasant surprise." Sarah flowed to a cushioned chair opposite William's and sat gracefully. William stood, still consumed by inexplicable awe.

"Please, William." Sarah indicated the chair and he once again sat.

"Are you well, Sarah?"

"Yes, thank you, I am quite well, William."

"That is good."

"I understand I have you to thank. I have been very remiss in not expressing my gratitude until now."

"It was fortunate that I saw you from the other side of the street, that is all. I am a very early riser and most mornings I would have been inside the barns by then, but what with the previous day's events, I had afforded myself another hour in bed."

"Of course. Then in some ways I have her Majesty the Queen to thank for my rescue."

"Indeed." William relaxed and realised the humour in her statement. "In truth, yes. One could say that she is a protective mother, not just of the Empire, but of us all"

It was poor humour, but it was the best he could do. He knew that the longer he was in Sarah's company, the more at ease and relaxed he would feel.

"Eliza tells me you ventured out for the first time yesterday?"

"I did. Only as far as the top fields, mind, it was the loveliest of evenings."

"Ah, yes, but not to be repeated this evening, I think."

"My walk?"

"No, the evening, there is a change in the air. Our sunny hours may be put on hold for a few days, I think."

"But the harvest is in."

"Yes, as you say, the harvest is in. A good harvest too."

"Indeed."

As often happened in their conversations, a silence ensued, as William thought of what to say next, and Sarah considered him again. She could not be anything but polite to him, she could not be faulted for liking this man, she could not bring herself to discount him. She knew John and she knew when she regained touch with him, he would understand and he would undoubtedly forgive her for allowing her mind to stray.

"What of Samuel and Catherine? I understand they progress well, even without your expert assistance."

"I believe Lottie is proving her worth as my second. I saw them all briefly yesterday and they spoke extremely highly of her. She is a very bright girl, Lottie, although a little talkative. However, in these circumstances, that is probably a good thing, as this will enable her to supply them with just as much information as I would have been able to."

"I'm sure," William suddenly remembered the reason for his visit. "which reminds me."

"Reminds you of what?

William leant forward in his chair, arms balanced on the top of his legs, hat between his hands.

"Of why I have come round."

"Ah yes, Wilbury Hills."

"Wilbury?" Sarah's statement had thrown him.

"The trip that we had to postpone."

"Of course, Wilbury Hills, yes. We will indeed need to reschedule that, most definitely."

"That is good. I am sorry that it did not go ahead as planned."

"Yes, but that isn't the reason for my visit. I am afraid I am the reluctant bearer of some sad news."

"News? Regarding what?"

William had become more solemn as he approached the subject of his visit.

"We have found Beggar."

"You have?"

"Yes, or rather two of my lads did."

"Where?"

"The other side of Walsworth, by the roadside in a hedge."

"A hedge?"

"Yes, Sarah. I'm afraid Beggar's dead."

There was a stunned silence as Sarah put her feeling for William and her desire to regain John to one side, and her humanity surfaced supressing all else.

"They were coming down the Willian road and one of their dogs found him. When my lads got to him it was quite clear that he was dead. Had been for some time too. William hesitated, not sure if to say more but knew he should not keep it from her.

"His throat had been cut."

Sarah said nothing.

"I'm so sorry, Sarah, I truly am."

The main door to the hall was situated at the foot of the new tower

Chapter Eleven

It was a strange feeling that everyone experienced, regarding the loss of Beggar. The dog had not been theirs by rights and he had only adopted them a year past, but when Sarah informed those in the yard, a great sadness affected all of them. Neither was the response a momentary regret, but rather a sincere mourning that in some ways seemed out of proportion to its facts. It was as if a chapter had been turned that could never be read again. Many an eye welled up, from the young girls to some of the most hardened of the men, who you would not have thought would have been so affected.

However, none took it so badly as little Lucy Hutchins, who blubbered and wailed as if she had lost one of her numerous siblings. She sat clutching the lead she had fashioned for him and was inconsolable. Hilda, who had recently returned, took her under her maternal wing and saw to it through conversation and good humour, that Lucy's obvious grief for Beggar would not be everlasting. 'Time,' thought Sarah, 'would eventually heal the little girl's wounds.'

It was strange that, as Sarah thought these things, she did not recognise the similarities to herself. It did not enter her mind for even an instant that the healing process of the passing of time, as a cure to grief, might also apply to her.

She had walked to the shop to inform Samuel and Catherine of the tragic event as soon as William had left. Catherine thought it only right, with the full agreement of Samuel, that it should be Sarah that divulged the sad news. All were gathered in the yard and were informed as previously described. Sarah had decided not to mention the cause of death, and simply inferred that Beggar may have been hit by a passing wagon or had suffered from some other similar misfortune. She saw no reason to paint the whole harrowing story and cause even more upset. It would suffice that all were aware of the event without the additional details of cruelty. In time this fact would become common knowledge to all through the conduit of conversation, but now was not the appropriate moment.

It was late afternoon before Sarah set out to Letchworth Hall along the Willian road. She had swapped her grubby parasol for hat and shawl as the sun had not shown its face that day and was unlikely to. It was possible it might rain before nightfall but she fully intended to have returned home long before then.

Three years previously, Alington had increased the size of Letchworth Hall substantially. This included the erection of a large mock medieval tower. An expensive construction which he had built simply because he could. His eccentric sense of grandeur and his fascination with the courtly life of bygone ages, had seen him litter the house with eclectic relics that he thought enhanced the hall's standing. Having inherited greater wealth than most men could dream of, he had lavished it on unsavoury characters that littered the house and grounds and squandered it on frivolous follies.

His reputation was well known throughout the county and Sarah was quite aware of the scandalous rumours attached to Alington and his followers. Not only was he wild of mind and nature, which might pose a danger to a woman unescorted, but he also favoured Lazzy Smith as a trusted lackey.

Sarah made her way through the hall gates beneath overcast skies. Although unsure how Alington would react to her visit, she reminded herself that, despite his libidinous infamy, he was not renowned for being violent. Even at his notorious parties, it was said he would stand for no brawling in his house and any that should indulge in fisticuffs were quickly evicted. Furthermore, she could see no reason why he would object to her request to see Old Jinnepen, for it was an innocent enough request. She felt convinced this legendary old sage would prove the answer to her dilemma and she would be devastated if her request were turned down.

Before John's passing, she would have scoffed at the very action she now took, but John's reappearance had changed her views on all such mumbo jumbo. She knew now that nothing was impossible in the unpredictable world and that all teachings, learning and wisdoms were simply what was believed to be the facts. She knew differently, she had proof that the established view of the boundary that separated life from afterlife was flawed, if not blatantly false. However, there must be keys that unlocked the doors to these windows, these corridors that allowed things to be seen and journeys to be made. If this were indeed the case, then it followed that some gifted people that lived would hold these secret keys. It was quite plausible that Old Jinnepen's reputation for special powers derived from her being one of these spiritual janitors.

The main door to the hall was situated at the foot of the new tower, a tower built from recycled brick to render it seemingly 'ancient' to those that beheld it. She was pleased to see that the lever mechanism to ring the bell that she had pulled in her dream, did not exist. In fact, the means to announce one's arrival was by use of a large brass door knocker in the shape of some fearsome gargoyle. Sarah lifted the heavy beast and knocked hard with unafraid confidence. She looked to summon the Saturnalian master of the house and was undaunted and unrepentant in doing so. If what she desired could only be achieved through making a deal with the devil, then so be it. If the Christian world was wrong in their view of life after death, which she knew to be the case, then it could just as easily be wrong about Lucifer and the torment of his hell.

The door was opened by a Romany girl. An extremely pretty, pleasant girl; grey gypsy blouse revealing naked shoulders, her legs draped in a bright red flowing skirt that hid cream petticoats and which swirled about dainty ankles even as she stood still.

"Would it be possible to speak to the Reverend Alington, please?"

"Come in lady, the parson, he's expecting you."

Sarah entered the hall to no party, no revellers, no fiddlers, no writhing bodies strewn upon the floor, saturated in the dew of lust. The only similarity to her dream was the fireplace at the far end of the hall, where a small and insignificant fire burned.

"He'll be down soon, lady." The girl walked away with a swagger that saw her hips move in a way that caused her skirt and petticoats to sway around her, as if they had a life of their own. Sarah suddenly remembered the girl saying that Alington was expecting her. How? She had sent no letter.

"Mrs Perks!" She turned to see the slender Alington, middle aged, thin shoulder length hair, wild and greying, descending the stairs. "What a pleasant and delightful surprise, madam."

"Mister Alington, thank you for seeing me, I will not take up much of your time, sir."

"You, madam, will take up as much of my time as you so wish. I do not have many distinguished visitors, so I will enjoy your company whilst you are here."

It sounded to Sarah like a comment of sarcasm but looking at him, no such sign was evident. He did look genuinely pleased to see her.

"The young girl said you were expecting me?"

"Yes, indeed."

"How, may I ask?"

"Ah, I see. You suspect that some magical power I have conjured up in some musty dungeon, allows me this insight. That I have possibly gained the power of foresight and prediction through some bedevilment. Which of course would be most befitting of such a depraved place as Letchworth Hall?" Sarah was slightly disconcerted at his words, as if she may still be in her dream.

"Rest assured, madam, I possess no such gift. However, I do possess an extremely efficient telescope which I have had mounted at the top of the tower."

"I see."

"It is powerful and a far-seeing piece of equipment, but a piece developed through the wonder of science and engineering rather than borrowed from Lucifer's loft. Come please, let us sit by the fire and you can tell me what brings you to Letchworth Hall."

"In truth, sir, all I request is to be furnished with a glass of water." said Sarah as Alington led her to chairs situated either side of the fireplace.

"Water? Of course, my dear lady." Alington stopped and looking back called out, "Hester?"

The young girl who had shown Sarah in appeared from a far door. "A glass of water, if you will?"

"Yes, parson." answered Hester before exiting once again.

"A delightful young girl is Hester and the most enchanting of dancers. Do you like dancing, Mrs Perks? I suspect you do for I hear you and your late husband once encouraged it, even in your yard at home. You are no dowdy Quaker, I think, and no doubt have time for the true joys of life. To dance and to sing is to liberate oneself nearly as much as the sexual act itself. Did you know that the Romany dances have their origins in the Andalusian area of southern Spain? A fiery region that excites like no other. It is a hothouse of burning instinct that produces love and hate in equal measure. A land where lust governs the body and love is left to rule the heart. Are you aware of Andalusia, Mrs Perks?"

"I am not, no... I mean, I have heard its name by all accounts, but that is all. I have never visited the place."

"I must confess, for my part, that I have been there and witnessed many things, Mrs Perks, things that should never be repeated in certain company."

"I see…"

"Certain company such as yours, madam. I can be guilty of forgetting myself, so, I beg you, if my language and

excitement for the human basic needs should offend, tell me
and I will cease forthwith."

He gave her no more than a split second in which to register
such a complaint.

"And Hester is the most sensual of exponents."

"She is?"

"She is, indeed. I have many Romanies staying on my lands
and even several in the house. I find their company
stimulating and unpretentious. I realise that many of the
local populace suffer from extreme prejudice concerning
their race, but I do not."

"Neither do I, Reverend Alington. I employ several each
year to work the harvest."

"So I hear, Mrs Perks, so I hear and good for you I say, for to
my mind they are much put upon."

"It would be advantageous to us all if we could live with
each other more civilly."

"Exactly. My thoughts entirely, madam, my thoughts
entirely. I do my utmost to have them here as often as they
will and I try constantly to integrate them with my own
tenants."

"And do your efforts bear fruit?"

"In truth, Mrs Perks, no. No, they do not, which is most
disconcerting. But I will continue to strive, Mrs Perks, I will
continue to strive."

"That is very admirable, sir." She feared her comment may
have sounded tinged with sarcasm, but she had not meant it
that way and smiled at him to show her sincerity.

"Yes, I think so, too." he replied unconcerned.

Sarah had not noticed the approach of Hester with her glass
of water. "Lady?"

"Thank you." Sarah took the glass from her and drank.

Alington watched Hester walk away, lingering his look upon

her for longer than good manners would normally allow. "The most exquisite dancer…" Sarah heard Alington mumble as he continued to watch Hester exit. Sarah was aware of his stare and so was Hester, who's swagger was increased and intensified so that her skirts flung themselves energetically around her curvaceous figure.

"The water is greatly appreciated, sir, but I should explain my presence here."

"As you wish, but there really is no need."

"I was taking a walk for my health and whilst deep in thought, regarding mundane matters, I somehow lost my way. Although regaining my bearings quite quickly I had, by then, caused myself a great thirst."

"Indeed?" he replied, returning his gaze once more upon Sarah now that Hester had finally disappeared from his sight. "That is most unfortunate, madam, and somewhat surprising."

"And so, I thought to call upon you… Surprising? How surprising, sir?"

"Well, what with you being so familiar with the area..."

"It was for a moment only, but enough to put me on the wrong path."

"I see."

Alington looked at her closely. He was curious and had his suspicions. To his mind, it was an odd visit from such an intelligent and respectable lady. Although it was a fine-looking woman that sat opposite him, he would not be diverted from his present thinking by his normal considerations for the flesh. He knew perfectly of his reputation and how respectable people would do much to shun and avoid him. Yet, she was here, unannounced and unescorted. Something to his mind did not make sense but he was slowly putting the pieces of the puzzle together and if he were right, her visit may prove advantageous.

"When I espied you through my extremely efficient telescope at the top of my new tower, you seemed in total control of your surroundings and seemed to be heading directly to this house."

"Well, yes…"

"In observing your direction and speed, you did not create the impression of somebody who was lost and in need of sanctuary."

"I did not say sanctuary, sir…"

"It was quite evident that you had come up the hill from Hitchin and were seemingly intent on this as your preferred destination."

"It was only for a moment that I was lost…"

Of course, I might be mistaken."

"Do you doubt what I say, sir?" said Sarah, hardening her precarious position.

"I most certainly do, madam. But it is of no importance to me, you are just as welcome, whether you are here by design or good fortune."

Alington smiled at her reassuringly. Sarah noted that when he smiled at women, whether at her or the retreating Hester, it was not the usual man's look of desire or judgment. More of a scholarly look of observance, an academic weighing up what was good and what was not so good.

"You see, I am aware of my reputation, Mrs Perks. Some think me as mad as old Lucas at Redcoats, the deranged hermit who people travel from afar to view, like some caged animal. I make no apologies for the goings on here, madam, for I am an unashamed advocate of free love. I embrace rather than shun all the taboos that such a mindset would usually entail. I see the attitudes of our Christian society to such a normal human function as copulation, as suffocating.

In my studied opinion, it is a repressive doctrine, that will only lead to physical and mental turmoil, not to mention severe sexual frustration. Which may even manifest itself into the odious assault of rape."

Still looking at her like some lecturer on human sciences, he paused for a moment before continuing.

"Putting my perceived eccentricities to one side, I am a harmless and well-educated man, a scholar of high degree and a fellow of Oxford. My point is, Mrs Perks, I am not a fool."

Sarah realised her excuse for being there was a pathetic, ill planned and poorly executed one. Once again, she knew that her recently chosen strategy of covering her track with lies, was proving inadequate and dangerous. The more she lied, the more she was disbelieved.

"I will be honest with you, sir."

"That would be most refreshing, madam."

"I seek someone who I believe shelters on your lands, and I simply seek your permission to visit her."

"Would I be correct in surmising that Old Jinnepen is this person you seek?"

'Yes. Yes, you would." answered Sarah, deciding that now the best policy to follow was one of honesty and not deceit. Silence.

He said nothing, thinking, still intrigued. But he needed to know more.

"Why?"

A pause.

"I cannot tell you."

This time a very, short pause before he spoke again.

"I would suggest that you can, Mrs Perks, but that you would rather not, is probably closer to the truth."

Alington stood and with the dignity of a thoughtful politician that had not been originally evident, he stood with his back to her, looking down at the fire.

"You intrigue me, madam." He turned round to face her, with his back to the fire. "Greatly."

"I don't see why I should, sir, what I ask is of no great importance."

"Is it not? So, if I denied your request and asked you to leave my house and lands, it would not trouble you unduly?"

Sarah's heart sank. This was something she had never considered possible, but she could not divulge her true reason. This curious and astute man would not be easily deceived, especially by another ill constructed lie. She fought hard to hide her desperation, she prayed that this inquisitive man could not see into her heart or read her mind.

"Mrs Perks, I do not receive visitors of your intelligence and beauty very often. Mistake me not, I adore, indeed, revel in the decadence and licentiousness my Romany friends bring to my table. On occasions though, I sincerely wish for more intellectual and sophisticated company, such as yours." Sarah did not comment. She had nothing to say.

"The old lady that you seek, does indeed dwell in a small cottage on my estate. She has done so for some time now, but she is frail and old. Because of her longevity, there cannot be many days left for her to bear witness to and when she passes, I fear much of the knowledge gathered in her wise old head will be extinguished with her. I understand that she wanders the woods during the day and only returns to her cottage of an evening. So, there is no point in your attempting to visit until she is returned. I am afraid you do not deceive me with your denial of the importance of your request. No one seeks Old Jinnepen for trivial or unimportant matters. Their reasons are always of a desperate nature and of the utmost significance, as I assume are yours."

Sarah sat still, waiting to see where this speech was leading. For now, she would admit nothing nor deny anything.

"If you will do me the honour of joining me for afternoon tea and provide me with the intellectual conversation that I crave, allowing me to court you for an hour or so, then in return I will grant your request and see that you are escorted safely to her cottage.

Sarah knew she had no option.

So, it had come to this, she would have to deal with this softly spoken parson without a parish and sign in his devil's book if she were to regain her special world. Her Faustian desire would be accomplished through the giving of her company. But what of this 'giving'? What of his desire to 'court' her, however briefly? Should she have cause for concern or did she worry unnecessarily? Was she reading too much into these seemingly innocent words or were they cleverly framed, and intimated darker obligations on her part? More importantly, was she truly contemplating playing the harlot to achieve her aims? Possibly. She felt so close that she would not stumble and fail now.

Having agreed to his proposal, a table was promptly set up in front of the fire. Logs were added, as the weather was turning rapidly like it often can in England and the air temperature had fallen noticeably. Windows, high up, revealed a blackening sky and a failing light, despite the sunset still some way off. Hester and another stunning girl, whose name was Selina, brought in plates, cups, saucers, cutlery, napkins, pots of tea and fruit cake, all set up as if for an indoor picnic. Candles were lit around the hall to accompany the lambent light issuing from the fire. Hester poured the tea and Selina cut and placed a slice of cake on each of their plates. As the two young women worked around them, Alington watched their every move, as if assessing their ability to serve. He gestured to them both when all was done that he was satisfied and, thanking them politely, dismissed them from the hall. As before with Hester, he watched them both go until they were out of sight.

The tea was duly sipped and drank, and the fresh fruit cake was savoured and eaten without a word spoken. Sarah would play her part but not with any false enthusiasm, just enough cordiality to be agreeable to this unusual man. If more were required from her, she would decide how to respond to that demand if, and when, it should arise. Eventually, Alington, content that enough cake and tea had been consumed, removed his napkin, folded it back on to the table, smiled as if satisfied with affairs and leant back in his chair.

"Mrs Perks?"

"Sir?"

"Have you ever had the good fortune to visit Paris?"

"Paris? No, I haven't had that pleasure."

"Then you should. Finances and opportunity permitting, I would strongly recommend that you do so. It is the intellectual and artistic centre of the human mind."

"Above London?"

"Very much so. Even as we sit here, many of our greatest writers, poets and thinkers gather there in Parisian coffee houses and evening soirees. They are soaking up the thoughts of those who may one day change the world for the better. Several years ago, and due to my wealth and academia, I was invited to attend a particular club in Paris that numbered men of vast intellect; men who readily expounded the most stimulating theories on life."

"I see."

"It is called the Club des Haschischins. It is possible that you have heard of it?"

"I'm afraid not."

"No? Well, that is hardly surprising; they are recently formed and their fame travels slowly. For the most part their numbers are made up of the social elite, mostly rich philanthropists, who look to highlight social injustices that befall the less fortunate."

"Such as gypsies?"

'Indeed, such as gypsies. Amongst them are the writers Alexandre Dumas and Victor Hugo, but more significantly the revered scientist Jacques-Joseph Moreau." Alington paused.

"I am unaware of this scientist, sir, although Dumas is a familiar name to me."

"Indeed. Well, Moreau is a most interesting character." Sarah's fears of what might be expected of her were slipping away. It increasingly seemed evident to her that this man was honest to his word. All that he required from her was a higher quality of conversation than he could receive from his Romany favourites. This was not as severe a bargain as she had originally thought she might have struck.

"He has led several studies on the positive and negative effects of drugs on the human mind. Particularly, an ancient drug called hashish."

Once again Alington paused in order that Sarah could comment.

"I have heard of this drug, yes, although I know little of its value."

"It is a remarkable drug, madam, made from the ground flowers, leaves and stems of the Cannabis plant."

"Similar to opium?" asked Sarah, looking to engage more civilly now that she felt herself safe. "My late husband was a chemist, as indeed is my brother in law. I hear of the names of many drugs, although I am not always aware of their individual properties and uses, especially those that never enter the pharmacy."

"Indeed, the influences can be quite similar in form to those contracted by the taking of opium. But it is thought by many that the attributes of hashish transcend all others. It also has the added advantage in that it does not kill."

As Alington continued to talk, Sarah was becoming increasingly surprised at his behaviour. A man whose reputation had meant she had set out to the hall, weighed down with unease and trepidation. But she was not finding him as she had originally thought. He was learned, well-mannered and genuinely content to pass the time with intellectual dialogue. She was not mistaken, however, by the nature of his stare upon her or the way he watched the two gypsy girls as they had moved about their work. But this was no more than a woman would expect from most men. The more she thought about her situation, the more relaxed she became. He perhaps was not the scandalous demon he had been portrayed.

"Mrs Perks?"

"Sir?"

"Do I bore you?"

"Not at all, sir."

"I think I talk too much and for too long, let us pause for some entertainment."

Sarah became concerned and Alington noticed.

"There is still time, she will not have returned yet. Believe me, this dimming light is caused by the dreariness of the day not the onset of night."

Alington turned from looking at her and his gaze transferred to the centre of the hall. Sarah also turned to look. She saw, standing on the empty hall floor, the young girls Hester and Selina. To one side of them, close by, were two men that she had not noticed before. One sat perched upon a chair and leant over a small guitar. The other man stood behind him, straight backed, violin and bow in hand. They were looking at Alington, as if waiting upon a signal. Sarah did not see the signal when it came, nor did she hear it, but it must have been given for the two girls suddenly stamped hard upon the wooden floor and the gypsy musicians began to play their evocative music.

The girls' dancing was hypnotic. Stepping, swirling first as individuals, taking turns to strut, before then coming together as if challenging each other. But challenging each other over what? She knew something of these people's dances from those that John would invite to perform in their yard. The old gypsy lady who visited once a month had also explained their roots and meanings. For Sarah's adored husband had been no staid man, neither priggish nor prudish. He was a man full of passion in the privacy of his home and even more so in their bedroom. He had loved the freedom that the gypsy culture proclaimed and lived by. If he had sat with her, watching this spectacle as she now did, he would not condemn it as deviant but would rather praise it for its true worth. A performance that had no time for lies, the suppression of heartfelt feelings or social pretence.

Many dances contained ancient stories that were told with wild, vivid movement rather than the dulled spoken word. Tales of betrayal, warning, adultery, tales of love professed, love requited and unrequited. They contained movement and gestures that could shock. There was a physical 'coming together' in ways that would seem inappropriate to many.

But this was an honest portrayal of desire and intent, rather than one suffocated by sophistication and acceptability.

The dance exploding before Sarah was one such passionate piece. They glided past each other, then up to each other, tempting, smiling, encouraging, their faces so close to each other, lips relaxed apart, and breathing heavily from their exertions. They almost touched, entwined, kissed, forever daring each other to go further, but never doing so. They were working around their musicians whose strings had originally set the tone but now moved indiscernibly from leading the performance to following it. Skirt hems were lifted and swung from side to side, teasingly, revealing ankle and leg before being dropped once more. She found herself being drawn in and seduced by its eroticism. She could not take her eyes from them even if she had wanted to, and she did not want to. She was content. With the heat of the fire and the visual energy of the ritual playing out before her, she felt a strange comfort that was not unlike that experienced on exiting from a pleasurable dream. But she was not dreaming. Not this time.

The dance climbed and climbed to a great crescendo in sound and vision before eventually reaching its climatic end. Beside her she could hear Alington applauding, crying out the traditional 'Bravo!' Then she was aware of another voice shouting similar praises and the sound of another pair of hands just as enthusiastic as Alington's in their clapping. She looked around, but no one else was there. It was her voice, her hands, her cheers.

She looked up, towards the gallery. A face looked down at her, watching her as she watched the others. A face not unfamiliar. Then she felt Alington's hand upon her arm, leading her gently back to her chair.

She sat, exhilarated but still. In her mind she was dancing as they had, with the same gay abandon. But as her energy simmered, she could see that the dancers had gone. The musicians too had disappeared as mysteriously as they had been conjured. The face that had looked down at her from the gallery high above, had also vanished. She was once again alone with Alington. He sat in his chair opposite, looking at her. His face, just as before, scholarly. His brow furrowed only by his desire for intellectual understanding.

"Their dances are unique, with some movement directions of my own. The lifting and dropping of the skirts, I saw in the flamenco of Andalusia and the Cancan halls of Paris. It is a fair fusion, I think."

Sarah said nothing but was aware that she was smiling. Almost grinning.

"Mrs Perks? How do you feel?"

She heard herself answer. It was her voice but not her intent, she felt detached from it, as her mind and logic rallied to help her to explain. She looked at Alington, who was not rushing her, waiting, happy for her to come to realise in her own time.

"Sir," asked her voice, "Have you drugged me, sir?"

"Yes, madam, I cannot lie to you, I have indeed. But you must not worry, for I mean you no harm, and the drug that takes hold of you will not harm you either."

"You have taken a liberty, sir, you have rendered me helpless. Why should I not suspect that you mean to harm me in some way?"

"Because harming you, madam, is the last thing I would want. You will find you are not helpless.

You are quite able to stand, able to walk out of the door and leave if you so wish. What is curtailed a little is your willingness to do these things, not the ability to accomplish them. But that will change and lessen and within the next couple of hours, you will regain all your faculties completely. I promise."

He did not move towards her, remaining settled into his chair. His manner that of a doctor giving wise counsel, rather than that of a man who had captured her for purposes diabolical.

"Please, see this as an experiment, an experiment that will satisfy me, whatever its outcome and at the same time might aid you greatly in that which you seek. I have drugged you, yes, but it is a measured amount you have eaten and drunk, just enough to assist and not hinder. Yet, I swear you will not be harmed in any way."

Sarah felt a little concerned at his words, even more so regarding herself as she was aware that she still grinned.

"To me the nature of your visit to see Old Jinnepen is obvious. As I have said before, people do not seek out the old woman for triviality or novelty. Her reputation is not that of a fortune teller, a charlatan that tells you what colour your lover's hair will be, but something much more inexplicable in nature. I do not know if her abilities can transcend this world as they say, but I know some believe that they do. These are desperate people who have exhausted all other routes and see her as their last port of call before hopelessness overwhelms them, sending them mad or into an untimely grave.

You are a respectable woman, madam, who would not risk soiling her reputation for anything else but the ultimate. Mankind is and always has been obsessed with three questions: Who are we, why are we here and what lies beyond. You seek the third, I suspect, possibly regarding your late husband. I do not know and I do not need to know."

He paused.

"The French scientist, Moreau, whom I told you of earlier, has suggested that the hashish that circulates within you now, may enhance your experience at a seance."

A séance was something that Sarah had considered before dismissing such a notion as foolish. It was odd to hear such words coming from a man whose opinions seemed to be based on scientific proof rather than superstition.

"In a few moments, I will honour my promise to you and see that you are escorted to Old Jinnepen's cottage safely. All I ask is that you return here when you are done and inform me whether your quest was successful or not. I do not need to know the question you ask, nor the answer given, just the success or failure of your experience. I wish to know whether the drug works as is suggested. As I have said, it is on my part, an experiment."

Sarah could hear everything he said, and she understood.

"That is all?"

"That is all, madam."

Carefully, slowly, as if her bones were tired, she leant forward in her chair.

"I have your solemn promise?"

"Yes, you do, as a gentleman or a madman, accept whichever you will."

They sat for several minutes more. Sarah gazing into the flames, picturing all her past and present and Alington, patiently waiting for her answer. It was what it was, Sarah concluded. It was an easy price to pay, simply relaying to him the success or failure of her encounter. Her secret would remain safe. More importantly, if this drowse-inducing drug helped her at her meeting with the old lady, then she would be forever grateful to Alington, Moreau and the grounded leaves of the cannabis plant. In the far reaches of her mind, she heard the rumble of approaching thunder. Looking up at one of the high hall windows, she waited for the next tell-tale flash of heavenly light and when it eventually came, she counted the seconds. She reached sixteen before the warning sound rumbled once again. Time enough she thought. If the cottage were near enough as Alington had inferred, there would be time enough to meet and return before the rains fell. Placing her hands on the table in front of her, she stood steadily, without too much effort and gave Alington his answer.

"It is agreed."

"Good. Thank you, madam. Let us hope we are both happy with the outcome."

"Is it time to go?"

"As good as."

She turned and cautiously walked towards the door. A door that in her dream had seemed to grow to colossal size, on her arrival earlier had been observed as being of normal size and now seemed quite distant. Her walking was not an arduous experience, just time consuming, as if she were treading water in some deep space.

From behind her she heard Alington's voice, as he followed her across the hall to the door.

"I will send someone with you, to support you in case you should need it, but you should be fine. It is not too far to the cottage and if you take your time, it will cause you no great effort."

A hand reached in front of her, turned the handle on the door and opened it for her. She stepped out on to the doorstep and looked ahead.

"When you return, madam, I will see that you are taken home by carriage. With good fortune, the rains will hold off until your return."

"Yes..." answered Sarah, still reconciling herself to the

surreal state she found herself in, elation and apprehension mixed confusingly together.

"The path straight ahead of you will bring you to the ancient lady's abode."

Sarah felt a supporting hand under her elbow as she stepped down and began her walk along the path indicated. As she walked through the woods, she found herself concluding that there might be much in what Alington had said about the properties she was experiencing. Her sense of euphoria resembled almost identically the rapturous feeling she encountered when meeting John at the edge of the fields. The ecstasy of John's touch before all went wrong and before her wickedness had taken hold. Watching the young women dancing, closing in on each other, she had wanted them to touch. She could sense what they would gain from each other if they had and wanted them to sense it too. She had always felt it with John and as Alington's hand had guided her, she had felt it. The hand that supported her now as she walked along transmitted similar vibes of sensuality. Her thoughts were wild, unrelenting, heightening her craving to be touched. To be loved.

There was a slight bend in the path and as they rounded it, her thoughts turned to the identity of her escort, the person who Alington had nominated to see her safely to the cottage. The blood within her that had been flowing fast and hot, now slowed and chilled. Her heart found no comfort in her thoughts of realisation and her mind threw away its optimism and took upon itself the coldness of warranted fear.

She stopped.

Waited.

Then she turned to face whom she thought it would be. Whom she knew it would be. And it was.

"Keep going, Mrs Perks," he sleered, "we're almost at the old hag's cottage."

She put up no resistance as Lazzy Smith took her arm and encouraged her to continue walking. She had been resolved to sign a deal with the devil for what she wanted, but instead had come to think of Alington as a kindly benefactor. Perhaps Lazzy Smith was the devil and Alington was God. Was her soul being vied for, between these two great powers. It was difficult to distinguish whether her thoughts were the product of a troubled mind or the rantings of induced hallucination. She was fighting to keep her thinking on level ground, as a small, rustic cottage came into sight.

"Nearly theres, Mrs Perks," came Lazzy's voice from behind her, "Although, I'm a thinking, most times than not, she has smoke a-coming from the chimney."

There was no smoke coming from the chimney. Did that mean the old woman was still wandering the woods and yet to return.

"Are we too soon?"

"No. Mores like she ain't got around to it yet. She's old as the earth and twice as hard. She'll be in there, I reckons… see? I can sees a candle lit at the window."

There was, as Lazzy said, a small pin prick of light in the lower corner of the window, put there by wisemen as if to guide those forsaken to its shelter. A stable where all would be answered. They got closer and the candle grew to its recognisable shape. Once they reached the door, he leant past her rudely and knocked. No answer. He knocked again.

"Deaf as well, damn the hag!"

Sarah was becoming worried. The air, though still quite humid and desperate to be broken by storm, had awakened her senses a little. She stepped forward and turned the door handle and pushed. The door was unlocked and it gently swung a few inches open.

"Oi! You has a visitor!" Lazzy shouted from behind her.

He turned Sarah roughly to face him.

"Alington says I'm not to go in with you, so's I won't. But be aware, Mrs Perks, that I'm not one for standing out here forever. You be quicks about your business or I shall drags you out, do you hear me?"

Sarah refused to answer. The man that had once raised carnal longings within her, excited cravings in her mind and body for the most unholy of attentions, now instilled merely contempt.

He shook her hard by grabbing both arms at her side.

"Does you hear me?!"

The harder he shook her the more she wanted him to. As if liquid common sense had been poured in at the top of her head and his shaking of her would unintentionally ensure it filled her from top to toe.

"I says, did you hear me!?"

Again, she did not answer and with his anger spilling over, he would wait no longer. Pulling her into him he kissed her deep and violently, hard, numbingly hard upon the lips. Forcing her mouth apart with his searching, probing tongue; snake-like, serpent-like, devil-like with no passion. There was no reasoning, no love, no real desire, just the bullying venom of a man denied. His intention was only to cause hurt and shame. She did not respond and he felt her coldness, her utter contempt. Hate, unbridled hate. For she knew now that she hated him as much as she loved John and she wanted Lazzy to know. Finally, he stopped his vicious, unfeeling assault and released her. His purpose was unfulfilled, for he saw and felt her undaunted and knew she was impervious to his spite and malice. Looking into her eyes, he could now see the loathing that he had sensed and it unnerved him.

"In! Go in and you be quick about it!"

He threw her against the unlocked door and it opened wider as she stumbled in, falling to her knees. The door slammed shut behind her and the draught from the slamming almost put out the solitary candle. But it survived, bending first beneath the rush of air, then flickering before regaining its destructive strength and burning as before.

She stood up, her eyes adjusting to the dimness and looked around, but saw no one.

"Hello?"

She let her eyes drift from wall to wall, expecting any minute to see the old lady asleep in a chair.

"Is there anyone here?"

But no one spoke and there was no one to be seen.

"Please? Please be here…"

As her words faded on her lips, dampened by her disappointment and just as she began to fear the worst, the room was lit violently in a steel blue! Immediately, deafening thunder rolled and cracked directly above. Loud, with an angry, giant grumbling as if the sky demon had been disturbed untimely from its sleep.

In that moment, a curtain had been revealed on the far side of the room. A single curtain on a wooden rail, drawn closed as if protecting an unseen room. A bedroom.

Sarah moved cautiously towards it.

"I apologise for disturbing you…"

She now stood directly by the curtain but with still no response to her calling out from the other side. Reaching nervously forward she stretched out to pull back the curtain, taking and gently pulling it along its rail until it gaped as wide as it would. She could now peer into the tiny space, but little was revealed in the darkness of the windowless room. She took the candle from the windowsill behind her but before she could even turn round, another all-encompassing flash of blue scorched the room from floor to ceiling and from corner to corner, with nothing escaping its exposing brilliance! Simultaneously, thunder roared, as if within the cottage itself and surely heralding the advent of a tumultuous downpour. Outside, her impatient escort thumped hard upon the door demanding more haste.

"Quickly! Be about it, woman!"

This last flash had revealed to Sarah a bed against the far wall and maybe the outline of a person in it. If there was someone there, Sarah pondered, then it was a person with the tiniest of frames. She moved in closer. There she was, the old woman who held the keys to the secret ways, laying peacefully in her bed, fast asleep. She slept, seemingly oblivious to both the storm that was raging outside and the fact that she was destined to be Sarah's saviour, her angel of mercy. The light from the candle flame danced across the old woman's face and even though her skin was leathered, and stood wrinkle upon wrinkle, with a mass of brown aging blotches ingrained and spread plague-like, Sarah thought she recognised her.

She moved even closer and though it had been sometime since she had last seen her, Sarah knew it to be the old gypsy woman who had for years visited the Perks yard in Bancroft. Once a month she had come and her visit had always been looked forward to by all, save perhaps James, who never had time or inclination for idle chatter. She had been making her visits long before Sarah had married, long before John had been born and even before Sarah senior had married into the family. She had no name that they knew but all referred to her simply as the old gypsy lady.

All believed her to have passed on, yet, here she was. The old gypsy lady and Old Jinnepen were one and the same.

Sarah suddenly remembered her purpose and that time was at a premium. She had to wake her, but the old woman slept deeply, so deeply that her body hardly stirred with her breathing… hardly stirred at all…

Sarah stood back a little and observed her in more detail. Her face was towards Sarah and her right arm hung down from the bed, fingers almost touching the floor. Sarah placed the candle on the ground close by and took the old lady's dangling hand into hers. It was cold. Un-responding to Sarah's touch. The candle highlighted the hand's coat of lifeless grey; an unmistakable result of blood no longer pumping through now stagnant veins.

She carefully lowered the hand back down and it swung gently for a moment by the side of the bed until coming to a final halt. Sarah looked at the wizened old face that had once cracked and stretched with laughter, the eyes that had reacted accommodatingly to everyone's chatter and gossip. The thin grey-blue lips that had told so many stories and yarns and maybe, just maybe, had answered questions that no one else could ever know the answers to. She might have known where to find the key that Sarah sought.

But Sarah knew that she would now never know.

All had been for nothing, her last great hope had shattered and vanished with the passing of Old Jinnepen and there was nothing she could do about it. In the hollowness of her despair, Sarah contemplated whether to cry or scream. As she did so, the heavens above opened-up at the behest of the storm cloud's fury, desperate to vomit, for they were bloated with great quantities of disposable water. With one last crack of thunder and one last stark streak of lightening, that lit up and shocked the universe in perfect unison, a great torrent fell upon the land and drenched all those below, so completely, that the human tears and rain that gathered there merged into one great deluge.

There was no smoke coming from the chimney

Chapter Twelve

Her eyes were fixed upon the ceiling as the downpour crashed on to the roof of the cottage. The constant thud reminiscent of standing under some great waterfall rather than an English storm. As she tried hard to resign herself to Old Jinnepen's death, the door flung open wide and her escort's dark and menacing figure stood in the doorway, silhouetted by a splash of lightening; a stance not unlike a dramatic pose of villainy from a theatrical melodrama. He stepped inside, drenched and shut the door behind him, the closing making small difference to the storm's volume.

He walked over to where she stood, glared at her and then turned his attention to the old lady.

"Dead?" he snapped looking back at her.

"Yes."

He looked again at the silent woman. His profile revealed his stank hair soaked and flattened, his soaking jacket collar up and stuck against the nape of his neck and rain dripping from his forehead and nose. He stared at the old lady for a moment then returned his gaze to Sarah.

"Well, we ain't venturing out too soon, I'm a-thinking. We'll have to sits it out in here."

"I'm supposed to return to the house."

Lazzy ignored her and moved towards the small table in the centre of the room. He wrung out his sopping cap before flinging it down and then proceeded to remove his clinging jacket."

"I promised the Reverend Alington I would return."

He didn't speak as he threw his jacket to join his cap upon the table.

"He'll be expecting me."

Without looking back at her, he walked to the closed door and opened it wide, shouting above the roar of the rain.

"If you want to goes, then I suggest that you does!!"

Sarah could see the storm outside raging. The deluge was falling with such ferocity upon a ground so hardened by months of baking sun, that each raindrop bounced fully one foot back into the air before dissipating. He waited, she did not move and so he slammed the door shut.

"I thought not."

He moved back to the table which housed just two chairs.

"Best we sits this out, I'm a-thinking."

He pulled a chair out and sat on it, wiping his forehead with the sleeve of his woollen shirt, a shirt sleeve that now dripped and sagged from his arm as if three sizes too large. He sat facing her, his legs wide apart, his hands clasping the top of his knees, fingers splayed. The hands and fingers that she had once looked to welcome. But not now. Now she shuddered at her stupidity.

He looked at her, daring her to speak. No sleer accompanied

his grin this time, just contempt and scorn for a woman that he had grown to hate.

"This storm ain't to be stoppin' too soon, lady."

It was an unfortunate but undeniable fact.

"You can sit upon my lap if you wish?" With this, the sleer returned and dug deep into her guilt.

Sarah knew she was in danger from this unpredictable man and would need to tread carefully, give him no added reason to anger more. She made a slow, nonchalant move towards the other chair, but he was ahead of her. Standing up quickly, he grabbed the rickety chair from under the table and with sudden fury he raised it up then smashed it down upon the floor. The chair shattered into several pieces, scattering around the room as if looking for somewhere to hide. Without a word he returned to his seat, resumed his position and stared her boastfully in the eye. Waiting.

"As I says," he eventually sleered, "you can be sitting on my lap, if you cares to."

Sarah did not answer, her silence backed by the rain. He did not expect her to answer and so the pair stood and sat as they were, looking at each other for several minutes, both planning ahead, neither speaking a word.

A particularly aggressive flash of lightening ignited the room and held their stand-off tableau in its hands for longer than normal. She saw him sitting like some Canute, waiting for his wishes to be granted and he saw her like some ridiculous heroine, stoic and statue-still, but helpless in his prison. She was his captive, his prize, to do with as he saw fit.

"You despise me now, Mrs Perks, ain't that true?"

She did not reply.

"But you didn't always lady, did you? I knows that and you knows that."

She wanted to scream at him, tell him how vile she thought him to be, but could not risk re-kindling his rage. So, she did not answer. Their stillness and silence contrasted with the violence and deafening concert playing outside. He waited so long to speak, that when he finally did, Sarah had almost forgotten what it was he now referred to.

"We both knows that, Mrs Perks."

He waited to see if she would respond, not that he needed her to. He knew what he said was the irrefutable truth and her silence confirmed that truth.

"I can feel your hate, lady. I'm a-wondering if it's a-burning you just as hot as it burns at me?"

He took his hands from his knees, laying one loosely across his leg the other he placed on the table next to him, as if relaxing. She stood before him, defiant, but like some mute conquest.

"It doesn't matter none, 'cause I'm likewise hating you the same. Shall I tells you why I'm a hating you? Shall I?"

Sarah refused to be drawn, refused to acknowledge him in any way. That would only give his pathetic court of trial credibility that it did not deserve.

"It's on accounts that you looks down at me. Not like you folks always looks down at us gypsies, that's much different. I'm used to that, we all is. No, you looks down at me 'cause of the man I am. Now, I'm a-thinking, why would that be so? What's she a-thinking that makes me someone to look so down upon? I never done nothing to her, nothing that she didn't want me to do, anyhows," he took another opportunity to sleer.

"I think I now knows what it is. You thinks I'm not good enough to be your man. You thinks you can do better than Lazarus Smith. But I tells you, Mrs Perks, I'm as good a man as any around and plenty good enough for the likes of you."

Sarah could feel the need to defend herself welling up inside, screaming to be voiced and to put this repulsive man in his place. But she stayed frozen, looking through him rather than at him.

"Here's a truth, Mrs Perks. For all your fine clothes, fine speaking and fine airs and graces, you're just the same as any woman in the bed. When you strips it all away lady, you're nothing special." Looking to test her patience and rile her more, he suddenly remembered the early death of her husband and so quickly added "Nor was your man."

Sarah eyes glared wide as she fumed inside, a wildness soared through her that matched the savagery of the raging storm.

"A weak man, he was, Mrs Perks, I tells yer, and that's why he died so young. No goodness comes from having yourself a weak man…"

Lazzy did not manage to finish his sentence before Sarah's mounting temper finally took her over the edge and her tongue lashed out.

"No! You are wrong! Damn you, you are so wrong!!"

The fierceness of her outcry startled Lazzy and shocked Sarah. He did not expect, nor thought possible, such an outburst from this haughty little woman. For her part, Sarah had no idea that such venom lay within her or that such anger could manifest itself so quickly, forcing itself to the surface. It was as if something inside her subconscious had been waiting for just such a moment to explode. An opportunity when everything she had thought regarding John, could finally be spoken. Out in the open where she would hear them and not be able to hide from hearing them. Everything that, until then, had found no place upon her lips. She was about to defend herself, the man that was so precious to her and more importantly, her special world. "You cannot even begin to understand what kind of man he was! He was kind, he was loving, he was passionate, he was considerate; a man of intellect and a man of great reasoning!"

As she ranted, however eloquently, it was not lost on herself that she was speaking of John in the past tense. She had never thought of him so in her mind. Yet, here she was talking of him as if he were no more, as if he no longer lived. "The heights he attained you could not even see for looking up! He loved! And his love brought joy and ecstasy. He was not a brute, an animal that pawed… and clawed and… smothered! You only know the lust and desire of an ignorant beast! Worse! At least animals can show affection and at times true tenderness. I do the animal world a grave disservice! An injustice! For you, Mister Smith, are not even worthy of being compared to an animal!"

It was Lazzy's turn to feel anger growing within. But his anger, unlike Sarah's, was an anger that he knew well. It was no surprise to him that it existed. It was an anger that had caused many a man to shudder and think to avoid him or even run. It was an anger that would quickly put an end to this woman's rantings, quell her impudent spirit and put her back in chains. But Sarah had not finished, her torment unleashed was now being carried along on a tide, rushing to be heard.

"He was strong! He had a strength that you could not possibly understand. He was never weak!"

She was defending a man that she now perceived to be gone. Still the realisation of this escaped her.

Lazzy moved towards her, resorting to his life-long tactic of bullying. Standing in front of her, letting his physical presence and strength threaten and intimidate. Quieten her.

Frighten her.

"Then tells me, why does he be dying when so young?" he snarled, gloating.

She could smell the stench of his odour and sweat, dampened by the rain. His breath, hot, sickly, poured onto her as he opened his mouth again and bellowed into her face, repeating...

"If he was so strong, lady, why does he die so young!? Tells me that if you can?!"

Her eyes widened, her mind egged on by the pain caused by her stress, she felt her common sense at last shouting to be heard and her special world struggling to survive. Yet, instead of giving ground and finally facing the truth, she reverted once more to defend her madness.

"But he didn't die! He isn't dead!"

There was a silence that stunned Lazzy and he gaped disbelievingly.

"That's right, he isn't dead. He is such a man of strength... that he has defied everything and everyone and returned to me. At night, he sleeps with me by the fields. No one sees us, but we are there. That's right, you heard me, he isn't dead!"

Lazzy had been stopped in his tracks, thrown by Sarah's deranged proclamation. He looked into her eyes and saw a lunacy he had never seen before in anyone's eyes, man, woman nor beast...

"You talk madness, lady. Why do you say such cracked things? I knows him to be dead and you knows him to be dead!"

His words hit Sarah like a hammer, full in the face, unsparingly.

"Not only dead but lying buried and rotting in your great St. Mary's Church!"

Sarah now likewise stopped in her tracks.

"He's no more alive, than I am dead, lady."

His simple words of spite that were meant to hurt and mock, had a much more profound effect on her. Unintentionally, his simple statement of truth would begin the release and recovery that her mind had so craved. A recovery that she had prevented herself from accepting, by refusing to admit it was needed.

"You talk madness! Madder words than even she over there ever talked!" he shouted, pointing at the lifeless old lady behind her. "I heard her say some rum things, mind, but she never says to anyone that she knows how to cheat the grim reaper."

"You're saying…?" she murmured, her voice broken, her defence in ruins.

"I'm saying, dead is dead, that's what I'm saying! You divvy gadji!"

He looked at her to see if her expression would change because of his cruel bluntness. Yet, all he saw was a woman in shock, trying desperately to come to terms with some great mystery that was unravelling before her eyes. As if the answer to this great mystery had always been there, never hidden from her, in fact, shouting out to be heard. But she had not heard it because she did not want to hear it.

"I did not want him to leave… I wanted his love for me to be so strong, stronger than death itself. But there isn't such a thing, is there?"

Sarah whispered her words, her strength and resolve crumbling as she spoke them. As if she was dying and only her shadow remained. She heard her words, but who was she talking to? They were not directed at Lazzy, for in that moment he was not there. They were being spoken into the air so that she could hear them for herself.

"He's dead, isn't he?" she whimpered.

He said nothing.

"He is, isn't he…?"

Lazzy knew Alington had drugged her. Was this some effect lingering on, causing her to act so strangely, staring into some dark void?

"Listen, mad lady, dead is dead! No one comes back. Aren't I named Lazarus? Aren't I? And if I'm thinking my chances is slim to none, what be the chances of your scrawny man, eh? Eh?!"

A huge grin clouded his gnarled face, greatly satisfied with his own humour and now joyful in Sarah's fall from superiority. Having subdued and tamed her, he was determined not to let go. He would have total revenge now as she wavered, helpless, drowning in self-pity.

"What is to become of me…I believed he had returned... I made myself believe…"

"Enough, mad lady!"

"I have been so foolish, have I not… have I not been so foolish…?"

"I said, enough!"

"I have caused my own torment…"

As her voice and wits began to forsake her, as her past doings began to taunt her, just as those of Lady Macbeth's had haunted her, she broke completely and sobbed at what she now knew to be the truth. Her head dropped but was immediately lifted again by Lazzy. Grabbing her by the jaw and looking into her ghostly eyes, he slapped her hard across the face. The blow hurt, stung, shocked Sarah back into the present.

She stared at him in anger and disbelief. He saw her stare as an act of disobedience and, raising his hand, he struck her hard again.

"I'll shows you the strength of a man, a man who's alive,

lady!"

Having slapped her, drawing blood to her lip, he let her go and as she stumbled back in her shock, he turned his back on her, unbuttoning his waistcoat as he did.

"Mad lady, who thinks mad things…who would lie with a dead man…"

He threw his waistcoat to one side and as he slipped his braces from his shoulders, the chair that Sarah had picked up, smashed down upon the back of his head. The force sent him sprawling forward on to the floor.

In an instant, Sarah was at the door and out into the heart of the storm. She ran along the path, a path now flooded and puddled by constant rains. Where was she going? She would run back to the hall, seek refuge there and tell Alington what had taken place. He would be sympathetic. He would protect her, wouldn't he? Sarah had not travelled far, yards only, before her progress slackened rapidly, her running quickly being reduced to a stagger.

The water in most places was now two or three inches deep, and still filling. Her skirts dragged, collecting brown muddied rainwater as she willed herself on. Ahead, the path had all but disappeared and was now swamped by a river of squelching sludge. She tried to step quicker in her frantic determination to get further away from the cottage and, in doing so, she stumbled, turned her ankle, forcing her to fall painfully to her knees. Her hands had disappeared completely as she had stretched out on the ground to protect and support herself. She knelt there, her knees submerged and sinking and there, in that position of submission, her mind and body admitted defeat.

She could not halt the whimpers of self-pity that stumbled from her throat, as she looked down at the pool of water in front of her. The blazing skies above reflected repeatedly upon the surface of the puddle and in this muddied mirror, she saw her face distorted, manic, laughing at her own downfall. Unable to support herself, her arms gave way and she fell forward into the shallow water. Her face half in, her nostrils flooded, her mouth searching for air. Absurdly, she recalled the night in the fields where she had cried herself to sleep, when thinking him gone from her. 'Thinking him gone!' she thought, mocking herself, 'When in truth, he had never been there in the first place!'

A hand grabbed the neck of her dress and turned her over in the quagmire, so she now lay face up in the swamp of sludge. She spluttered and on opening her mud-caked eyes she saw it was him, standing above her, his face crazed. He reached down and ripped at the top of her dress, where earlier she had so neatly and foolishly parted the lace and undone the top buttons.

"Tell me, Mrs Perks, how's that dog of yours? Not dancing as much, I'm guessing!"

Soaked, with the rain pouring from his body on to hers as if he were a conduit, he ripped at the flies of his trousers, unable to undo them by hand and then dropped to his knees upon the ground. Leaning on to her, he lifted her weighty, drenched skirts, pushing them up her body and exposing her nakedness to the elements. He then pushed his rough hand between her legs.

"This may not be to your liking, Mrs Perks!" he screamed at her above the sound of the torrent, "But it is very much to mine!"

As he fell forward on to her, thinking to complete her humiliation, he was lifted into the sky as if winched up to the clouds by God himself. With shock and horror etched upon his disbelieving face, she witnessed him fly away from her, his head smashing in mid-air against a sturdy branch and then his body crashing against a great, dripping oak tree. Making no sound that was audible, with his head limp upon his neck, she watched him slither down the trunk, lifelessly, before coming to rest against its sodden base.

Sarah thought Alington or his men had come to her rescue, come out to see what had kept her so long. Through the mist of her waterlogged eyes, a face appeared looking down at her, a face she instantly recognised, but now in unfamiliar setting, seemingly painted on the storm clouds as a heavenly portrait. It was the giant and familiar face of her soft-spoken protector.

James bent down without a word and lifted her up as if she were a doll, then carried her through the unrelenting rain to the little cottage. Pushing the door open with his foot, he carried her in and laid her down gently in front of the unlit fire. Going back to the doorway he looked out into the night, studying the storm. It was not going to end any time soon, neither would any sane man be venturing out until it did. They would hold fast for now, he thought. He looked towards the side of the path where he had thrown Lazzy and, peering through the blanket of rain, he glimpsed the body against the tree, unmoving. There would be a price to pay, he knew, but he would worry about that some other time. He remembered, however, that when he had dragged Lazzy from Sarah, he had no jacket, which was odd, considering such weather. Looking back into the room, he noticed the cap and jacket on the table and the waistcoat on the floor. Picking them up, he went back out into the tempest to deposit these items by their silent owner. Returning to the cottage, he glanced out once more and then, satisfied, closed the door.

Sarah watched this huge man who had saved her from her humiliation. He was unaware of her gaze and intent on making their stay as comfortable as possible.

Seeing the candle still burning upon the floor by the bed, he bent to pick it up and, noticing the old lady's hand hanging limp and helpless, he carefully, tenderly, lifted it up. Pulling back her blanket he placed her hand upon her chest. With the blanket restored to just below her chin, he stood for a moment and studied her face. A face he knew so well from her visits to the yard. The old gypsy woman who, as far back as he could remember, had bided her time within the Perks' family yard. Moving away, he searched the single cupboard for matches, found some and lit the fire. As it spat and crackled into life, he ripped the curtain that acted as a door to the bedroom from its rail and draped it over the now shivering Sarah. Content that all that could be done had been done, he sat on the floor with his back to the wall alongside the fireplace. He sat there and she laid there, both looking into the flames, both grateful for the growing warmth, both in deep thought.

Minutes passed.

Finally, still looking deep into the friendly fire, Sarah spoke. "James?"

James looked at her.

"I have been most foolish."

He continued to look at her but still said nothing. If she wanted to talk, James thought, that would be a good thing. It was time she talked, and he would listen. He was a good listener and he would happily be the sponge that soaked up all her demons.

"So foolish that I cannot think it possible of myself, but it's true."

Then, with the fire's generous heat drying her damp clothes and liberating her soul to speak, she did. And he listened.

She told him everything because he was there, but in truth she was telling herself. Speaking out loud all her longings for John, her refusal to let him die, her mind's creation of their special world and all the torment it had caused her. Striving to keep the two worlds separate, fearing to lose the special one that did not exist, if anyone should learn of what she thought. And that was the whole point. Somewhere inside, part of her knew it all to be nought but a lie. Deep down, she knew that if she ever spoke out loud, the world that she had created to enable John's return would shatter, disintegrate like some great glasshouse. Yet, it was not something that could ever be destroyed by others. Only she had the power to destroy it, because only she believed it existed. While she did not speak its name out loud, she would never realise the absurdity of what she did and she would continue to believe in its existence. She knew in the depths of her buried and banished common sense, that the spoken word would force her to confront her false paradise, then reason would rise within her like Lazarus of Bethany and she would be well again.

How foolish. How sad.

Surrounded by beautiful relations, steadfast friends and well-wishers, it had taken the evil doings of Lazzy Smith to bring her violently to her senses. How tragically it might have all ended if James had not happened upon them.

"Is he dead?"

"Yes, Miss Sarah, I believe him to be."

Her story told, her heart relieved of all its pain and despite her impoverished surroundings, for the first time since John's passing, she felt at peace. The fire comforted and warmed the body, but only truth can calm the soul.

Sarah looked at James. The man who was sixty-three'ish looked older than she remembered. The features and strength that belied his years, looked aged now and tired. The exertions and elements of the day, no doubt.

"Thank you, James. I am most grateful."

"It's good to be talking, miss."

James smiled at her with a beautiful smile that she had never seen before. The old man's face lit up, as if her story had relieved some heavy burden in his own heart.

"How is it that you were here?"

"Good fortune, miss."

He sat thinking, she watched him think as if he were thinking on whether to say more. He did not decide one way or the other but found himself doing so anyhow.

"I think's it's promises that can cause consternation, promises made in the heat of the moment, miss. When emotion spurs them to be made, rather than good reason."

He paused. She was content to wait.

"I knew not of my birth, Miss Sarah, as you know, but I knew of the love and care I received from Edward Perks as I was growing up. I cannot remember me ever being told so, I cannot recall a moment, but I grew up assuming I had been left at the foot of the door by some unknown persons. Abandoned for reasons unknown. I was content with that, for my wants were few and my pleasures countable on one hand. It was Edward's father, Harry, that had found me. I did not know him well, him dying when I was young, but I was close to Edward and a bond grew between us, long before he married your mother in law. When he was taken ill, he called me to him, for him thinking he was close to dying, he thought there was something I should know. Something that his father had thought best kept from me, but him thinking I deserved to know."

For a moment James did not speak. His mind was travelling back to that day, sitting by Edward's bed, ill at ease, for he recognised that his old friend's time was coming to a close and he was sorry for it.

"I had not been found as I previously thought. Old Harry had been out on his wagon near Charlton pond. It was late of an evening and a day of rain, not as heavy and vicious as this, but drab and dreary none the less. Approaching the pond, he sees another wagon, a vardo. Nearby a couple were kneeling by the water's edge and a young girl stood yards back from them, watching what they did. They sees Harry approaching and quickly boards their vardo, calling that the young girl board as well. But she was looking at the water, as if transfixed and as Harry drew nearer, the vardo moved away, the girl still standing there. Then she turns to look at Harry, tears in her eyes and her face full of confusion. As Harry halted, the girl turned and ran after the vardo and they were gone. He watched the gypsies disappear out towards Offley. Then his eyes goes to the water's edge, where they had all been so concerned and occupied. There was a small bundle just below the water's surface. On instinct, Harry steps in and picks it out. Unwrapping the small bundle of cloth, he finds a baby, just hours born, wet from its soaking but very much alive."

"It was you."

"Yes, miss, it was."

"James…" Sarah was not sure what to say, but it mattered not because James looked to continue. He had started the telling and now he would finish.

"A couple of years later, a young gypsy girl turns up at the yard to see Harry. He recognises her despite the passing of time. It was the young girl that he had seen at the pond, she had come to thank him and inform him of matters. She had been taken against her will, she said, and that had resulted in her falling pregnant. Her parents' honour would not let her keep the child and they were in the midst of disposing of it when Harry happens along. She could not take the baby back, but it was agreed between them that Harry's family would take care of it and raise it and the young girl could visit once a month, on the pretence of selling products. She asked that I should not be told who I was, nor what had happened."

James reached over to a battered basket, with a few small logs in, and placed one on the fire. They watched it take and become wrapped in eager flames, hungry for more food. "That was twenty-six years past, miss."
Another moment.

"When he told me, I was gripped with hate for her. I felt that she had been wicked in agreeing to me being drowned and again by agreeing that I would be brought up by strangers. I promised myself I would not speak to her, nor remain in her company whenever she visited from that day on. I now knew her visit were but a pretence to see me and watch me grow, so I did everything in my power to deny her that satisfaction. I always found excuses not to remain in the yard when she was there. I never let her know that I knew who she was, ever."

His thoughts of regret caused him to pause. Sarah, moved by his story, lay patiently to see if he would say more. "There you have it, Miss Sarah. A great regret and something that will never leave me. All because of a promise, a rash promise made in time of hurt. A promise made when I was suffering the unforgiving and cruel pain of abandonment."

The relevance to Sarah's own story was not lost on her.

Perversely, in knowing that James had also suffered because of a promise made, she was comforted. She looked from the fire back to James who sat silently looking through the cottage to the bed in the other room. To the bed where his mother lay sleeping, never to wake.

"Was it her fault?" continued James, "That she was taken against her will? I think not. As time passed, I learnt more of her story from others. She had not teased the man and had done nothing to encourage him, but he was of evil stock as some are and he would have his way. At no time did I think of her pain when I made that foolish promise. She had not chosen that path it had been forced upon her. She would not have wanted it so and no doubt would have changed things if she could. Yet, she was wise and she knew that change could not be made, however much she wanted it."

Sarah's eyes looked where James looked, at the old woman who she had put so much store in. She had wanted to ask this old woman a question, wanted an answer from her, to something that anyone of sound mind could have given.

She turned back to look at James. He was deep in thought, his heavy frame holding up the thin brick wall of the cottage, unaware that tears ran down from his open eyes. No shudder, no sobbing, just tears. Though they were few in number, they were powerful in their ability to heal. Moments passed, the tears stopped their flow and his face became quickly dried by the fire. He continued as if no pause had taken place.

"I'm guessing, Miss Sarah, that Mister John did not choose to leave you. Did not want to go but had no choice. He knew he would have to leave but you would not let him. Then in the heat of your hurt you too made a promise, a promise to bring him back."

"I have been very foolish."

"Maybe miss, but you were hurting."

James paused, looking at Sarah, his concern now for her.

"He's gone miss, but you keep a good and straight path and you'll see him again."

Sarah looked at him.

"Not in this world, but you will see him."

"I pray you're right."

"Of course, I'm right, Miss Sarah, for I hears tell I'm the wisest man in Hitchin and all the surrounds."

He smiled teasingly and she smiled back.

"I wonder where that wisdom came from?" posed Sarah, looking at James knowingly, then both turned to look at the bed.

"Would make sense. I never spoke to her again after that day, because of my promise. But I would often sit in my room at the yard, window slightly open so that I could listen to her. She spoke a lot of sense, I think."

"She did." agreed Sarah

"She spoke too much, mind, but much of what she said, I had to agree with."

Sarah's thoughts moved to another subject.

"James, how did you know?"

"Know what, miss?"

"That I was here."

"I'd been following you, miss, simple and as plain as that. Old Sarah asked me to keep an eye on you, though I already was. The other night I followed you to the Little Spinney. After you left, I spoke to Nick and he said you was asking after Old Jinnepen, so's I knew it was in your mind to come."

"I sensed you."

"You did?"

"Yes. But in my madness, I thought it was John."

"No, miss, it weren't Mr John, it were just old James."

"The Perks Protector."

"That's right, Miss Sarah, and proud of it." James said with all seriousness. "Proud of it, miss."

A slight pause ensued.

"Anyhows, I saw you leave and knew where you were bound. I waited a while then I sets out after you. But I got here before you. I couldn't hear anything from outside and on looking through the window, I saw you weren't in here. Yet, there she was, laying on her bed half on and half off. I didn't want to come in but felt I should."

He paused

"She was dead."

He paused again.

"Had been dead for an hour or so before I got here, I reckon. I placed her on to her bed properly and pulled the blanket over her. Then I sat and looked, forgot everything else and just sat and looked at her. I was thinking that you might have decided against the visit or had been diverted from your purpose…"

"I was detained by Alington." explained Sarah, but James was not listening.

"Couldn't bring myself to move, you see. So, I just sat here and thought thoughts. Maybe, like you, Miss Sarah."

"Like me?"

"Like you with Mister John, I sat here thinking that if I stayed long enough, she might wake. I knew her to be dead, mind. But I wished it otherwise, you see, I wished her to wake. There was so much I wanted to say to her, wanted to ask her, wanted…. wanted to hug her."

Sarah thought he might weep again and she watched, but he didn't. He was too deep in analytical study to weep, so she began to weep for him. Just a little, no sobbing, no wailing, just tears that would befit those that James would have shed, had he the mind to.

"The brain does mighty strange things to you when you're hurting, doesn't it, miss?"

Fortunately for Sarah, the question was rhetorical and James never looked at her.

"Yes." said Sarah, softly biting her lip.

"Mighty strange. At the time you knows it's strange to think such a way, but you can do little about it." He continued remembering the recent scene before moving on,

"Eventually, I stood and stepped outside, walked back round the rear of the cottage towards the wall that I had climbed over earlier. But I didn't leave. I stood there, lit up my pipe and thought on it. I had a lot to think on. Even then, even when I'd come to my senses and moved outside, I kept looking back, thinking that if I went back in, she might be up and about, busy lighting her fire and doing her chores. It's what they call 'hopeful thinking', Miss Sarah. There ain't no sense in it, but it's a powerful force when it catches you unawares and when you dwell on it in times of trouble."

"When one's hurting?"

"Yes, miss, when one's hurting."

Once again, he paused unintentionally before realising that he had and then continued.

"Anyhows, I stood there too long and hadn't noticed the storm brewing, too busy thinking to notice and it was upon me before I knew it. So, I stood back into the woods a bit and sheltered under the canopy of a great tree. Too late to make for home and in truth too late to run back to the cottage, so I decides to wait there till the storm abated some. Then I heard screams. Your screams, miss. Didn't know it was your screams at the time, but I knew they were a woman's screams and that she was in some danger. This shook me out of my stupidity, and I found myself running back."

James was reliving the moment, not for Sarah's information, not to glorify what he had done but to complete his own recovery, purge his own guilt.

"Coming round the side of the cottage, I could see in the middle of the lane, a man kneeling and in front of him, someone I could not see. I moved nearer to see better, making sure that what I was seeing was what I thought I was seeing. It was. There was no doubt in my mind. I saw a man and heard him cursing at a woman, ripping at her clothes, attacking a woman who was lying down unable to move, drenched and soaked and being taken against her will!"

His voice had risen, noticeably. The normally soft-spoken James was recalling the event with the angry energy of being there. He had sat upright, back no longer against the wall, with eyes staring out at the scene in his head, forgetting that Sarah lay beside him.

"She was being taken against her will!" he cried and as he did, the whole room was swamped with light, followed seconds later by a clap of thunder that signalled that its destructive power was far from waning. The sound had brought James back to his senses. He listened, he thought, he spoke.

"We must be gone, Miss Sarah."

"Gone? But the storm?"

James had stood and gone to look out of the window.

"We can't afford to wait for it to cease."

"I don't understand…?"

"A man lies dead outside, Miss Sarah, and you must not be found here when he is discovered."

Sarah stood as well, but now feeling the injury to her ankle.

"And I would not trust your friend Alington as far as I could throw him. He is a man of unpredictable humour, miss, and not to be fully trusted."

James had opened the door.

"I cannot walk, James, my ankle is turned and I cannot walk."

Without a word, James reverted to kind, scooping her up in his arms, curtain still wrapped around her and walked out of the cottage.

They walked through the trees. Branches now whipped and thrashing by the winds, looking to add their fury to the night's chaos. Through the undergrowth they strode, with saplings springing at them from every direction, wickedly aiming to scar. Sarah fended them as best she could with her free hand and James did likewise ducking and weaving to avoid their sting. At last they reached the boundary wall. Lifting her on to it, James climbed over and once more picking her up, strode on to the Willian road and headed for home.

The rain did not cease and his stride did not falter nor slacken. Hope for a passing carriage or wagon was forlorn thinking, no human walked the watery gauntlet that night, as they did. Two fools caught in the mayhem. The storm continued its rage and the rains continued to fall, never ending. As if all the water from the planet's oceans had been sucked skywards and was now being poured back to earth in one colossal, never-ending cascade.

Along the lanes, tracks, roads, all flooded in every direction, James walked on as if immune to the ferocity of nature. Down the hill to Walsworth and as they neared the hamlet, it became evident that the River Purwell had flooded both its banks and the track leading to the bridge was submerged. But James waded on through with his precious cargo, at times up to his knees, until reaching the bridge that had been built only twenty years previously, to replace the ancient ford below. Over the Purwell, up the hill and under the new bridge that served the Railway Station. Down the Nightingale Road past Nightingale Cottages and Ransom's cow meadows, over the Hiz at Starlings Bridge, past the gas works then on into Bancroft, finally passing the Adam & Eve public house, before reaching the safety of home and the waiting arms of Eliza. A shocked Eliza who was beside herself with worry. A distraught and hysterical Eliza who was in the process of organising search parties. A truly relieved Eliza that they had managed to return safely.

They were home, both soaked, both grateful and both better for living through their torment.

Walsworth Bridge over the Purwell

Chapter Thirteen

The day after the events at Letchworth Hall and the worse storm people could remember for many a year, the sun came out. Bright and brilliant as it always did in Hitchin. The hours of sunshine then continued for several more days, nowhere near as humid and unbearable as before the storm, but above average for September. It had been decided by Sarah and James that their story to all would be a simple one. That they had been walking separately and met on the road, Sarah had fallen awkwardly and twisted her ankle and then they had got caught up in the storm. Fortunately, none questioned it or even doubted it. The ease of their being believed was helped in no small measure by the violence and power of a storm that all had witnessed.

Within days, Sarah's body recovered from her injuries and her mind continued to settle and heal. She knew she would eventually make a full recovery, although it would take strength and perseverance to hang on to legitimate memories, yet at the same time, avoid falling into the pit of obsession. But she was on the right path and time is a good healer, someone once said.

Although Sarah had made good progress, James had not been quite so fortunate, having come down with an annoying cold that was taking its time to shift.

"You're not a spring chicken anymore, James," Doctor Hawkins had said on attending to him, "I fear your days of running around in the rain, clad in nought but a jacket and a desire to be young again, are over."

For his comfort, he had been moved into one of the spare rooms in the house where, to his annoyance, he was fussed over by Sarah and Eliza especially. He was also visited often by the Perks children, who demanded to know when he would be up and about again, as there were serious repair works required in the Navy Dockyard. It seemed the storm had played havoc with the barrelled ocean, with timbers falling on to it, cracking the sides and emptying it of water. There were also two damaged ships that needed completely rebuilding.

Sarah visited him each day and as often as possible on her own. They would talk quietly, knowing that Eliza would always be close by and that she was renowned for lingering at doors longer than was socially acceptable. In their hushed tones, they would relive the day and talk to each other to ease and hasten their journey of recovery. As always, James insisted that talking was a good thing, although Sarah tended to talk for the most part and James would patiently listen.

It helped Sarah tremendously. He was able to keep reminding her of her foolishness and the torment she had imposed upon herself. On one of her visits, he made her promise that if anything should ever happen to him, she was to choose a new confidant. Someone she could trust. Someone who would listen and be as supportive as he had. She must talk and never sink back into her shell. She should share her memories of John constantly, with friends and her children. She must remain vigilant until she was convinced her demons would not return to torment her.

One of her first tasks was to cover her tracks, to dis-spell any need for unwanted questions. She wrote to the Reverend Alington, for despite everything, she had made a promise to him which she had not kept and there were questions regarding her visit that remained unanswered.

Dear Reverend J. Alington,

I write to sincerely apologise for not returning after my visit to the old lady. We both know the 'old lady' whom I refer to. I was unwillingly prevented from fulfilling my promise, for the wretched and sudden storm made doing so virtually impossible. Besides, after exiting the said lady's cottage, my escort could not be found anywhere. It is possible he had wisely found shelter elsewhere, as I understand you had insisted that he should not enter the cottage under any circumstances.
As to your request for certain information regarding my visit and the effectiveness of the 'aid' you kindly supplied me with; I can confirm that I learnt nothing from my visit, as the lady in question was fast asleep throughout and did not wake. Consequently, your aid neither hindered nor helped. Your faithful servant,
Mrs Sarah Perks

P.S. Thank you for your hospitality and entertainment, they were both most enlightening.

In writing this letter Sarah had allowed herself a few little white lies, though nothing too far from the truth. She prayed that the letter would suffice and that her time on the Alington's estate would not be questioned further. James had listened to the letter before she sent it and he felt it served its purpose well.

"I'm thinking, Miss Sarah, that you will probably hear nothing more from the man. They say he is as unpredictable as the wind and probably does not even remember your visit. They also say he has a liking for certain drugs and young gypsy girls. Too much of both, to my mind, will render the mind forgetful."

Sarah agreed and saw to it that the twins delivered it directly to the hall, she would not send pretty Lizzie for fear she might not return for a few days. Or if she did, she might not be in full command of her faculties. She was growing quickly into an attractive young woman and Sarah thought best not to put temptation in the parson's way.

However, James was wrong. Something that was quite a rarity, but on this occasion, he had misread the Reverend Alington completely. Not only did the eccentric master of Letchworth Hall remember Sarah's visit, but he kept the boys waiting whilst he wrote so that his reply was immediate.

Dear Mrs Sarah Perks,

Thank you for your letter of explanation and apology, which I humbly accept.

You may be interested to know that a couple of unusual incidents occurred around your visit, or just after. At the time of writing it is difficult to ascertain which of these is correct.

In the first instance: Your escort, whose name was Lazzy Smith, had indeed stepped into the woods to shelter. Unfortunately for Mr Smith, a branch had fallen upon his head, no doubt ripped from its trunk by the ferocious winds and rendered him very much dead.

In the second instance: Yesterday, after some concern had been raised by others on the estate that Old Jinnepen had not been seen for three days, it was thought wise to enter her cottage and enquire unto her health. Unfortunately, she too had passed on. According to the Doctor who issued her death certificate, her life ended about three days previously. This timing would put the moment of death around the time of your visit. I do not wish to upset you unduly, but it is quite possible that when you tried to wake her and she did not respond, it was not because she was in a deep sleep, but because she was, in fact, dead.

But as Mister Smith's demise was obviously caused by an unfortunate freak of nature and the old lady's through being of such an old age and, consequently, having used up all the years available to her, I will not be investigating either death further.

If you are of a mind for company and conversation in the future, you would be most welcome here at Letchworth Hall, at any time.
Your obedient servant,
Reverend J. Alington JP

James thought it would be wise that she did not accept the Reverend Alington's kind invitation anytime soon and Sarah tended to agree.

The day after receipt of the letter, she had visited the Perks

Pharmacy to see how all went in her absence. Samuel was lunching with William Ransom

"I believe, Sarah, that they discuss the purchase of a steam powered threshing machine. An American model, which Samuel tells me is far superior to that which Britain produces at present."

"Well, Catherine, perhaps they do, although it does sound…"

"Expensive, Sarah, to my mind it sounds very expensive."

"I wouldn't worry. William is of an extremely sensible mind and I'm sure he will settle Samuel's wonderful enthusiasm for everything to be done yesterday."

"Of an extremely sensible mind, say you?" teased Catherine.

"I believe him to be so, yes."

"Have you seen him since your escapades in the storm?"

"I might have…"

"There is no 'might have' Sarah Perks, either you have, or you have not?"

"Very well, Catherine, I have, yes. He has visited to enquire on my ankle, so now you know."

"Once?"

"Twice."

"Twice?"

"Catherine, you are being absurd. He is my neighbour, our neighbour. William is of a naturally charitable character and simply enquires regarding my recovery."

Before Catherine could ask or tease more, Lottie entered from the yard.

"Miss Sarah!"

"Lottie, it is so good to see you, are you well?"

"I am so well, Miss Sarah, that I can't help myself!"

"Well, Lottie, that is good news, I am pleased for you and how goes the romance?"

"Lottie, I think you should let Miss Sarah in on your good

news."

"Yes, Miss Catherine. Miss Sarah, be kind enough to close your eyes, if you will?"

Sarah closed her eyes, but no sooner had she done so, than Lottie commanded her to open them again. On doing so, Sarah found Lottie's hand dangling just beneath her nose with a brass ring on her engagement finger.

"Lottie!"

"I knows, miss, he's a very lucky boy, says I. And I told him as much."

"For fear of dampening your good news, Lottie, it's not too quick I hope…?"

"Oh no, miss, we ain't planning anything till at least next Autumn. Plenty of time for me to change my mind."

"So, Annie gets to be a bridesmaid."

"No miss, Annie gets to be a bride! We're having a double wedding at St Mary's! And before you start enquiring of me, no Robert didn't ask her, but Annie tells him, and he says, 'yes'! She even got the brass ring for him and gave it to him to give to her. She won't have no nonsense, will Annie."

"Well, well, Catherine?"

"Sarah?"

"I'm not sure if you're having a bad influence on Lottie and the girls, or a good one."

"There are still four single girls working in the yard, Sarah, my plan is to get them all engaged before Christmas."

"Lottie, I could not be happier for you. A double wedding. How wonderful!"

"Yes, Miss Sarah. Well it seemed to make sense what with Albert and Robert being cousins."

As if on cue, Annie knocked and entered the shop from the yard. Sarah beamed as she saw her.

"Congratulations, Annie!"

"Thank you, Miss Sarah, I ain't actually got to tell anyone in person as of yet, 'cause Lottie is always diving in and opening up her mouth afore me."

"Nonsense, Annie." defended Lottie.

"It's true, miss, I think she even told me mother afore I did."

"That's just not true…"

"Anyhows," said Annie, returning to why she had knocked on the door in the first place. "We got a bit of a problem in the yard, Miss Catherine."

"In what way, Annie?"

"It's with little Lucy, miss. If you got one minute? I'm thinking, it'll be easier explaining in the yard than in the shop."

Lottie, Annie, Catherine and Sarah all exited into the yard where they found Lucy sitting on a box with a blanket wrapped up in a ball on her lap. Hilda sat next to her and most of the yard stopped work and moved towards Lucy, as Sarah and Catherine came out.

"Whatever is the problem, Lucy?"

"I'm not sure, Miss Catherine, Cedric says he found this over by the gate."

"Lying on the pavement by the gate post it was, Miss Catherine. It had a note attached, in scrawling writing and it said, 'To Lucy.'"

"Well, Lucy, it is obviously a present from some well-wisher. Have you unwrapped it?"

"Yes, Miss Catherine."

"Well child, what is it?"

Lucy carefully reopened the cloth with a little help from Hilda, revealing its contents. Painstakingly, as if it contained some priceless treasure.

"It's a puppy, miss, the tiniest of little baby puppies."

And it was.

"Oh…" sighed Sarah, then upon catching a glimpse of a note peeping out from behind the puppy's head, she carefully pulled it out whilst the conversation continued.

"He's beautiful, Lucy."

"Yes, Miss Catherine."

"But I do not understand why you should think there is a problem?"

"I don't know what to call it, Miss Catherine, that's the problem."

As all those in the yard laughed heartily at Lucy's endearing innocence, Sarah had unfolded the note and could see instantly that it only had two words written upon it. Two words in scrawled and unschooled handwriting, just as Cedric had described the first note.

"Sarah? What does it say?" asked Catherine.

"'From Rosa', that's what it says. 'From Rosa'."

Sarah looked at Lottie and smiled and Lottie smiled back.

Sarah later discovered that Nick and Rosa had delivered the puppy. They had heard what had happened to poor Beggar and were convinced he would undoubtedly have suffered his fate at the hands of the wayward Lazzy. Nick saw the gift as an opportunity to show their gratitude for Rosa's brief bout of nursing at the Perks Yard. When Lavender, for that is the named Lucy has chosen for her puppy, grows to a reasonable size, Nick will visit the yard and instruct Lucy and Lottie on ways of training her to do a few basic tricks. He warned that the puppy is unlikely to reach the incredible standards of the wonderful Beggar, but with love, care, patience and an abundance of treats, anything is possible.

On a sadder note, the cold that had plagued James from the day of the storm, turned into acute pneumonia from which he never recovered. James Smith passed quietly away, peacefully, in his sleep.

For Eliza, it was an insurmountable loss. During the six years that she had known him, they had grown close and she had become very fond of him. It was not until he died that she realised how fond.

"I will miss him dearly, Miss Sarah," she said, sniffing back the tears.

"We all will, Eliza."

"He could be a contrary old soul when he chose, miss and never one to rush around. I says to him once, I says, 'If your trousers were on fire, James Smith, you wouldn't know until they were burnt to a cinder.' Do know what he goes and says to me, miss? Well, I'll tell you, he says 'I'll be fine, Eliza, 'cause I has another pair.'"

With this, Eliza once again burst into floods of tears and it took Sarah some time and two glasses of Madeira to calm her.

"Thank you, Miss Sarah. I'm so sorry to be such a blubberer, but I shall miss him something terrible."

"I know, Eliza, I know you will."

"'Cause I saw him day in day out, miss, he was always here and he never strayed far from the yard, as you knows. He was as regular as the sunrise, miss, and now he ain't here anymore."

Eliza was about to collapse into another emotional mess but managed to hold herself together on this occasion.

"But wise, Miss Sarah? I knew no one wiser, miss. No one did. Sometimes they came from as far away as Clifton, miss, further! I knows one person who travels all the way from other side of Langford, just to ask James' opinion on something or other. I mean, Langford? Why that's all the way over in Bedfordshire, miss!"

   Eliza had seemed to have forgotten that both her and
Sarah originated from Bedfordshire, for that is where the
village of Henlow lies. Sarah decided not to point this out, as
Eliza might then think James reputation not so widely spread
as she had originally thought.
"He had the most wonderful reputation for wise counsel,
Eliza."
"He did, Miss Sarah, he did. I knows he didn't know who is
mother was, nor father as it happens, miss. But whoever they
was, I tells you, one of them must have been a wise old soul,
cause I'm thinking he had to get his gift of wisdom from one
of them."
Sarah thought to herself that no truer word had ever been
spoken.
"That sort of wisdom, yer don't find growing on trees in the
woods, miss. No miss, you certainly don't!"
   There was a brief pause, as Eliza thought on what she had
said and on how much she would miss the man. Then once
again, she burst into a genuine flood of tears and anguish
that could only be supressed by yet another glass of fine
Madeira.

Sarah had lost her confidant and loyal friend, but she had not
lost nor forgotten his wise words. She would choose a new
confidant to take his place and, in fact, she had already
decided on who to ask. Catherine had offered her a shoulder
on which to cry and Sarah would make use of her kind
gesture at the very next opportunity. She would find the right
moment and divulge all that she had gone through to her
beautiful sister in law. Sarah was convinced she would make
an excellent, close and trustworthy friend.
"Never stop speaking of it, Miss Sarah." James had
constantly advised her over his last few days. "Not to the

whole world mind, miss, you don't want to be going putting it in the broadsheets, but one or two close friends will do no harm, but only good. It has to be spoken, Miss Sarah and not kept to yourself."

As Sarah reflected on his words, it became apparent to her that he knew he was dying. Why would he not know? He was wise and knowledgeable about others, so why would he not be just as aware of himself. He knew, he most certainly knew.

Sarah senior has travelled to her second home in the Lake District, content that all issues concerning her family are now resolved. Although she would have happily taken her granddaughter with her, it was thought best that the young girl should return home to her mother and siblings. As soon as Anne was through the front door, she immediately took on the role of 'cot rocker' to little John. Her maternal instinct to care for a small child had propelled her willingly into this age-old role. Her cot rocking is accompanied by the gentle singing of nursery rhymes to help lull and soothe her baby brother to sleep. This was something her predecessor had been forbidden from doing as Eliza's singing had the reverse effect of keeping the baby tormented and awake, not to mention the rest of the household. Eliza had happily relinquished the time-consuming task to her young apprentice. Although when Anne is tucked up at night in her own bed, Eliza resumes this important work, but without the lull-a-byes.

Thomas has volunteered to fill the void left by the sad passing of James, chief ship builder to Edward's Navy. He had watched the gentle giant at work, carefully observing the man at his craft and had made several ships of his own for his younger siblings at home. This quick promotion has been to the great relief of Edward, who feared life would never be quite the same. It has also pleased Thomas' twin brother Toby, for it has seen the teasing regarding his blossoming romance with pretty Lizzie lessen, if not cease altogether.

As for little John, progress is slow. One day of promise and recovery is followed by another of relapse and suffering. Sarah is fully aware of the fact that her youngest child may not see Christmas tide and is resolved to this possibility. With this in mind, she spends many an hour with the child as all the family and servants do. When he is awake, they all see to it that little John is smothered with as much love and giggles as is humanly possible. If his stay in this world is to be a short one, it will not lack for joy and contentment.

As an addition to her therapy and recovery, for the first time in months she pulled out an old chest from beneath her bed. After John's death she had stored many artefacts away, mementoes and any other small objects that reminded her of him. Looking back now, she realised that she had incorrectly thought it would signal to others that she had moved on, put the past behind her and that they were no longer important to her. What madness. She had found the key, still hidden in the vase on her sideboard, and taken out every item from its hiding, returning them all to their original placings throughout the house. At the bottom of the chest was an item of great importance, of special significance. John had bought it for her whilst honeymooning in the Lake District and she now remembered placing it there. It was a white parasol with tassels.

Saturday evening around seven o'clock, Sarah, armed with her parasol with tassels, walked as she always did, to the fields. Not to see John, for she knew he was not there. She went to think her thoughts and enjoy her memories. If John rested, waiting for her in God's heaven, he would surely hear her thoughts and share the joy of them from afar.

She walked familiar paths and at the infamous corner that her incident with Lazzy had occurred, she stopped, not to regret, not to try and exorcise any ghosts, because there were no ghosts. She instead stopped to pick blackberries. She had always done so as a child at her home farm outside Henlow, she had done so with John and she would do so with her own children, when they were of a sensible age to avoid the brambles. Staring into the hedge she spied a berry in its fullness of time, at its peak and ready for harvest. She picked the beauty from the branch, ready-ripe from the constant sun and, luckily, missed by the greedy magpie. It tasted sweet, gloriously sweet and with its juices rewarding her taste buds, she walked on round the next corner and up to the edge of the fields.

She stood looking, not hoping he would join her, for in a way he was always with her, but thinking of the days to come, just as much as the days that had passed. God willing there was much life still to be lived. Her life was good. She thought of things that elated and pleased, rather than those that challenged her and tested her sanity.

Unchained, her thoughts now turned to William. The following day was Sunday and she was travelling by carriage, with young Willian Ransom, to the excavation site at Wilbury Hills. Originally, they were to be accompanied by Samuel and Catherine. However, Catherine had decided that Sunday afternoon would be an excellent time for the two of them to cost out some of the machinery that Samuel said he intended to buy.

"I really cannot see why this cannot be attended to at another time." bemoaned Samuel as he explained to Sarah why they would not be joining her and William. "It really doesn't make any sense to me. But you know Catherine, when she gets a bee in her bonnet there is absolutely no persuading her otherwise."

Sarah was most definitely pleased with her choice of confidant.

On Sunday, she would attend church first, for she had returned to church and the God she had temporarily forsaken. Then afterwards she would accompany her knight in shining armour alone. Unchaperoned.

She would enjoy the day with William. Kind-hearted, charitable William. Good-looking and intelligent Mr William Ransom. She would have no expectations and place no unreasonable limitations upon herself. She would sally forth into unchartered waters, with no preconceptions and most definitely no regrets. If John were alive, he would have been proud of her.

Across the field, dipping on the horizon, the sun was once again beginning its descent to another land and the trees' shadows on the far side were visibly lengthening. The field, for now, was barren with all crops safely taken from its furrows and for a while it would lie that way, undisturbed and unworked. But soon there would be ploughing anew, sowing, planting, tending, until finally it would be time for cropping once again. The year would turn full circle, as years always have done and always will do.

The breeze was gentle and the air pure. Sarah determined to take in one last breath before making her way home. A last breath of golden air whilst standing in her most favourite spot. An intake of air that would remind her of all those things she treasured. It would conjure up sweet reminders of the people she loved, past and present, her friends, her family, all those at the yard, the sleepy little town of Hitchin and most of all, it would remind her of the smell of lavender.

THE END